SHOW ME A HERO

Other books by Alfred Coppel

Night of Fire and Snow
Dark December
A Certainty of Love
The Gate of Hell
Order of Battle
A Little Time for Laughter
Between the Thunder and the Sun
The Landlocked Man
Thirty-four East
The Dragon
The Hastings Conspiracy
The Apocalypse Brigade
The Burning Mountain
The Marburg Chronicles

Alfred Coppel

SHOW ME
A HERO

Harcourt Brace Jovanovich, Publishers

SAN DIEGO   NEW YORK   LONDON

Poetry from THE COLLECTED POEMS OF A. E. HOUSMAN.
Copyright 1922 by Holt, Rinehart and Winston.
Copyright 1950 by Barclay Bank, Ltd.
Reprinted by permission of Henry Holt and Company.

Library of Congress Cataloging-in-Publication Data

Coppel, Alfred.
Show me a hero.

I. Title.
PS3553.064S5   1987   813'.54   86-26961
ISBN 0-15-182080-5

Designed by Robert Bull

Printed in the United States of America

First edition

A B C D E

For Ann

One fair daughter and no more,
The which he loved passing well.
—SHAKESPEARE
Hamlet, Act II, Sc. 2

Prologue

[Front Page, *The New York Times*, January 9:]

AMERICAN AMBASSADOR AND MEMBERS OF HIS STAFF ARE KIDNAPPED

U.S. Marine Slain Resisting Attack

By **JAMES V. REICHAUER**

Special to The New York Times

BEIRUT, January 8—Ambassador Edward Lyman and eleven staff members were kidnapped this afternoon by a band of armed men who invaded the United States Embassy compound in West Beirut.

A Marine guard who attempted to resist the gunmen was shot and killed during the incident. His name is being withheld pending notification of next of kin.

Reports from intelligence sources are conflicting, but other members of the embassy staff who witnessed the attack say that the invaders penetrated both Lebanese and American security in an unmarked van and escaped with their captives in the same vehicle.

An embassy spokesman said that an investigation is under way to determine how this was possible. "Any further comment must come from the Department of State," the spokesman said. [Page A6.]

As yet no one of the many militant organizations operating in the Middle East has claimed responsibility for the action.

[Page A6, *The New York Times,* January 9:]

LAWMAKERS DEMAND EXPLANATION OF BEIRUT KIDNAPPING

By **STEVEN C. JANKLOW**

Special to The New York Times

WASHINGTON, January 8—Congressional leaders said today that they would demand an explanation of this morning's abduction of Ambassador Edward Lyman and members of his staff by gunmen who invaded the United States Embassy in Beirut.

Some lawmakers expressed dissatisfaction with the security measures taken recently by the Department of State to protect American diplomats serving abroad.

A spokesman for the Administration said that a meeting of the National Security Council has been scheduled. The President and the Secretary of Defense are returning to Washington from California.

Presidential Press Secretary John Steinhart issued a statement declaring that the Administration intends to take appropriate action the moment the kidnappers are properly identified. "At that time," Mr. Steinhart said, "we will do what is required to protect American interests and American lives."

[Front Page, *The Washington Times,* January 10:]

LOCATION OF AMERICAN
DIPLOMATIC HOSTAGES UNCERTAIN

By **ZACHARY LEWIS** and **ANDREW WILLIAMS**
The Washington Times

The whereabouts of Ambassador Edward Lyman and his staff, taken hostage by Islamic militants on January 8, is not yet known, according to a State Department spokesman.

Clayborn Grayson, Press Officer of the Beirut embassy, told *The Washington Times* today that early indications that the kidnapping was the work of Shiite fundamentalists are now being questioned. "We are not certain which of the many radical groups in the city is holding Ambassador Lyman and his people, or where," Mr. Grayson said. "It is even possible that our diplomats have been taken out of the country. There is simply no way to be certain."

Mr. Grayson then refused to comment on criticisms being made in the Congress about State Department security. In an earlier statement in Washington, a State Department spokesman said that "our embassies are as secure as we can make them without turning our diplomatic missions into fortresses."

[Page A3, *The Washington Post,* January 22:]

TV REPORT OF DELTA
MOVE ANGERS PENTAGON
Administration Denies
Mid-East Redeployment

A television news segment disclosing the departure of elements of Delta Force, the U.S. Army's anti-terrorist assault force, brought strong criticism from the Department of Defense today.

Departure of Delta Force units from their base at Fort Bragg, North Carolina, was broadcast on the CBS Evening News last night.

[Page 4, *The Baltimore Sun,* March 12:]

IRANIAN U.N. AMBASSADOR LAUDS HOSTAGE TAKERS
But Envoy Denies Complicity by Iran

(Special to *The Sun*) Ibrahim Rafsanjani, Iranian Ambassador to the United Nations, said today that the fighters who hold Ambassador Edward Lyman and his staff do so in order to restrain acts of overt imperialism by the United States. "They are perfectly justified in doing so," Ambassador Rafsanjani said in an exclusive interview with *The Sun.*

While willing to justify the taking of American hostages, Ambassador Rafsanjani denied categorically that Teheran is in any way involved.

Ambassador Lyman and his people were taken from the United States Embassy in Beirut more than two months ago. No recognized organization has claimed responsibility, and no demands have been made for their return.

[Page 1, Section 2, *Los Angeles Times,* April 10:]

SECRET DEMANDS FOR RELEASE OF U.S. HOSTAGES?
Rumors and Denials in Tel Aviv

(Special to *The Los Angeles Times* from our Correspondent)

Spokesmen for the government of Israel are busy denying that specific demands from the terrorists holding Edward Lyman, American Ambassador to Lebanon, have been received. A Foreign Ministry official describes as ludicrous a report out of Cairo that release of Lyman and his fellow prisoners, abducted four months ago, depended on specific concessions from the government of the State of Israel.

Yet rumors persist, and the *Times* has learned that a possible condition being set for release of the hostages has to do with the Israeli Ministry of Defense's supersecret installation at Dimona in the Negev Desert. Though it is categorically denied here, unconfirmed reports insist that Dimona is the assembly and storage place for Israeli nuclear weapons. The government of Israel had never been willing to confirm or deny their possession of any such weapons.

[Page 22, *The Wall Street Journal*, August 1:]

HOSTAGE FAMILIES HAVE FORMED A GROUP
Ambassador's Wife is Spokeswoman

Eleanor Lyman, wife of Ambassador Edward Lyman, who is being held somewhere in the Middle East by as yet unidentified radicals, was the featured guest on ABC's *Nightline* Tuesday.

Mrs. Lyman expressed the fears and frustrations being experienced by the hostages' families. "We are in constant contact with the State Department," she said, "but it is difficult to get any satisfaction from what we are being told."

Asked if she favored military action to free her husband and the other hostages, she replied that neither she nor any of the other members of the Beirut Hostages' Family Association wanted anything done that could endanger their loved ones.

Appearing with Mrs. Lyman were Elie Frankenheimer, an

expert on terrorism from the American Enterprise Institute, and Charles Covell, a spokesman for the Department of State.

Mr. Frankenheimer warned that continued inaction on the part of the United States was "a certain formula for disaster to American foreign policy," and recommended punitive strikes against known terrorist bases, such as those in the Bekaa Valley in Lebanon. He remarked on the Israeli policy of instant retaliation and put forward the recent Israeli air raid against PLO headquarters in Tunisia as an example of suitable action. "Terrorists must know that their actions will bring retribution," he said.

Mrs. Lyman said that the Israeli raid on Tunisia had depressed and angered the members of the Beirut Hostages' Family Association. "It must have put our people in great danger," she said.

Mr. Covell, speaking for the State Department, said that the Secretary of State has said many times that he believes in military countermeasures against terrorists. "But we must first be absolutely certain that we are striking the guilty and not killing innocent civilians. Indiscriminate retaliation would be counterproductive."

[Editorial: *San Francisco Chronicle,* January 9.]

A YEAR AND A DAY FOR LYMAN

One year and one day ago an unmarked van made its way through the concrete barriers and gates guarded by Lebanese government troops into the American Embassy compound in Beirut. Five minutes later a brave young Marine, Private Manuel C. Rivas of El Centro, California, was dead and the Ambassador of the United States of America and eleven of his staff were prisoners.

This is a sad anniversary for America. It is sad because our diplomats have been humiliated, possibly mistreated or worse. It is sad because our leaders seem unable to take any effective action. And it is saddest of all because we have grown so accustomed to outrage that it has lost much of its power to shock us. We are forgetting that somewhere out there people who served us bravely are waiting for their country to bring them home.

PART
ONE

He's of stature somewhat low—
Your hero always should be tall, you know.

CHARLES CHURCHILL, *The Rosciad*

1

The man carrying the rocket-propelled grenade launcher gleamed as though he had been burnished. Shafts of sunlight sliced through the jungle canopy like a shower of polished knives. There were animal rustlings in the dense growth, and when some unseen bird uttered a cry, he froze, listening. He was three times life-size, and the light artfully framed him against the green background.

The longish hair and the folded bandanna worn as a sweatband were Harry Redding's trademarks. Close up, his eyes were oddly opaque. Killer's eyes. Stallone had soft eyes. Not Redding. His could make Eastwood's look gentle.

He was doing it all wrong. Louis Brown whispered in my ear, "He's going to get himself greased standing there like a fool statue." Twenty years of soldiering backed Sergeant Brown's disapproval.

Almost as though he had heard Louis's murmured comment, Redding moved forward through the undergrowth. He was naked to the waist, apparently impervious to the insects of Vietnam. He glistened with sweat. You could almost smell him. Earlier we had seen the jungle rot on his feet, but he never limped or hobbled, not Harry Redding. Now he was knee-deep in the stagnant stream, ignoring the leeches we knew were there. A half-reel back we had seen him burning them off with a cigarette coal. The Vietnamese colonel whom Eagle Films had hired as a consultant hadn't told them that a cigarette could be smelled a hundred yards away.

Redding kept moving up toward the log bunker where we knew the Spetznaz officer, a Soviet assault specialist, had holed up with a half-dozen North Vietnamese regulars. Redding carried the RPG launcher cradled in one arm, and he wore a necklace of reloads like a string of black sausages. Rocket-propelled grenades are heavy, but he carried them as though they were nothing. The word was that he worked out with weights and a Nautilus machine for four hours every day of his life, and his physique suggested the story was true. He was put together like a Roman gladiator. In all my eighteen years in the U.S. Army, I had never seen any soldier built like Harry Redding.

In addition to the RPG tube and the reloads, he carried an Israeli-made Uzi rifle slung across the small of his sweat-slick back. Neither Louis nor I could figure where he had acquired it. Uzis were rare as chicken's teeth in Nam. I had always wanted one, but the best I could do was a captured Russian AK-47. The pockets of Redding's jungle fatigue pants bulged with ammunition. A canteen and a commando knife—Ranger issue—hung from a webbed belt low on his hips.

He had used the knife a while back, slipping it into a Vietcong soldier he had encountered a few miles down the stream. His technique had been perfect, right out of the *Special Forces Manual*: in under the ribs, sharp edge up. Private Harry Redding didn't take to army discipline, but he knew when to go by the book.

He was always a private, because he liked to cool noncommissioned officers. We discovered that when he sucker-punched a sergeant first class in a bar back in Danang. That scene had brought a growl of disapproval from Louis.

Louis had been a ghetto kid, raised in Watts. He was born with most of the survival skills he was ever likely to need, but the army had sharpened them and given him a sense of self-worth. Louis was a master sergeant when he retired, and proud of it. He didn't find the spectacle of raunchy soldiers fighting bar brawls amusing. But the hint of insubordination was part of the Harry Redding mystique.

"What's he doing now?" Louis whispered. "Why doesn't he use the RPG?"

Redding had a clear field of fire between himself and the bunker. A single rocket, well aimed, would reduce the bunker to rubble. But instead of using the launcher, he chose to charge the enemy position, screaming at the top of his lungs. He splashed up the stream, the heavy weapon in both hands. A jungle bird I had never seen in my two tours in Nam exploded from the greenery beside the water and flew away shrieking. Redding waited until the men in the bunker began to shoot at him before he got down to business with the grenade launcher.

The bad guys in the bunker opened up with automatic-rifle fire and a heavy machine gun. The bushes all around Redding shredded.Bullets frothed the water in which he stood. A tree shattered and fell. It was like Armageddon, but somehow the Russian adviser and his troops failed to chop him into dog meat.

Redding raised the tube and launched a round at the bunker. It hissed and roared its way to the log face of the bunker and went off like a two-kiloton nuke. Logs, branches, earth, and two enemy soldiers went flying into the air.

"Je-zuz," Louis muttered. "Beautiful."

The din of pyrotechnics overpowered the musical score. It *became* the score. Redding slipped another rocket up the spout and let go again. The explosion made our ears ring. From a dark corner of the screening room came a cry of "All *right*, Harry!"

Redding took cover behind a thin screen of jungle brush that wouldn't stop a tennis ball. From the wrecked bunker came moans and more automatic-weapons fire. He caught a round on the biceps—a flesh wound. He dropped the grenade launcher. It fell into the muddy water. He got the Uzi into action one-handed and used it like a garden hose. A North Vietnamese soldier tried to run for it, and he dropped him.

5

The Spetznaz, a mean-eyed blond Russian, reared up out of the rubble and lobbed a concussion grenade at Redding. It exploded a few yards away and knocked him down. When he pulled himself out of the brush, his nose was bleeding. But he still had the Uzi in his hand, and he sprayed the Russian adviser with it.

"Take that, you Commie rat," Louis said. He was enjoying himself now. Louis loved Harry Redding movies at their most violent. He disapproved of their message of indiscipline, and he thought the battle scenes were never really close to the real thing. But there was still a great deal of the thirteen-year-old in Sergeant Louis Armstrong Brown.

I had served for twenty-six months in Vietnam with Louis. I owed him my life. He was a remarkable man. Part child—witness the James Cagney imitation—but all man. He was, without exception, the best fighting soldier I had ever known. They say of some men "He found a home in the army." Louis had. The army trained him, educated him (he had developed an insatiable appetite for military history, and he could tell you things about history's armies few college professors ever bothered to learn), disciplined him. The army had made him into a formidable man. When he chose to retire and throw in with me after I had my trouble with the army, I resolved that he'd never be sorry. I said I owed him my life. I did. And more now that we were civilians.

Up on the screen, the Spetznaz officer was dying the hard way. Redding had put what must have been a full magazine into him with the Uzi, but the Russian (played by one of those second leads whose pale eyes and good looks had never quite made him into a star) still managed to shoot Redding's weapon out of his hand before passing out. So when the Russian T-55 tank suddenly came crashing out of the jungle, Redding had to scramble back to where he had dropped the grenade launcher and fumble around in the water for it.

He found it, of course, but it came out of the stream smeared with mud. Chances were ninety to one that the firing circuit was shorted and unserviceable. Field weapons are supposed to be waterproofed, but anyone who has used one for real can tell you what the promises in the field manuals are worth in real money.

"I bet it works okay," Louis said.

Only a sucker would take that bet. Redding jammed a rocket grenade into the tube, assumed the regulation sitting position (as the tank closed in on him), and let go. The round took off like a moon shot and hit the tank in the belly. Chunks of Soviet steel pinwheeled off into the trees. Flames erupted from the gunports. The hatch opened, and the crew came spilling out, all of them on fire. They ran off into the bush, and finally everything grew quiet except for the crackle of flames.

There was more, but none of it was what Louis and I had been hired to consult on. We were there, so Jerry Ziegler had said, just to look at the battle scenes.

After the credits had rolled and the lights came up in the screening room, Ziegler left the group of people with whom he had been watching the film. He ran the business end of Harry Redding's company. General Stanley had told me that Ziegler expected a great deal from Eagle's employees and consultants but that he was scrupulously honest. If the General believed that, it was good enough for me.

Ziegler came down the aisle and sat on the arm of the seat across from mine. He had a round, plump face that made him look younger than he was. His long, dark hair was thinning. He was dressed casually in jeans and an expensive chamois shirt, and had gold chains around his neck. He could have passed for a balding schoolboy except for his eyes, which reminded me of the eyes of the Russian Spetznaz in the film. General Stanley, a former Ranger who had been technical adviser on three earlier Redding pictures, had warned me that Ziegler was devoted to Redding and not to be too damned rough with my comments about the picture. "Remember, Casey," he had said, "if they showed what it was really like, no civilian would want to see it."

"What do you think, Major?" Ziegler asked.

I was thinking of our five-thousand-dollar fee when I said, "It looks to me as though your picture is complete."

7

Since they already had a technical adviser, I wondered why Eagle Films needed Louis and me. General Stanley, who was back in San Francisco waiting to hear from me, hadn't made it clear what I was expected to do for Redding and Eagle.

Ziegler gave me a slow smile. "You're right about that. *Covering Fire* is in the can and ready for distribution. The screening was just an excuse to get you down here." The smile grew broader. "But I can't help asking for an opinion. It's the producer in me. How was it?"

"Not bad," I said. "Just nothing like the way it really was."

"Fair enough. What do you say, Sergeant Brown?"

"With the bark on?"

Ziegler mimed a wince. "With it on, Sergeant."

"Okay," Louis said. "It's bullshit. But great bullshit."

"That's what Harry told me you'd say. He flew up to San Francisco yesterday to talk to the General about you fellows. Stanley said you'd level. About anything." He looked at me intently. "That means a lot to Harry Redding, Major." He lit a cigarette. One didn't see much smoking in Tinseltown these days. Not tobacco. He went on: "So I'll level, too. We really checked you out. All the way. But Harry wanted to hear it from General Stanley personally. He admires that old man."

I frowned. First because, sick as he was, General Stanley was only fifty-one years old, and with forty just over my own horizon I wasn't ready to accept fifty-one as "old."

Then there was the business of my military record. I got all the right medals and commendations in Vietnam, and I did pretty well in the years after that. But it was no secret that I had been passed over twice for promotion to light colonel in the last year. That was why I decided to leave the army. Eighteen years of my life went out the window with that decision, but the president of the selection board told me straight out that major was the end of the line for me. And he told me why.

My last posting had been to the War College, as an instructor in the strategic and political uses of unconventional warfare. And I had departed from the syllabus too often. When terrorists began to hit American targets, I started telling my students that diplomacy wasn't going to work unless it was backed up by force—a great deal of force, covert or overt. Despite some reprimands, I kept it up because I believed what I was telling my students. I probably could have gotten away with it until the end of my tour at the college, but I made the mistake of giving my favorite lecture to a group of visitors from the State Department.

I was called in to the Academic Commandant's office and told to drop my crusade. America's response to terrorism, I was told, was not a military decision, but a political one. And in the U.S. Army soldiers don't make political decisions.

I had no excuse. I'd had three years in the Philippines after the Miltary Academy. Then three years with the Fifth Air Cavalry in Germany, followed by a year at the Special Warfare School, and two tours as an A-camp commander in Fifth Special Forces Group in Vietnam. Losing the war—and that was what we did—had a bad effect on me, but no worse than on plenty of other professional soldiers. I did a short tour of duty with the military mission at our embassy in Israel and another slightly longer one in London. The army did its best for me. It even picked me to teach at the War College. So I should have respected the ground rules. But somehow, the spectacle of the United States floundering around trying to deal with terrorists and not being able to bite the bullet and hit back simply got to be too much for me.

Louis, whom I had managed to keep with me after Vietnam, had warned me. "Casey," he said one night as we shared a bottle of Chivas in my quarters, "you had better cool it or they are going to give you the heave-ho."

I said, "Centurion, mind your manners."

"Remember Varus and the three legions," he said.

I had to look up the reference after he left. Publius Quintillius Varus was the Roman general who got himself ambushed in the Teutoburger Wald along with eighteen thousand of Emperor Augustus's best troops. Trust Louis to know that.

He had been right about what was going to happen to me, too. The following March I went before the selection board and got passed over. Then in November it happened again, and I resigned. What I hadn't expected was that Louis, who had two more years in than I had, took his twenty and retired. At the age of forty-one. "We're a team, Major," he said simply, "whichever way it goes." And that is a rare thing. Since then I had been casting around for some kind of job that would earn us both a living. I even got in touch with Dieter Lang, a man I knew in Zurich who might find us positions as military instructors in any one of a dozen Third World countries. I specified countries on "our" side, and Dieter had said, with a grim sort of laugh, that such countries were getting hard to find, but he would see what he could do.

That was why I had been so quick to respond when General Stanley had called me to his suite at Letterman Hospital and suggested that Louis and I go down to Century City to see Jerome Ziegler of Eagle Films. There was a five-thousand-dollar fee mentioned for only a few days' work, and I figured that would give Louis and me a real travel fund in case Lang came through.

After the screening, Ziegler said, "I want you to meet someone."

A girl who had been huddled with some of the film technicians caught Ziegler's signal and came over. Close up, she wasn't just a girl. She was a woman, probably in her thirties, with a strong, pretty face and great legs. Her eyes were brilliant blue and large. Her hair was dark, smooth, and shiny as the fur of a seal.

"This is Ann Maclean," Ziegler said, "Eagle's publicist."

The moment she spoke I knew she was British. I learned that she had been living and working in the States for four years. Some British immigrants go back every so often for a refresher course in the London mumble, but not Ann Maclean. She still said "whilst" for "while," but she was on the way to speaking just like the rest of us, more's the pity.

"Ann is the keeper of the flame," Ziegler said, lapsing into the habit film people have of speaking in motion-picture titles.

10

The meaning was clear enough. It was her job to deal with the press and take care of Harry Redding's image.

And in fact she had been having some trouble doing that—with his peers in the business, not with the moviegoing public. Six years ago, Redding had won an Academy Award in a sleeper about a young lieutenant's escape from the Chinese Communists during the Korean War. The award had stunned his fellow actors, even those who had voted for him. But it opened doors for him. On a financial shoestring, he and Ziegler had formed Eagle Films and started making his war pictures. The paying customers had loved them. He did what Sylvester Stallone did: he gave a great many Americans a large dose of wish fulfillment. By now he was a millionaire dozens of times over. *People* magazine said so. One might ignore that as media puff, but *Forbes* and the *Wall Street Journal* confirmed his net worth. Redding's pictures made money, big money.

For the last couple of years the critics had been after him. Stories had begun to appear about how ironic it was that Harry Redding could "cash in" on pictures about the Vietnam War although he had no war record, no service record at all.

When General Stanley had told me that Ziegler wanted to talk to me about consulting on a picture called *Covering Fire*, Louis had filled me in. He showed me a copy of the *National Investigator* (a publication to which Louis was unaccountably addicted). It claimed that Redding had run off to Canada to avoid service in Vietnam. I didn't know whether or not this was true. Neither did Louis. A publication that specializes in kinky celebrity sex gossip and stories about newborns who talk to the doctor in the delivery room isn't my idea of a source of hard intelligence. Louis's only comment had been, "So what?" Sergeant Brown had always believed Vietnam—and any other war—should be left to the professionals.

"I've heard a great deal about you, Major Quary," Ann Maclean said with a dazzling smile. "What does K. C. stand for?"

"Kenneth Charles," I said. "But no one has called me that since my mother stopped tying my shoes."

Louis grinned at her. He made up his mind swiftly when

11

meeting new people, and he was seldom wrong. "You call him Casey, Miss Maclean. He won't answer unless you do. And you can call me anything you like, so long as you call me."

"I'm Ann, Louis," she said. Then to Ziegler: "Harry is waiting for us in Malibu, Jerry." Despite my height, she didn't have to raise her eyes much to look into mine. She was a tall woman. "Harry would have been here, Casey," she said, "but something came up at the last minute. It often does. He wants very much to talk to you and Louis."

Louis's face showed unalloyed pleasure. He loved movies; the more outlandish and inaccurate the combat scenes were, the better he liked them. In Nam, after a movie in camp, he would tell me: "Someday I'm going to get one of the cement heads who make these things and straighten him out." He'd have his chance now, he'd thought. But he'd been disappointed that Redding had not been at the screening. Well, the man was a celebrity, so why not?

"We have a company car outside," Ann said. "Is your car here, Casey?"

"No," I said. I had sold my TransAm and put the money in our travel fund.

"We can ride out together then," she said.

I stood next to her. She smelled of perfume that had to be expensive. I was glad that my only civilian suit was of decent quality and fit me well. At six three and two hundred pounds, you can't buy much off the rack.

Sergeant Brown always said I was a vain man. It is possible he is right. But it isn't too easy to be vain when your face has been scarred by a steel splinter, your nose broken, and you carry a piece of a Russian mortar shell under your ribs. In the army such marks aren't envied, but they are badges. In civilian life, I don't think so. I've seen ugly men who are great with the ladies, but most of them are rich. Ugly plus poor isn't attractive.

I found myself wishing that I could afford a woman like Ann Maclean. I couldn't. Not even close. With that depressing thought in my mind, I followed Ann and Ziegler out of the screening room and into the hot, smoggy afternoon of Century City.

12

2

The company car was a Mercedes turbo-diesel limousine, silver-gray, with dark windows. Inside, there was a television set, a telephone, a bar, and a temperature drop of about ten degrees. The driver, Sam, was a thin-faced black man I was reasonably sure had had a small part in *Covering Fire*. I found that interesting. He was, like so many others in Southern California, hopeful, however vaguely, of a career in the movies. Redding made a practice of giving his people, even his domestic staffers, a shot.

Louis sat up front with Sam, by choice. He and I had settled the race thing between us a long time ago. We were in a joint in Saigon, competing for the company of a doll-faced bar girl. I was a first lieutenant then, and he was a sergeant. He said, "Look, Lieutenant, we are friends, and I'll lay my ass on the line for you any time. You'll do the same for me. Okay, that's fine. But we're visibly different, and sometimes it counts. So why don't you take your white butt down to the Caravelle? This place is for the brothers."

I was offended, but Louis was right. I was in a black bar, and there were noncombat soldiers there who didn't know what happened when black and white actually fought side by side. He softened it a bit by putting my beret on my head and grinning at me. "Go punch out a television reporter," he said.

13

Louis and I served out the whole of our second tour together. First down in the delta, and then up north at Dakto. He saved my life up there when I was wounded. The North Vietnamese overran the camp, and he stood over me until the evacuation chopper arrived. I got him a DSC for that. "Great," he said when he heard about the citation. "Fair is fair."

Louis was one hell of a soldier. The army never should have let him retire.

Traffic was bumper to bumper on Santa Monica Boulevard, so Sam took us on a circuitous route through a part of Culver City and Ocean Park. The sun was still high in the west, looking dull red through the tinted windows of the limousine. The sky was cloudless, but the air was thick, almost viscous. There was a first-stage smog alert on, but as far as I could tell it hadn't kept Angelenos out of their cars. How could it? The Los Angeles basin is a sprawling urban complex of hundreds of square miles that had taken shape in the golden age of the automobile. There was no public transport worthy of the name, and if there had been, what Angeleno would have used it?

We passed through a tiny enclave of Vietnamese refugee businesses on the edge of Culver City: a market, a bar, a restaurant. The Vietnamese who have come to this country are a hardworking lot. We owe those people. We talked them into fighting and then bugged out on them. That might be simplistic (a stupid word for recognizing the obvious), but it is no more than the truth. I wondered how many of the people living over those storefronts and in crowded one-room apartments shared the same memories Louis and I carried.

Ziegler looked at the shop signs as we inched past and said, "There are a good many ex–South Vietnamese soldiers down here. Were they good, Major?"

"Some were, some weren't," I said. "They didn't lose the war because they couldn't fight. They lost it because Congress cut them off. At the end, their airplanes couldn't fly and they were rationing cartridges."

Ann said, "You sound bitter, Casey."

14

"It was just a bad deal from beginning to end."

"You mean it was a bad war?"

"That's a political question," I said.

That smile lit up her face again. "It is my impression that political questions don't frighten you, Casey."

"President Johnson and his brain busters lost the war the day after the Tonkin Gulf resolution was passed. It just took thirty thousand casualties to tidy up the loose ends."

"There's a lot of anger in you, Casey."

"I'm an infantryman, not a psychiatrist."

"Not exactly a diplomat, either."

Ziegler, who was listening to the conversation with interest, cut in. "Among other things, you told some State Department visitors to the John F. Kennedy School for Unconventional Warfare at Fort Bragg that it was a mistake to send Marines to Lebanon, that what was needed was a brigade of Special Forces to organize the Lebanese Christians against the Shiite militia."

I hope I didn't give away my surprise at how well informed these people were about my misdeeds in the army. It shocked me that the statements made by an obscure Green Beret officer to a bunch of striped pants from the State Department could find their way into some civilian's possession. When Ziegler said he had investigated me, he had meant "in depth."

"That was some time ago," I said. "Besides, no one took it seriously." No one, that is, but the Inspector General of the Army, who tucked away my indiscretions in my 201 file.

"You may well have been right," Ann said. "It certainly didn't work out well the way it was done."

"Marines," I said, and looked out the window at the gold path the setting sun made on Santa Monica Bay. Not fair, of course; it wasn't the Marines' fault they had been set up for a terrorist fanatic. They should have hit the beach in Lebanon as though it were Iwo Jima. Instead of that they were told not to look too warlike.

Ziegler glanced at his watch and turned on the television set. The local news was winding up. There were shots from a traffic

15

helicopter showing the clogged freeways. Some laughing and banter among the anchor people. Then a graphic showing a stylized bomb explosion and the superimposed word *Terrorism*. And, last, the solemn voice of the number-one talking head intoning the grim statistic—the number of days that the American diplomats had been held somewhere in the Middle East by some still-unlocated gang of guerrillas.

"And still nothing from the Administration or Delta Force," Ziegler said. "What do you think, Major?"

"You already know what I think," I said.

Ann asked softly, "Could something be done, Casey?"

"I don't know. Something might have been done a year ago. But now?"

Ziegler looked at Ann and then snapped off the television set. "What do they want, Major? Any idea? And who are they? They haven't behaved the way Islamic radicals usually do. They haven't played to the media. Isn't that damned peculiar?"

"Yes," I said. "Maybe they're on to something new. The old way got them plenty of newsprint and television time, but not much else. Who knows? I sure as hell don't."

"What would you have done, Casey?" Ann asked.

"I would have had a force ready. Marines. Delta Force. Whatever. I would have had it in place and ready to go, and I would have chased the bastards no matter where they went."

"That's not very practical," Ziegler said.

"You didn't ask me for practical," I said. "You asked me what I would have done. Whoever they are, they are going to ask for something, and when they do, there are going to be some tough questions that have to be answered."

"You believe the rumors about Dimona?"

"It doesn't matter what I believe or what anyone believes," I said. "The important thing is that we can't give them *anything*. If we do, then there's no end to it."

"What about the safety of the hostages?" Ann asked.

"Once they're hostages they *aren't* safe. Look at the record. And every time we yield to blackmail to save a hostage, we hand

16

out an invitation to take some more. Sure I'd want to save hostages. But at what price in future lives? It isn't fair, it isn't decent. But what the hell is fair or decent about terrorism? Chance puts the innocent hostage at risk, and that's the way I'd play it."

"A bit brutal," Ziegler said.

"I suppose it is. War gets pretty grisly sometimes."

"It is a war, isn't it," Ann said quietly.

"Believe it," I said.

A war it was. The Pentagon theorists called it "low intensity." And we were in a strange kind of limbo. There had been rumors inside the military that policy was changing or about to change. The decision to force down the hijackers of the *Achille Lauro* with navy fighters made it appear that the Administration was reaching a limit of tolerance. In my book, the program should now be to send Delta Force or some Rangers in hot pursuit of the next gang of hostage-takers. But *that* decision, if it was in the works, was still being debated.

Plainly, something had to be done, and soon. One day the hostage would be a chief of state or the bomb would be nuclear. What then?

But I was out of it now. Such things were a far cry from giving Harry Redding a critique of the combat scenes in *Covering Fire*.

I looked out at the traffic and the smoggy Southern California day sinking into evening. The weather and my sense of isolation depressed me.

Ziegler opened the refrigerator in the console and produced a frosty bottle of beer for each of us. Ann used the telephone to call Redding's house and talk to the houseboy. "Ming, please tell Mr. Redding the traffic is bad and we'll be a half hour or so."

Actually, it took us closer to an hour and another bottle of Michelob to reach Redding's Malibu beach compound.

3

Harry Redding lived well. His beach house was guarded from the Pacific Coast Highway by a high, long wall made principally of fieldstone. The cost of the wall alone would have built on-base housing for a battalion of wives and dependents. There was a handsome gate, the posts of which were topped by television cameras in concrete housings.

Sam tapped out a code on a black box in the front seat, and the gate swung open for us. A smoothly paved road angled down the slope of the seaward hill toward a handsome house of fieldstone, redwood, and glass. There was a satellite dish in a service yard, a half-dozen or so whip antennas mounted on the roof of the main house, a pair of small microwave dishes, and one of those spiky nondirectional antennas used for ham-radio reception. I had read somewhere that Redding was an amateur radio hobbyist. He hadn't spared expense for his equipment. It was all first-quality and neatly installed.

Beyond the house lay a terrace, with a swimming pool perched on the edge of a sheer drop of some thirty feet down to the beach and the Pacific. The sea was gentle, with placid waves washing up onto a shingle of white sand. The beach was public; the California Coastal Commission saw to that. But the only figure on it was a lone man in swimming trunks. A black Great Dane gamboled alongside as he jogged at the water's edge.

The sun was almost on the horizon, looking red and huge. To the south lay the darkening bulk of Santa Catalina, to the northwest the other Channel Islands. A sailboat, toylike in the distance, ghosted slowly toward Huntington Beach in the light air. Gulls soared on the barely perceptible updraft rising from the cliff face. It was beautiful. I couldn't even imagine what it would be like to live this way, in such surroundings.

The Mercedes had pulled into a paved court in front of the house. Being California, the garage was prominently featured. It should have been. It contained a vintage Ferrari Testa Rossa with one of those wonderful Scagliatti spyder bodies, bobtailed and droop-snooted. A large white circle decorated the Italian racing-red flank. It was the car Redding ran in the vintage-car races to which amateur drivers had turned when the professionals took over sports-car racing. Next to the Ferrari stood a black-on-black whale-tail Porsche, then an Audi Quattro, and the immaculate space for the Mercedes in which we had arrived.

As we alighted from the limousine, Louis murmured to me, "Rich or poor, Major, it's nice to have money." The whale-tail was Louis's dream car. He'd have wrestled a tiger to have one.

"The Quattro belongs to Ann," Ziegler said. That began to clarify her standing here. The Audi looked very much at home. So did she.

We were met at the door by a venerable Chinese in a white coat—Ming the houseboy.

"Mr. Redding is on the beach running Tarquin," he said. "Mr. Agron is on the terrace." His English was flawless.

We followed him through a living room dominated by a huge fireplace, over which was displayed what appeared to be a genuine Revolutionary War British Brown Bess musket. A priceless antique. From the high ceiling above our heads hung a mobile. It might have been a genuine Calder. It looked like one.

The living room was separated from the terrace by a wall of thermal glass and sliding doors. Beyond, near the low fieldstone wall, was a bar. Ziegler headed straight for it, with only a wave to the thin, tanned man in casual clothes who lounged in one of the chairs scattered about the flagged terrace.

19

From the bar Ziegler said, "Major Quary, Sergeant Brown, meet Gershon Agron. Gershon is our agent in Tel Aviv. You have things in common. He used to be a paratrooper."

Agron got to his feet and silently shook hands with me and with Louis. He raised Ann's hand to his lips. It was not a gesture one saw often these days and certainly not one expected from an Israeli. But it looked right when he did it.

Ziegler asked what we wanted to drink, and Louis and I settled on Scotch. Ann asked for straight tonic. A very controlled young woman, I thought.

She went to the fieldstone parapet and waved to the man on the beach. The black Great Dane came bounding up the steep stairs to greet her, tongue lolling and tail lashing happily. One more indicator of her status in this elegant house.

Redding came jogging up the stairs as though they were part of his daily regimen.

That early evening in Malibu was my first experience of meeting a celebrity. I suspected even then that it wasn't typical. Harry Redding had a rare quality of warmth and sincerity that came across strongly from the screen. Even rarer was the fact that it came across in person. When he spoke to you, you were *important*, and not, it seemed, for any self-serving reasons but because he was genuinely interested in what you had to say.

He was forty-four years old. I wouldn't have known that if I hadn't read the Eagle Films biography Ziegler (or was it Ann?) had taken care to send to me.

He was a native Southern Californian, and had attended the University of Southern California in the 1960s. At some date unspecified by the handout, he had gone to New York to study acting with the shaggies of the Method school. The bio jumped, with an oblique reference to Off-Broadway work and summer stock, to a dozen years ago, when he had surfaced in Hollywood and started playing small parts in low-budget pictures and some science-fiction films that Louis, the movie buff, had told me he remembered. Like dozens of prime physical specimens, he had taken what parts were offered and hoped for a breakthrough.

20

Then he had met Jerry Ziegler and through him got the lead in a sleeper called *Chosin*, a kind of antiwar, oddly artistic film about Korea. For a parcel of different reasons, it had captured the critics. Redding had carried the whole story by the brilliance of his performance, and the role won him an Academy Award for best actor.

From that moment on, Harry Redding was what the film people call "bankable." Meaning that if he's in it, financing will be no problem.

But Redding—even I could see Ziegler's hand in this—had realized that if he was bankable, he could now make films for himself and for the people he wanted to pull into the movie houses. It wasn't a new idea. Stallone and Eastwood had done it before him. But Redding did it just as well as they did, and with a special touch. A Redding film had a way of reversing the judgments of history. Losers became winners. Battles lost became victories. Moral victories, to be sure, but victories. There was always a touch of irony in a Harry Redding picture. One critic called him "a celluloid Kipling," and maybe that said most of what needed to be said about him. He waved the flag, but with such sincerity that even the most hard-bitten paying customer left the theater moved. Film was Harry Redding's medium.

The first Eagle film was a blockbuster called *Freefire Zone*. Young people who had been children during the worst of the Vietnam War flocked to see it. What followed was a whole series of pictures about Americans at war, and the money rolled in. Redding didn't glamorize war exactly. He glamorized heroism, and the public loved him for it the way they had once loved "Duke" Wayne and Errol Flynn.

Even soldiers who knew better crowded into post theaters to see Redding's explosive fantasies. George C. Scott playing Patton said, "Americans hate to lose." Redding somehow fixed on that and gave the public what it wanted. Of course, the critics began to turn on him. They resented his skyrocketing success, his money, and what they had begun to think was his conservative political slant. Most of all, I think, they were embarrassed by his patriotism. Some thought it was phony and commercial. Others were even more distressed by the thought that it might be genuine.

But the moviegoing, video-cassette-buying public wanted heroes. Redding gave them heroes.

I had come to meet him with some reservations. Louis and I had discussed it before we left San Francisco. I wondered about the values of a society that rewarded make-believe more generously than the real thing. Louis, more tolerant than I, said, "Hell, Casey, that's the veteran's lament. It's just the way things are, the way they've always been. The Athenians ruined Miltiades, who fought the Persians for them, and made a hero out of Aeschylus, who wrote a play about them. So what else is new?"

Harry Redding had the same open friendliness that Tarquin had shown. He could have entered a body-builders competition that very evening, and he would have done just fine. He wore minimal trunks and stood solidly on large, broad feet. He was as handsome in the flesh as he was on the screen, with regular features and dark hair bound with the familiar folded bandanna. He had flat, smooth cheeks and a surprisingly small and delicate mouth, saved from weakness by a square, dimpled chin. He was shorter than I had expected him to be, not more than five eight or nine. Both Louis and I loomed over him as we shook hands.

The Great Dane romped over to him and buried his nose in his crotch, the way big dogs often do, whipping the air happily with his tail. Redding spoke to him, and he immediately flopped onto the flagstones, still thumping his tail and regarding his master with worshipful brown eyes. Redding's eyes were exactly the same color, flecked with similar shards of yellow.

Ming appeared from inside the house with a thick terry robe, which Redding draped over his shoulders as he took a frosty glass from Ziegler. Tonic water, just like Ann Maclean.

When everyone was seated again, the Israeli still silent, Ann with a hand on Redding's arm, Ziegler said, "The Major and the Sergeant didn't think much of the combat scenes, Harry."

"I would have been surprised if they had," Redding said. "People who know the real thing have different standards." He looked directly at me as he spoke, as though measuring my response.

"They were as good as any I've seen on the screen," I said. "Your Vietnamese colonel did a decent job."

"Tactful Casey," Ann said, smiling at me.

"What do you think, Gershon?" Redding asked. "You saw all the footage."

The Israeli shrugged. "It's make-believe, Harry. Make-believe bores me." His English was accented but fluent.

"And you, Sergeant Brown?" Redding asked.

"Hell, I love noise," Louis said. "Where did you get the Russian tank? It was the real article."

"We bought it from the Israelis," Ziegler said. "At great expense. Nothing we get through Gershon comes cheap."

"We get our money's worth," Redding said. He turned to Ann. "Before I take our guests downstairs, we have to arrange things for tonight. Jerry and I have to see those gonifs from United Artists. Can't get out of it. And Gershon's got to catch a plane for Washington. Will you look out for the major and Sergeant Brown? You'll have things to discuss, I think."

Ziegler said, "Sergeant Brown was drooling over the Porsche, Harry. Maybe he would drive Gershon to the airport, if you want to let him use it."

"Try me," Louis said happily.

Ann looked at me. "Dinner tonight, Major?"

"My pleasure," I said.

"Done, then," Redding said. He put down his glass and said to me, "Is there any reason you and Sergeant Brown can't stay over? There's plenty of room, and I think we may want to talk some more tomorrow."

"All right," I said. For a moment no one spoke. Agron was looking at me with a coldly speculative expression in his black eyes. He seemed strangely familiar. I had served only briefly in

23

the American military attaché's office in Tel Aviv, but it had been long enough for me to recognize the scent of Mossad or Shin Beth counterintelligence. Agron might act as agent for Eagle Films, he might even broker captured Russian equipment to the movies, but somehow I felt that wasn't all he did.

He seemed to read my mind and gave me a slow smile.

We couldn't stay in Malibu among the rich and famous for long, but until tomorrow was within reason. And the idea of having dinner alone with Ann was very appealing.

The silence seemed to make Redding nervous. He got to his feet. For a moment he stood at the balustrade looking west. The sun was slipping below the horizon. Lights were coming on in the offshore rigs down the coast. The Channel Islands were purple mountains rising from the calm sea. Overhead, the gulls wheeled and uttered shrill, sad cries.

"Jesus," Redding said softly. "This is a beautiful country."

Ann excused herself and went into the house. I put down my unfinished drink, and we followed Redding inside. He led the way down a flight of stairs and into a room built into the hillside under the main house. The room contrasted with the opulence of the house. There were only narrow horizontal windows facing the beach. The walls were concrete where they were not covered with bookcases and maps. There were no chairs other than a few high stools spotted around several large steel tables. One corner was dominated by Redding's radio gear. I am not an expert, but even I could recognize a powerful short-wave transceiver, television monitors of professional quality, and other expensive equipment.

The workroom—that was what Redding called it—was at least thirty feet by fifteen. Part of one wall was devoted to one of the most lethal displays of firearms I had even seen in civilian hands. There was an assortment of automatic weapons, American, Russian, and Israeli. In a place of honor was his famous rocket-

24

propelled grenade launcher, with a dozen rounds neatly racked beneath it.

Louis was drawn to the hardware immediately and stood inspecting it with admiration. "Christ," he said. "You could start World War III with all this. Have you got a nuke hidden away somewhere?"

Ziegler looked at Redding and then put a hand on Louis's shoulder to draw him away from the arsenal. "No, Sergeant, no nukes. But I'm working on it," he said, all smiles and affability.

The low ceiling, the fluorescent lighting, the slit windows overlooking the sea, the *coldness* of the room made me think of an old German bunker I had once explored above the Normandy beaches.

There was a knock at the heavy door, and Ziegler opened it. Ming had left a serving cart on the landing. Ziegler wheeled it in and served the coffee. Inky and without sugar or cream. I half smiled at Louis, who loved his coffee sweet enough to attract bees and who disliked playing the Spartan unless it was absolutely necessary.

"Well, Harry?" Ziegler said. "Do we begin now?"

"Do it," Redding said.

Ziegler went to a locked cabinet, opened it, and took out an armload of maps, papers, bound files, photographs, and computer print-outs. He also took out a flat metal briefcase, which he left closed on the table.

I walked over and looked. There were six Operational Navigation Charts, 1:1,000,000 scale. ONCs are intended for the use of pilots and air navigators, and are usually called simply air-navs. They are the best and most detailed large-scale charts available to civilians. These covered all of North Africa from Morocco to the Red Sea. In addition to the air-navs, there were a dozen or so smaller maps, some of them Egyptian.

Since most of northern Africa is either desert or mountains, all the charts were spotted with colorless areas marked "Limits of Reliable Topographic Information." I wasn't a jet pilot, but I was a qualified helicopter driver and knew that sort of thing on a chart is always bad news.

There was a stack of photographs taken from high altitude, possibly from orbit. There were National Ocean Survey charts of the Moroccan and Red Sea coastal areas and of the Gulf of Sidra, all generously marked with restricted zones and areas and notices that unauthorized approach to these would result in vessels being fired upon without warning.

Ziegler had spread out a variety of colored folders labeled LOGISTICS, TRANSPORT, SUPPORT, UNIT ONE MAINTENANCE, UNIT TWO MAINTENANCE, PRODUCTION, and PERSONNEL.

And there was a stack of eight-and-a-half-by-eleven books bound in red plastic and labeled "*Kasserine: A Screenplay* by Harry Redding." These bore the embossed logo of Eagle Films.

I looked across the table at Redding. "That's what all this is about, Redding? You are going to make a picture about the war in North Africa?"

I was tempted to say that a man had to be infatuated with American defeats to make a film about the battle of Kasserine Pass, where green American draftees in obsolescent tanks were bloodied by the veterans of the Afrika Korps in 1943. But, of course, defeat into victory was Redding's thing.

"We are going to make *Kasserine*, yes," he said. "In fact, the project is already under way. We have the cooperation of the government of Tunisia." He grinned in an almost boyish way. His ability to produce that grin out of an expression of sullen anger was one of the things, I had read somewhere, that made him so attractive to women. "We're getting twenty genuine Heinkel-111 bombers from Spain. The same ones used in *The Battle of Britain* and *Patton*. And a thousand soldiers from the Tunisian Army, along with some old Sherman tanks. All authentic equipment, Major."

"Obtained at great expense," Ziegler added. "Unit One is already on the water. They'll be in Bizerte within a week and on the way to Kasserine about a week after that."

"There are dozens of people you could get better qualified than I as technical adviser," I said. "Not that Louis and I couldn't use a legitimate job, but you could get people who fought at Kasserine. There are still some of them around."

Ziegler and Redding exchanged glances. Then Ziegler said, "We have someone—a retired colonel who was a captain in II Corps when Fredendall was in command."

"I'm impressed," I said. I *was* impressed. Someone connected with Eagle Films had done his homework. The name of Major General Lloyd R. Fredendall, a U.S. Army officer whose star had briefly risen when the Americans went ashore in Morocco that long-ago November of 1942, was not exactly a household word. He had commanded the Center Task Force during the landings and II Corps for several months thereafter. But the American defeat at Kasserine Pass had finished his career. A rich California martinet named George Smith Patton, Jr., had taken over II Corps and later went on to other glory.

"Don't play games, Ziegler," Agron said impatiently. "He's the man we selected. He's here. Get on with it."

Bending over the littered table had given me an ache under the ribs where my gift from Soviet State Munitions Factory Number Six at Semipalatinsk nestled near my heart. I knew what it was because X-rays showed it clearly. It was a fragment of a mortar shell's fuse. I knew where it was made because I got it from a North Vietnamese mortarman at Dakto. I was warned that I would have to have it removed one day because it could migrate into something vital and finish me. But I was in no hurry whatever to surrender my body to a Veterans Administration surgeon.

I straightened and said, "I think that's a fine idea. You ask us to come down here to see a picture that's finished and ready to be distributed. Then you tell us about another picture that already has a technical adviser. So I assume you want to talk about something else. Let's just do it, shall we?"

Louis gave me a warning glance. He knew how short-tempered I could be when people got mysterious.

Redding said, "Major Quary, you are here because General Stanley thinks you are the best available man to handle a project we are planning. The General thinks the world of you and Sergeant Brown."

I had served off and on under General John Stanley during

my military career. He was an unconventional-warfare specialist, one of the best the army had ever produced. He was retired now, and ill enough to be living in a suite at Letterman Army Hospital, but he was one of those men the military never quite releases. To me, personally, he was a source of encouragement, support, good advice, and friendship. If the General thought I was the man to do a job, I was going to listen.

"Gershon," Redding said, "show them the other material."

Agron opened the metal case and extracted a sheaf of photographs. He spread them out on the table.

When I examined them, I received a shock. *These* were not ordinary low-orbit pictures. These were something very different, taken from a military satellite. It was as though the observer floated a few dozen yards above the features on the ground. The terrain was desert. I could see camels and tents and what appeared to be a Bedouin settlement. Tribesmen stood around or were caught in the act of walking, eating, defecating. The resolution was fine enough to distinguish the features of one face from another. Behind one of the tents women were making pita, Arab bread. You could almost reach down and take it from their hands.

There were eighteen pictures. Some showed galvanized-iron buildings—warehouses, actually—with piles of old drilling gear scattered around. On an oil drum I could read the legend "British Petroleum, 100 Imperial Gallons." The nose of what looked like an armored vehicle protruded from a shack. All the men were armed. Not with old surplus weapons, but with Soviet assault weapons.

The colors were sharp and clear. I could see patterned rugs in the tents and make out the labels on the cans piled in a shallow pit near the camp.

Rusty cans that once held meat and fruit and Western goodies? What sort of Bedouins carried that kind of supplies with them? I looked at Agron. His expression said, "Interesting?"

Interesting wasn't the word. *Fascinating* would do better. Then I found the set he had been waiting for me to find. Taken at a low sun angle, they showed a pattern of dunes that were not dunes at all. They were the sand faces of some very sophisticated strongpoints. You couldn't see the weapons inside, but they were undoubtedly there, with overlapping fields of fire in every direction.

And then the *pièce de résistance*: two men in Western dress kneeling in conversation with an armed Arab. The faces were bearded. Agron tapped a finger on a last photograph, a blow-up of those faces. The print was grainy, but considering how it had been made it was a technological marvel.

"That is Ambassador Edward Lyman and his chargé d'affaires," he said. "You can compare it with some shots Ziegler collected of him at a White House reception two weeks before he left for Beirut."

I had no reason at all to doubt him.

I flipped the prints over. They were stamped in Hebrew. From my Tel Aviv duty, I recognized the Israeli Defense Force MOST SECRET rubric.

"How did you come by these?" I demanded.

"I got them," he said.

"Israel has nothing that could produce stuff like this," I said. "These are American surveillance-satellite pictures."

The black eyes regarded me steadily. "Of course."

I was nonplused. I'm a soldier and I know the value of good intelligence. I also know that there is much secret wheeling and dealing between intelligence services. The American intelligence community was still regarded with apprehension by foreign services because of the Freedom of Information Act, among other things. But foreign spymasters were willing enough to *accept* intelligence from us. We had, after all, the finest "national technical means" (bureaucratese for spy-satellite technology) in the world.

These pictures had been taken by a very sophisticated military surveillance satellite. The men and women in the Blue Cube—the satellite control headquarters—at Sunnyvale, California, had found the missing hostages.

"How fresh are these?" I asked, Redding's movie forgotten.

"The head shots were taken last Friday," Agron said.

I stared at him hard. "When does Mossad send someone looking for this stuff?"

He shook his head. The gesture was oddly, economically eloquent. Israeli intelligence had allowed him—or someone—to remove these sensitive pictures from the files. It shook me badly when I realized what this implied.

It meant, simply put, that our government knew—had probably known for weeks—the location of the hostages taken from the Beirut embassy. A satellite search was difficult and time-consuming, so the people in CIA or NSA had to have known, in general terms, where to search.

But nothing had been done. Nothing at all. No doubt "policy" was still being debated.

The information had been shared with the Israelis, though. I wondered why. Were there people in the Administration who hoped that the Israelis would pull off another Entebbe, snatching *our* people out of terrorist hands? And, incidentally, taking all the blame if in the process hostages died?

No. Whatever the plan had been, that wasn't it. The Israelis were not naïve.

Now enter Gershon Agron. What were *his* connections with Mossad, I wondered. He had been given access to the highest secret classification of military photographs and allowed to make off with them.

And bring them here. To Harry Redding's house in Malibu.

I said, "Where is this place?" Wherever it was, it was in the deep sand sea. That meant either Saudi Arabia or Egypt or Libya. Given those choices, I knew the answer would not please me.

"It is an old British Petroleum concession. About three hundred miles from Tripoli. The coordinates are 27° 29′ North, 12° 22′ East."

"Libya."

"Yes."

That answered my question about why no military action had been taken to retrieve the hostages if their location was known. I had heard, not once, but several times, a rumor that there was a uranium diffusion plant in that part of the northern Sahara. The story was that Leonid Brezhnev had built it for Colonel Qaddafi and staffed it with Russians. The Soviets had always claimed to believe in nuclear nonproliferation, but apparently Brezhnev had believed in appeasing Qaddafi's militant pan-Arabism even more. This was changed now. Mikhail Gorbachev apparently *did* worry about proliferation, but he could not simply dismantle the plant and pull out. His compromise had been to deploy Soviet troops there.

If any of this was true, the concealed plant would be ringed with defenses as sophisticated as the Soviets could contrive. The politics of the situation were tense, the implications grave. The Soviets had put themselves in a dilemma of large proportions. Policy or not, they could not allow Qaddafi to make a weapon with his enriched uranium. It was quite possible they were flying the stuff out as quickly as it was made. But they could not simply close the place down without losing an important foothold in the Arab world. So, the story went, they sat on Qaddafi's diffusion plant, looted it regularly, and stood ready to defend it against all comers.

The United States, for all its power, was in check. An assault into the Libyan interior to rescue hostages would look like a preemptive strike on a nuclear installation. To penetrate central Libya with a force of gunships, assault troops, and transports would be certain to trigger a violent Russian response. There was plenty of Soviet power in the area. The Black Sea fleet spent more time in the Gulf of Sidra than it did in its home waters around Odessa.

"Where, exactly," I asked Agron, "is Qaddafi's diffusion plant?"

Agron's narrow eyebrows arched. "You know about that?"

"There's been some talk," I said.

"It's at a place called Barqin. A hellhole near the Wadi Zallaf. They built it there because there is water from a *qanat*, a desert aquifer, about two hundred feet down. The uranium ore comes north from Chad—almost a thousand miles—by truck. Barqin is less than a hundred miles from Point X. There are Spetznaz at Barqin. Soviet Special Forces." He glanced at me ironically. "Point X has a name, by the way. Turab al Jadjah. But no one remembers to call it that any more."

"Point X," I said, "doesn't look too pretty. Have you pictures of Barqin?"

Agron lifted his shoulders and spread his hands. "Ah, no. Everyone pretends Barqin doesn't exist. It is easier to deal with the Russians that way."

"And I thought we came here to talk about movies," Louis said.

"*Kasserine* is real," Redding said. "Principal photography is scheduled to begin in two weeks." He paused, watching Agron and then glancing across the table at Ziegler, who nodded. Then he said, "I don't know if you've heard of Ross Perot, Casey."

Of course I had heard of Perot. Who hadn't? He was a millionaire Texas businessman and something of an American hero. His company had been selling computer systems to the government of Iran when the fundamentalist revolution rolled over the Shah. Some of Perot's executives had been trapped and arrested in the wave of anti-Americanism that swept the country. When all else failed, Perot had organized a personal and private penetration of Iran and snatched his people out from under the noses of the Pasdaran. The contrast between his swift action and the inability of the United States government to rescue its own embassy staffers was marked and invidious.

Redding said, "Well?"

"Am I reading you right?"

"Eagle Films will have more than two thousand people working in Tunisia. Isn't that a perfect cover for—well, for whatever we decide to do?"

"God save us from amateurs," I said. "Your precious Point X has to be almost two hundred miles from the nearest point in Tunisia. Miles filled with sand, nasty Libyans, and Russian Special Forces."

32

"No. It's in the armpit of creation, Major," Ziegler said. "There's nothing but desert between Point X and the border."

I said, "This isn't anything like the Perot situation. Are you seriously proposing to do what the United States Army, Navy, and Marine Corps won't tackle?"

"They *can't* tackle it," Redding said. "I can."

"You? You don't know what you're saying."

"We didn't start planning this yesterday," he said.

I began to laugh. I couldn't help myself. I had never heard anything quite so harebrained and ridiculous. Not even after eighteen years in the army.

"Hell's fire, Major," Louis said. "We can listen, can't we? Listening doesn't hurt."

He was wrong, and I should have known he was wrong. I should have said to Redding that this wasn't about grease-paint blood and glycerine sweat, but the real thing, the sort that hurt and make you stink as you die. But I did not. Against all sense and judgment, I said, "All right, Redding. We're listening."

4

The slit windows of Harry Redding's personal war room showed the last of the fading daylight as we began to talk seriously.

The first thing I wanted to know was whether these people understood that what they were planning was illegal, not only in the United States but just about anywhere in the world. It was a minor point, but it needed to be discussed.

"You are proposing," I said, "to put together an assault force of real soldiers under cover of your *Kasserine* operation and invade the sovereign territory of an unfriendly state. Have I got that right so far?"

"It could be viewed in that light," Ziegler murmured.

I looked at Agron. "How many in that Bedouin camp?"

"Fifty, perhaps. Not more than sixty, counting the women."

"All right, let's take that as an estimate for now," I said. "What kind of a force would do the job? Louis?"

Sergeant Brown was all business now. "Two hundred regulars. A hundred fifty infantry, fifty in support."

"For fifty ragheads?" Ziegler demanded.

"Shut up, Jerry," Redding said. "This is their business."

"Of course, with a couple of gunships running interference," Louis said, "you could get by with half that many in the assault force."

I glanced at Ziegler to see if any of this was really getting through to him. Renting soldiers and military equipment from Third World governments for use in making movies was something he knew about. He had no idea how much more costly it could be to hire real soldiers to fight real battles. I thought if we enlightened him, this whole scheme would dissolve into what it surely was, a film hero's pipe dream. But Agron knew exactly what I was doing.

"Let's say seventy men in the assault force," I said. "Trying to make it overland would be impossible unless the unit traveled only at night. There are always some surplus military choppers available in Europe. Dieter Lang might be able to get us what we need."

"We'd need at least three, Major," Louis said. "Big ones. Cost an arm and a leg."

"I'm just laying out your small-budget invasion, Sergeant Brown. An economy action. Say, a couple million dollars or so."

Redding was looking at me peculiarly. "Go on, Major," he said.

"All right, let's add it up. We could put together a pretty fair assault team. Seventy people. Figure twenty thousand dollars a man. We could get by on, say, five hundred thousand dollars' worth of ordnance, though that's cutting it fine. The choppers would come from a legitimate government, so they would have to be bought outright. I don't think you could get them for under one hundred thousand each. What else? Some ground transport. Say twenty-five thousand dollars. Wheels are cheap. Fuel, uniforms, food, water. Another fifteen thousand? It depends on the operational plan, of course. How long the assault team has to stay in the field. And travel, shipping, graft, and bribes—not less than another hundred and fifty thousand dollars. Let's see. That comes to two million two hundred and ninety thousand dollars, right? All cash, of course. The money up front, as I think you film people say. How does that strike you, Ziegler?"

Ziegler looked at Redding and shrugged, and the latter, speaking almost gently, said, "Major Quary, do you know what the

budget for *Kasserine* is? Twenty-five million. And we are prepared for it to run as much as thirty-five percent over budget.
Eagle's first picture grossed eighty million in its first release.
Freefire did thirty-seven million its first *week*. *Covering Fire* will
do even better. Dollars are not the point here. What I want to
know is: *Can it be done?*"

Ziegler half smiled at me, a mean-eyed cherub. "Those are
real numbers." To Redding he said, "I think you've shocked
the Major." Too true. He *had* shocked me. Unless he works in
the Pentagon, a professional soldier does not deal in sums of
such magnitude.

Redding said, "I am prepared to spend whatever it takes. I
am serious about this."

"Well, now," Ziegler cautioned. "So long as it doesn't run
over five mil. We could run into cash-flow problems then, with
Kasserine in production."

"Holy Jesus, Major," Louis said. "For that kind of money we
could start World War III."

"It might be best if we didn't go quite that far," Agron said
laconically.

Redding was looking at me. I had heard, of course, that film
people who were "hot," the way Harry Redding was, made huge
amounts of money. I had never really given it much thought,
since I lived in a different world.

I said, "I'll want to think about it. A lot."

"No problem, Major. Think it over tonight, and we'll talk in
the morning. Gershon, isn't it about time for you to saddle up?"

The Israeli nodded. "Are you ready, Sergeant Brown?"

Louis was looking at intently, and I knew from that wild look
in his eyes what he was thinking. He was *impressed*. And he
wanted to do this operation. Very much. It was an unconventional-warfare specialist's dream mission.

"Ann will get you the keys to the Porsche, Sergeant Brown,"
Redding said.

"Call me Louis, Harry," Louis said.

He started for the door with Agron and looked back at me

pleadingly. I could read him five by five. He was saying, "Casey, do it. Do it."

When they had gone, Redding said, "Jerry and I have to go, Major. Stay here as long as you want and look over our—" there was that film star's smile again—"intelligence. Ann will put it away when you are done with it. Jerry and I will see you in the morning. We'll be late, so don't wait up for us. And don't be gallant. Ann will take care of the dinner tab tonight. It's all deductible, anyway."

When he had gone upstairs to dress, with Ziegler trailing along behind him, I sat on a stool and looked at the materials spread over the surface of the worktable. Deductible, was it? Harry Redding's private war.

I was left alone for about an hour. Redding and Ziegler were shrewd judges of human nature. They had read my doubts about this scheme, and my hidden wishes, too. Their investigation of me must have been thorough. They knew me to be aggressive, good at my job, and absolutely at loose ends, adrift from my profession.

The more I studied the intelligence spread out on the table, the more I became convinced that, with luck, secrecy, and money, the hostages *could* be retrieved. But it would be critically risky for everyone involved. A single mistake could turn a rescue into a massacre.

And that set me to wondering about Redding's motives.

It was possible that they were as simple as a desire to justify his patriotism. Or maybe just his bankroll. Did it really matter?

I was thinking about that when Ann appeared at my side with a fresh pot of steaming coffee.

The hard light made her sleek hair gleam. I noticed now that there was a faint spray of freckles over her nose. She had changed into a black dress that suited her boyish figure perfectly.

I said, "What do *you* think of all this?"

Her smile was solemn. "You mean do I think Harry is crazy?"

"He really means to do this, doesn't he?"

"Yes. He does. It is important to him, Casey."

"I never liked leading men over cliffs."

She smiled at that. "Is that what you are being asked to do?"

"All this," I said, indicating the scatter on the worktable, "has the makings of a fiasco."

"You mean it can't be done?"

"I didn't say that."

She walked to the windows and looked out at the night and the sea. A quarter-moon was in the sky. We couldn't see it, but as the day faded into night the misty Southern California air took on a silvery tint.

"There is something you should know about Harry, Casey," Ann said. "He's a coward. I know that sounds cruel, but it's true. He is afraid of pain and death."

"Everyone's afraid of pain and death," I said.

She turned to look up at me. "Don't misunderstand me," she said. "Harry is a dear man, and I care about him very much. Most people in his position become impossible. He's not like that. He's real."

"All right," I said. "I'm prepared to believe that."

"It's important that you do, Casey. And if you do this thing, it's important that you understand why he is backing it."

"Can you tell me?"

"I think so. I think I know Harry Redding as well as anyone does. He isn't what one automatically thinks of when one thinks of a 'movie star.' He is vulnerable, Casey. Terribly so." She regarded me intently, willing me to understand.

I could think of nothing to say to that. My feelings about Redding were all impressions. I knew almost nothing about the man himself. But there was one thing that needed saying, and I said it as plainly and positively as I could.

"One thing, Ann. *If* we go ahead with this—adventure—there can be no question of his actually taking part in it. It won't be anything like a Harry Redding movie. It will be a job for professionals."

She smiled ruefully. "Oh, Casey, that's the last thing in the world you need worry about. Harry won't even swim in the ocean, because it's too dangerous. Did you see the Ferrari in the garage? Harry drove it in the antique-car races at Laguna Seca last year and frightened himself so badly he hasn't touched the car since. I told you Harry is a physical coward, Casey. A lovely man, but a very easily frightened one."

I thought about Redding's movie image: the supermacho man, the fanatically brave soldier. Well, since when was it the received word that a man's film personality had to reflect the real man?

Then I found myself wondering about the relationship between Harry and Ann. What did a woman feel about a man whose fault she could readily disclose to a relative stranger?

Ann said, "Are you finished in here?"

"For now," I said.

She began to gather up the materials about Point X, putting them back into their proper folders.

"Is it wise to have those photographs here?" I asked.

She returned them to the metal case and carried it back to the cabinet and locked it in. "You don't know what Harry has spent on a security system," she said. "These things are safer here than at the Pentagon."

"That isn't saying very much. Not these days."

I waited to see if Ann would volunteer more information about Harry and, not incidentally, about her feelings for him. But apparently she felt she had given me enough to ponder for the time being.

"Ming doesn't cook," she said. "I've made reservations for us at the Breakers. It's a restaurant a few miles up the coast." She added: "It's one of the few places Harry can go without being bothered. He swears by it." A half-smile. "But the food is only fair. I hope you aren't a gourmet. Jerry is, and he drives us all mad with his talk about food and wine."

I followed her upstairs and outside into the still-warm, salty evening.

"Do you want to drive?" she asked.

39

"No," I answered. Suddenly I didn't want to drive a car I was sure Redding had bought for her as a fringe benefit.

"All right," she said, and climbed into the left-hand seat of the Quattro.

She drove fast and well, with the seat moved back and her hands in the approved ten o'clock–two o'clock position on the wheel. The Quattro traveled as though it were on rails.

I asked, "Will you be going on location with the *Kasserine* company?"

"I'm Eagle's publicist," she said. "I'll be on location part of the time and traveling some. It depends on how much publicity Harry wants for *Kasserine*."

"Too much attention wouldn't be good," I said.

She glanced at me, her face momentarily illuminated by the headlights of approaching traffic. "Unit Two won't draw attention. I'll see to that."

"Really? How?" I detected just an edge of hostility in my tone, and I wondered whether it was her competence or her relationship with Redding that challenged me.

Her smile was swift and bright. "The Purloined Letter, Major Quary. There will be a thousand Tunisian soldiers and fifty or so American and British actors milling around on the *Kasserine* location. Where better to hide soldiers than among more soldiers?"

I had to smile back at her assurance. And she was right, of course. An assault force of seventy or so men, even if they were professionals, could easily be hidden in a mob of Central Casting make-believes. Suddenly, for all the obvious problems involved in an attack on Point X, the whole mad scheme looked possible.

We rode in silence the rest of the way to the restaurant, which turned out to be a rambling structure of driftwoodlike boards and glass overlooking a bluff. The sea below was illuminated by floodlights. There was no beach; the waves broke on the rocks, all white froth and diamond-bright spray. The restaurant itself was lighted mainly by the candles in storm lanterns on each of the small tables.

The staff knew Ann and were plainly accustomed to giving her the finest table in the house: a small booth facing the window and the last hint of color from the sunset, which etched the distant marine horizon. I wondered how often Ann and Harry had been here.

We ordered drinks and then a dinner of rex sole, which the waiter guaranteed had been flown down fresh from San Francisco that very evening.

We were working on a bottle of California Chardonnay, and I felt relaxed, or nearly so, for the first time since getting off the AirCal flight that noon.

There was no one nearby. The Harry Redding table was deliberately isolated from the ruck of the Breakers' ordinary clientele.

I told her about my tour in England. I had worked with some people from the Special Air Service Regiment at Hereford. They were good. At their particular job, which was assaulting well-situated small enemy units, they were quite possibly the best in the world. Already I had been planning that *if* Louis and I signed on for the Point X operation there were some SAS people I would like very much to recruit.

Ann said, "My father was a brigadier in the British Army. He was serving with the Rhine Army when he died four years ago. I know something about soldiers."

I regarded her with deeper interest than I had before. "Somehow I thought of you as Oxford, British Broadcasting, that sort of background," I said.

"Cambridge, actually. And I did a tour with the BBC. But it was boring. And the pay was terrible."

"It's better now, I suppose."

"Much better," she said.

And there were fringe benefits, I thought. Well, damn it, Quary, what business is it of yours?

Despite our isolation, I didn't really feel free to talk about the Point X thing in a public place. And presently it didn't seem to matter. There was always tomorrow for that.

41

"Right now," I said, "Louis is probably showing that Porsche off to his old friends."

"I think it's in safe hands with the sergeant," Ann said.

"None safer," I agreed.

"You and Sergeant Brown," Ann said, "you've known each other a long time, I take it."

"Yes. There's no better soldier in any army, nor any better man."

"You wrote him up for a Distinguished Service Cross."

"You didn't get that by using the Freedom of Information Act," I said.

"No."

"I think it bothers me that personal information can be bought so easily," I said.

"It wasn't bought easily. Or cheaply," she countered.

Secrecy these days was something people joked about. But if, assuming I took on the operation, on the morning of H-hour there was a leak—what then? How many dead?

Redding's sources of information would have to be looked into.

Ann said, "You aren't married, Casey."

"No," I said. "I never met anyone who would have me."

"Really? Or is it that you feel more comfortable in a man's world?"

"The army isn't exclusively a man's world, Ann. Not any longer."

"Combat is."

"The last bastion of macho," I said, making a joke of it.

"The lady soldiers stay with their computers whilst the boys go out to play together."

I smiled at her, but without amusement. I had heard all this before, many times. It was a source of quarrels in army families and in officers' clubs in twenty countries. I was tired of it. Liberated women made me nervous. I never knew whether to make a pass or throw a punch. The relationship between the sexes should be simpler and pleasanter than that.

"Are you asking me if I'm gay, Ann? Because I like to get out in the field with the boys?"

"*That* is not a question I'd ever ask you, Casey. What I mean is, why do some men prefer to fight rather than do anything else? My father was like that, and I could never quite understand it. Neither could my mother. She had a miserable life, Casey. But he loved his, every day of it."

"You have to love soldiering, believe it serves an essential purpose in a dangerous world. I know that sounds *simplistic*, but that's the way it is, Ann."

"And so, never a Mrs. K. C. Quary."

"What can I say?"

Her mood changed with startling swiftness. "You can tell me how you broke your nose."

"That wasn't covered by your investigation?"

She shook her head and looked at me across her wineglass.

"A fight in a bar in Danang," I said. "A Marine with a nifty right cross. Berets on American soldiers really upset him."

She laughed and put her hand on mine. I turned mine over and held hers.

On the drive back down the Coast Highway we were silent. I rode with my hand on her shoulder, and once she leaned her cheek against it.

I could not remember ever having spent an evening with a woman I liked better than Ann Maclean. Then the image of Harry Redding strode into my mind. I took my hand away.

She looked at me directly and just as directly asked, "Why?"

"I don't poach, Ann."

She turned back to watch the road. Looking straight ahead, she said distinctly, "God damn you, Casey."

The evening collapsed all around me. I felt I'd had to say it, as stupid and wooden as it had sounded. But I should have known how it would sound to Ann.

When we drove down to Redding's house, neither the Mercedes nor the Porsche was in the garage. We walked to the front door in silence, and when Ming opened it, all Ann said to me was "Ming will show you where you sleep," and she was gone.

I followed him to a room encased mostly by glass facing the moonlit, misty sea and containing an enormous king-size bed. Fresh shaving and toilet articles had been laid out for me in the bathroom. Feeling very low, I stripped, showered, and got into bed.

But I couldn't sleep. The moon was brilliant. It illuminated the Pacific, the ghostly white beach, the pale wall of the room.

It was well past midnight, by the luminous hands of my watch, when I heard the door open and close.

Ann was there. She dropped her robe and stood naked in the moonlight.

"I'm my own person, Casey," she said. "No one owns me."

She walked to the side of the bed as I got up. I could smell her perfume and something else, a sexual sweetness that had to be hers alone.

She stood close, her knees against mine. "Don't ever use a word like *poach* in relation to me," she said, and pulled my head against her. I kissed her small breasts, feeling the hard nipples rise against my lips.

We didn't sleep much that night. We made love often and only dozed in between. And we talked. Lord, how we talked. It was as though we were trying to fill in a lifetime because we knew hours like this would be rare.

I was leaning against the softly padded headboard with Ann's head resting on my shoulder. I ran my hands over her breasts, cupped them. She had a body like a runner's, and those fine breasts. Her skin gleamed in the moonlight.

"I started to tell you why Harry wants to do this," she said. "I never did."

I thought about Redding, wondered if he was in the house. I hadn't heard him arrive, but he could have come in at any time. While we were making love I hadn't been listening to anything but Ann's feral little cries.

It would not have been my choice of a time to talk about Redding, but if she wanted to, I was willing to listen.

"I told you Harry isn't a brave man," she said quietly.

"Bravery is overrated, Ann. Courage is something else."

She smiled a bit ruefully. "All right. Yes, I understand that. But we are speaking of Harry, Casey."

"You are," I said.

"Harry ducked out on the war in Vietnam."

"Is that supposed to shock me? Plenty of people managed to miss Vietnam, one way or another. I used to worry about that, but time passes. You don't forget. It just matters less."

"Is that really true? If you are going to work with Harry, you have to be certain, Casey."

"When I was over there," I said thoughtfully, "I despised the movie stars and politicians who went to Hanoi to have their pictures taken with General Giap and sitting on antiaircraft guns. I guess I still do. But it's one thing to run away from a war your government keeps trying to pretend isn't serious and another thing to be a traitor. Harry was never that, was he?"

"Of course not. I told you, Harry was afraid. I didn't say he didn't love his country."

"All right. Now you've told me," I said.

"The ironic part of it is that he was never drafted, never called up. He went north to Canada because he was afraid he would be, but it never happened. I've always thought maybe he was more afraid of being a coward when it really mattered than of anything else."

After that we didn't speak again about Harry. We spoke very little about anything. It was early in the morning when we finally fell asleep. And when I awoke in the gray dawn, I was alone.

5

When you have spent most of your adult life in the army, you learn to sleep when you can and to get by with little or no rest when you must. It was only eight when I rose and dressed. The glare coming through the undraped window-wall of the guest room was harsh with white light and blue sea. There would be smog and reduced visibility later in the day, but at this hour the morning sparkled.

I left my room and paused at an open door. It was a room exactly like the one in which I had spent the night. Louis lay in a relaxed sprawl on the bed. His scarred, dark body looked too massive for the soft furnishings and the pastel walls. He was soundly asleep, and I made no move to wake him.

I walked into the high-ceilinged living room, where the big metal mobile rotated lazily in the air from the open doors to the terrace. I could see a white-uniformed woman preparing breakfast in the kitchen. She smiled at me across the open counter. Ming appeared and said Mr. Redding and Mr. Ziegler were out on the terrace and would I join them there please.

There was another man with them. The three were bent over a scatter of papers on the glass-topped breakfast table. As I approached, Redding stood to introduce me.

The newcomer was short, thick-shouldered, with thin reddish

hair and a sunburned face. He was about my age, perhaps a few years older, well muscled and robust in an outdoorsy way. He wore a bush jacket and khaki trousers that were clean and pressed but obviously not new and just as obviously not purchased at some Rodeo Drive boutique.

Redding said, "Major Quary, this is Rod Strachan, our location coordinator."

Strachan had an open smile. "That's film talk for freight agent and gofer, Major Quary. I see to it that things get to where they are supposed to be when they are supposed to be there."

"Sit down, Major. Ming will bring breakfast. Have some coffee." Ziegler poured black brew into a fresh cup.

The papers scattered on the table seemed to relate to *Kasserine*. They were tables and schedules and shipping printouts.

Strachan's grip when we shook hands was firm, his hand rough. Whatever else he might be, he was not playing dressed-up executive. No gold chains, no Gucci loafers worn without socks.

Redding looked the part of the film star this morning. He wore skin-tight jeans, a white cotton cable-stitched sweater, sleeves pushed up to the elbows. His feet were bare. There probably had been a time when picture people greeted the morning in fine tailoring, but no longer. The desired look was informal, even half-dressed.

Redding sat down across the table from me. I couldn't help but wonder if he knew how Ann and I had spent the night. And where was she this morning?

"Rod," Ziegler said, "is our resident genius in charge of getting the right gear to where it's wanted. *Any* kind of gear, Casey."

This indicated that Strachan was no stranger to Redding's Point X project. All right, I thought. Logistics officer. But how many other people had taken a look at the file in the war room?

Redding said quietly, "Rod used to be with British Petroleum. He had to keep the concessions supplied."

"In Libya?" I asked pointedly.

Strachan grinned. "Ah, no, Major, more's the pity. In Saudi Arabia. But if you need any old Libya hands, I think I could locate some for you."

Ming brought me ham and eggs and croissants. I ate like a wolf. When I had finished and the dishes were taken away, Ziegler asked if I wanted a drink. I said no. He made himself a Bloody Mary and rejoined us at the table.

"Well, Major? Have you given our project some thought?" Redding asked.

"Quite a lot," I said. "But."

"There's always a but," Ziegler commented.

I continued: "I won't ask you if you've considered what you are getting into, Mr. Redding. I have to assume that you have. And you know what sort of expenditures we're talking about. My quick estimates yesterday could have been too low. Do you want me to do a detailed operational plan for you?"

"Only a cost sheet, please. So that I'll know how much money we'll need to put at your disposal."

"All right," I said. "What happens if the ragheads decide to reverse their field and set the hostages loose?"

"Is that likely?"

"I don't think so, but it is a possibility."

"Well," Redding said, "if our people turn up somewhere safe, we simply shut down the operation." His gold-flecked brown eyes looked suddenly hard. "Until the next time. There *will* be a next time, Major."

"Agreed," I said.

"Then you'll do it?"

"I seem to be saying that I will," I answered with a faint smile. "But now we get to the ground rules."

"I'm listening."

"You pay the bills. And after it's done, you do what you please about the publicity or whatever. But *until* it's done there's to be no talk—none at all—not to anyone who doesn't have a specific need to know. I'll do a cost estimate, and you'll put the money in a Swiss bank in a numbered account. Ziegler can keep track of the balance, but there will be no questions about how the money is spent. None."

"That's asking a great deal, chum," Ziegler said.

"Either you trust me or you don't. If not, get someone else."

"All right," Redding said. "Go on."

"Time," I said. "This operation has to be organized and carried out while your people are in Tunisia, because that's our only hope for cover."

For the first time Strachan joined the conversation. "How long, Major?"

"Three weeks from today. Four at the outside."

"No problem."

"What about men, Major?" Ziegler asked. "Are you thinking of hiring mercenaries?"

I had to smile grimly at that. I hadn't realized that *mercenaries* was still a magic word among the dream merchants.

"The age of the mercenary is long gone," I said. "Back in the fifties and sixties there were such people, but they operated with the tacit approval of governments. In those days you could have a private war for a half-million dollars. Not now. We don't want a war. We simply want a neat, surgical strike to get our people out, if possible, in one piece."

"What does that mean, exactly, Major, 'if possible'? It sounds ominous." For the first time Ziegler really looked concerned. But these people had to know what it was they were starting.

"What I say. *If possible.* We are proposing to attack a fortified base in, of all places, Libya. If we are fast and lucky, maybe we won't lose hostages. But there are no guarantees." I wanted them to understand that the primary reason Delta Force had become an exercise in futility was the demand—on the part of the media, the relatives of hostages, and the Administration's political enemies—for guarantees that no hostage would be hurt or killed. "If you insist on guarantees," I said, "it can't be done."

"Jesus," Ziegler muttered, looking at Redding.

"It could finish you, Mr. Redding," I said. "If this goes sour, it could wipe you out. I don't care how much money you have. You have to understand this."

Redding looked steadily at me. "I do understand."

"And let's have one thing more understood," I said. "There will be no amateurs in the strike force. None. Amateurs get people killed. Is my meaning clear?"

"Very clear, Major," Redding answered, avoiding my eyes now. After what Ann had told me, I thought I knew why.

"But we can film, can't we?" Ziegler pleaded.

I looked at him in disbelief.

Redding broke into a smile, and some of the tension oozed out of the meeting. Even Strachan was smiling. "How are you with a Panaflex, Major?" he asked.

"I don't even know what a Panaflex is," I said.

"A camera. A big one."

I decided to bring the meeting back to earth. I said, "If we go in by helicopter, there won't be room for things or people who don't shoot bullets. Let's talk about filming later."

Ziegler looked disappointed.

"The first thing we're going to need," I said, "is an intelligence officer."

Ziegler asked, "Wasn't Gershon's material what you need?"

"It was fine as far as it goes. But I want someone available to act as CIC." Faces went blank, and I explained: "Combat Intelligence Center."

"Won't Gershon do?" Ziegler asked.

"You seem to have a lot of faith in him," I said. "Tell me why."

"Gershon is—well, a kind of entrepreneur," Redding said. "He's been our distribution agent for Israel for a year. And he has good connections with the Israeli Defense Force. All the Russian equipment we use comes from them. They have a mountain of captured weapons and vehicles."

"He seems to have good connections with Mossad, too," I said.

"We don't ask him about that. The pictures you saw last night are the real thing, aren't they?"

"If they aren't," I said, "I'll soon find out. We don't move without confirmation."

"Confirmation?" Ziegler asked. "How do you plan to get that?"

"General Stanley," I said.

"He's a sick man, Major," Redding said.

"He's also one of the best G-2s in the army. If he says Agron's material is accurate, then it is. I'll go back to Letterman and talk to him. He may be the CIC we'll need."

"He can't leave the hospital," Redding protested.

"He won't have to," I said. I didn't want to pursue it then. I had begun to have doubts about Gershon Agron. There was something disturbing about the way this operation was beginning to rely so heavily on him. "What is Agron doing in Washington?"

Ziegler shrugged. "Contacts. Gerson is into a number of things. He's very active in the Russian *refusenik* community, the Jews who have managed to get out of the USSR. He was one himself, Major. Gershon Agron is his Israeli name. He was born Feliks Kopinsky. It took him eight years to get out of the Soviet Union. His family was arrested when the Russians discovered some of the things he was doing in Israel. He has paid his dues." Ziegler's tone was bristling.

"All right, Ziegler," I said. "I'm not making any judgments about Agron. I just want my own intelligence officer. Now let's talk about personnel."

For the next hour we discussed the kind of people I felt we could get for the operation. What it came down to was that I wanted men who had recently been soldiers in elite units—Rangers, Special Forces, Marines. I had already decided that the force should be international, but not *too* international. I knew a number of Britishers who might well jump at a chance to twist Muammar Qaddafi's nose. After all, they had that bloody mess at the Libyan People's Bureau in London to remember. A British policewoman had been murdered by a shot from an embassy window, and the Brits had been forced to endure the humiliation of watching the killers go free because they had diplomatic immunity.

"One other thing I'd like from the UK," I said to Strachan. "Can you locate a British Petroleum man who knows not only Libya, but also the old concession at Point X?"

Strachan smiled broadly. "Ask and ye shall receive, chum."

"We have one thing going for us," I said. "Everyone is watching Delta Force. The media are just waiting for the army to make a move. Any move. Delta Force hasn't been forgotten. But no one will be looking for an assault group in a movie company in Tunisia. That's our asset."

"Right," Redding said.

"Now the bad news," I said. "Barqin. The minute the Russians at Barqin discover a force moving in their direction, they'll react. If they do, there will be hell to pay. We must not create a superpower incident. So, security is the number-one priority. I want to take the force in and out without a Russian stirring."

"It's my impression," Strachan said, "that the comrades have their dicks in the zipper at Barqin, Major. The present party line is all for test bans and nonproliferation. But they can't pull out of Barqin without losing their grip on Qaddafi."

"Well, let's just plan our operation so that we don't disturb them. The Barqin situation is strictly theirs. Let them stew in it."

I looked up to see Louis standing in the doorway, yawning.

"How long have you been standing there, Sergeant Brown?" I asked.

"Long enough to know we're going soldiering again, Major Quary."

"Come have some breakfast, Louis," Redding said.

Louis settled his substantial bulk into a chair and spooned sugar into a coffee cup. "What's my job, Casey?"

"What else?" I said. "Sergeant Major, you'll have to turn a reinforced company of casuals into a fighting unit. In four weeks or less. Can it be done?"

"If we get the right men. I know where to look."

"I think you'll be doing some traveling, Louis."

"Say where and when."

"Fort Bragg, to begin with. Maybe Benning. Then Parris Island."

"Jarheads?"

"We can use some," I said.

Louis shrugged agreement. The rivalry between the services is largely fantasy among soldiers trained in unconventional warfare. He drank his sweet coffee and looked around. "Where is Miss Maclean this morning?"

Redding smiled and said, "Film people go to work early, Louis. She took a seven o'clock flight to London this morning."

That shook me. I didn't know why it should. Ann had made it clear that she kept her own schedule and her own counsel. If she had work to do in London—and the business of Eagle Films did go on, regardless of the Point X project—why should she feel she had to tell me about it? Nevertheless, it stung me.

"Can I ask some questions?" Louis said.

"Feel free," I answered.

He addressed himself to Redding. "Why us?"

"Fair question," Redding replied. "I've known General Stanley for quite a while now, ever since he was technical adviser on the first Eagle picture. I admire him. He says K. C. Quary is the best man for this kind of job and he's available. I call Jerry, and Jerry sees Quary. Good enough?"

Louis grinned broadly at me. "Casey, for a passed-over major you have a fair reputation."

Ziegler laughed. "He's not really the Nigel Green type, is he, Harry?"

Redding and Strachan joined the laughter.

Then Redding took pity on me. "Nigel Green is a fine British actor, Major. He was the bad guy in *The Ipcress File*. That's what they called him: 'a passed-over major.' You know your films, Louis."

Louis said, still grinning, "Will you really pay each of us twenty thousand dollars, Harry?"

"Yes. The same to officers and noncoms."

Ziegler winced visibly.

Louis gave a shout. "I like your style, Harry. The next time I drive a Porsche, it will be all mine."

I hope so, Louis, I thought. I most fervently hope so.

"Let's go over the charts again," I said.

6

Down in the war room Louis and I gave the maps a second, and much closer, look. It was as I had feared. Barqin, where Qaddafi's Soviet sponsors had built the uranium diffusion plant, was surrounded by a menacing-looking polygon of blue crosshatching that indicated what the makers of the chart euphemistically called a "Special Use Air Space." In simple terms this means that any aircraft crossing into the zone will be attacked and shot down.

This nonpleasantry was of no particular significance, since *any* unauthorized aircraft entering *any* Libyan air space would be treated exactly that way. What Special Use Air Space on the chart meant was radar, surface-to-air missiles, antiaircraft artillery, and quite probably a hot line to the nearest fighter base. Which in the case of Barqin was at Gurdahbiyah on the Gulf of Sidra—about eleven minutes from Barqin by MiG-27. It could even be worse. There was an airfield with runways capable of handling fighters at Sabhah, much closer to Barqin. A MiG-27 could cover that distance in 230 seconds—less than four minutes.

The chart that covered the southern tip of Tunisia, where the national borders of Tunisia, Libya, and Algeria meet, deep in the saheer—the Arabic name for the deep-sand Sahara—showed an oil-pumping station about twelve miles from the frontier. There was nothing else shown on the chart for miles in any direction. If the place was really as desolate and isolated as it appeared to be, and if there was water there in sufficient quantity, it looked like a reasonable staging area.

The roads through the deep sand sea were largely imaginary, no more than wheel ruts in the desert. But there was a range of low hills just inside the Libyan border that would have to be traversed if we decided to move overland. The roads marked the passes. There was another airfield shown at Ghadames East, at about 30° 10′ North, where Libya's western border made a small bulge into Algeria. That might simply be a small strip used by petroleum geologists for light aircraft. Or it might be suitable for fighters. It depended on the way the runway was surfaced. Given Qaddafi's paranoia and the nearness of Ghadames East to Algeria, I suspected the worst.

"This is going to be a bitch, Casey," Louis said. "It's at least five hundred miles by road from that pumping station to Point X, and we'd be bracketed by airfields. One pass by a hot jock and we're dog meat."

I measured the air distance off the scale in the margin of the chart. "Four hundred miles and change by air," I said.

Redding, Ziegler, and Strachan watched us without comment.

"Could Dieter find us choppers?"

"It shouldn't be impossible. If he can't, maybe Agron can. He seems to have all the right connections." I looked at Ziegler as I said that and got a shrug in return.

"This looks like work for Rangers, Major. I know a few who might be interested."

"Stockade hard cases and dishonorable discharges?"

"Some," Louis said reasonably. "You can't expect Boy Scouts to line up for a job like this."

Through the rest of that day Louis and I worked in the war room, and when we finished, we had a rough operational plan and a table of organization. We had cut the force down to sixty men, which was very light, but to make up for it we would give the force the fire power of a full company of Rangers. That meant an Uzi automatic and three thousand rounds for each man and one of Harry Redding's favorite rocket-propelled grenade launchers for each platoon of twenty. In addition to the Uzi, each soldier would carry a dozen concussion grenades, emergency water for three days, and whatever personal weapon he favored.

To Strachan, who was accustomed to moving heavy gear in and out of semifriendly countries, I delegated the task of transporting the weapons and equipment to Bizerte as part of the tons of military props he was moving for the filming of *Kasserine*.

"Tonight I'll go back to San Francisco to see what I can do about setting up some sort of CIC," I continued. "There's a retired air force colonel I know in Portola Valley who served at Wheelus Air Force Base before Qaddafi's revolution. His information won't be new, but it will be useful. After that I'll hop a plane to Zurich to see Lang about the weapons and aircraft." I asked Strachan what port he was using to keep *Kasserine* supplied. He told me Naples, which made sense. It didn't hurt that the Italians tended to be reasonable to the point of laxity about freight moving through their ports. As long as it was bonded, their curiosity was nearly nil.

"If I can get choppers in Europe," I said, "I'll have them flown to Naples and disassembled for shipment by sea. You'll have to charter a ship, Strachan. We can't take the chance of having other shippers' cargo aboard. But it's only two days to Bizerte, so the cost shouldn't be too high. There's one small problem about the aircraft. Anyone who knows about *Kasserine*—and I suppose that is just about everyone in your business—might wonder what we are going to do with helicopters if we're making a picture about the war in North Africa in 1942. Can we say they are camera platforms?"

"I don't see why not," Strachan said. "Harry?"

"Hell, yes. What about pilots?"

"I'll get pilots. Europe is thick with ex-military chopper drivers hungry for work. I'll use your name if I have to."

"You'll need money," Ziegler said.

"Quite a lot of it. Can you wire the first hundred thousand

to the Zwingli Bank in Zurich today? I'll give you my service number. That will do for identification. And as soon as I finish with Lang, I'll be going to London. I'll need another hundred thousand sent to Lloyd's Bank. Deposit it in an Eagle Films account and give me a letter authorizing me to draw on it. I want to locate one or two Brits I once served with and see if they are interested in a few weeks' work, sight unseen."

To Louis I said, "Your job is going to be a bit tricky. We want experienced men. Offer twenty thousand, with a possible bonus. Tell them only that it means working out of the country for five or six weeks and that it can be hazardous. Recruiting is the soft spot in our security, so try to impress upon them that they are to keep talk and speculation to a minimum. With luck, we can have everyone away before we draw too much attention."

"Can I use Harry's name?"

"No. I don't want anyone asking questions about *Kasserine*," I said. "Just tell them what I told you."

"I read you, Major."

"I'll try to get us a medic," I said. "We're liable to need one. A medical officer might be hard to shake loose from his practice, but Stanley should know where I can find a 32 Bravo medical specialist." I straightened up and said to Ziegler, "That is about all we can do right now. I need to get myself established as working for Eagle as a technical adviser. So I'd like you to have your secretary book me on AirCal back to SFO this evening, then to Zurich on Pan Am. I'll need a room in Zurich—whatever looks right for the job I'm supposed to have with Eagle. The same in London. I'll take it from there. By that time maybe I'll believe I'm a technical adviser on *Kasserine*. By the way, who is the adviser you hired?"

"Colonel Jonathan Cathcart. Retired fifteen years ago but still talking about the fight at Kasserine Pass," Ziegler said.

"Where is he now?"

"In Bizerte, getting things set up."

"You'd better talk to him and say you've hired me to do something. Supervise demolition, something like that. I don't want him sweating about some new man taking his job. But make certain he understands I work exclusively for Redding. Colonels have a way of using up a major's day. We haven't time for that."

"Done."

"You'll arrange travel for Louis. He will need to advance money to his recruits. Forty thousand cash should take care of it until we can see how the force is shaping up."

"R Force," Louis said, grinning. "R for Redding."

"Why not?" I said. The excitement was getting to me as well as to Louis and the others. "Let's saddle up, then."

"I wondered if you Yank soldiers really said things like that," Strachan said.

Redding turned suddenly to Ziegler. "Jerry, book Quary into the Stafford in London. He'll want to see Ann."

He said good-bye standing in the doorway, with his black Great Dane beside him. As we pulled out, heading for the airport, I wondered why any man sought self-inflicted wounds the way he did.

7

As in every large, structured organization, people in the military are watched and personally evaluated by their superiors. There is the regular chain of command, with its efficiency reports and selection boards. And then there is something very like what civilians call the Old Boy network.

Some officers, the fortunate ones, are taken under the sponsorship of more senior commanders. The generals and colonels, if they are observant, begin to guide and back junior officers they think show special talent. Dwight Eisenhower, when he was only the Camp Dowd commander during World War I, attracted the attention of General John J. Pershing, who took the American forces to France, and from that time on he was on a special list for high command if war should come again. The air force's General Lauris Norstad made it from second lieutenant to lieutenant general in record time because "Hap" Arnold, the air officer at the top of the pyramid in World War II, thought him remarkable. Norstad retired as the youngest chief of staff the air force had ever had.

In my recently terminated army career, I had had the sponsorship of Major General John Stanley. I was no longer a prospect for the Joint Chiefs of Staff, of course, because I had been unwise and too outspoken. But Stanley still stood by me, and it was through his friendship with Redding that I now found myself commander and organizer of R Force.

General Stanley might have gone far higher in the military hierarchy if his health hadn't failed. The years in Southeast Asia had infected him with a particularly vicious form of malaria, and the illness had done bad things to his heart. Technically he was not retired, but to all intents and purposes his active career in the army was over. He lived in a two-room suite at Letterman. He still rated a noncom orderly (a grizzled old six-striper, Sergeant Rubin Balch) and the services of an aide (Captain Joe Weeden, who was technically a member of the Plans and Training Staff of the 91st Division, the command cadre of the California National Guard's infantry).

Stanley might be immobilized, but he knew everyone who mattered in the army, and most of those who did in the intelligence community. He was a man who could pick up a telephone, call the Secretary of the Army, and get an answer.

I walked into his room on the third floor at Letterman and gave him a soft salute.

"I figured you'd be back, Casey," he said. "Sit down and pour us a drink." He indicated a bottle of Chivas on the dresser. Stanley was never far from a bottle of good Scotch, but I had never seen him drunk.

He was a large man, or had been before the malaria began to wear away the muscle and sinew. He had a thin, deeply lined face, with eyes as bright as a hawk's. His skin had a sallow look from the Atabrine he still took. Standing, he would have been well over six feet, and once would have weighed in at over two hundred pounds. He was down to three-quarters of that, and he looked like a skeleton in his blue hospital bathrobe.

I put my briefcase on the bed and poured Scotch. One of the three telephones in the room rang, and he shouted to Sergeant Balch in the other room to answer it and hold his calls. He had organized his hospital suite like a commanding general's office, complete with orderly room and message center.

He raised his glass and said, "Here's to the infantry." It was

61

a familiar toast to all who knew him. He had done many things in his military career, but he never forgot that he was, when everything else was worn away, a dogface infantryman.

"The poor bloody infantry," I said, and drank the velvet-smooth liquor down.

"All right, let's get to it," Stanley said. "You talked to Redding."

"Yes, sir, I did."

"And what did you decide?"

"To go ahead with his project. If I can get what I need to do the job."

The bird-of-prey expression in his eyes sharpened. "What have you got? Have you worked out a table of organization? An order of battle? Show me."

I held off for a moment. "You know about Gershon Agron?"

"I never met him. Ziegler gave me a rundown on him. I checked him out. So far, he seems genuine. Does he bother you?"

"So far, you say. How far is that, General?"

"As far as Defense Intelligence. They don't know anything that would suggest he isn't what he says he is."

"Can you push a little harder?"

"If you want me to. That is, if you are going ahead with Redding's operation."

I stood up, walked to the window, and looked down on a peaceful street. The night air was balmy. Pale moonlight dimmed the stars. Out over the bay, an airliner climbing north made a pattern of flashes. The bridge was a looping line of amber lights. I said, "Is Redding's operation really his? Or is it something else?"

"It's not like you to ask foolish questions, Casey."

"Is it foolish? I'm talking about taking sixty or so men into Libya on a clandestine operation that could get them all killed, General. I would just like to know that my own government isn't going to pull the rug out from under us and leave us up to our asses in sand. Can you give me that much assurance?"

He showed no change of expression. The mention of Libya hadn't fazed him. He obviously knew most of Redding's plan. It was even possible that he had helped set it up.

"There is no United States government involvement in any of this, Casey," he said flatly.

I opened the briefcase, took the satellite photographs of Point X out, and dropped them in his lap. "Who took these, General?"

"They came from Agron."

"You've seen them before, General?"

"Of course I've seen them before, Major."

"Ex-major," I said, with a not-very-warm half-smile.

"Something might be done about that, Casey. After you get our people out."

"I see," I said. Stanley's meaning was clear. The U.S. government was not *involved*, so the General was not exactly lying. He wasn't exactly telling the whole truth, either, and I was expected to have the military sense to understand why. Any clandestine operation must have one thing above all: the quality of *deniability*. What he was telling me was that my government would cooperate to some unknown and unspecified degree, but that was as far as it would go. If we ran into trouble, we were not to look for an American rescue. Despite the legendary profligacy of some branches of the government, the military did not send resources in to rescue bunglers.

On the up side was the suggestion that if I was successful, the army might be willing to have me back.

"So there's a chance—let's skip the odds—that I could return, sadder, wiser, and forgiven. But what about Louis?"

Stanley cut in. "Sergeant Brown? Hell, Casey, he could come back right now. In his case there's nothing to forgive."

"Fair enough," I said. "Now I know where we stand."

I laid out my table of organization and the rough battle plan Louis and I had cobbled together in Redding's war room. We discussed them like the two experienced professional soldiers we were.

63

"It looks sound, Casey," Stanley said. "But you are going to be operating blind."

"I want to do something about that," I said.

"What's your idea?"

"I need someone back here to act as my intelligence officer. I don't want to rely on what Agron can lift from Mossad."

"That won't be an easy spot to fill, Casey."

"I agree. There is only one man who can do the job on such short notice."

"See if you can get him, then."

"All right, General. You. You are the people's choice to act as CIC."

Stanley stared at me out of his drawn, skull-like face. "That's out of line, Major."

"You know the plan. You can get me whatever information I'm likely to need. There isn't anyone else."

"Casey," he said, "I'm a dying man. You know that as well as I do. So don't give me any bullshit."

"You have telephones in here. If necessary we can set up a satellite radio link with an SCR 1220." A Signal Corps radio model 1220 was one of the neat new gadgets of sophisticated field equipment. It was a backpack radio link to a satellite that could give a soldier coordinates for his location anywhere on earth. And, even better, it could communicate through the satellite with a ground station a third of the way around the globe. The poor bloody infantry had a deep bag of tricks. "Of course," I said, "you would have to locate a set for us and see to it that Rod Strachan has it on hand before we leave for Tunis."

The sallow face broke into a grimace that could pass for a smile. "You have more goddamn brass than any snotty major I've ever encountered, Casey. You are enlisting me in your guerrilla army?"

"Why not?" I said. "You're still a soldier, aren't you, General?"

Stanley broke into wheezing laughter, which seemed likely to finish him. "I'd like to see the face of the Director of Central Intelligence if he could hear this," he said.

Blandly, I used the phrase with which one limits the disclosure of any classified bit of information. "He has no need to know, sir."

"Casey," the General said, "a great highwayman was lost in you. Bring that bottle over here and pour us another drink. You just got yourself an intelligence officer."

I arrived at Zurich's Kloten Airport after having slept my way across the pole in the first-class section of a Pan American 747LR. I carried a light bag and a heavy shopping list, and I was on my way to see my old acquaintance Dieter Lang.

He was a seller of military equipment, but he didn't fit the merchant-of-death stereotype. To begin with, he was a Swiss, and the Swiss are basically peaceful people. This doesn't stop them from turning a profit wherever one is legitimately to be made, and there had always been money in the business of supplying weapons to suitable nations. The word *suitable* is the key. Lang and men like him (dealers in surplus arms, mostly) acted under the tacit imprimatur of the anti-Communist West. Third World countries that lined up squarely with the West got their weapons from the United States and Europe in a straight-forward way. Soviet client states got theirs direct from the USSR or the East Bloc countries. But the nonaligned nations (those that were truly nonaligned, as opposed to those that claimed to be) had theirs through the efforts of Lang and his peers.

Despite the superpower competition going on in the world, there were always small countries that needed arms but chose not to risk the embrace of the Russian bear or the American eagle. Lang and his friends did a good business with such nations. I had always suspected that he also supplied arms to approved groups such as the Afghan Mujahadeen and Jonas Savimbi's Unita, with the blessing of the CIA, but such suspicions were better left untested.

One of the things I had done as an instructor at the War College was to invite Lang to lecture, to the officers undergoing training, on the clandestine weapons trade. I guessed that my choice of lecturer managed to find its way into my personnel file, too.

Secretary of War Henry Stimson, when informed that the navy had cracked the Japanese codes before Pearl Harbor, is reported to have said disdainfully, "Gentlemen do not read one another's mail." There were still officers in the army capable of such magnificent rectitude, and having an arms merchant as lecturer at the War College had probably offended them. The military is the most conservative class in every period of history, or so Louis liked to say. He was right, of course. It was probably a good thing, considering the damage they could do if they became radicals.

———

Before leaving the San Francisco Bay area, I had driven down to Portola Valley, near Stanford, to see Colonel Dan Sales, the retired USAF officer who had once been stationed at Wheelus, in Libya.

He was willing to talk to me about the place, which had once been our major air base in North Africa. He had collected an enormous amount of memorabilia, most of it useless to me, and some aerial photographs of the base that were years out of date but that gave me some idea of how big the place was.

"The Libyans," he said, "have at least three squadrons of new Sukhois and probably that many MiGs there. But their pilots aren't much. The navy took out a pair of them a while back without even working up a sweat." He regarded me speculatively. "Why so interested, Major?"

"I'm doing a military history," I said. "One section is about U.S.-built facilities that are now available to the Soviets. Camranh Bay, Wheelus, a few other places."

"Not a very happy chore," he said.

Unfortunately, Sales had no information about the Libyan saheer, the deep desert. He had never bothered to have anything to do with either the desert or the Bedouins who lived there. A fairly typical American attitude. We have always had a bad habit of making American enclaves in foreign lands and living there as though we were in the suburbs of Indianapolis.

After a couple of not-very-productive hours with the colonel, I returned to San Francisco airport. From the international terminal there I telephoned an ex–Green Beret doctor I had served with in Nam and asked him if he could find me a discharged medic, airborne-qualified. He said he thought he had a man and would I check with him in two or three days.

An hour after that I was at forty thousand feet, heading for Europe and Dieter Lang.

8

The weather in Zurich was overcast, with occasional periods of rain so fine it was almost mist. An hour after leaving the airport I was signed into the Zurich Continental, a glass-and-steel tower that was oddly at home in a city of Swiss Gothic churches, narrow cobbled streets, and elegant avenues. The Swiss seem always to mix the old and the new and get away with it. No other Europeans have ever quite had the knack.

I telephoned Dieter and made an appointment to see him that afternoon at five o'clock. Then I showered, had a meal brought to my room, and lay down to sleep for an hour, to take the edge off the jet lag.

At three I dressed and walked through the cool drizzle to the Zwingli Bank to confirm that the money I had asked Jerry Ziegler to deposit was, in fact, on hand. Dieter Lang was a friend, but Swiss francs and plenty of them would stop speculation far better than personal cordiality.

As I made my way down the Rämistrasse through the throng of pedestrians I noticed that a man in a black leather coat was keeping pace with me on the other side of the street. My first impression was that he was a policeman. There was no reason to think that, except, perhaps, for the leather coat. In spy films, policemen and enemy agents often wear such impractical things.

Under ordinary circumstances I would have smiled at my own sense of the dramatic and concluded that I had been seeing too many George Smiley miniseries. But my circumstances were far from ordinary. There were at least a few people in Washington who already knew far too much about Harry Redding's Point X operation, and if a thing was known in Washington, the chances were that information about it could already be leaking.

It was three-thirty as I passed the Grossmünster, and suddenly high above in the great towers, the bells rang the half-hour. At the same moment, a line of Mercedes tour buses materialized out of a side street and pulled up in front of the church, presumably to collect the tourists who began to come out of the great double doors at the stroke of the bells. It had the precision and timing of any Swiss outing, and it flooded the street in front of the Grossmünster for just the smallest interval of confusion.

I broke into Hottingerstrasse at a rapid walk, and when I paused in front of the Zwingli Bank building to look back, the man in the black leather coat was nowhere to be seen. He had been overwhelmed by the torrent of tourists debouching from the church.

I stood for a time searching the crowds walking by to see if the man would reappear. He did not, and I concluded that my imagination was getting the better of me.

I walked into the bank and asked the uniformed security man to guide me to a bank officer. When he did so, I identified myself and asked whether or not the Eagle Films deposit was now on hand in my account.

The officer, a portly vice-president named Kügler, assured me that it was. I had never been greeted in a bank with such affability before. Herr Kügler led me into an inner office, where coffee was served us in porcelain cups. I wondered if film people were all accustomed to such treatment from bankers. When I had floated a loan to cover the purchase of my TransAm in California, no one had spooned sugar into my coffee from a silver bowl.

Kügler asked how he could now serve me. I told him that

starting today and for several weeks to come I would be making a number of purchases that would be paid for out of my numbered account. I showed him my letter of authorization on Eagle Films stationery, signed by Jerry Ziegler and countersigned by Harry Redding.

That, I think, impressed him more than did the amount in the new account, which was, after all, only money and far from a huge sum as Swiss bankers calculate such things.

Kügler, it seemed, was a heavy Redding fan. He had seen every one of his pictures and, he said, loved them. It may well have been no more than the truth. Under many a sedate three-piece suit hides a hero wishing to do great deeds. Redding and a few others like him had touched a deep spring in the American psyche, but it didn't stop there. I had heard that his pictures were runaway hits even in the Arab world, where Americans were supposed to be the very hounds of Satan.

Kügler would have kept me there for hours answering questions about Redding and the new project he was undertaking— the epic about the battle at Kasserine. I gently disengaged myself. It was nearly time for my appointment with Dieter.

It was raining in earnest when I left the Zwingli. The sky had darkened, deepening the approaching dusk. Lights were on in the shops, and the cobbles glistened from automobile headlights. I raised the collar of my green trenchcoat and walked back toward the lake and the Limmat Quai.

Before I reached Dieter's offices I had some moments of sober contemplation. I had committed myself—and Louis—to Harry Redding's private war. So, it seemed, had General Stanley and whatever shadowy types stood behind him. I had the uncomfortable feeling that I was about to cross the border into a dark land of spooks and covert actions where professional soldiers didn't set the rules. It made me nervous. On a street in a Swiss city, one of the most civilized places on the planet, I had actually imagined I was being followed. That was no way to begin. In a short time men would be counting on me for leadership. I had to think of the coming action simply as a military necessity. We knew where our people were. It was up to us to get them out. The army had passed me by, but I was still what I had always been, a soldier. A. E. Housman, a soldier's poet if there ever was one, said it better than I ever could:

I will go where I am wanted, where there's room for one or two,
And the men are none too many for the work there is to do.

Dieter Lang, like most German-Swiss, is far from a jocular man. But the news that I had come to buy rather than to ask for employment set his small blue eyes to dancing. He rose from behind his desk and led me to a pair of deep leather chairs and a table on which stood his favorite schnapps and glasses. He poured and gave me his favorite toast, which he imagined Teutonic soldiers had spoken since the Crusaders raped Pskov.

"Hoch!"

I raised my glass and drank, then looked around his office. Like a law library, it was book-lined and low-key, with an old Persian rug on the floor and green mohair drapes over the tall, narrow windows. The only thing that might have given a stranger a hit of Dieter's profession was the handsome brass model of an American Civil War Dahlgren gun on the credenza behind his desk. That, and the chatter of a Telex machine in the outer office, where his secretary held sway.

"Now sit and tell me how it is with you, Casey," he said. Dieter was always tactful and soft-spoken. He was as greedy as most men, maybe more, but his faults were well leavened with courtly manners. "Have you seen General Stanley recently?"

"I saw him yesterday," I said. "He is as well as can be expected."

"And that Sergeant Brown? Is he with you?"

"Louis is still with me, but he didn't make this trip."

"Ah. Perhaps next time."

71

"Perhaps."

"And now." He poured more schnapps. "How can I serve you?"

"I've been retained by Eagle Films to advise and assist in the making of a picture in Tunisia," I said.

Dieter brightened perceptibly. "You know Harry Redding? You have met him personally?"

"I report directly to him."

"This new film. I have heard talk about it. It is about the Americans at Kasserine, I believe?"

"Yes. The advance people are already in Bizerte. What I require is sixty Uzis and one hundred and twenty thousand rounds of nine-millimeter ball ammunition for them. Can you supply them?"

Dieter's eyebrows arched. "Uzis? Not to be used in the film, certainly!"

"Of course not. I plan to arm a security force for the company. We will have two thousand people on location, and a couple of hundred of them will be Americans and Brits. Redding wants to be sure they are protected."

"Are you expecting trouble?"

"I hope not. But some of the filming will be in the south, near the Libyan border. Redding is hiring four battalions of Tunisians as extras. Security is being left to us. To me, actually."

Dieter regarded me thoughtfully. "Can I assume that the Tunisian government is willing to let you bring in so many weapons?"

"My understanding is that the government is only too happy to leave security in our hands. I would buy the Uzis directly from the Israelis, but that would open up a whole different can of worms. The Tunisians couldn't allow a direct shipment."

"Naturally," Dieter said, spreading his hands. "We live in a complicated world. Sixty, you say. And one hundred and twenty thousand rounds. That's impressive fire power."

"Can you supply what I need?"

"How soon do you need it?"

"As soon as possible. A week. Ten days. Delivered in bond to Naples. I can let you know the name of the ship before then."

"There is a premium on Uzis right now," Dieter said.

"How much per weapon?"

"Can you supply me with an end user certificate?"

This document, issued by a sovereign government or other recognized authority, was to assure the arms dealer that the weapons he supplies will not be resold. It is intended to prevent arms from falling into the hands of criminals, terrorists, or revolutionaries. It provides a fig leaf of legal protection to the dealer if his weapons are found to have been used in illegal or paramilitary actions.

"We can obtain one from the government of Tunisia," I said, "but that would commit us to sell them the weapons when we leave the country. What I had in mind was to sell them back to you—at a discount, of course—when filming on location ends."

"Ah," Dieter said, steepling his hands. "Perhaps a certificate from Eagle Films would suffice, then. After all, everyone knows Harry Redding, no?"

"We can give you a company commitment," I said. "In fact, I am authorized to sign such a document."

"Well, then, I would be comfortable with that. Let's talk price." He produced a pocket calculator and let his manicured fingers fly familiarly over the keyboard. "Sixty Uzis at five hundred sixty dollars U.S.—"

"I can buy them for less in a sporting-goods store in California, Dieter. Think again, please."

He shrugged. "The quantity, Casey. The quantity. I will have to order them direct from Israel and have them shipped by air. Let's say four hundred apiece—"

"Let's say three seventy-five, Dieter. Remember, you'll get them back at a discount."

"All right, Casey. Let's not argue. I tell you what I'll do. I'll sell them to you for three fifty each if you agree to sell them back to me for two hundred. Is that fair?"

"Done," I said.

"And the ammunition. Will you be returning that to me as well?"

"I hope so, Dicter."

"But no guarantee. Well, then. Let's say one hundred dollars per thousand rounds."

"Ninety," I said.

Dieter shrugged. "Agreed. Ninety per thousand. That is, let's see—" He did his act on the pocket calculator, although I knew he had the figures in his head. "That comes to thirty-one thousand eight hundred. Plus two thousand for air freight charges and three thousand for documentation and incidental expenses brings it to thirty-six thousand eight hundred."

Two thousand rounds per man was not a surfeit of ammunition, but I didn't want to order more from Dieter. I didn't want him to think that my "security force" was going to start a limited war. I knew that his operation was under constant surveillance by NATO intelligence, but the story of a security force to protect a world-famous film star's company on location in a potentially dangerous place was believable.

"A few things more, Dieter," I said. "Redding likes to film from the air. He asked me to see if you could locate two large helicopters."

"He is not bringing machines from the States?"

"Why bother if they are available in Europe?"

Dieter frowned, pressed a buzzer, and spoke to his secretary. "Will you bring the AviaAlpha file, *liebchen*?"

We made small talk while the secretary brought the file and retreated. Dieter examined the contents dubiously. "This firm reconditions used military helicopters. Converts them to civilian use. According to their latest bulletin they have some Sea Stallions. Two that were damaged in a collision and are now ready for use again. But they are very large, Casey. Expensive to operate."

I suppressed my excitement. Sea Stallions were not the most reliable machines. It had been the failure of a U.S. Navy Sea Stallion that had set off the chain of disaster at Desert One back in 1979. But if these were in good condition, they would be perfect. Two could carry all of R Force with room to spare.

"This AviaAlpha—Italian?"

"Yes. Their facilities are in Milan. The managing director is a former Italian Air Force officer named Marini."

"Call him for me, please. Set up a meeting. I'll fly down to Gallarate to see him if he will meet me there. Make it tomorrow."

"I will leave a message at your hotel. Is there anything else I can supply you?"

"One more item," I said. "I require three Czech RPG-7s and fifty rockets."

"For a security force, Casey?"

"For a security force, Dieter," I said.

"Those will look very odd on the end user certificate."

"I would prefer it if you listed them simply as collector's weapons."

"Collector's weapons. I see. Difficult but not impossible. Expensive."

"I can see that they would be," I said. "But Redding wants to add them to his collection."

"With rockets."

"Of course."

It was a moment of truth. Dieter Lang was a legitimate dealer in arms, but he was also a member of a profession in which the bending of rules was common. One of the reasons he operated in his home city of Zurich was that the Swiss *never* extradite. Switzerland was the home of both private banking and the arms trade for good reason.

"Well," he said, pursing his lips thoughtfully, "the price will be $15,000. I can't bargain on that, Casey. You understand."

I did understand, of course. I also understood that since the weapons I wanted were Czech in origin they would almost certainly be undocumented, though they would probably have a fascinating history. Often the Soviet and Warsaw Pact soldiers stationed in Eastern Europe stole weapons and sold them for drinking money. There was even one case, reasonably well documented, of a pair of Soviet Army soldiers selling a T-80 tank to a Polish scrap dealer to finance a week's binge.

"Agreed," I said. "Deliver them with the Uzis to Naples."

Dieter drew a deep breath. "About payment, Casey."

"I will give you a draft on the Zwingli Bank now for $25,000. The balance when the merchandise arrives on the dock in Naples."

"That is acceptable," Dieter said, pouring out another schnapps. We drank, and I stood to leave. Dieter put a hand on my shoulder. "I was sorry that you were forced to leave the army, Casey."

"The fortunes of war," I said.

He studied me somberly. We were not close, but we were friends, after our fashion. "Are you certain you are doing the correct thing?"

I stared him down.

"I mean, taking this position with a film company," he said. "I can always use men like you and Louis Brown. I cannot pay like Mr. Redding, but the work is steady."

"*Danke*, Dieter," I said. "But I probably wouldn't make a very good salesman. I will have a certified check sent by bank messenger before the close of business tomorrow."

"Fine."

I clapped him on the shoulder. "*Wiedersehen*, Dieter."

"*Glück auf*, Casey," he said.

———

I dined in a café on the shore of the Zurichsee and returned to the Continental at eleven. There was a message from Dieter that I had a meeting with Alfiero Marini of AviaAlpha at Gallarate at noon tomorrow. He had taken the liberty, he said, of booking me a seat on the Alitalia flight leaving Kloten at ten-fifteen.

I called Alitalia, confirmed my booking, and reserved space on their Milan to London flight at seven in the evening. Then I went to my room and telephoned Louis at the Holiday Inn in Fayetteville, North Carolina. He was out, and I left a message for him to call me when he returned. Next, I called Ziegler at the Eagle Films office in Century City. It was early afternoon in Los Angeles. I gave him a résumé of what I had accomplished so far. I disliked speaking over an unguarded line, but I was reasonably certain we were still secure.

I was surprised to hear that Redding was in the office. I didn't know his working habits then. He wanted to talk to me, and when he came on the line he wanted to know when I would be in London. I told him tomorrow night.

"I'm calling Ann in an hour," he said. "I'll tell her when you're getting in."

There it was again, I thought, that self-inflicted wound. Was it possible that I had misjudged the affection between them? I didn't think so. So what was it—some sick desire to be a cuckold? Whatever it was, it was no bribe. I was already committed to leading R Force.

"Everything is on track, Harry," I said.

"Good," he said. "Good. Here's Jerry again."

I gave Ziegler a list of equipment that he could pass on to Strachan, who would be leaving for Naples within three days. These were things that could be air-shipped with photographic gear without attracting attention: night sights, light-enhancing binoculars, a half-dozen or so infrared scopes that could be adapted to the Uzis. I told him that Louis would be arriving back in Los Angeles with some other things, and that if he was going to miss Louis to arrange for the articles in question to go air freight to Naples as supplies for Unit Two. I suggested that they not be opened by anyone but him.

I also told him I thought I had a line on two Sea Stallions and to tell Strachan to make certain there was deck space for them on whatever vessel he chartered to move R Force to North Africa. Strachan had the native Scot's dour efficiency, and I was confident that if we ran into trouble, it would not be because of any mistake made by him.

I was awakened by Louis's call at about three in the morning. Without preamble, he said, "We have twelve ex-Rangers and a couple of straight legs so far. I'm talking to some blood tomorrow. Six more, almost for sure. How is it with you?"

"The tools are taken care of. I'm seeing about birds tomorrow noon. There are some things I want you to pick up. Get two Barnett Thunderbolt crossbows and a dozen hunting flechettes for each." Hunting crossbows could be bought at almost any sporting-goods store, but it would be better to buy them from an outlet near Fort Bragg, where off-duty soldiers often bought such weapons. "Have them air freighted to Eagle Films in Culver City. Private carrier, Louis. Overnight service."

"Right, Major."

"When are you going down to the jarhead kingdom?"

"Tomorrow night. I have a line on a retired gunny and another half-dozen guys."

"Sergeant."

"Yes, Major?"

"Try to pick a few white guys, will you?"

"I'll give it some thought, Major."

"See you back in L.A. in three or four days."

"Whatever's right, Major."

"Take care, Louis," I said. "When you get down to Parris Island, don't insult the jarheads."

Louis laughed. "Casey?" he said.

"What is it, soldier?"

"How do you feel? Good?"

"Yes," I said.

"I'm glad. I was beginning to think you'd let the bastards grind you down."

"Never, Sergeant," I said. "Now let me get some sleep. It's three in the morning here."

"Right," Louis said, and broke the connection.

9

At noon the following day I met Colonnello Alfieri Marini in the terminal building at Gallarate, the airport just north of Milan.

The colonel had retired from the Italian Air Force at the age of fifty because he had discovered that it was far more lucrative to repair and lease obsolete military aircraft than it was simply to fly them.

I realized how lucrative his business was when he led me to his Maserati in the parking lot and then drove me to Monza. There, his employees labored in a jumble of prefabricated steel-and-aluminum buildings containing an astonishing assortment of military aircraft, mostly trainers and light attack craft of the sort being phased out by the NATO air forces now, but still useful. His facility was almost in the shadow of the racecourse on which Phil Hill, the first American ever to become Grand Prix champion, had won his title in 1960. Marini told me that he employed twenty-eight sheet-metal workers and nine qualified air mechanics. Most of the aircraft he reconditioned were sold or leased to Third World governments.

"Even the inconsequential have needs, Maggiore," he said, lifting his narrow shoulders. "If neither East nor West will give people aircraft, they must buy them from people like me. I do not take advantage of them, I assure you." But judging from the gleaming custom-designed racing car crouching outside his office, I took his disclaimer with some skepticism.

On the airstrip behind his factory stood two Sea Stallions: large, ungainly machines. I had not flown in a Sea Stallion since the last time my Special Forces A team had been delivered to the Viet highlands by a marine cargo-chopper unit from Danang. These looked scruffy, with the Italian Air Force paint and markings chipped and peeling. But as I inspected them I could see that the engines had been reconditioned, the rotor hubs (the most vulnerable part of a helicopter—a machine that ought not to fly at all) were sound.

"These splendid Stallions can be had immediately for only two hundred fifty thousand dollars apiece," Marini said. "A coat of paint and they will be worthy of Eagle Films and Signor Harry Redding."

"We do not plan to buy, Colonnello," I said. "What I had in mind was a month's charter, beginning next week."

There was considerably more discussion than that, but in the end we came to an agreement. AviaAlpha would lease us the Stallions for fifty thousand for a period of four weeks. Marini's pilots would deliver them to Naples and oversee their dismantling for shipment to North Africa as deck cargo. I asked him if there were any former military pilots available who would be willing to remain with the helicopters throughout the charter. His own people would be unable to oblige, he said, but he would make inquiries.

The fliers were apt to be the Achilles heel of the assault on Point X. If I had been looking for fighter pilots, I had no doubt I would have had more candidates than I could possibly use. But helicopter pilots were a more cautious breed. In a pinch I could fly one of the Stallions myself. I was not Stallion-qualified, but after three thousand hours in Hueys and Loaches one can fly almost anything.

The day in northern Italy was sunny but as smoggy as Los Angeles. The Po Valley has had an air-pollution problem ever since the Marshall Plan rebuilt Italy's industrial north. In return for America's generosity, the workers of Lombardy have voted Communist for forty years.

Marini insisted on having his engineering test pilots give me a short flight in each of the Stallions so that I could be reassured of their condition. I was satisfied with them. Each aircraft could carry thirty men and a crew with ample room for stores.

When we landed, I told the colonel that I would make an advance payment of $10,000 by bank transfer from London, and I asked him to paint the Stallions flat desert tan.

With sand-colored aircraft and World War II Afrika Korps desert uniforms, R Force was going to resemble a military unit caught in a time warp.

Colonel Marini drove me to Milan in his red beast. We had a fine meal in the Galleria near the Duomo, and then he drove me back to Gallarate to catch my plane to Heathrow.

The flight across Europe was smooth, the ground hidden beneath a solid cloud deck. We landed at 2300 hours in a driving rain. By midnight I was through passport control and customs, and an hour later I was checked in at the Stafford and bedded down for the night.

I thought about Ann Maclean somewhere in the warren of elegant rooms around me. And I thought about Harry Redding, too, before I fell into weary sleep.

———————

I didn't call Ann's room in the morning, but when I went down to the small breakfast room overlooking St. James's Place, there she was at a window table, with three men. One of them was a middle-aged English actor I recognized from a BBC series currently being shown on American public broadcasting. The other two were young men I took to be film-company executives. Savile Row clothes with a touch of Carnaby Street. Ann looked fresh and beautiful. I was surprised—and a little dismayed—by the turn it gave me to see her sitting there with the rainy London morning light on her ebony hair.

81

I went to her table, and she looked up at me with an expression that gave no indication she was glad to see me. When I considered that the last time we had been together she had been naked in my bed, the change did not warm me. She was polite and businesslike as she introduced me to her companions. When the two executive types stood to shake my hand (the actor remained seated, his mouth filled with croissant and marmalade), I felt oversized and unpolished. They seemed to regard my scarred face and broken nose with apprehension. I guessed that they were gay. In fact, it turned out I was wrong about their profession and right about their sexual preference. They were film critics from two of the London dailies. My manner may have been more brusque than I intended, but I had hoped that when I encountered Ann in London she would be alone.

She asked me to join them for breakfast, but the offer was clearly made out of British politeness. I said no thanks, that I hadn't time for more than coffee.

"Harry said I was to make myself useful to you," Ann said. "Any orders?"

That drew a giggle from the critics and a munching stare from the actor that seemed to say: "Who is this oversized Yank?" I felt more than ever out of place.

I said, "Meet me here at seven. If that's convenient." I didn't know why Ann had gone brittle on me, but then, I had never seen her working.

She said to her companions, "Sorry, darlings. Duty calls. We will do the screening for you Wednesday." So it wasn't convenient, but she had been told by Redding that I had precedence.

As I left them I heard one of the youngsters (neither could have been more than twenty-four or -five) say, "He's a *big* one, your Yank friend, Annie."

I was seething. I didn't know much about women like Ann Maclean. They were largely outside my experience. And I had allowed a one-night stand and a few pleasant hours to make me vulnerable. I didn't like that. It had never happened before.

I ordered a pot of coffee and some toast and sat in the empty lounge. Jesus, I thought. Annie? I gulped the scalding coffee down, made a mess out of the toast (which was served cold, in the British manner), and stomped out to order the doorman to find me a taxi. I had work to do. It didn't occur to me that our one-night stand might have disturbed Ann's equilibrium as much as it had mine.

10

I have often thought that if some World War II warrior had been given, during a lull in the fighting, a one-minute vision of future time circa, say, 1985 and had seen the living rooms of America and Britain and France with their Sony and Hitachi television sets and high-fidelity radios, and the streets of London and New York bumper to bumper with Japanese economy cars and German luxury sedans, he would have thrown down his rifle and said to the troops, "It's all over, men. I don't know who fucked up, but we lost the war."

I had that thought again as my taxi carried me down Knightsbridge in a steady downpour. Through the rain-smeared windows I could read the news placards on the kiosks where the London dailies were offered for sale. Some of the old traditions still survive in the UK even in the age of the telly and the VCR. There had been another car bombing in Beirut. Either the Shiites had done it to the Sunni or the Christians, or the Christians had done it to the Sunni or the Shiites. The signs made no distinction, and, logically, none was needed. The world had become so numbed by terrorists murdering the innocent that the factions became blurred. Hezbollah, Amal, PLO, Fatah, Red Brigades, Red Army Faction, Direct Action, Provo IRA, Japanese Red Army—the groups splintered and renamed themselves so swiftly it boggled the mind—as it was intended to do.

My guess was that if I stopped to buy a copy of the *Times* or the *Guardian* or the *Evening Standard*, there would be not one word in any of them about the American diplomats held hostage in some secret place. I was struck by the thought, as my taxi inched along through the heavy traffic, that whatever Redding's real purpose in bankrolling a rescue attempt, it would break the apathy. Whatever Harry Redding did was news.

I had given the cab driver the Knightsbridge address of a former officer of Royal Marines I had met when he was an exchange officer at the JFK Center at Fort Bragg. His name was Albert Ware. He was about my age and had served in the Falklands war. We had corresponded sporadically over the last few years, but it had come as a surprise to me when he had written to say he was "now in civvie street."

I would have preferred to fill out the ranks of R Force with less haste, but there was barely enough time to transport and train an effective strike force, even one as small and specialized as ours. I had to rely on such notoriously imponderable factors as war records and a simple willingness to serve.

I was let into the Ware flat by a colorless, prematurely aging woman in her late thirties. Her name was Jean, and she had the strained look, familiar to professional military people, of the woman living with an active, angry man suddenly deprived of the only career he ever wanted.

Ware was not at home. He was at the Rover agency, where he sold cars. It was difficult to speak to Jean Ware until I realized that she would give anything to have Bertie gone, at least for a time. I could understand that. Living with an unwillingly retired soldier can mean living in hell for a woman.

I sat with her for a time, a teacup balanced on my knee, while we covered the polite ground, reminiscing about the few occasions when we had met in the States, once a British Embassy party we had both attended in those days when Bertie Ware's career—and mine—was still on track.

The gloomy sitting room was decorated with Ware's military memorabilia: framed photographs, decorations, officer's sword, a captured Argentine's bullioned epaulets. All of it grossly out of place in this tiny, genteel flat at a "good" London address.

I didn't want to speak to Ware at a car dealer's showroom. Somehow it seemed to me it would demean him and make my offer seem melodramatic. So I said, "I must leave now, Jean. I'm sorry I missed Bertie. I should have called. But would you ask him to telephone me at the Stafford this evening? I have an offer of employment that might possibly interest him."

I felt guilty putting it that way, because selling Rovers was at least steady work with no one seeking to kill you. But I wasn't prepared for her rushing gratitude. "Is it soldiering, Casey? If it is, let me say so to him. You don't know how he hates what he's doing."

"I need a few good professionals," I said. And then, because honor demanded *some* honesty, I added, "It's only a few weeks' work, Jean. But it is soldiering."

"Bertie will be so pleased," she said, her face transfigured. I'd swear she looked younger. I was offering her an interval of peace by taking her husband to war. There was a fine chance I was offering her widowhood as well, but she didn't sense that and I didn't suggest it.

———————

Because I didn't know what else to do—and the appointment I had made to see some other British military castoffs at Aldershot was not until tomorrow—I went to the Imperial War Museum. I spent three hours there wandering among the Chieftain and Sherman tanks, the World War I aircraft, the Bren-gun carriers, and the row upon row of Victoria Crosses displayed in glass cases—awards going back to the Crimean War. The British military, I thought, had once been so certain that it was the standard-bearer of Western civilization. Now, all that remained to it were endless cruel skirmishes in Northern Ireland. And memories of past glory that lay here, under glass, unvisited by the heirs of the brave men who had carried the tattered battle

86

flags hung on these walls and who had worn the quaint colorful uniforms displayed on the faceless mannikins.

It was not that the barbarian had gone from the world. It was that he had outlived these ghosts. I left the museum a thoughtful, and slightly depressed soldier.

I stopped at a pub to wash down a sandwich with a pint of warm, bitter ale. As I made my way back to the Stafford, I passed a cinema showing Harry Redding in *Freefire Zone*. The restless line stretched down the street and around the block: young Londoners standing in the rain of a dark afternoon awaiting their turn to see an American film hero refight a lost war.

At the Stafford two messages were waiting for me. One was from a Mr. George Sawkins, of a firm called Sawkins Explorations, and the other was from Colonel Marini in Monza.

I returned Marini's call first. He had bad news for me. The pilots he had half promised me would not, after all, be available. His own company pilots would deliver the Stallions to Naples, but the others he had solicited had refused the job with Eagle Films. Tunisia was too much for them. I thanked the Milanese and assured him that his failure to get pilots wouldn't affect the leasing of the helicopters. He would receive his initial payment on schedule.

To make up for his inabililty to produce willing airmen, he told me that the Sea Stallions were being made ready immediately. His people were working overtime. Did I want the Eagle Films logo painted on the machines? I said thanks, but no.

Next I called Sawkins. He was a petroleum engineer with wide experience in Libya. He had received a call from Rod Strachan asking him to telephone me. I arranged to see him early the next morning.

––––––

It was a few minutes after seven when I went down to the lounge to meet Ann. She was waiting there for me, a gin-and-it on the low table in front of her. There were other hotel

87

guests there, but I looked only at her. She wore a blue dress that clung to her figure and made her eyes look like sapphires.

"Hello," I said, suddenly at a loss.

I ordered myself a Scotch and sat down across the table from her. She looked cool, self-possessed. I wondered what had happened to the woman who had made love with such abandon in Malibu.

There were a hundred things I wanted to say to her, and almost none of them had to do with the job I had taken on for Redding. But she gave me no openings to speak of personal things, and so I simply told her, in the briefest way I could, what I had done in Switzerland and Italy.

She said, "I spoke to Jerry today. He said to let him know if the funds deposited were enough. What next?"

"I am going to Aldershot tomorrow." I hesitated. "Care to come with me?"

"I don't think so, Casey," she said. No explanation. Just a refusal.

It went that way for most of the evening. We had dinner in the hotel dining room—which is probably as good a restaurant as you'll find in London, though I'm certainly no judge. The staff knew Ann. The Stafford was Eagle Films' home base in England. We were treated royally, but I was in no mood to enjoy myself. The misgivings that had depressed me all day, ever since leaving Ware's Kensington flat, in fact, lay heavily on my mind, and being close to Ann and yet so far from her made the depression worse.

When dinner was finished, it was still only nine o'clock, and I said, "Let's walk a bit, Ann."

She looked at me oddly. "It's raining, Casey."

"Not hard," I said. What I really wanted to do was take her up to my room and try to reinvent the woman in Malibu. But I knew better than to suggest any such thing.

She said, "All right. Let me get my mac." Some little warmth came through her half-smile, as though I were a little boy and she was, reluctantly, indulging my foolish desire to walk in the rain.

I waited for her on the front stoop of the hotel, belted into my old green trenchcoat with the holes in the epaulets where major's leaves had once been pinned. The rain was falling gently now, and it was not really cold. The air smelled damp and fresh.

St. James's Place, a small cul-de-sac walled in by the Stafford on one side and old and elegant town houses on the other two, was cluttered with cars. There were the inevitable Rolls-Royces, two of them, probably belonging to owners of elegant flats in the town houses, a Rover saloon, a Mazda RX 7, and a Toyota sedan that looked vaguely out of place parked among its betters. Two men sat in the Toyota, one of them smoking. I could see the cigarette smoke curling up and out through the open window.

The doorman, always willing at the Stafford, offered to trot out to St. James's Street and find me a taxi. I thanked him and said no, that what I had in mind was a walk through Green Park. As though it were a warm summer evening, he said pleasantly that it was a fine night for it, sir.

I was smiling at that when Ann came out to meet me. She was wearing a beautifully cut raincoat, black and shiny as a dolphin's pelt. Her head was bare.

We headed across St. James's Place to the tunnel that runs between the old town houses for a block and emerges on the edge of Green Park—more properly *The* Green Park, though I've never heard a Londoner call it that.

We walked in silence through the narrow tunnel and then down Queen's Walk toward The Mall. All around us were the soft sounds of London on a rainy evening. The overhanging trees made spidery patterns against the overcast that glowed soft amber with reflected light.

I said, "I went to the Imperial War Museum today. We call that a busman's holiday."

"You miss it, don't you, Casey?" Ann said quietly.

"The army? Yes. I miss it. It's all I've ever really known. Army brat, you see."

"I know something about that sort of life. I simply never loved it," she said. "I found it too expensive."

"Expensive?"

"Not in money. In other things."

I thought about Jean Ware and all the women like her who spent their lives following their men around the world from miserable post to miserable post and were paid for their loyalty with loneliness and boredom. That was one reason I had never married.

Ahead of us we could see the lights of the automobiles on The Mall and the shining windows of Buckingham Palace beyond the Victoria Memorial. The broad expanse of the green, dotted with old trees, made a plain of darkness crossed and recrossed by gravel walks.

"Is that why you are doing this, Casey?" Ann asked. "Because you miss the life?" There was no mistaking her meaning. She was asking me why I had agreed to Redding's plan. "There won't be any glory in it. You'll get no medals."

"I don't expect any."

"I don't just mean bits of bronze and ribbon. I mean any sort of credit. Or thanks," she said.

"I thought you were in favor of it," I said. "At least I thought so in Malibu."

"Malibu is far away, Casey. Malibu is make-believe."

Hearing that from her turned me cold, bitter and cold.

"Does Redding know you feel like this?" I asked.

"No. Harry wants me to be on his side. He wants me to understand. In a way, I do. It is just that I suddenly am very afraid of what it might cost." She slipped her arm through mine in the first gesture of concern or tenderness she had made since California. "You could die, Casey. Or end up in a Libyan prison," she said.

"That won't happen."

"So speaks the professional soldier. But professional soldiers *do* die." There was pain in her voice, and I didn't know why— until she said, 'My husband was a professional soldier, Casey."

That shook me. I didn't know why it should, except that I'd had no idea she had ever been married.

"Ian was an officer in my father's regiment. The Provos blew

90

up an officers' mess in Armagh. Eighteen officers were killed. Ian was one of them."

"Ann," I said, "I am truly sorry. I didn't know."

"I didn't tell you. How could you know?"

"It's mad, Ann," I said as gently as I could. "It's a war. We don't call it that, but it is. Someone had to fight it. I think Redding realizes that. Does he know about Ian?"

"Yes. He thinks I should be angry. I was. In a way I still am. But I'm uncertain, Casey. I hear what our governments say they'll do, and I see those lines of people who see Harry's movies and listen to them cheer him on the screen. Is any of this real? I know the hostages and the terrorists are real, and so are the maimed and dead innocent bystanders. People *say* they want action, but do they? Then along comes Harry to pay you to do what no one else will. Or can. It frightens me, Casey. There is something medieval about it. Rich men hiring condottieri to do what politicians are afraid to do."

"Is there another way, Ann?" I asked.

"There should be."

"But *is* there? You can't stop these killers with tough talk," I said. "Every time we make threats and do nothing we make matters worse. It has to stop."

"That's what Ian said."

"He was right."

"He was right," Ann said bitterly, "and he is also dead."

"It costs, Ann."

"That's what frightens me. I don't know if Harry really understands that it costs lives as well as money. He won't be with you, you know, when you go into Libya."

"The last thing I want is Harry Redding in R Force," I said.

"No fear of that. Nobody died in *Freefire Zone* or *Covering Fire*. When the director said 'Cut,' the dead got up and walked off the set. That's the difference."

We moved in silence through the soft rain. It felt fresh on my face. It glistened in Ann's hair like tiny diamonds.

"It can be done, Ann," I said.

"Perhaps it can be done," she replied quietly. "What will you do about the Russians at Barqin?"

"I hope we won't have to do anything about them."

"But if?"

"If they intervene, we'll fight them. Our job is to get the hostages out."

I felt Ann shudder against me. "Sometimes you frighten me, you professionals."

"The politicians frighten me more," I said. "How many Munichs can we stand before we bring everything down? Some things are not negotiable."

"Ian said that, too," Ann murmured.

We reached The Mall and turned to walk slowly by Clarence House. There was traffic there and on Marlborough Road, lights gleaming wetly on the pavement, but we were the only walkers. As we turned up Marlborough Road toward Pall Mall, I caught a glimpse of a single figure in the shadows behind us. When we paused, he paused. When we moved again, so did he, keeping his distance.

"What is it, Casey?" Ann asked.

"I'm not sure. But don't look back."

We took shelter in the colonnade of St. James's Palace facing Marlborough Road. It was very dark in the shadows. I said to Ann, "Walk on slowly. Up to the sentry box on Cleveland Row. Wait for me there."

She did as I told her without a murmur.

The man behind us could be a stroller, out, as we were, for a walk in the rain. Except for one thing. As he passed under a streetlight, I saw that he was wearing a black leather coat. The man I had seen two days earlier on the Rämistrasse in Zurich? I felt certain of it.

As Ann slipped around the corner, the man in the leather coat passed me. Perhaps if I had not become increasingly worried about the shaky security that surrounded the Point X operation I would have been more restrained. But I *was* worried, deeply so. I had a feeling that we were being watched, perhaps even manipulated by forces outside our control. I stepped into the light and confronted the man.

"Who the hell are you?" I demanded. I was half a head taller and fifty pounds heavier, and I must have startled him. Even so, he handled himself better than I did. He threw a karate blow that spun me around and almost felled me. And before I could recover, he was running across Marlborough Road, his footsteps loud on the paving.

I started after him. There were automobiles passing down on The Mall, but the streets near St. James's Palace were oddly empty. I heard Ann's voice calling after me.

A car swept past me, accelerating. Its headlights illuminated the man. He looked back over his shoulder and leaped for the safety of the walk.

That safety was purely an illusion. The car—and suddenly I realized it was the Toyota I had seen waiting in St. James's Place when I stepped out of the Stafford—put a wheel up on the walk, swerved, scraped the stonework of the building with a shrill cry of metal. It hit the running man, lifted him into the air. He spun like a pinwheel, all arms and legs, struck the building, then the walk, and lay still. The Toyota skidded back onto the roadway and sped away in the direction of Admiralty Arch.

From several places, all at once, a crowd materialized. Automobiles were stopping on Pall Mall. I was not the first one to reach the sprawled man, but I was the first to know he was dead. Soldiers recognize death: the slackness of muscles that were, only moments ago, in violent action, the peculiar angles the limbs make with the body, the sudden changes that overtake a human being when he becomes a damaged assortment of parts and no longer a living man.

People were murmuring in shock, some voicing outrage at the callous wantonness of the hit-and-run driver. In the distance I heard the odd whistle London policemen use.

I felt someone touch me as I knelt beside the dead man. I looked up. It was Ann. Her face was drained, a bloodless mask. Her eyes looked enormous. I stood and stepped back, letting

93

the crowd close in around the shattered man. I put an arm around her. She said something I couldn't hear, and I leaned closer. "Is he dead?" she asked.

"Yes," I said.

"Let's leave here," she whispered. "You mustn't be seen."

What she'd said was true enough. If nothing else, it might take me more time than I could afford to explain to the Metropolitan Police how it happened that I was chasing a man who became a hit-and-run victim. I could even be detained as responsible for the accident.

But it was no accident. The driver of the Toyota had driven up onto the sidewalk to take out his target. Ann had seen it, too, and she looked sick and shaken.

We walked quickly toward St. James's Place, away from the crowd and the dead man. I had my arm around her shoulders, and I could feel her trembling. I wanted to comfort her, talk to her, see if we could make some sense of it. But when we reached the lobby of the Stafford she looked at me and said, "I don't want to talk about it, Casey. Please." She was obviously agitated and, I sensed, frightened and vulnerable.

"You need a drink. So do I," I said.

"No, please," she said. "I don't want anything. I'm going to my room." It was as though a steel door had slammed in my face.

"Ann—"

"No, Casey. Please. Just leave me alone." Her voice was thin with strain, but she meant what she said. I was being pushed away, shut off. I felt the sting of it and backed off.

"Good night," she said, and asked the desk clerk for her key. When he handed it to her, she hurried up the stairs, unwilling even to wait for the lift to arrive.

The desk clerk asked me, "Is Miss Maclean ill, sir?"

"We saw a traffic accident," I said. "A bad one."

"How dreadful, sir."

"Yes," I said.

"You had a telephone call, sir." He handed me the message.

It was from Bertie Ware. I took the lift up to my room and called him.

"Casey," he said excitedly. "When Jeanie told me you'd been round, I could scarcely believe it. Whatever is happening, old boy? What's all the mystery?"

"There's no mystery, Bertie," I said. "A chance for a few weeks' work, that's all. Better not discuss it on the telephone."

"Where are you stationed, chum?" he asked.

"Here and there. I'm a civilian now. It's a long story. Can we talk about it tomorrow?"

"Is seven o'clock too early?"

"How about ten?" I said. Before he could reply I asked, "What's happened to Bill Tinker? I heard he was running a pub in Aldershot."

William Stuart Tinker was an officer in the Scots Guards with whom I had become friendly during my tour of duty in England. He was older than I, a marvel with tactical organization. The story was that he later spent two years with the Special Air Service Regiment and then had been promoted to lieutenant-colonel and discharged from the army, because the table of organization of that supersecret elite outfit couldn't use anyone in that rank except the unit commander. It was a typical bit of military weird-think. I had an idea that Tinker would leap at a chance to join R Force. It depended on his current commitments.

"That's what he's doing, chum. Being a gracious landlord. Are you going to see him?"

"I thought I might. What's the name of his place?"

"The Robert Bruce. What if I drive you down there tomorrow?"

"Can you get away?"

"I'd like to see anyone try to stop me. It'll be good to see the old Brown Job again." Bertie never forgot he was a Marine. Army people, no matter how competent, were always Brown Jobs.

"I'll meet you on the corner of Pall Mall and St. James's Street at ten."

"Bless you, chum. Look for a blue Rover saloon."

After I broke the connection I wondered whether or not I should call Ann's room. I couldn't shake off the vision of the corpse in the leather coat sprawled on the sidewalk. The possibilities were endless and all of them nasty. Was the man one of Mossad's watchdogs? Agron could certainly have told the Israelis I would be in Zurich and then in London. Israeli intelligence wasn't known for its trusting ways—they could have put a man on me. But that opened up an even more troubling possibility. Had the men in the Toyota been Arab agents watching *him*? My mind ran in circles.

Our security was amateurish at best and fatally flawed at worst. And it could only degrade as time went on. Each man Louis recruited was being warned about security and told as little as possible. Even so, they would talk—they couldn't help it. A wife or a girl friend would want to know about the new job, where it was taking him and for how long. When it came to keeping secrets, soldiers were their own worst enemies.

Since there was no way to keep our people from leaking snippets of information, our best protection lay in speed. I had to get R Force operational so swiftly that any opposition wouldn't have time to organize.

I thought yet again about the man who had died. Could the men in the Toyota have been one of the notorious Libyan hit squads that had been in the news so much a year ago? The media had scoffed at the idea until the British policewoman was killed not a quarter of a mile from where I was sitting.

If that was the case, it was quite possible the leather-coat man had been mistaken for me. I thought for some time about that. I had spent a good part of my military life being shot at, but I had never become the target of assassins. It was an unnerving idea, even though it made a kind of dreadful sense.

I picked up the telephone and direct-dialed General Stanley's rooms at Letterman. It was five-thirty in San Francisco. The telephone was answered promptly after two rings.

"Captain Weeden."

"This is Casey Quary," I said. "Is the General available?"

"I'll see, Major," the aide said.

Stanley came on the line immediately. "Casey? What can I do for you?"

I gave him a swift rundown on what had happened.

"That's not good. Who was with you?"

"Ann Maclean."

There was a long pause. "Having second thoughts, Casey?"

"We have a security problem," I said. "If it was me they were after, we have a *bad* security problem."

"I'll do some checking. Where will you be?"

"I'll be back in Malibu day after tomorrow, in the afternoon."

"I'll talk to you then," he said, and hung up.

That was all I could do for now, so I undressed and went to bed. For a long time I lay awake thinking about the General and Bertie Ware and Louis Brown and Bill Tinker. Soldiers. All over the world there were people like us. Some deep thinkers believed it was the military mind that was the cause of most of the world's problems. Because, as Ann had said—rather bitterly, I thought—we loved what we did. But it wasn't so. We were only the clawed paws out on the end of a very long limb.

And I gave Harry Redding some thought, too. There was something almost touching about him. I could imagine him as a child, sitting in a dark movie house and watching Errol Flynn conquer Burma, Humphrey Bogart fight the Afrika Korps to a standstill with one lone tank, John Wayne lead his horse soldiers deep into the Confederacy. I had watched many of the same things. Only, I had become a soldier, and he had become a hero.

I wondered if he had ever read Housman:

I 'listed at home for a lancer,
Oh who would not sleep with the brave?

After an hour of restless tossing, I fell asleep and slept until dawn.

11

Sawkins came to see me at eight o'clock. I was up and had breakfast laid on in my room. He was a slender, weathered-looking man with a mop of gray hair. His skin had the burnished look a man gets from years under a desert sun, but his features were regular, and he carried himself with the assurance of one who is good at his job and pleased with what he does.

"Rod Strachan says you are interested in the Libyan saheer," Sawkins said. "I've done my time down there among the wogs, Major. I brought some things that might be of use to you." He opened a battered briefcase and laid out geological charts and tables and a thick stack of photographs.

We bent over his material, and I located Point X for him. "This place," I said. "It's an old British Petroleum concession. Do you know it?"

"I know it," Sawkins said. "But there's not a ruddy thing there. If you're thinking oil, forget it. The place was test-drilled, and it's no go. Not above twenty thousand feet, anyway. Not economically feasible. BP did the test drilling back in 1967."

"You have actually been on the ground there, Sawkins?"

"Too right I have. The saheer is grim enough almost anywhere south of 30° North, but that place is dry, dry, dry. No oil. No gas. No water. Particularly no water. It has to come in by lorry

98

from Waddan. That's more than two hundred kilometers. I think there's water—a *qanat*, so they tap for it—at Barqin. But the area is restricted. Military only. I don't know what the wogs are up to there, but whatever it is they don't want anyone to see it. There are rumors, of course."

"What sort of rumors?"

"When one works for BP, Major, it's best not to repeat gossip. I'll be going back to Libya one of these days." Sawkins studied me with interest. "There are plenty of your chaps working for El Supremo and the oil companies. You could ask them."

"I'm not really interested in Barqin, Mr. Sawkins. I'm only interested in 27° 29′ North, 12° 22′ East. What's the country like between there and the coast?"

"Mostly sand sea. Some grungy little mountains." He pointed out the Jabal al Sawda. "Almost nine hundred fifteen meters, three thousand feet, at the highest point. But of course if you were going down from Tripoli you wouldn't need to mess with them at all."

"And between there and, say, the Tunisian border?"

"Scrub desert for the first fifty kilometers or so, then sand sea again. Dry wadis. That sort of going. Not too difficult if one has proper transport. But there's nothing there, Major. The concession never even had a name. Dry Hole is what I call it."

I glanced at the pictures. They looked very similar. Sand dunes. More sand dunes. Like a scene from *Beau Geste* without the Foreign Legion or Fort Zinderneuf. One or two of the shots showed galvanized-iron buildings, others had men in Arab headdress standing by or sitting in jeeps bearing the BP logo.

"I'd like to keep the charts and photos for a few weeks, Sawkins. Would that be possible?"

"No problem at all, old chap. Anything to oblige an associate of Roddy Strachan." His gray eyes looked at me from beneath thick gray brows. "This is about films, isn't it, Major? Are you chaps actually thinking about making a picture in Libya?"

I grinned at him. "A life of Colonel Qaddafi," I said.

"He'd love that, the bloody twit. But he hates you Yanks."

"Maybe Allah will be compassionate," I said.

We ate breakfast together and there was more talk, but the photographs were what I wanted. Sawkins ate heartily, drank four cups of coffee, and then bustled off to his office in Southwark Street, on the other side of the river.

When he had gone, I telephoned Ann's room.

"Did you sleep at all?" I asked her.

She sounded tired, but she said, "Yes. I took a Seconal."

"Are you all right?"

"Yes, I'm much better now, Casey. It was an accident, that's all. A dreadful accident."

I thought, Does she really believe that?

"May I see you when I get back from Aldershot?" I asked.

"I don't know, Casey. Harry wants me to get down to Cannes to review the campaign for *Covering Fire*. The poor man, *Fire* hasn't a chance with those so-called critics down there, but he wants it in the festival next June. So I really have to go."

I couldn't imagine a Harry Redding film in the Cannes Film Festival, but there was no point in saying anything.

"Did you speak to him last night?" I asked.

"Yes. I telephoned him as soon as we got back here." She paused, as though uncertain, then she said, "I didn't mention the accident, Casey. I didn't see any point. He has enough on his mind right now."

A flame of jealously flared. *Harry* had enough on his mind, did he? She sounded so protective, and positively tender. I said nothing. After all, what right had I to comment?

"Can I come down?" I asked.

"I'm not dressed, Casey."

She had not been nearly so modest in Malibu. But Malibu, as she had stated clearly yesterday, was make-believe and far away.

I said good-bye.

It wasn't raining, but the air was misty, heavy with the threat of a real storm, as I walked out and joined the brisk crowd of Londoners going about their business.

I had not intended it, but I found myself walking over to pass the exact spot where the dead man had lain last night. The pavement had been washed clean of blood, but the place where the speeding car had scraped the stonework of the building was a perfect marker.

Was it possible the man had been simply an innocent bystander I had flushed out of the dark? Was he really the man I had seen in Zurich? How could I be sure?

There is a military phrase for injuries inflicted on innocent bystanders: "collateral damage." When you bomb a gun emplacement and some of your bombs take out the school next door, that's collateral damage. When the enemy hides himself among civilians and you attack anyway and innocents are killed, that's collateral damage, too.

Sometimes the collateral damage is far, far greater than the damage you do to your objective. War is far from precise.

And then there is the moral judgment a soldier has to make again and again in the real world of combat. In the Great War, now called World War I for an obvious reason, the battlefields had been swept clean of civilians, and the soliders were left to butcher one another in the mud without hindrance. But our modern age was not so elitist. In the aerial bombing of Rotterdam, Dresden, and Hiroshima in World War II there were few military targets destroyed. But even that war hadn't reached the current level of bestiality. Now it was doctrine to hide among the innocent. The presence of one soldier or guerrilla could precipitate the destruction of an entire village. My Lai proved that, if it had needed proving. Islamic guerrillas lived and trained among women and children in the Bekaa Valley and a hundred other places.

I thought about the Bedouin women and children in the satellite photographs. Some of them were likely to be killed. When we hit Point X I wouldn't hesitate to wipe out every terrorist.

101

But women and children? The fanatics counted on that Judeo-Christian ethic which burdened the West. Did I have the hardness of soul needed to put it aside?

It was ironic that when we went into action we would be dressed in the uniform of the Nazi Afrika Korps. Maybe the God of Battles was trying to tell me something.

Bertie Ware arrived in a flurry of spray and a roar of exhaust aboard a blue Rover shaped like a large wedge with sharp edges—Britain's not-quite-adequate answer to Italy's Ferrari. But an impressive set of wheels, for all that.

He swerved through the traffic to come to a stop inches from me, opened the door, and shouted a greeting in a most un-British burst of enthusiasm. Ex-Captain Albert Ware of the Royal Marines dearly wanted to go soldiering.

He was a short barrel of a man with a ruddy face and brick-colored hair. His eyes were blue and lost in a nest of wrinkles and pale flesh well dusted with freckles the color of his hair. He was dressed in flannels and a navy-blue blazer with a bullioned Royal Marines patch on the pocket. An open shirt and the almost inevitable ascot in Royal Marines pattern completed the outfit.

"If I'm going down among the Brown Jobs, I have to show my colors, right, Casey?"

We dispensed with the amenities while he was powering the Rover—an agency demonstrator, he said—through the London traffic and onto the M3 Motorway. We got as far as Richmond before the sky opened up and the rain came down in a torrent. "Welcome to Britain, Casey," Bertie said. "The Falklands were never like this. Bloody London."

In the first ten minutes we were together he made it clear that he loathed his job, hated trying to sell cars, and preferred Jaguars, in any case. "It's a miserable way to spend one's days," he said. "It's getting under my skin, Casey. And I think I'm getting under Jeanie's. Tell me what in bloody hell you have going."

So I began at the beginning, with Louis's and my trip to see Harry Redding and ending with the arrangements I had so far made on the Continent for the arming and organization of R Force. But I dealt solely with the military ingredients of a hazardous rescue mission. Intelligence material, precise locations, timing—all that, I avoided. Bertie heard enough, though. He listened as though I were his fairy godmother come to change his Rover into an armored personnel carrier.

When I had finished, and after I had told him there was a place for him as one of the platoon leaders in the force, he said, "I always knew you Yanks were dotty, Casey. I love it. I love it." He laughed and banged his hand on the thickly padded steering wheel, making the Rover swerve on the wet surface of the motorway. "Redding? That wild man with the bandanna and the bloody RPG? He's paying for this?"

"Under cover of the army he's hiring to make his picture in Tunisia," I said. "It's so logical it's simple. We train for two weeks, move south as a second unit, to film backgrounds or whatever, move in the Stallions, and go in at night. Out the same way."

"I always loved Redding movies, bad as they are. Now I know why."

"It isn't for our personal enjoyment, Bertie," I said. "I want our people out. Safely, if possible. But out and free."

"Too right, chum. Your Sergeant Brown—how many troops will he be able to round up?"

"He'll get what we need, but we can always use a few more."

"How are you fixed for chopper pilots?"

"I'll take whatever you can find as long as they are Sea Stallions–qualified."

"Piece of cake, chum. The navy and RAF Coastal Command just turned a batch of the lads out. I think I can do some good there," he said happily. "I can promise you a wizard company sergeant major for sure, and maybe a gunner or two. Are you going to ask Billy Tinker?"

"I want him for executive officer, if he'll do it."

"Redding's International Brigade is it?"

"Well, English-Speaking Union, anyway."

"Tinker will sign on. I can't see an SAS man spending the rest of his days being the jolly host of a pub in Aldershot." Bertie grinned. "There was some talk of dropping him from the Army-Navy Club because it wasn't fitting for a former officer to be running a gin joint. He told them to jump it and resigned."

Our business with Colonel Tinker went perfectly. We found him at the Robert Bruce, and he turned out to be as restless as we all were. He was a man some five years older than I, but still a long way from being ready to retire. I always thought there was a touch of C. Aubrey Smith in Bill Tinker. He looked as though he should be leading a squadron of Lancers through the Khyber Pass, but, alas, he, like most of us, was born out of his proper time.

Tinker sat us down by a roaring fire and had his bar girl bring in hot ale. He had been married, but his wife had long ago left him. He regarded this as a kindness on her part. He would not have been allowed in the Special Air Service Regiment if he had not been single. He was quite alone now. The Robert Bruce was a favorite drinking place for young soldiers from the various units scattered nearby.

I repeated what I had told Bertie about the R Force operation. And I cautioned him about security. "We can't keep it secret forever," I said. "I just want to keep it secret long enough."

"It's so bloody outrageous," Tinker said, "that most people wouldn't believe it."

"The ones who can hurt us would," I said.

"I wouldn't miss it for the world, Casey."

"You are XO then," I said. "We'll assemble in an Italian port. I'll be in touch to tell you where and when. You'll have a draft on Lloyd's Bank for travel expenses. Each man will get twenty thousand dollars." I looked at each man in turn. "So you understand there is risk involved. All the men are being told that— and as little else as we can manage until we are ready to stage."

To seal our bargain we had dinner at the Robert Bruce, and Tinker produced an ex–Scots Guards pipe major to serenade us. We ate, drank Irish whiskey, and the piper strode around the table in his tartan kilt and dress jacket skirling.

Bertie and I suffered in that small private dining room, but thanks to Tinker we suffered in style.

I was back at the Stafford by midnight. The minute I arrived, I called Ann's room, only to be told that she had checked out late that afternoon. No, there had been no message left, sir.

By eight the following morning I was aboard a British Airways flight from Heathrow to Los Angeles International. Lulled by the constant drone of the jets, eased by two tots of more than passable cognac, my mind drifted beyond the visible vista of soft clouds and the dark gray-green ocean. I thought of Redding and Ziegler, of Agron, of Ware and Tinker, of Ann, of Louis and me—of all of us, those I knew and, in some shadowy way, those billions of strangers. One way or another, we were all hostages. But it's one thing to be a hostage to fate, quite another to be a hostage to terrorists, assassins. There is a difference.

One hell of a difference.

PART TWO

*Show me a hero
and I will write you a tragedy.*

F. SCOTT FITZGERALD, *The Notebooks*

12

My return to Los Angeles started with a surprise. I was met by Harry Redding's white Mercedes limousine with Redding himself waiting for me in the back behind the tinted windows. I had begun to get some idea of the way people like him were regarded in their own world, and my picture of it did not include their waiting for the late arrival of an intercontinental jet.

It had been less than a full week since I had seen him, but he seemed changed. His face appeared thinner, and there were lines of strain around the eyes and the mouth. Peculiarly enough, these small imperfections did not detract from his good looks. His profile seemed cut with a sharp blade, his tawny eyes more intense, his lips firmer.

Ann had told me that when the time to start a new project was upon him, he grew tense, his artist's nerves (and he *was* an artist) made taut by the responsibilities he piled on himself. Eagle Films was his personal creation, and though he hired the best, he hired no more than were needed to help him get the job done. *Kasserine*, for example, was really an enormous project, involving hundreds of people—technicians, actors, cameramen, stunt men, prop men, logisticians, and God knows what other specialists. Yet it was Redding who was in charge, and there was no mistake about who made the decisions. Within days of our meeting again, I realized that, except for his one critical flaw, he would have made a remarkable troop commander.

At the beach house, the Ferrari and Ann's Audi had vanished from the garage. The space was filled with canvas duffel bags, crated equipment, and a large number of sealed boxes. On several of the boxes I recognized the company name of the outfit in Fayetteville where I had told Louis to pick up some of our silent weapons.

Redding stood in the sunlight, dressed in what I began to understand was his personal uniform—sweater, jeans, and, today at least, Topsider moccasins—and explained that all of this would be picked up tonight and sent to Los Angeles International to be stored until it could be loaded aboard the chartered jet. Meanwhile, it would be replaced by another load of stores and personal gear. It was clear that he checked each item personally before it was put on the shipping lists.

Ming opened the door, and Redding's black Great Dane, Tarquin, was there to greet him with lolling tongue and lashing tail. The animal obviously loved him, and I found it touching that he responded by kneeling and letting the monster lick his face. "I wish I could take him to Tunis with us," he said, looking up at me, "but that's out." He addressed the dog directly, rather like a teen-age boy with his beloved pet. "You have to stay with Ming, old Tar. I'm sorry."

We went directly down to the war room, and I gave him a briefing and showed him the charts and photographs that Sawkins had lent me. In the late afternoon Jerry Ziegler arrived, and we went over the material again. I was forming a battle plan in my mind, but I had no intention of revealing it to either of them.

"We need pilots for the Stallions," I said. "I can fly one in a pinch, but I'd rather not. It's likely to be a night penetration at low altitude. We don't need a disaster."

Ziegler looked at me apprehensively. I showed him the sections left uncolored on the Operational Navigation Charts, the large areas of the Libyan saheer marked "Limit of Reliable Topographic Information."

"It doesn't matter," I said, "if a hill is only fifty feet high. If you are flying contour and don't see it in time, you're just as dead as if you flew into the Matterhorn."

Ziegler looked as though he had swallowed something very sour. Fear? Or did he know something I did not?

"There's something else we should talk about," I said. "Security. Did Ann speak to either of you?"

"She called me today," Redding said, "and was able to talk about that terrible business in London."

"I would like to know what your friend Agron knows about it," I said. I looked at Ziegler.

"Well," Ziegler said, and stopped. He had connections in Israel, undoubtedly contributed generously to the annual appeals for Israeli charities, and had introduced Agron to Redding. How much did he really know about Agron, and what had he told Redding? If Agron's cooperation was genuine, having him involved was vital. But intelligence officers of whatever nation make me uncomfortable. Their dealings are like medieval clockworks, wheels turning within wheels. They work for their services and for their countries, and quite often they leave broken bodies behind them. I didn't plan to be one of those, and I had an absolute responsibility to the men I was recruiting for R Force.

"I asked Ann to tell you to talk to Agron," I said. "Did you do it?"

Ziegler said, "He knows nothing about it."

"Our security is weak," I said. "If the Libyans find out what we're up to, they'll pulverize us. Without surprise, Point X will be a deathtrap for us and for the hostages."

Redding nodded thoughtfully. I had impressed him. I thought I had better press the point further. "As far as we know, only about a dozen people have the key details of this operation. Each one is in the 'need-to-know' category. There's no question that U.S. and Israeli intelligence have a damned good notion of what we're up to, and we have their blessings. And nothing more than blessings. We're doing what they can't—or believe they can't, which amounts to the same thing. So we have their silence. But we're still in hazard."

I paused and looked at them. I had their rapt attention.

"Soldiers are not cloak-and-dagger types," I went on. "They talk. Mostly among themselves, because they don't really trust civilians. But they do talk. And Louis and I have been recruiting. And ordering some potent equipment. The word is bound to get around. But so far it's a guessing game. That's why I was followed in Zurich, then in London. That's why there's probably an unidentified corpse in the London morgue. Somebody's looking damned hard for an answer—and hasn't got it. Yet."

I paused again. My audience of two seemed to be hanging on each word.

"So let me make it plain and simple. My job is to get the hostages out and to get my men out. Your job is to maintain security and give us cover. So when I ask you to put a clamp on Agron, it's not because I don't like him. It's because he knows so much. Maybe too much. And if our security is seriously breached, I swear I'll pull the plug and let the mess go down the drain. Think about it, Harry. There's still time to call it off."

He gave me his photogenic smile. "All bets are still on, Quary. From here on in, my concern is the success of the raid and the safety of the men."

"And *Kasserine*," Ziegler added.

"You take care of your troops, Major," Redding said. "I'll deal with security and *Kasserine*." His smile broadened, and he looked like a boy. "After all, Jerry, as Alfred Hitchcock once said, 'It's only a mooo-vie.' "

13

Louis Brown arrived in the morning. In his luggage he carried photocopies of forty-eight service records, one-third of them belonging to people we had served with at one time or another in Vietnam. Eight of the new men were ex-Marines, one of them a gunnery sergeant so freshly out that he was still on terminal leave. Two others were former Seals, navy commandos with experience in the Riverine Forces in the Mekong Delta. Underwater specialists were unlikely to need their aquatic skill at Point X, but scuba qualification was only a part of what made the Sea Air Land navy teams. In unarmed combat it was hard to find better, tougher fighting men.

Over breakfast on the terrace, Louis gave us a report on his trip. "Now I have to make up travel packs for each one of them," he said. "Airline tickets and money and a schedule, so they all get to Naples in time. How is Strachan doing with our boat charter?" Louis wanted to get the troops on the water, so he could begin working and briefing them.

"Rod is onto a two-thousand-ton steamer. Liberian registry," Redding said. "It sounds like a rust bucket, but it's available."

"How did you do with the weapons, Major?" Louis asked eagerly. "Can Lang supply what we need?"

I told him that Lang would deliver the Uzis and one hundred twenty thousand rounds to Naples, with the RPGs and rockets. "Do you remember Colonel Tinker and Captain Ware? Ware was at JFK with me, and Tinker did a course at Benning."

"Sure. Who could forget Ware? Built like a fireplug and sunburned all the time?"

"That's the one," I said. "Ware is bringing his company sergeant major and a corporal gunner." Turning to Redding, I explained that these were former Royal Marines, who had fought in the Falklands.

"Counting those and that medic you promised," Louis said, "that's fifty-five. It still leaves us short."

"Tinker may be able to get a couple of SAS people," I said.

We spent the rest of the day in the war room (maybe it was a measure of how completely the idea of R Force had taken us over that we all called it that naturally now) making up the travel packs for the men Louis had recruited. Redding, on the telephone, relayed to a secretary in Century City the ticket requirements. With each pack went a thousand dollars of expense money and a contract from Eagle Films hiring the man as a consultant.

I called Tinker in Aldershot, gave him Strachan's address in Naples, and instructed him to get down there fast, so he could make billeting arrangements for the men who would shortly be following. I asked him to make certain they were scattered in various hotels catering to seamen, with no more than two of them in any one place.

Next I called my Special Forces doctor friend in San Francisco, who told me he had lined up a former 32 Bravo medical specialist. I told him I'd come up and interview the candidate personally. The man who is charged with patching up your wounds is special to any combat outfit and needs extra consideration.

Finally, when I was alone, I telephoned General Stanley to ask if he had been able to discover anything significant about the man killed in London. He said that he had not, but that he had some incidental intelligence that might be useful to me. I arranged to meet with him that night.

At six o'clock I caught a commuter flight to San Francisco, and by eight I was interviewing our medic, former Sergeant Jimmy Green.

He had been working, until a month before, as a paramedic with a south bay city fire department. He was on suspension now because he had attended a teen-age accident victim, nearly dead at the scene and impossible to save. The parents of the boy were suing the city because the city police department had failed to arrest the boy when they stopped him fifteen minutes before the accident, at a time (the parents said) when it must have been obvious the boy was too drunk to drive, and because Paramedic Green had displayed "gross incompetence" (their lawyer's words) in dealing with the boy's injuries. These, Green explained to me, consisted of a fractured skull, a fractured pelvis, a collapsed lung, ruptured spleen, bladder, and liver, a broken neck, compound fractures of both arms, and torn femoral arteries in both legs.

Green was bitter and at loose ends, without the possibility of reinstatement before the case was settled—which, given the condition of the California courts' calendars, might be in two years or quite possibly five. He had served thirteen months in an A Camp in the delta in Nam and owned two Purple Hearts and a Bronze Star. The lawsuit was, he said, the last goddamn straw. I signed him up for R Force on the spot, telling him exactly what the others were being told—that the job was hazardous and that it would take him out of the country for a few weeks. Former Special Forces men don't need a building to fall on them to realize what that might mean. I issued Green travel money and told him he would get his airline ticket by Express Mail, together with instructions.

I drove to the post at the Presidio at nine-thirty, to see the General at Letterman.

Stanley's appearance had deteriorated even in the short time since I had last seen him. His skin was gray, and there were hollows in his cheeks. There were oxygen tanks in his room. But he had added another E-6 sergeant to his staff, and a computer terminal had been moved into the anteroom. I had always been impressed with Stanley's ability to move the lethargic monster of the military establishment. In Vietnam he had accomplished miracles. I was even more impressed now. Behind the ailing old soldier one could sense the tall shadows of the powers that be.

I was troubled as well as impressed. How much of all this was the result of the coming into being of R Force, I wondered. And how secure would it remain for the time we needed to do what Redding was hiring us to do?

The General was propped up in his bed, writing a memo on a pad, when Captain Weeden ushered me into the room.

"Close the door, Casey," he said. "How much is left to do?"

"You haven't spoken to Redding, sir?" I asked.

"There won't be any contact between me and Redding from now on," he said.

That made sense. I didn't know how much was known in Washington about Redding's wild scheme, but whatever was known was enough—probably too much. And then there was the need for absolute deniability. If we failed, the CIA and the Department of Defense would never have heard of us. This dying old soldier was the perfect cut-out. A fragile link that could be snipped like a loose thread. None of this came as a shock to me. Project Omega in Vietnam—an operation run inside North Vietnamese territory against Communist cadres—had been organized this way. There was nothing in the orders to indicate that it had been controlled by the CIA. There was nothing in the records to prove that it had taken place at all.

I told Stanley what I had managed to get done.

"You'll be going in mighty light, Casey. Can you take the objective with only sixty men?"

"If we hit them before they know we are in the country," I said.

"One slip and the hostages are goners."

There was no denying that. I didn't try.

"About the incident in London," he said. "I've done some

nosing around. Our British cousins are pretty tight-lipped. They think there are still Libyan hit squads operating in London." He regarded me with those deep-set, sick man's eyes. "I couldn't get much without stirring up a wasps' nest. But it is possible the man who was run down was Special Branch. Or possibly MI-5 or MI-6. No one will confirm or deny."

That shook me a bit. It suggested that our security was even worse than I thought it might be. The British security services tended to be very nervous about people recruiting British subjects to fight private wars—particularly against Arabs.

Stanley continued: "My sources think that he may have been taken out by a Libyan team. It's only conjecture, but the car was found abandoned out near Heathrow. A Mideast Airlines flight left that morning for Damascus."

"It's too pat, General," I said. "I saw the man in Zurich. He was following me. Why should Libyans hit him like that?"

"The ragheads could have made a mistake, Casey. They often do."

"You mean we've been penetrated, and I was the target."

The General shrugged. "It is a possibility we can't ignore." His sunken eyes glittered as he watched for my reaction. "It might be best to stand down. Have you given that any thought?"

"No, sir. I don't think we have it right yet. Maybe the fellow *was* Special Branch or MI-5, but if he was, what was he doing in Zurich? The Brits aren't organized that way. And what was he doing tailing me? If we've been penetrated, it isn't by any Arab group."

"So you don't buy the hit-squad theory."

"I have nothing better to put in its place, sir. But no, I don't buy it. If the Libyans have any idea what we're planning, they'd be raising hell with the Tunisians about letting a movie company and a lot of military hardware into the country right next door to Point X and Barqin."

"Why do you mention Barqin?" The question was harshly put.

"We can't ignore it, can we?"

"Rumors," Stanley said.

"With respect, sir. More than rumors. Ziegler's friend Gershon Agron says that the uranium diffusion operation there is real enough, and that the Soviets are getting more and more jittery about what they've done by building Qaddafi a potential nuclear-bomb facility. I believe him."

"Redding told me about Agron. I'm doing some checking on him."

"I was going to ask that you do just that. But the material he has produced so far is prime stuff. Ours, by way of Mossad."

"So Redding claims. I'll check out the *refusenik* story. But I want you to think carefully. That whole business in Zurich and London has a nasty smell to it."

"I agree," I said. "But I can't wait around to check it out. I'll have to rely on you, sir."

Stanley essayed a bleak smile. " '*L'audace, l'audace. Toujours l'audace.*' Napoleon would have made you a marshal of cavalry. What was it Murat always said? 'I ride to the sound of the guns.' "

"I hope not, General. The first gunfire I want to hear is that from R Force."

"For Redding? Well, why not. Redding is going to earn it. How are you getting on with him, by the way?"

I shrugged. It was a difficult question to answer. There was such a gulf between my life's experience and his that we could communicate only by signals. And then, there was Ann. I wanted her badly, and she was his girl.

"I managed to obtain the SCR-1220 you wanted," Stanley said. "I've had it sent down to the prop department at Eagle Films. Have you ever used one?"

"No, sir."

"It has a computer keyboard. No voice link. The computer scrambles your signal before it gets sent up to the satellite, and the on-board computer in the bird encrypts the signal again before sending it back down. I'm having Weeden set up a dish on the hospital roof. Nothing gets sent through land lines. It

118

will be as though you were in the next room. I hope it's worth the trouble it cost to get it."

"I hope so, too, sir." I looked at the emaciated figure in the bed and wondered what I was doing to him by using him as my personal intelligence officer.

I thought about that on the way to Los Angeles and Malibu.

14

Preparations began to pick up momentum now. Jerry Ziegler was impressive in his command of the financial details. And Rod Strachan came through with the name of the ship he had chartered, the SS *Kaliph*, which now waited for our arrival in the port of Naples. Then Tinker telexed that he had an ex-RAF pilot with Sea Stallion time.

Redding put on such a show of energy that I was left wondering how he managed it. He had all the tag ends of the film company's move to Tunisia to take care of, and he still managed to pay close attention to every move Louis and I made in the final organization of R Force.

I was more tired than I was willing to admit, but presently the organization of R Force was complete—or as complete as it could be until I had actually assembled the people and the weapons.

But Redding's tasks were still not done, nor were Ziegler's. They had people and equipment scattered from California, across Europe, to North Africa. There were still things that needed to be cleared with the Tunisian government: visas to be obtained, schedules to be agreed upon, fees to be paid for the use of Tunisian troops, agreements to be made with film unions, actors' agents, banks, and insurance companies. All of this was customary in the organization of a foreign shoot and enormously time-consuming.

On the day before we were scheduled to depart from Los Angeles in Eagle's chartered jet, Redding told me at breakfast that he and Jerry would have to spend the entire day at Century City. "You have done wonders, Casey," he said. "Take the day off. Use the Porsche. Unwind. Say your good-byes."

He took off with Ziegler in the Mercedes, leaving Louis and me alone in the beach house with Ming and the cook to look after us.

Louis made some calls and then came in and asked me if it would be all right if he ghosted out for the day. I told him to take the Porsche and to be back by midnight. Our departure was scheduled for ten the next morning.

"You won't need the wheels, Major?" he asked dutifully.

I said no, and he took off.

The cook had departed, Ming had vanished into his own quarters, and I found myself alone.

It was a foggy morning, with the air gray and damp. Standing on the terrace overlooking the beach I could just see the waves rolling up onto the sand shingle below the house. The air was very still. The only sound was made by the waves.

Suddenly I was chilled by loneliness. The truth was that, unlike other men, I had no personal resources. No relatives, no plans for civilian life. Without the army, I was adrift.

One can know a thing and not know it. I had lived so long without reserves that I had mistaken dedication for completion. I had tried to be the perfect soldier. And what, in fact, had I become? A condottiere, a soldier of fortune. Harry Redding had offered me this ridiculous, quixotic venture to lead, and I had snapped at it like a famished predator. It was near madness, unreal.

Would I have done it, I asked myself, if I had been less empty and alone?

I started down the steps to the beach, restless and disturbed. I was pathetically grateful when Redding's dog, Tarquin, appeared at my side, loping across the sand with his pink tongue lolling and his tail wagging at the prospect of a run on the beach.

I walked through the soft sand to the tide line. Behind me the house on the bluff faded in the fog. The beach—what I could see of it—was empty.

I was wearing a heavy cardigan of Redding's, and I jammed my hands into the pockets and strode along as though I had somewhere to go.

The truth hit me hard that foggy morning. Redding and Ziegler had things to do, people to see. Despite the importance of the operation we had planned, they had other concerns as well. I had none.

I found myself remembering the women I had known since leaving the Academy. A long line of brief encounters—not one of them touching me. Claire, the daughter of a lawyer in Washington—an affair that had lasted six weeks when I was at Command and General Staff School. Dana, the southern belle who occupied my off-duty time when I was at Benning. Margarete, who took up a month of my time when I was in Germany. Names. I had some trouble putting a face to each name. A man should have more than that to remember, I thought.

And friends. Redding had said, "Take the day off. Say your good-byes." But I had no one to bid farewell, no friends, not the kind he meant.

Even Louis. In a way that was deeply felt, I loved Louis Brown and he loved me. But it was a soldier's bond. We *served* together. He had put his life at risk for me. I had done the same for him. But even Louis had a life. I tried to imagine him at this moment, surrounded by his friends.

I walked for an hour before I turned back. When I reached the beach house again, I climbed the stairs and roamed through the rooms as though I were seeing them for the first time. I was surrounded by evidences of wealth. There was the rare Brown Bess over the fireplace, the Calder hanging from the ceiling, the handsome appointments, and the steel, glass, and fieldstone house itself.

Down in the war room I took the time to inspect the collection of weapons. Redding had a fortune in guns. The bookshelves were lined with one of the finest collections of books on military history I had ever seen. His ham-radio equipment shamed some of the gear I had seen in the Pentagon. He had everything money could buy. And then I asked myself, But has he a life, any more than I?

He had things to *do*, that was obvious. But what about the inner man? Was he as alone as I was? Were we, each of us, looking for one act that was meaningful and fulfilling beyond the ordinary definition of such cant words?

I walked upstairs again and stood in the doorway to Ann's rooms. The scent of her was in the still, moist air. It struck me that she had sensed my emptiness almost immediately. She had come to me in the night. Why? Simple lust? Or had she been performing an act of generosity to a lonely, displaced man? And did she do the same for Redding?

It is the right of the hero to be fulfilled, I thought. Was Ann Maclean the instrument of that fulfillment? And to whom would she turn when our adventure in the saheer was finished?

I am not much of a drinking man, but suddenly the prospect of sitting alone, with only Redding's dog for company, in Redding's house for an entire long, foggy day was more than I could face.

I helped myself to a bottle of his Chivas Regal, sat down in his living room, with Tarquin at my feet, and steadily, deliberately drank myself into oblivion.

15

I awoke feeling like an old boot. When you are six three and weigh two hundred pounds, it takes a fair amount of Scotch to put you down. I had started early and finished late, before stumbling into my room and locking myself in.

When the pallid sun woke me, I felt physically terrible but psychically cleansed, having availed myself of the immemorial anodyne of the licentious soldiery. I have no doubt that the Duke of Cumberland's professionals had done the same thing before Culloden and so had Ramses III's charioteers before Karchemesh.

The house was filled with people and activity when I went out to the terrace for breakfast. Redding introduced me to a half-dozen people, most of them young, all of them excited and ready for departure. Louis took me aside and said, "You all right, Casey?"

"Never better," I said.

"Harry asked me if you did that often. I said only once in a while."

I shrugged and went down to the war room to collect the charts and satellite photographs. While I was down there, Redding appeared. He said that he had spoken to Ann in Cannes, but there was no mention of whether or not she would meet us in Naples. The plan was for those of us directly involved with R Force to travel to Tunis by ship from there, while Redding and the film people went to Bizerte by air.

I still had the feeling that he was putting Ann up as a kind of prize. But surely, I thought, he must know her better than that. I thought I did.

He looked fit and alert. This morning he was dressed as though for a safari, in tropical whipcords, desert boots, and a bush jacket open to display his developed pectorals and his muscular neck. His face was flushed with anticipation.

He paused for a moment in helping me pack up the charts and photographs and said, in an almost intimate way, "Casey, I want you to know how glad I am that you are in charge of this project. I feel good about it. It is going to succeed."

"Yes," I said. "Count on it."

"I will," he said, and gripped my arm.

———

By nine o'clock the company people had been packed into two Eagle Films vans, and Redding, Ziegler, Louis, and I were in the Mercedes, all heading for Los Angeles International Airport. Ziegler looked overworked; his round face had a sheen of sweat and his clothes were rumpled. He had copies of the morning edition of the Los Angeles papers and the *Hollywood Reporter*.

He said, "Casey, did Harry mention we talked to Gershon again?"

"Is he still in Washington?" I asked. Lolling about the Agency in case there were newer pictures, no doubt, I thought.

"He's meeting us in Naples."

I said, "I know you've relied on Agron for a good many things in the past, but I don't want him on shipboard with the troops."

Ziegler looked offended. "Gershon has been invaluable to us."

"So he has. But he's an open wound to R Force. Through him, every move we make will go straight to Mossad."

Ziegler bridled at that. "You don't know that for certain, Casey."

"I do and you do. Leasing you captured Soviet equipment for your pictures is one thing. Those photographs he gets are something else. They came from the Israelis. You've asked yourself where *they* got them, I assume. I don't want the CIA swarming all over us. This is our operation, not Mossad's, and for damned sure not the CIA's."

"All right, Casey," Redding interposed himself between Ziegler and me. "If you don't want him on the ship, that's the end of it. Forget it now, Jerry."

Louis had followed the conversation with arched eyebrows. Like any of us who had been in Special Forces in Vietnam, he did not remember Central Intelligence Agency projects with any affection. The boys from Langley had a way of stirring up trouble and then vanishing into the night mist. It was standard behavior for clandestine services, but it had never won them friends among the soldiers who had to stay and fight, or among the refugees who were left behind when the last helicopter departed.

More to change the subject than for any practical reason, Redding showed me a single-column story in the second section of the *Los Angeles Times*. The rumor that the kidnappers of Ambassador Lyman and his people were making secret demands of the Israelis had surfaced again. Our State Department had issued a curt statement to the effect that it was "fruitless and counterproductive" to attempt to link the missing Americans with questions that were of interest "only to the government of Israel." Nevertheless, the reporter who wrote the story reminded readers that Israel, not too long ago, had released unconditionally some thirteen hundred Arab militants convicted of terrorism and murder, and had subsequently released three hundred "detainees" in exchange for the Amal militia's release of American airline passengers taken hostage earlier. The linkage had never

126

been acknowledged by either the United States or Israel, but as far as the press was concerned it was a fact.

The story was short and buried in the back of the thick paper. Hostage stories had a very short shelf life these days, I thought.

By eleven the Eagle Films charter was climbing out of LAX on a great-circle route to Naples. The staffers were partying in the main cabin of the DC-10; Louis was with them, having the time of his life.

In the first-class section, where Redding had settled his personal party, I sat beside him while he mulled over the story in the *Times*. Presently he jammed it into the pocket of the seat in front of him and said intensely, "We are going to break the cycle, Casey. We are going to shake those bastards up good." It was precisely what the sweat-burnished Harry Redding of *Covering Fire* would say: *This time we win.*

There is the moment in any operation when doubts have to be put aside, the moment of total commitment.

"Yes, Harry," I said. "That's exactly what we are going to do."

The dicey weather of a week earlier had cleared, and we landed at Capodichino in the middle of a crystalline, starry morning. Strachan had arranged transport in a fleet of vans, and we moved like a mechanized division through the dawnlit streets of Naples to the Hotel San Germano, on the outskirts of the city.

Our early-morning arrival had been planned to discourage the *paparazzi*, the free-lance photographers who traveled Europe in packs searching out celebrities. It did not. The word that Harry Redding would spend a day in Naples before flying on to North Africa had got around, and the lobby of the San Germano was swarming with shouting, shoving, shaggy young people with cameras and tape recorders.

Even though he was tired from the long flight, Redding handled the pushy crowd like the veteran celebrity he was. He was a man who knew the value of publicity, and, unlike many other film stars, who treated the free-lance press generously only until they became "hot" and then backhanded them, he displayed a remarkable tolerance.

It was an incredible scene. I had never experienced anything quite like it. The *paparazzi* pushed at one another and at Redding's people, who had gathered around him like a bodyguard, lifting their Leicas and Nikons over their heads with strobes flashing. There were an unbelievable number of pretty Italian girls mixed in with the throng, some of them with their agents and others with, I suppose, their mothers, all of them hopeful that Redding or one of his executives would recognize them or at least notice them enough to offer work in *Kasserine*. It was quite hopeless, actually; *Kasserine*'s script called for an all-male cast. But that didn't discourage them or their agents or their mothers or whatever. A role in a Redding film could make an unknown actress into another Sophia Loren, and there was not one of them who didn't see it happening to her.

I looked through the seething crowd for a glimpse of Ann, but she wasn't there. Louis stood beside me, wide-eyed and grinning. Ziegler, with two young assistant producers, was opening a path for Redding to the elevator. Eagle Films had taken over the entire top floor of the hotel, and the manager was doing his best to make it possible for the star to move across the lobby.

"Casey, have you ever seen the like?"

Suddenly, close by my side was Bertie Ware, his face redder than ever and a wide grin showing his excitement. He said something by way of greeting to Louis, but the noise level in the lobby was so high I didn't hear it.

Strachan pushed his way to us and said, "Follow me. We'll go the back way."

It took us five minutes to push our way out of the lobby and down a hallway to the service elevator. Even then we had to shove a pair of *paparazzi*, more enterprising than others, out of the elevator before we could use it to reach the top floor.

Activity was at a high level. Carts of food and drink were being trundled down the hallways by nervous waiters, maids were still preparing rooms, assistant managers were scurrying about carrying bouquets of flowers and buckets of iced wines. At six o'clock in the morning! Harry Redding's arrival in Naples had rearranged the Neapolitan clock.

Strachan led us to a corner suite, handed me the key, and said, "This is yours. I'll be back straightaway. Make yourselves comfortable."

The suite consisted of two bedrooms and a large sitting room containing, among other things, a buffet with the makings of breakfast, utensils, and an enormous and complex Italian coffee machine.

Ware examined the table with a gleam in his eyes. "We get nothing like this in my flytrap down on the waterfront, chum," he said.

Louis poured coffee for all of us and threw his great bulk down on a softly cushioned sofa. "I could get used to this, Casey," he said.

"Don't," I said. "There won't be time."

Ware had already helped himself to eggs, bacon, tomatoes, cold meat, and cheese. When ex-Captain Ware was unhappy, he drank; when he was not unhappy, he ate.

Between mouthfuls, he gave me an account of what had been happening in Naples over the last few days. Colonel Tinker, our executive officer, had arrived in Naples with a Stallion-qualified RAF reject. Our weapons had arrived in bond, so there had been no problem with the Italian customs.

"Tinker and Strachan have already got the goods on board the rust bucket," he continued. "I've put my sergeant major and my clerk to making us a proper inventory. We're bloody rushed, you know, Casey."

I agreed that we were rushed. I also pointed out that the speed with which we assembled our men and equipment was likely to be the best barrier against intelligence leaks.

"What about the Stallions?" I asked.

"They arrived at Capodichino yesterday. A mechanic came with them and started disassembling them straightaway. They'll be trucked down to the dock today."

"And loaded tonight," I said. "You see to it personally, Bertie."

Ware grinned around a mouthful of cold meat. "Beat you to it, chum. Strachan has the deck space and the derricks ready. He's quite an artist with freight, that haggis."

"Is there a warehouse near the ship where we can assemble for a briefing tonight?"

"All of us?"

"All."

"I don't know. Strachan could probably tell you."

I said to Louis, "See if you can find him. Tell him we need him here for a few minutes."

Louis got to his feet and left the room.

Ware watched him go. "I'd forgotten how bloody big he is. Fifteen stone if he's a pound. Getting gray, though, isn't he?"

"Aren't we all," I said. "Don't worry about Louis. He's our sergeant major, by the way. Tell your people. I'll take one section, you take one, and Tinker takes one. Twenty men to each commando. I want to be clear of Naples no later than the day after tomorrow. Strachan will truck us south from Bizerte as soon as we can get all our gear ashore. I want to start training five days from now."

"Where, Casey?" Bertie asked.

"There's a pumping station on the Jenien pipe line just north of 30° North. If Qaddafi's flyboys aren't violating Tunisian air space this month, it will be perfect for us."

"Speaking of the crazy Colonel," Bertie said, "I hear he's pissed at the Tunisians again. Threatening to ship all the Tunisian workers back home."

"Who told you that?" I demanded.

"Why, Strachan, I think."

"You *think*?"

"Well, for Christ's bloody sake, Casey. Yes, it was Strachan. Why should that rile you?"

"Because what we don't need is a division of Libyan tanks clanking about the saheer making threatening gestures at the Tunisian Army," I said. "There's been nothing in the papers. Where did Strachan get his information?"

"From that Jewish wallah, I suppose. He wandered in yesterday with three Israeli ex-paras."

That stunned me. Agron? Already? Yesterday I—and, I believed, Ziegler and Redding—thought Gershon Agron wasn't yet within five thousand miles of Naples.

"Something wrong, Casey?" Bertie wanted to know.

Was there? Or was it all in my imagination? There was something about Agron that gnawed at my insides. Silent, competent, vaguely mocking. It was unusual for me to make such judgments on so little information about a man. After all, I'd seen him for only a few hours that first night in Malibu.

Well, suppose Agron *was*, in fact, a Mossad agent. Was that so bad? Given our situation, wasn't a pipe line to the best intelligence service in the world exactly what was required?

I was certain that the photographs of Point X were American. And the fact that they were in my possession was, I reminded myself, an indication that Redding's army had the tacit backing of the United States government.

But there was something more, something hidden that I could *feel*, deep in my belly. And it troubled me. When we boarded the helicopters and penetrated Libyan air space, we would be pointed straight at Qaddafi's uranium diffusion plant a few dozen miles from our objective. And there were Russians there at Barqin, at least a full battalion of Spetznaz soldiers, the best in the Soviet Army. If the Soviets at Barqin discovered us and reacted, it could turn into a massacre. We and the hostages we hoped to rescue would find nameless, secret graves in the saheer. Under those circumstances did I have the right to dismiss the

131

services of the one man available who could supply us with fresh and accurate intelligence?

Louis returned with Strachan, and I asked the Scot about the availability of a place where I could assemble the entire force for a briefing without alerting the Italian authorities.

"There's a warehouse on the dock," Strachan said. "It's where we've been storing stuff for the shoot. It will be empty by to-night."

"How long will this madhouse be like this?" I asked.

Strachan grinned. "As long as Harry is here."

"I want the Stallions on board the ship tonight," I said.

"They'll be loaded by six this evening."

I couldn't quite let the matter of Agron go. I asked if Strachan had seen him.

"Yes. He arrived last night on an El Al freighter with three rough-looking blokes. And three cases of something or other he didn't want to show me. He said they were gifts for you, Major."

"Where is he now?"

"On the ship, stowing his gear."

I flushed with anger at that. I had made it plain to Ziegler that I didn't want Agron to travel with the force, that if he was going to Tunis he should travel by air with the picture people.

"All right," I said. "Louis, I want you and Ware to make the rounds and be certain that everyone has arrived and is ready to go aboard the *Kaliph* tomorrow. Count noses. I want every man accounted for. Where is our dock, Strachan?"

"In the Beverello basin. The short pier opposite the Castel Nuovo."

"Take Brown and Ware with you and show them. Then you, Bertie, have Tinker's Stallion driver oversee the loading of the helicopters. Louis, look over the warehouse. We will brief at ten tonight. Detail some of your own people for security."

"Sir."

"All right. Move," I said. "I'll go down to the ship as soon as I have a word or two with Ziegler."

Louis and Ware left with Strachan, and I called the concierge to ask where Mr. Ziegler was. The man sounded harassed. I could hear the continuing hubbub over the telephone. But presently he located Ziegler in the confusion and put him on.

"I want to see you," I said. "Now."

"Things are pretty hectic, Major. Won't it keep for an hour or so? We can do lunch together."

"*Now*, Ziegler," I said, reining my anger. "And here."

"All right." He heard the harsh ring in my voice. "Do you want Harry there, too?"

"Just you," I said, and hung up.

I poured myself more coffee and ate some cold meat on bread. I had lost whatever appetite I had brought with me from the airport, but I wasn't sure when I'd get to eat again.

When Ziegler arrived, I didn't waste time with pleasantries.

I said, "We agreed Agron was not to travel with the men on the ship. He's down there now."

"We didn't exactly agree, Casey," Ziegler said, trying a friendly tack.

"Redding and I did."

Ziegler sat down on the sofa, looking suddenly worn and weary. "Casey, I'm going to be honest with you."

"Better late than never," I said.

"There are some things about this operation that it would be far better Harry didn't know."

"Go on."

"Listen, I don't blame you for being angry. But, believe me, I'm leveling with you now. Gershon is putting a lot of resources into this thing. More than you realize."

"I don't deny he's being helpful," I said. "I just want him helpful from a safe distance."

"The people Gershon represents regard the Point X operation as vital. I mean, there are things involved here that we can't even guess at."

"I'm glad that 'the people Gershon represents' want us to pull this off. I'm even willing to grant that we couldn't manage any of it without his information. But he's a goddamn spook. It sticks out of him like spikes. It's bad for the troops to have a spook around, Ziegler. It makes them damned uneasy. People like Agron have their own agenda."

"We've dealt with him often."

"You've leased captured Russian junk from him. This is different," I said.

"I've known Gershon for a long time," Ziegler said heavily.

"You think you know him. But nobody ever knows a spook."

"We need him."

I had involved General Stanley specifically to do what Ziegler thought we needed Agron to do, but I couldn't say so. I wasn't that sure of Ziegler.

"He means to be part of R Force, Casey. Is that such a bad thing?"

It depended entirely on his motivation, of course. But I didn't like the way he was going about it. The trouble was that I had control over almost everything else, but not Agron. He knew the Point X operation from start to finish. That left me with a choice. I could kill him or I could swallow hard and include him. There was no middle ground. I couldn't leave behind a man I didn't trust.

"He can get us later satellite pictures, Casey. He has promised to produce them before you take the force down to the border."

I had to admire Agron's shrewdness. He had foreseen my objection to his presence and had come up with the one bribe I couldn't afford to reject. "When did he tell you about these new photographs?"

"By telephone before we left Los Angeles."

"It would have been more honest to put it up front," I said.

"Casey, let me tell you. Gershon is a man of honor. You can rely on him. I promise you," Ziegler said with deep feeling.

"Maybe that makes a difference," I said. "But if it does, I don't know it. You say we can rely on him. All right, maybe we can. But to do what? Get this through your head, Ziegler. Agron isn't working for us. He isn't working for Harry."

"That doesn't mean he isn't giving us something we need."

"Right," I said. "Okay. Spook, *refusenik*, whatever. If he goes into Libya with us and makes one wrong move, I'll shoot him. That's not an empty threat."

I left Ziegler staring at me. I hoped he believed me, because I meant what I said.

I went down the stairs and pushed my way through the throng of movie and media people to where the taxis, a long line of them, waited—their drivers alert to see and to serve a big-tipping celebrity.

16

If my interview with Ziegler was calculated to put me in a black mood, my visit to the dock where *Kaliph* was loading was a bracing reprieve. Strachan's long experience with shifting movie companies from one exotic location to another had honed his natural gift of efficiency. I had served with dozens of transport officers who could have learned how to do their jobs from Rod Strachan of Eagle Films. And, of course, what I was seeing at the Beverello basin was only part of the miracle Strachan so competently performed. He had already established a good part of Redding's location units in Bizerte and in a self-contained compound near the village of Kasserine.

But the smoothness with which he had organized the loading of our war gear onto *Kaliph* was balm to my jangled nerves. The warehouse in which we would hold our first briefing was nearly empty already, and it was not yet noon. The crates containing the Uzis and the ammunition for them were already stowed in the hold of the angular old ship moored at the pier, as were the boxes containing the RPGs and special weapons.

The two old Sea Stallions stood on the dock, their rotors disassembled and their ample fuselages trussed up ready to be hoisted aboard as soon as *Kaliph*'s forward hold was closed.

A young man I took to be Tinker's RAF recruit climbed down from his perch on one of the Stallion's pylons and ambled over to me. He was a freckled youngster, not more than twenty-three or -four, with a long English face on which grew an enormous RAF mustache. "I say, sir," he announced himself, "you must be Major Quary. I'm Derek Penny. I've been hired to fly one of these beasties by Colonel Tinker. If you agree, that is, sir. Colonel Tinker made it quite clear you are the officer commanding."

I shook hands with Mr. Penny, who, it turned out, had been until six months ago a pilot officer in the Royal Air Force Coastal Command.

"Are you married, Penny?" I asked.

"Will be, sir. When I've put by a few pounds," he said cheerfully. How much of his cheer was due to the dollars he would earn by flying a Stallion for us and how much was due to the anticipation of action, I wondered. Whichever it was, he seemed keen, and that pleased me. There is hardly anything worse than commanding troops being committed to a hot landing zone by a frightened pilot. There were times in Vietnam when the chopper pilots started to leave the LZ while troopers were still jumping from the aircraft.

"How much Stallion time have you?" I asked.

"Eight hundred hours, sir. We used them for air-sea rescue until about two years ago. They're temperamental sods, but these look in good condition."

He returned to his task of watching over the helicopters, making sure the Italian stevedores didn't damage them while preparing them to be hoisted aboard.

Strachan come up and said, "Tinker is in the warehouse office, Major."

I followed him across the booming empty space to where Tinker, dressed in British Army work clothes, was poring over our shipping lists.

I perched on a stool and briefed him on the command setup. From ruling a battalion of the crack Special Air Service Regiment to leading a section of twenty men in a strictly illegal raid, a blatant violation of intenational law by anyone's standard, was a comedown. But plainly Colonel Tinker didn't see it that way.

"You rank me," I said with a grin. "I hope that won't trouble you, Bill."

He grinned back at me, showing large, irregular teeth under his straw mustache. "Being a subaltern makes me young again."

"You're an odd lot, you Brits," I said. "But you've got style."

I turned to Strachan and said, "Where's Agron?"

He indicated the ship, which could be seen through the open door of the warehouse, its derricks and rigging etched against a sky of startling Italian blue. On the deck below the bridge, I saw Agron leaning against the rail smoking a cigarette.

"You carry on, Strachan," I said. "I want a word with our spook."

"Problem, Casey?" Tinker asked.

"None I can't handle."

I left Strachan and Tinker together and walked across the pier to the accommodation ladder slanting down *Kaliph*'s rust-streaked topside. Agron saw me coming and waited at the top of the ladder.

"Welcome aboard, Major," he said. The slightly languid bearing of his slender, wiry form and his cool, appraising expression set my teeth on edge.

Sweat-streaked members of *Kaliph*'s crew of eighteen went to and fro on the decks, helping to guide the loading nets being warped aboard by the ship's hoists and derricks.

"Let's talk," I said.

"The saloon?" The narrow door to what might be called that was hooked back to the steel bulkhead. I stepped over the coaming and walked into the constricted, cluttered compartment. The air smelled of fuel oil and garlic.

I looked hard at him and said, "Who the hell are you?"

He leaned against a grimy leather couch and stared back at me. His black eyes were as opaque and unreadable as stones.

"I don't understand you, Major Quary."

"I think you do."

He lifted his shoulders in a graceful shrug. "I am an Israeli businessman. I do deals with motion-picture people."

"I want to know about your connections, Agron. Those pictures you gave us in Malibu came from Mossad. True or not true?"

"I can't tell you that, Major. Believe me, I would if I could. I can let you draw your own conclusions, but I cannot confirm or deny them. I'm sorry. But I can tell you they are genuine."

"They had better be, Agron. If we buy it, so do you."

"We all want the same thing. We want your countrymen out of hostile territory and safe."

"Has your government received any demands from the kidnappers? I need to know *that*."

Agron sighed. "I believe so, Major. I cannot be certain."

"All right. That's good enough. Maybe it explains your interest in all this. Maybe there's more. We will find out. Believe me." I looked straight into his veiled eyes and said, "I told Ziegler this morning that if you get out of line when we are committed, I'll kill you. I want you to believe *that*."

Agron gave me a slow smile. "Oh, I do, Major."

"You will travel with my commando."

"Of course."

"Your bodyguard will travel with Ware and Tinker."

"Very well, Major."

"Ware told me you arrived with some sealed cases. Where are they?"

"In the forward hold, Major."

"Let's go look at them," I said.

"Certainly, Major."

I followed him out of the saloon and down the cluttered foredeck to where the hatch gaped. A steel ladder had been hooked to the coaming. I looked into the hold. The crates and cases were neatly stacked, and the interior of the space was lit by feeble electric lights in wire cages. Three burly young men, stripped to shorts, were at work down there. Agron called to them to steady the ladder.

"After you, Major Quary," he said.

Looking down at Agron's three ex-paras, I found myself wishing I was carrying a weapon. I lowered myself into the hot, steamy interior of *Kaliph*. The three Israelis were as large as I was, but they were younger.

When Agron reached the catwalk he said, "Major, these are Avram, Elie, and Ariel. My contribution to R Force. Here is another." He picked up a crowbar and went to one of three identical cases, each about three by three by one and a half feet. He lifted the wooden lid and stepped back. Inside, racked and preserved in cosmoline, were twenty silencers for the Uzis. I had to be impressed. I had wanted to ask Lang for silencers, but I hadn't dared risk it.

"Show me the other cases," I said.

Agron grinned. "Of course, Major."

He pried up the lids and displayed another forty beautiful silencers for our Israeli weapons.

"Right," I said, and, to the paras, "Close them up."

"Is there something else?" Agron asked.

"Yes. You have fresh photographs. I want to see them."

"Of course. They are in the captain's safe."

We climbed the ladder out of the hold and into the brilliant Neapolitan day. A prickle of relief traveled down my spine.

Kaliph's captain, a purple-black Liberian in a shabby dark-blue jacket, greeted us as we came on deck. Strachan was with him, and he made the introductions. The Captain's name was Woodrow Wilson. We all smiled at that, and some of the tension between me and Agron seemed to ease. It was an illusion, of course, and we both knew it.

But we went with the Captain to retrieve the new pack of photographs and accepted a drink in his cabin. We made no attempt to hide the pictures from him. Only we—and those who had taken them—would know what they were.

Then Agron and I went back to the saloon and spent an hour going over the photographs with a large magnifier. When we were done, and the pictures were returned to the Captain's safe, I was as convinced as I could be that nothing had changed at Point X in the interval between the first satellite pass and the last.

As I left the ship, Agron said, "I will try to obtain one more set of pictures before we cross into Libya."

I wondered how he intended to obtain a final set of photographs in Tunisia before we climbed aboard the Stallions.

Nothing had really been settled between Agron and me. All we had accomplished was the establishment of an uneasy truce.

———————

Back at the San Germano some semblance of order had been established by the hotel management and a detachment of the Neapolitan police. The *paparazzi* had been urged out of the hotel lobby and now stood behind barriers erected on the far side of Via Domiziana. A television van and crew waited there, hoping for a glimpse of Harry Redding.

Getting back into our suite was like getting in to see the Joint Chiefs at the Pentagon, but I finally managed it.

I had with me our table of organization and the equipment lists, as well as a chart of southern Tunisia and northwestern Libya. What I needed now was a few quiet hours to go over the tentative battle plan and study the terrain in detail, but when I had ordered up a meal and settled down with the chart and tables, the telephone rang. It was Redding.

"I understand you had words with Jerry, Casey," he said. "I'm coming over to talk."

It was his show, and he had rights.

He arrived alone, dressed again in his off-duty uniform of sweater, jeans, and Topsiders. Somehow, what he wore seemed to set him in his frame of reference—whatever it might be. There was a chameleon quality to him that was, I suppose, a part of his art. He could play the star, the celebrity, the businessman, the low-key, laid-back artist, the good fellow, the younger brother. And all of these characterizations were genuine, a part of the man's true personality, the source of his mass appeal. Some movie pundit once wrote about him that "what you see is what you get, and for one hundred minutes in a darkened theater it is real." In London, Ann had told me that even Harry's acceptance speech at the Academy Awards dinner—a gathering accustomed to the most egregious sentimentality and self-promotion—had been received with astonishing respect and attention. If he could achieve that among his peers in the world of illusion, what chance did ordinary people have to doubt his sincerity?

Here he was in my suite, the celebrity as supplicant, almost touchingly eager for my approval and forgiveness.

"I can't tell you how sorry I am about the misunderstanding over Gershon, Casey," he said.

"He makes me uneasy, Harry," I said. "I don't like spooks."

"He's dedicated to the plan, Casey. I believe that."

"He's dedicated to *a* plan. That's certain."

"Jerry is worried that you might back away. You wouldn't do that now, would you, Casey?"

"No," I said. "I wouldn't do that."

He sprawled on the sofa by the balcony window, the bright Italian sun illuminating him like a klieg light.

"Thank you, Casey," he said. "I can't tell you how I appreciate that. Getting those people out means a great deal to me. More than I can say. I'll speak to Gershon myself if you want, and explain to him that what you say goes—in every situation."

"That won't be necessary," I said. "I'll handle him."

My meal arrived, and the waiter set up a table, all the while looking sidelong at Harry.

While I ate, Harry sat with me. He talked of many things, but I had the feeling that there was something more on his mind. Finally he got to it.

"I'll be going on to Bizerte tomorrow on the charter," he said.

142

"But would you object to having me at your briefing tonight?"

"Who mentioned a briefing," I wanted to know.

"Rod told me. Is there any reason he shouldn't have?"

I suppressed a feeling of irritation. Our security was a joke. The sooner the people could be embarked and away from here the better. But I had to accept the fact that I was working, not for the United States government, as I had for eighteen years, but for Harry Redding now. And when a man was spending millions of his own dollars and risking his reputation, he was entitled to know what was going on.

"So far the only reason the Italian government isn't on our backs is that you've funneled tons of people and equipment through this port for *Kasserine*. The fewer people who know about us the better, Harry." How did one explain to a man whose career depended on constant publicity and attention that a word to the press could result in a fiasco or possibly even a massacre? It was so obvious that it was almost an insult to explain it to him, and it was, of course, useless to do so. To Redding, spies were people like James Bond, soldiers were George C. Scott, and blood was grease paint or tomato ketchup, or whatever they used. So I said only, "It will be better if we keep the briefing quiet."

"I'd like to be there, Casey."

"Jesus, Harry," I said. "That's a terrible idea. You can't make a move without drawing a crowd."

I pointed out to him that there was no way at all a person as well known as he was could move through a city as movie-crazy as Naples without being recognized, and that even if that were possible, having him appear in all his movie-star glory among the ex-soldiers and Marines we had gathered would be bad for morale. The men of R Force had to know from the outset that what they were about to do would be dangerous. The presence of a celebrity at the first briefing would give the operation an aura of make-believe. I finished by telling him that it was impossible, and that I hoped he understood. "Later," I said, "when we've moved down to the pumping station in the desert, you can come down and meet the troops. But not before."

I thought I had convinced him. He suddenly and radically changed the subject. And it seemed to me that he did it with an instinct for the jugular vein that surprised me.

He said, "Ann is finished with her work in Cannes. She's joining us in Bizerte." His tawny eyes were fixed on me. "Are you in love with Ann, Casey?"

I stared back at him. In my world, men don't speak so openly of love. Not to other men.

I said flatly, "I don't fall in love quickly, Harry."

For a moment tension and antagonism flared silently between us. It seemed to me that he had pushed Ann at me for days and now was snatching her back, restaking his claim on her. It made no sense, but the feeling was real, just as all emotions became real when Harry expressed them. And it angered me, because I was left with the notion that he had used Ann to make me eager, the way a mare is used to lead a stallion into the paddock. It was demeaning to Ann to imply that she could be used that way. "I'm my own person, Casey," she had said. "No one owns me." What sort of relationship could she have had these several years with Harry if he didn't understand that?

He got to his feet and rested his hand on my shoulder gently, almost tenderly. He said in a sad, quiet voice: "Don't be angry with me, Casey. I needed to know, that's all." Then he was gone, the door closing soundlessly behind him.

———

Louis came back to the San Germano in midafternoon, and I set him to work studying the chart and sketches I had made of our lines of approach and retreat. He had one of the best minds for terrain I had encountered in the army, and I wanted all the information printed on that chart engraved on our sergeant major's brain. I also wanted him to select the men who would be given rocket grenade launchers.

I left him there with orders to report for a last-minute officers' conference after the ten o'clock briefing. I took the pack of service records with me. I had only those of the Americans; I would have to rely on Ware and Tinker for a summary on the Brits in the force. And I wondered, without amusement, what Agron would tell me about the battle experience of his trio of sabra toughs.

I arrived back at the dock just as one of the Stallions was being hoisted onto the deck of the *Kaliph*. It was nerve-racking to watch, but under the supervision of former Pilot Officer Penny and Bill Tinker, I was sure the cumbersome beasts would be settled safely into place on each side of the forward cargo hatch, now closed and battened for sea.

The warehouse was empty except for a dozen or so heavy cardboard boxes, which contained our uniforms. A touch of marvelous irony there. They were authentic replicas of the German desert uniforms worn by Rommel's troops in that long-ago spring and summer of 1942. They had been made in Italy and, of course, there were hundreds of them already in Bizerte, together with American field uniforms of the same vintage. Some wag—I suspected it was either Ware or Penny—had painted small white palm trees, the insigne of the Afrika Korps, on the flanks of the Stallions. A forty-five-year anachronism.

The specialists we had recruited had appeared at the dock early, the way specialists will before an operation. Our medic, Jimmy Green (a pale string bean of a boy who didn't look old enough to have spent a tour in Vietnam and four years as a paramedic) had arrived before noon and had gone over his supplies with Strachan item by item.

Our American Stallion pilot, an ex-Marine Louis had found dusting crops in California, had drifted in a couple of hours later. He was tall and built like a light heavyweight, and he showed his twenty years in the Corps in his nearly skinned head and his ramrod bearing. His name was Luther Washington, and he was the color of black coffee. He and Penny were going over the aircraft, checking their deck moorings and telling each other the war stories flyboys love to share.

I went into the warehouse office with Ware and Tinker

to study the personnel list and make individual assignments to each of the three commandos. We were now sixty-three. There were thirty-eight former U.S. Army soldiers, all with Ranger or Special Forces training; eight former Marines; two ex-Seals; two pilots, one British and one American; two ex–Royal Marines, both with experience in the Falklands; two former Special Air Service Regiment antiterrorist commandos; three questionable Israeli paras; one medic; and Ware, Tinker, Agron, Louis, and me.

I would happily have done without Agron's Israelis, but I compromised my objections by splitting them up, one to each commando. Louis, in addition to his other duties, was going to get the job of keeping an eye on Agron.

We spent the next two hours in a staff meeting over the satellite photographs. In its early days, Point X had been a concession camp where a crew from BP had punched fruitless holes in the ground looking for oil. The holes were long since filled in by drifting sand. All that remained were three galvanized-iron buildings, in one of which I believed the American hostages were being kept prisoner. I could imagine under what conditions they were being forced to live. The nights were near to freezing, and at midday the temperature in that part of the saheer reached one hundred and twenty degrees. The kidnappers—and I was reasonably convinced that they were Shiite militiamen from Lebanon, and not desert Arabs—lived in Bedouin tents around the perimeter of the original concession camp. Some of the people there had to be real Bedouins, because the photographs clearly showed women and children. It was a standard device, practiced by all guerrillas, to mingle with a civilian population.

There was a moral problem again, the problem of people who claimed to be civilized. Reluctance to murder the innocent had kept the United States, for all its great power, helpless and indecisive. Someone had to decide the moral level of any war—even this low-intensity, protracted war. It was a sickening thing to accept, but eventually it had to be accepted. I told myself I was a soldier, not a philosopher or a clergyman. Those Bedouin

146

women and children at Point X were no more and no less innocent than the schoolchildren of Malot or the bystanders in the baggage bays at Narita. There was a new truism: In terrorist combat zones, there were no noncombatants.

I intended to take my countrymen out of Libya to freedom no matter what the cost.

17

At six in the evening we ate a meal aboard *Kaliph* and I met with Captain Wilson. The loading was almost complete, though the air still reverberated with the sound of the ship's donkey engine and the rattle of hoists and derricks. Our Liberian skipper seemed perfectly willing to accept us as a part of the film crew for *Kasserine*. The magic of Redding's name was working for us. Wilson had heard the waterfront talk of all the war gear that had left the port of Naples earlier, destined for Tunis. If there was ever a convincing cover for an operation like ours to Point X, the filming of a large war epic was it. Who could tell real soldiers from make-believe?

"Will we be ready to sail day after tomorrow, in the morning, Captain?" I asked.

"We can sail anytime after noon tomorrow, Mr. Quary," he replied.

I thought about that. The option tempted me, but I made no immediate decision. A great deal depended on Strachan's arrangements to get us through Bizerte and down to Kasserine as part of the general movement of the movie company.

I stayed with Wilson for half an hour, discussing billeting arrangements for the company. *Kaliph* did not have accommodations for sixty-three passengers, and he planned to turn his crew out of the forecastle and give us that compartment. Even then it would be tight, and the seamen would be without shelter for the duration of the voyage. But it was just over three hundred nautical miles from Naples to Bizerte, and *Kaliph*, I was told proudly, steamed at "nearly ten knots," which meant a voyage of only thirty to thirty-five hours. "Hardly more than a ferry trip, Mr. Quary," Wilson said. The weather, he added, would be good all the way.

I left Wilson and toured the ship, looking for Agron. I found him in the saloon with his three shadows.

I said, "This is a private conversation, gentlemen. Out."

The Israelis looked to Agron for confirmation, and he nodded. They filed out of the tiny compartment.

"I want it understood," I said, "that when I give them an order, they are to obey it without checking with you. Either that or they stay in Naples." I disliked making an empty threat, but I felt it had to be done. The threat was empty because I couldn't leave loose ends behind us.

But Agron simply said, "I will tell them, Major."

I straddled a chair and looked into those unreadable eyes. Mossad was still the best secret service in the world, but Israel was weary of its long war of attrition with the Arabs. Its people were overtaxed, tired of casualty lists, tired of military obligations, tired of killing. Who could blame them? They had repeatedly fought and defeated Arab armies, but they had never been allowed to win a peace. There was no military solution to their problem. It might be that there was no solution of any kind to it. They had established their homeland by force and guile in the midst of an Arab world that was medieval in its thinking, implacable in its hatred, hungry for martyrdom. There were more Muslims willing to die than there were Israeli citizens. Faced with that kind of bottomless opposition, Israel's resolve was understandably difficult to sustain.

Henry Kissinger had once accused the West of "a failure of nerve" in the face of the challenge from the totalitarian East. His accusation implied that all would be well if only we were convinced of the rightness of our cause and willing to defend it at any price. As a soldier, I had always believed that. I still believed it. But, like the Israelis, I had begun to wonder and to doubt. We Westerners, products of a rationalist political system created by elegant idealists in the eighteenth century, were raised to believe that there was a reasonable solution to every problem humanity might encounter. What if we were wrong?

"Agron," I said, "I can't prove you are a Mossad agent, but I am going to proceed on the assumption that you are."

He gave me a slow, mirthless smile. "Very well, Major. What follows?"

"A number of things. First, that the governments of both Israel and the United States know what we are going to attempt and will do nothing to hinder us. Comment?"

"An interesting hypothetical assumption, Major."

"Second, that both governments, although determined to avoid accepting any responsibility for a fiasco, are willing to offer assistance. That, in fact, they have done so. Through you."

"I couldn't say, Major. I am only a businessman."

"What I want to know is *why*."

"Why, Major?"

"Individuals often act irrationally," I said. "Governments, almost never. Why should a private venture financed by a film star—a venture that is illegal by any standards you care to apply— be tacitly *assisted* by our two governments?"

Agron rose from his seat and walked to the open doorway. Below, on the pier, lights were burning now. The ship's hoists were lifting the boxes containing our uniforms aboard in cargo nets. Reflections glimmered in the water of the basin. Across the bay could be seen the lights of a cruise ship making for sea. The position lights of a jet newly departed from the airport moved against the darkening sky.

Agron turned to face me. "I can give you no specific infor- mation, Major. I have none. But, like anyone else, I can sup- pose."

"I'll settle for that just now," I said.

He leaned against the table in the center of the saloon and lit a cigarette. The smell of the tobacco was harsh, bitter in the still air.

He said, "I put it to you, Major, that terrorism is coming of age. What began as a series of isolated acts of rage against what certain persons considered oppression has, over time, become an organized war, a low-intensity war. I believe that is the current jargon for what is happening."

"Agreed," I said.

"A few years ago organizations such as the Fatah, Black September, the Popular Front for the Liberation of Palestine, others—some with a thirty-day half-life, some with even less—conducted hijackings, bombings, machine-gun attacks in airports and supermarkets on a somewhat random, haphazard basis." He stared at me with those basilisk's eyes, as though he expected some comment. I made none. What he said was quite true.

When I remained silent, he went on: "Against such activities there could be reprisals—air attacks on Palestinian camps, for example—and other military options. The German recovery of hijacked Lufthansa passengers at Mogadishu. The Israeli raid on Entebbe." He shrugged. "All that the terrorists gained was martyrdom. In some cases that appeared to be all they really wanted. A week's attention in the media throughout the world, and then death or capture. Their real demands, the things they hoped to accomplish—such as the release of comrades or the payment of great ransoms—were seldom achieved." He studied the glowing coal at the end of his cigarette. He did it so coldly that I had an image of his using it on the flesh of some terrorist.

"But over time two things have happened," he continued. "The terrorists have become more sophisticated, better organized. And the West has become softer." He regarded me icily. "You Americans are the worst, of course. You have your Vietnam adventure to blame for that. Your rhetoric has become fierce. You have organized your famous Delta Force. Your President makes repeated threats. But you *do* nothing. Terrorists have blown up your embassies, and you have threatened. Shiite

151

fanatics have murdered your Marines, and you speak of retaliation and do nothing. Oh, yes, your ship *New Jersey* threw a dozen sixteen-inch shells into the Chouf Mountains and killed a few villagers. I recall there was an orgy of recrimination about it in the Western press and on American television. When a black aviator was shot down and captured by the Syrians, one of your black ministers rushed to Hafez Assad to promise eternal friendship in return for the young man's release. Great drama, Major. Marvelous theater. But not a very effective way to discourage acts of war against your country. You agree?"

I did agree. But I was tempted to remind him that Israel, in the best Western humanistic tradition, had no death penalty and so was in a position to supply terrorists with an unlimited number of prisoners whose freedom could be demanded to keep the pot boiling. I didn't, because American-Israeli disputes served no purpose. We were as we were. Powerful, confused, vulnerable.

It may be that Agron read my thoughts, because he shrugged and said, "Oh, I shouldn't blame you Americans too much. When there are no neat solutions, the Western mind grows weary and impatient. Israel suffers the same malaise. We retreated from Lebanon after we drove out the PLO because we hadn't the stomach to stay and pay the price. We traded thirteen hundred terrorists for three Israeli prisoners of war because we imagined it would improve the—what is the Washington expression?— the *atmospherics* in Egypt and Jordan. It did not. When Amal hijacked an American airliner and held its passengers hostage, we retreated again. We denied that was what we were doing. You denied it, too. But the fact is that the Amal and their Hezbollah accomplices, after murdering a young American sailor in the coldest blood and holding the other passengers hostage for only seventeen days, got exactly what they demanded. We pretended that our release of three hundred, and then three hundred more, prisoners was an act of simple, generous humanity. But who believed that? Not I, Major. Not your American media. Not the terrorists who watched with interest in Lebanon, in Syria, in Iran, in Central America, in Puerto Rico—

But why go on? You didn't believe it either, Major Quary. All over the world there are armed fanatics who watched, learned, organized, and found friends. Am I boring you with my lecture on the geopolitics of terrorism?"

"No, but there's a point coming, I assume. Get to it," I said.

"All right," Agron said. "I don't state this as a fact. I only offer it as a supposition. Let us say that in this most recent kidnapping of Americans—and it is now Americans who are most at risk, because America is the nation *least* likely to make reprisals, being the most moral nation in the world"—the sarcasm was heavy—"let us say that in this case there are demands being made. There are always demands, Major. Always. And let us further assume that the nature of these demands makes this hostage-taking a special circumstance, a unique case."

"Go on," I said.

Agron complied, his voice flat and controlled. "There is a facility in the Negev desert. It is no longer a secret installation, thanks to the diligence of a free press in my country—another gift of sweet reason from the democratic West. This facility might possibly be a place where nuclear devices are manufactured, assembled, and stored against the day when some Arab fanatic succeeds in building a bomb to use against the Jews. I say it *might* be such a place, Major. Now consider how this latest kidnapping of your diplomats differs from similar kidnappings. The hostages do not appear on your television at flower-decked tables surrounded by smiling gunmen. They do not send taped messages to your newspapers. They are not interviewed by your network anchormen. Instead, they *disappear*. They are spirited out of Lebanon and secretly taken to Libya, and there they are held in total silence. Don't you wonder why, Major? Don't you ask yourself why this time it is so—different?"

"I get the feeling you are about to tell me," I said.

"Please remember that I am describing a purely hypothetical situation. But let us suppose, Major, that demands have been made. Let us further suppose that these demands have resulted in negotiations. Negotiations that are far advanced. For the sake

153

of argument, let us say that there are secret talks going on in Geneva and heavy pressure being applied in Tel Aviv. Remember, Major, that the government of the State of Israel is almost totally dependent for its security on the United States of America. We can pretend, for the sake of Western sensibilities, that Israel is a sovereign nation. It would outrage sabra pride for me to suggest otherwise. But I am not a sabra, Major. I am, shall we say, a citizen of the real world. I know that if the United States says, 'Our people are worth more than your atomic bombs,' the government of Israel must listen. *Must*, Major. But geopolitics is never simple, not even for naïve Westerners. There are always factions, disagreements, cliques. So let us suppose that in this hypothetical situation I am describing there are some highly placed individuals in your government and mine who resist the notion of giving in to terrorists. Such persons might say, 'Before we surrender once again, before we strip Israel of her most potent defense, let us make a military attempt to retrieve our people.' Still with me, Major?"

Condescending bastard, I thought. "Yes," I said.

"Now we must suppose that through the miracles of technology the location of the hostages is discovered. Happy to say, they are found not scattered throughout a rabbit warren of a ruined city like Beirut but in the deep desert, where a strong force can be deployed against the kidnappers. One can almost visualize the joy in Washington and Tel Aviv, can one not, Major? But wait. Why have the Libyans, who undoubtedly planned and financed this hostage-taking in order to strip Israel of her nuclear capability, sequestered them so near a Libyan nuclear diffusion plant? The Libyans are fanatics, Major, but they aren't fools. Barqin was built for Qaddafi by Soviet technicians. Brezhnev was concerned about nuclear proliferation—as all Soviet leaders must be—but he was also determined to hold Libya in the Soviet sphere. This is all hypothetical, remember. The Soviet Navy could not operate in the western Mediterranean without Libyan bases. Libya was—and remains—of vital importance to the network of Soviet surrogates that will assist the Motherland

154

to project Soviet power into Africa and eventually across the Atlantic. Hence, Comrade Brezhnev and his successors continued to guide the Libyans through the complex problems of making enriched uranium. But in order to make certain that the process remain under Soviet control, they staffed Barqin with Soviet scientists and garrisoned it with Soviet troops."

Agron paused, looked at me with a fixed stare.

"Now where does that leave Washington and Tel Aviv? If Delta Force or the Sixth Fleet Marines strike at Point X, they must overfly Barqin. In order to keep their bargain with Qaddafi, the Russians *must* react. Now the hypothetical risks have been escalated by orders of magnitude. I told you the Libyans are not fools. It enriches the joke that now the Kremlin's policy of nonproliferation is genuine. Comrade Gorbachev has changed the party line because he recognizes, as apparently neither Andropov nor Chernenko did, that the mix of Libyans and weapons-grade uranium is extremely dangerous to everyone, including the Soviet Union. Yet the need for Libya to stay fixed in the Soviet orbit remains a fact of military life to the Kremlin planners. The Soviets are caught, as I believe you Americans like to say, between a rock and a hard place."

He walked to the door of the saloon and flicked the bitter-smelling cigarette over the side.

"So there you have it, Major. My purely suppositional scenario. The Russians at Barqin—who do not, by the way, exist officially and whose deployment there is a typical imperialist fantasy—make a strike by your government or mine too dangerous. Option one is therefore unworkable. There are two other options. Israel can dismantle the Dimona weapons facility, or a small, privately financed force can make a secret attempt to rescue the hostages. Those are the options. The *only* options. You see, our little group has what you Americans like to call deniability. If we fail, who would believe we had even tried? We were hired by a film star, Major, *a film star.* Who could take us seriously?"

"The Libyans," I said.

155

"Ah, yes. That. Well, as they must have taught you at your Military Academy, Major, no plan is perfect."

"You were the one who talked Redding into this."

"I encouraged him."

"Encouraged, hell. You must have put the idea into his mind."

"It took very little effort to convince him, Major. Harry Redding is a simple man, believe me. I don't mean that unkindly. He has a straightforward sort of mind. His emotions are very near the surface. I suppose that is what makes him successful as a film personality. One looks at that beautiful face of his, ten times life-size on a screen, and you can see into the depths of his soul. The depths are perhaps shallow, but the seeing is clear and true. He is not a duplicitous man, Major. Surprising, really, considering the gutter morals of his profession—"

"You have a lot of gall to stand there talking about morals," I said.

"Yes. Well. We won't go into the morals of my profession. Or yours," Agron said calmly. "But if you think about it, you will see that Harry Redding was born to be the benefactor of R Force. He waves the flag so convincingly. He plays the warrior hero so well. We are giving him a chance that comes to few men these days—a chance to be real. At no risk to himself, he can be a genuine hero. He understands that. If we succeed, he succeeds. If not—well, all he has lost is money, and he has plenty of that. You and I and the others, of course, may be dead or buried for life in a Libyan jail, but Redding will be quite safe in Tunis, making his new film, still being the celluloid soldier."

It seemed obvious that Agron despised Redding. I had not sensed it before.

"How much of all this does Redding know?" I asked.

"Not very much. What's the point of perplexing him? He quite probably imagines it will be a simple matter to slip in and out of Point X without arousing the Russians. That's the way it would happen in a Redding film, isn't it?" He smiled thinly and offered me a cigarette. I took it but did not light it. Agron was as cool a bastard as I had ever encountered.

Was it as straightforward as he said? It might well be that the deep-seated antagonism between us was what made my doubts persist. In a way, I should have been reassured. If what he had told me was true, then I could believe that neither the CIA nor Mossad would do anything to prevent our mission. Still, Gershon Agron, part-time movie salesman and entrepreneur and full-time Israeli spook, made my blood run cold.

"Ziegler must have told you what happened in London," I said. "Have you any explanation for it?"

Agron shrugged indifferently. "The British might have got wind of what you were doing over there. They might have put a special policeman on you, even in Zurich. They get very nervous, our English cousins, when someone appears and starts meeting with potential mercenaries. They do business with Libya, after all. Quite a lot of business." His voice was as cold as a hanging judge's. "The people who took him out might have been mine or yours, Major. We will never know for certain, will we?"

I had had more than enough of Agron and headed for the door. "Briefing in the warehouse at 2000," I said. "Be there."

18

The men started arriving at the dock in twos and threes after dark, about nine-thirty. As they arrived, Tinker checked their names against his list and sent them into the now nearly empty warehouse. As the ranks filled in, I had a sense of *déjà vu*. I remembered other briefings held in warehouses like this or in empty hangars at Danang. For the most part the men were a mature lot, in their late thirties, and had been soldiers for a good many hard years. Some, those who had enlisted when they were in their teens, were retired, with twenty years or more of experience. Some had joined us for the money, of course, but many had come because they found life outside the military difficult or boring or simply too complicated to cope with. Among the Americans there had to be thirty or more Purple Hearts, at least that many Bronze Stars and Silver Stars, and probably a half-dozen Navy Crosses or Distinguished Service Crosses. A civilian would probably think I make too much of the decorations the people had won, but to a soldier they are more than metal and ribbon. They are the talismans of success, the only way the military services have of saying to an individual that he has performed well. The citations always speak of gallantry, merit; even so high-flown a word as *intrepidity* turns up from time to time. But remember that, in the words of General Keegan, a military writer much quoted by Louis, "an army always contains a crowd trying to get free." It is the discipline civilians hate so that keeps that crowd under control, and all soldiers, of whatever rank, know it. The parades and flags and medals and ceremonials all serve the purpose of reminding the soldier that he *is* a soldier and that things are expected of him that would outrage any civilian. That expectation is what held the three hundred Spartans at Thermopylae and the Welsh Borderers at Rorke's Drift. The men who filed into the warehouse on the dock beside the SS *Kaliph* that night in Naples all understood this.

At a quarter to ten Louis arrived with a group of his hand-picked volunteers. Tinker checked them in—all but Louis and a grizzled character built like a prize fighter who walked with a slight limp and had a lumpy, thick-lipped face and graying hair under a black watch cap. I took him for a sailor, perhaps one of the *Kaliph's* crewmen, and I wondered why Louis had brought him to the warehouse. Apparently Tinker was having the same kind of thoughts; he was talking quietly to Louis, and he was backed up by his two Special Air Service Regiment recruits, who were acting as security guards for the meeting.

I went to the door and asked, "Trouble?"

"Sergeant Brown says this man is all right, but he's not on my list, Casey."

Louis looked at me with a barely suppressed grin. "I got me another body, Major. Picked him up in the hotel parking lot."

I looked at the stranger. He was almost a head shorter than I, but there was muscle under the black, oil-stained sweater. He wore black dungarees and scuffed boots. The longish graying hair that had escaped from under the watch cap was unwashed and stringy. He held himself oddly, with a slight twist of the body that implied some long-standing injury for which he had compensated. His face was dark and blemished.

I said, "You can't come in here. *È vietato. Capite?*" It was the best I could do with my pidgin Italian. I was angry with Louis. He should have known better than this. I couldn't understand what had come over him.

159

The sailor said, in a heavy, accented voice, "I speak English, Maggiore, a little."

I started to make a curt reply, and I was ready to take Louis aside and tear a strip off him for bringing this stranger to the briefing, when it struck me, and I looked again. It was the tawny eyes that gave him away, but they were the only thing that did.

"Son of a bitch," I said.

"Good, isn't it, Casey?"

It was more than good. It was perfect. He could have walked through the crowd of *paparazzi* outside the San Germano and not one of them would have recognized him. He had probably done just that.

I was still angry, but I was, once again, impressed with Harry Redding.

I said to Tinker, "It's all right. I know this man."

"You *know* this bloke?"

"You'll get to know him, too, after the briefing." To Louis I said, "We'll talk about this later, Sergeant."

"Sir."

I gave the Italian sailor my best military glare and said, "And you, *marinaio*, stay out of the way. And don't speak."

"*Capito*, Signor Maggiore," he muttered, removing the watch cap and twisting it in his oil-stained hands. It was a cameo part, but it was an Academy Award performance.

I went back to the center of the warehouse floor, where we had set up easels with hand-drawn maps, with no place names, and sheets of plywood with a set of photographs.

"All right," I said, "gather around me."

As I began the briefing I caught the coldly amused smile on Agron's face. Redding had fooled me, but not Agron.

————

I kept the meeting, in fact as well as in name, brief. The personnel assignments were read out, the pilots, medic, and officers introduced. The only men present who were not a part of R Force (the name was already in common usage among the volunteers) were Rod Strachan and our grimy, silent guest, the Italian Sailor as played by Harry Redding. He, at least, was enjoying his incognito enormously. It reminded me of a fraternity prank. I was impressed but far from delighted.

Of the nature of the mission I said little except that we would be crossing a hostile border at night to effect the rescue of a dozen men. "If that tells you something more than has actually been said here tonight," I said, "keep quiet about it. Don't discuss it with anyone, not even with one another." That was asking the impossible, but I wanted to put that pressure on them so that they would not bridle at what came next. "There will be another briefing aboard ship before we reach Tunisia. You will be given more information at that time. You will also get a chance to familiarize yourselves with your weapons." There was a murmur of approval at that. A soldier gets serious about "aim and mission" when he has the tools of his trade put in his hands. Before that happens, everything is talk and theory.

"All right, one last thing," I said. "From here you will not be returning to your billets. You will form up by commandos and go aboard *Kaliph*. We will not be sailing as originally told you, day after tomorrow. We will get underway at noon tomorrow."

That brought them up sharp, because it was unexpected, and that was fine with me. Louis and the officers looked a bit startled, too. Agron regarded me with an appraising, even approving, expression.

"You are entitled to one explanation from me, and here it is," I said. "Security is vital on this mission, and it is impossible to remain secure as long as we are in Naples. Therefore, Captain Ware and two men will make the rounds of your billets to pay your tabs and collect your personal gear. Colonel Tinker will break out weapons for his troopers, and the gangway to *Kaliph* will be guarded. No one will be allowed ashore, and no one will board the ship after 2300 hours without specific authorization from Colonel Tinker or me."

I was, in effect, making them prisoners aboard the ship, and if there was going to be a problem of insubordination or complaint, now was the time it would surface. This was not a national army, after all. I didn't have the sovereign power of a state to back up my commands. What we had here was a twentieth-century version of a Renaissance *condotta*, a mercenary band. From this point forward they would obey me absolutely or they would be kept under guard until the mission either succeeded or failed. The thought of having to do so crippling a thing chilled me, but I was prepared to carry it through. There was no road back.

I waited, watching them. There was some murmuring but there were no complaints, no arguments. Their faces, most of them American and a third of those black, showed only that the game had turned serious.

"All right," I said. "See Captain Ware and hand over your room keys if you have them. Turn in your passports. He will hold them until we have completed our mission."

One of the ex–Special Forces men who had served with Louis and me at Dakto said, "Banta, Major."

"I remember, Sergeant," I said.

Sergeant Banta gave me a sheepish smile. "I don't suppose any of us will actually be in the movie they're making?"

"I wouldn't count on it, Sergeant," I said. And I remembered that when we had first started discussing the project in Malibu, Jerry Ziegler had wanted to send along a cameraman. I wondered if he still intended to try. Actually, I didn't care if he did.

I called for their attention again. "As soon as Captain Ware checks you off, go aboard *Kaliph* and find your billets." I looked across the warehouse floor to where Agron stood with his three paras. "Ariel, Elie, and Avram know the ship," I said. "They'll help you get settled. They will stay on the ship with you." I addressed that statement directly to the Israelis. They murmured something to Agron, and he replied and then nodded at me. I went on: "The pilots will bed some of you down in the helicopters." I looked them over. "That's it then."

In the office I explained to Tinker and Louis why I had moved the sailing date up to tomorrow noon. Redding, still playing the misplaced sailor, had been relegated to sitting on a crate near the warehouse door.

We waited until Ware had collected all the keys and passports, and then I sent him off, with his Royal Marines, on the round of waterfront hotels.

There was a peculiar moment at the warehouse door when the Italian sailor stood to join us. I said, "Colonel Tinker, meet Harry Redding, prankster. Harry, stay as you are until we're back at the San Germano."

I don't know what sort of impression his masquerade had made on Tinker. I didn't ask. I was still angry that it had happened. It had been a fool thing to do.

Tinker posted his SAS security guards on the dock, and then the four of us, plus Agron, headed back to the hotel in Strachan's van.

———————

Back in my suite at the hotel, we settled around a table for one last critique of the mission profile.

We would land at Bizerte as a second unit of the location company and move straight on to Kasserine. We would be housed there separately from the picture crews for a day, not more. It was there, too, that we, along with all the extras and Tunisian soldiers, would put on our Afrika Korps uniforms. The following day Unit Two would be posted on the company bulletin board as being moved south "to film special segments." And without further fuss, we would load up in the two Stallions and two support trucks (driven by our own people) and head south past Jenien, the tiny village that gave its name to a pumping station on the pipe line from Algeria. There we would stage and exercise until it was time to go.

"I take it," Agron said, "that most of the exercises will be done at night?"

"All of them," I said.

"May I make a suggestion?"

"Go ahead."

"I suggest we keep daylight activities to an absolute minimum."

"Is there likely to be Libyan air activity in the area? Would the Libyans cross into Tunisian air space?" I asked.

"Ordinarily, no," Agron said. "But, as you have heard, there is quarreling between Libya and Tunisia. The Libyan Air Force could be patrolling the Tunisian border."

"Wonderful," Tinker said, fingering his mustache. "Bloody marvelous."

"I'm on good terms with General Mohammed Fayad, the man who's renting us the Tunisian troops," Strachan said. "I could ask him for a radar crew."

"No," I said. "They'd pick up radar on the other side of the border, and it would draw them like flies. We can do as Agron suggests and keep activity during the daylight hours to a minimum. We'll be going in at night anyway." I looked over to the sofa where Redding, stripped now of his make-up, sat in fascinated silence. "Are you sure you want to hear all this, Harry? You might end up testifying in front of some committee of Congress. It might be better if you didn't know details."

"I want to stay, Casey," he answered.

"It's your army," I said, and turned back to the military discussion.

"There is one thing we should talk about plainly," I said. "The Russians at Barqin."

I looked directly at Agron but spoke to the others. "Agron, here, has some interesting theories about our Soviet friends at Barqin. He was very eloquent this afternoon. I want him to tell you what he told me."

Agron ran through it all again, beginning with the history of the uranium diffusion plant Brezhnev gave Qaddafi and the shifts in the party line up to the present situation, in which, he believed, the Russians found themselves in a cleft stick—unable to dismantle the plant because they could not afford to alienate

164

Qaddafi, yet unwilling to let any sort of real military force from a Western nation approach it without reacting.

Louis said, "You mean that in Brezhnev's time they said they were against nuclear proliferation and they were *not*, and now they say they are against nuclear proliferation and they really *are* but they can't shut down the plant because Qaddafi'll get pissed?"

"That is it exactly, Sergeant Brown. You put it far more succinctly than I do," Agron said, steepling his hands.

Louis shook his head in disgust over the ways of politicians.

"And that, gentlemen," I said, "is the problem presented by Barqin, which is the only thing in all the Libyan saheer that is close to Point X."

"How close, Casey?" Tinker wanted to know.

"There's the chart. Step it off," I said.

Tinker did. "A hundred and sixty-five kilometers."

"That's what I make it."

"They'll have radar, of course?"

"It seems likely," I said.

"They keep a careless schedule," Agron said.

"How would you know that, I wonder," I said.

Agron smiled thinly. "As you know, Casey, I have friends in high places."

"Very high," I said, and tossed the satellite photographs on the table.

Tinker snatched them. It was the first time he had seen them close up. "I say, bloody marvelous, Casey. You can tell what the ragheads are wearing, what they are *eating*."

You could see their children, too, I thought, and their animals. I reined myself sharply. You could see the Russian assault rifles the masquerading militiamen carried and their emplaced anti-tank weapons as well.

"One thing more," I said. And I told them about the encounter in London. They had a right to know.

"Now Agron, here," I continued, "says we can disregard it. He thinks someone was watching my back."

"That is what I believe," he said evenly.

"Bloody *hell*," Tinker said suddenly. "I'm a careless bugger, and that's a fact. Has anyone gone over this room?"

"You mean with a snooper?" I asked. "No."

The Colonel fished about in the copious pockets of the military-style anorak he was wearing and came up with a small battery-powered bug detector. Regular issue for SAS officers, whose assignments were so secret they were required to sweep their quarters with detectors twice each day.

"Better late than never," he said, and began to pace about the suite with his debugger in his hand. He looked like a Pennsylvania dowser searching for water.

It wasn't water he found.

"*Christ!*" he hissed. A red light was flashing on the face of the device. It flashed ever more swiftly as he moved it toward the telephone. We were all on our feet as he lifted the receiver and unscrewed the cover on the mouthpiece.

"Damn. Damn and blast!" He held the tiny transmitter between his thumb and forefinger. "The telephone. The bloody damned *telephone*. It's so elementary, a child could have done it." He dropped the microdevice on the table, and we all looked at it. Well, not all. *I* looked at Agron. But he was genuinely shocked. I didn't think he was a good enough actor to fake it. And I almost broke into bitter laughter. The bastard must have been thinking that if anyone was going to bug my suite it should have been he. Instead of that, someone else had done it. He had competition.

"What does this mean, Casey?" Redding asked, his face suddenly pale.

"It means we had better get the hell out of Naples and down to Jenien as quickly as we can," I said.

I had Tinker run his detector over the rest of the suite, but the single bug in the sitting-room telephone was the only one that had been planted. There could be a dozen reasons for that. The bug planter could have been interrupted. He could have known where we would gather. Anything. The bug itself told us nothing. One bought such things at electronic supermarkets these days. Spying had become a game as moral and as legal as Trivial Pursuit. I crushed the transmitter underfoot.

"All right," I said. "Let's get packed and out of here. It's nearly one o'clock. We spend the rest of tonight on *Kaliph* with the troops." To Redding, I said, "We'll see you in Bizerte. Or if not, then in Kasserine."

Strachan handed me a file of papers: the bills of lading, the customs clearances, the lease and insurance papers on the helicopters.

Within the hour Tinker, Agron, Louis, and I were climbing the gangway up the side of the SS *Kaliph*. An hour later Ware and his Royal Marines reported aboard with the personal belongings of the men who were scattered about the ship sleeping.

I went to the Captain's cabin and knocked. Wilson was still awake, working at his tiny desk.

"Is your crew aboard, Captain?"

"Most of them, Mr. Quary."

"Are you cleared by the captain of the port?"

"We are cleared for noon departure, yes."

"Do you need a pilot?"

"No, Major. Not in the Beverello."

"How long would it take you to get up steam?"

"Two hours, not more, Major, but—"

"I will pay you one thousand U.S. dollars if we are at sea by 0400 hours, Captain," I said.

His soft brown eyes studied my face intently. "A thousand dollars?"

"Cash."

He removed a cover from a speaking tube and blew into it. "Engine room? Bridge. Stand by. I'm coming down."

Two hours and twenty minutes later, in the darkest part of the early morning, the SS *Kaliph* cleared the Beverello basin, destination Bizerte, Tunisia. I stood at the stern rail watching until the lights of Naples had vanished below the dark horizon. Then I went into the saloon, stretched out on the ancient leather couch there, and went to sleep.

167

19

I stood on the bridge wing with Captain Wilson and watched the exercises on the foredeck. Two Commando, Ware's lot, was doing calisthenics on the port side, and Three Commando, Tinker's group, was gathered around Agron and one of his sabras as he field-stripped an Uzi and showed them how to assemble the weapon with its silencer.

Wilson watched the proceedings in tactful silence. One did not earn one's keep running a seedy Mediterranean tramp without using discretion.

Washington and Penny, our pilots, sat atop the fuselage of the Stallion on the port side of the foredeck hatch making remarks about the quality of Two Commando's deep knee bends.

The day was filled with bright sunlight, the sky was cloudless, and the sea was a marvelous blue. *Kaliph* was making her ten knots across an almost waveless expanse of water, leaving a smear of thin smoke and stack gas behind her. From horizon to horizon not another ship could be seen. High above us, the contrails of a jet liner made a white line across the sky. I wondered if it was Redding's charter. The course was right. Straight as an arrow to the southwest.

One Commando—we were using the proper terms at last— was on the fantail being shown the special weapons we would use. Earlier Louis had displayed his virtuosity with the hunting crossbow, our silent partner, and now he was expounding the care and maintenance of the Czech RPG-7, a weapon Redding could have lectured on if he had been with us.

I heard Louis call for a sailor to drop an old oil drum over the side, and then I heard the characteristic whoosh of the rocket grenade and the thump of the explosion as the missile hit the floating drum and shredded it. I didn't need to look. Louis was an artist with the rocket launcher.

One Commando was the group I would lead, but I let Louis handle the familiarization. He would rotate through all three groups, because if anything took me out when we went into action, he would be in tactical command. That was one of the advantages of running our own mini-army: we could establish a flexible chain of command that had nothing whatever to do with military rank.

I told the Captain we were a private security force. He believed me because any skepticism on his part would only open up an unwanted tangle of complications for him and his owners.

I leaned on the rusty rail and thought about Ann. There was no chance I'd see her in Bizerte. I wanted to move R Force through the port city as quickly as possible. But she might be at Kasserine.

"Major?"

I turned and found our medic beside me, the breeze made by *Kaliph*'s headway ruffling his shaggy hair. He carried a newspaper with him.

"I forgot to show this to you, sir," he said, grinning. "We're in the papers."

That hit me like an M-16 bullet. "The hell you say, Green. Let me see that."

He handed me a three-day-old copy of the *New York Post* folded to show a piece by their film reporter. He had picked it up at the international newsstand at Capodichino.

Harry "This Time We Win" Redding is pouring millions of his own money into his newest epic battle film, *Kasserine*.

Redding, who has made a lucrative career of refighting

169

America's lost battles, has assembled an army that Erwin Rommel might envy for his revisionist treatment of the U.S. Army's shattering defeat at Kasserine Pass in 1943. He has enlisted ex-soldiers and military experts by the hundreds to achieve what he calls "absolute authenticity." Eagle Films has hired half of the Tunisian Army and a quarter of the Spanish Air Force in addition to his battalions of U.S. veterans.

Budgeted in the $30 million neighborhood—a neighborhood previously inhabited only by the likes of Michael Cimino and George Lucas—*Kasserine*'s location crews will have enough fire power to make even Harry Redding happy.

For everyone's peace of mind [she finished archly], we hope that Libyan strongman Colonel Qaddafi, a nervous type living right next door to the Kasserine company, has been warned that it is all make-believe.

"Wild, isn't it, Major?" Green said, grinning foolishly.

"Wild," I agreed grimly. "May I keep this?"

"Sure, Major."

I signaled for Agron to leave the instruction session below and come up to the bridge. When he did, I handed him the newspaper.

He read it and then looked at me, dark eyebrows arched. "What a wonderful thing is a free press, Major," he said. "Let us hope that Qaddafi is not a regular reader of the *New York Post*."

"It's a truism that no battle plan survives contact with the enemy," I said. "Or perhaps we should add, the American media."

"There will be reporters at Kasserine, of course," he said. "But they will all be people who write about films. Still, it could be a problem."

"We will have to keep the force isolated until we can move down to the south. Once we're at Jenien we can control security."

"I believe it will be up to Miss Maclean to keep the press away from our people. Can she do it?"

"If anyone can."

"Yes," he said, resting his elbows on the rail and looking out at the empty sea. "A very competent young woman. One wonders where she learned to *be* so competent."

I regarded the Israeli speculatively. Now what was he suggesting about Ann? Whatever it was, I didn't like it. I thought again that I disliked Gershon Agron very much.

That evening Louis and I sat on the foredeck hatch under the bulk of one of the Stallions. Darkness was rising over the eastern sea. We could feel the deep, cranky thrum of *Kaliph*'s old engine. Above us, the first stars were breaking through the dusk.

From somewhere aft came the sound of singing as the men lay about drinking beer. Old airborne songs. I liked that. It meant that they were coalescing into a group.

I said to Louis, "Remember that one?"

It was a song set to the tune of the "Battle Hymn of the Republic," and was learned, along with others, at jump school. It was part of the trainee hazing, and *everyone* was hazed in jump school, regardless of rank.

Louis laughed and joined in. It was a lament, as soldiers' songs tend to be when they are not obscene. It was the sad tale of a young paratrooper's first—and last—jump.

He counted long, he counted loud, he waited for the shock.
He felt the wind, he felt the breeze, he felt the awful drop.
He jerked the cord, the silk spilled out and wrapped around
     his legs.
He ain't gonna jump no more!

Then came the chorus, and I could now hear the Brits joining in, indulging their national penchant for sing-alongs.

Glory, glory, what a helluva way to die!
Glory, glory, what a helluva way to die!

171

Glory, glory, what a helluva way to die!
He ain't gonna jump—no—more!

Louis grinned at me and said, "Have you forgotten the words, Casey?" He picked up the verse in a fine, round baritone, as deep and full as Darth Vader's.

The days he lived and loved and laughed kept running through
*   his mind.*
He thought about the girl back home, the one he'd left behind.
He thought about the medics and he wondered what they'd
*   find—*
He ain't gonna jump no more!

Some of the others, members of One Commando, had drifted forward to hear Louis sing. He looked at me and said, "All right, Major. Sing for the troops!"

I felt twenty years old again, and I remembered a green second lieutenant standing in the door of a C-130 twelve hundred feet above a clearing in the Carolina pine woods called Drop Zone Bravo. The lieutenant's belly was a hard knot, as empty as the air at his feet. Lord, that was so long ago, but I remembered it as though it were yesterday. With Louis and the others I sang:

The ambulance was on the spot, the Jeeps were running wild.
The medics all rolled up their sleeves and showed their knowing
*   smiles.*
Why, it had been a week or more since last a chute had failed.
But he ain't gonna jump no more!

After that the song got much more graphic and gory. There is always a kind of gallows humor in the songs soldiers sing. The jokes and songs and pranks are all part of the defenses erected between the self and its extinction.

I glanced up at the bridge and saw Agron standing at the rail alone, looking down at us and listening. Somehow I doubted that intelligence officers sang wry songs about the risks of their profession. With the troopers around me and my friend at my side, with the smell of the sea wind in my nostrils and *Kaliph*'s rigging etched black against the darkening sky, I felt sorry for Agron. It must be a bitter thing, I thought, never to be unguarded, never to be free.

Then one of the men put a can of beer in my hand, and the singing began again. I gratefully, willingly, forgot about Agron, a man born in a hall of mirrors.

20

The presence of the great continent of Africa can be felt long before its coastline emerges from the sea. There is a heaviness in the air, a strange bitter smell in the wind that has blown over millions of square miles of forest, veldt, jungle, and desert. There is dust in the air and the flinty taste of the Sahara. But in fine weather, like that in which *Kaliph* approached the northern coast, the breeze has the smell of things growing, dying, rotting, of men and animals in their millions, a pungent slurry of odors that are unique to Africa.

There is something else, something sensed rather than seen. It is the oppressive loom of the continent. Standing at the rail of a ship and looking to the south, one can feel a great presence there. The light changes from the clear blue-tinged illumination of the sea to something harsher. The sun is silver, and it seems to strike hard at the unseen land. It is a cruel light. Then the land can be seen, rising from the sea, a narrow flat littoral that is deceptively fertile, almost benign. Beyond are mountains, with the tan emptiness of the desert hidden behind them. This is the Atlas Range, and it stretches like a rock wall from Cape Bon, in Tunisia, to Cape Dra, in Morocco.

Northeast of Tunis, on the Gulf of Tunis, lies Carthage, once ruler of the western Mediterranean, her heroes now deep in earth sown with salt by vengeful Romans. For a soldier, it is a land of ghosts. The Tunisian east coast veers steeply south, white beaches washed by shallow gulfs, a low, flat land with a deceptively kind face. From Nabeul to Sousse there are sparse woods and marshes, and from Sousse to Gabes there are grasslands capable of supporting cattle and herds of goats, which are tended by Bedouins whom the desert Arabs say have been corrupted by living a life of ease too long by the sea.

But the heartland of Tunisia is mainly tumbled, rocky mountains and sinks of sand that fall away deeper and deeper into the saheer and eventually into the immense emptiness of the Sahara. All of that lay before us as *Kaliph* approached Bizerte.

We had spent our time on shipboard as usefully as possible. Besides weapons familiarization, there had been tactical briefings (still using blind maps), a lecture on security by Colonel Tinker, and general assignment of military tasks. Jimmy Green had examined every man and pronounced them fit—though he showed what I thought was an unhealthy interest in my scars and in the chunk of Russian metal I carried inside me.

"It will have to come out eventually, Major," he said professionally. "I guess you know that."

"I've been told," I said shortly.

"You'll feel it first as pressure on the heart. Dull to begin, probably, then much more severe. There could be a lot of pain." His youthful face was intent. I never met a medic—most particularly a Special Forces–trained medic—who didn't half believe himself a surgeon. The United States Army took only the best for Green Beret medical training and gave them a year and a half to absorb their art. In Nam, soldiers like Green not only cared for the men in their own units, Americans and Mike Force Vietnamese alike, but also rode circuit through the villages, dispensing pills and delivering babies. A Green Beret medic was, in fact, the nearest thing to a country doctor remaining in our overspecialized world. Their training was a thousand times better than that received by the "barefoot doctors" of the People's Republic of China. Once we were at Jenien, former Sergeant Green would probably be the best—and possibly the only—doctor within a radius of several hundred miles.

I did my level best to think about Mother Russia's gift only when I could not ignore it. "I don't even feel it, Sergeant," I said to Green. That was not strictly true. He was right about the pressure. I felt it when I tried to run a long distance in full field kit. But I had no time to worry about it now.

The combat gear was all repacked in cases marked with the Eagle Films logo. Somehow, Redding or Ziegler or Strachan had arranged with Tunisian customs that all our equipment would pass through the Port of Bizerte in bond, without inspection. The money the *Kasserine* company was pouring into the Tunisian economy bought certain privileges. Even the section of Spanish Air Force pilots, who had flown their antique Heinkels across from Málaga to Algiers and then on to the improvised airstrip at Kasserine, had been given clear passage.

When *Kaliph* steamed into Bizerte and was properly moored at the pier in the narrow neck of the harbor, there was actually a Tunisian Army band playing on the dock and a swarm of stevedores dressed in dusty white waiting to move our equipment from the ship to the line of trucks Strachan, who had arrived a day before us, had organized. He even had two large flat-bed rigs standing by to take the Stallions.

I told Louis to assemble the men on the foredeck. The sun was harshly brilliant; the shadows cast by the two bulky aircraft were dark with edges as sharp as a knife blade. The air was heavy with the exotic smells of the port.

I climbed onto the hatch cover and looked for a moment at the sixty-odd men of R Force. None of them were really young; even Green was in his late twenties. And all of them had fought and survived a war or two in one form or another. Though American, British, or Israeli, black or white, they were curiously the same. In the Middle Ages, a mercenary was called a free lance. I was reminded of Housman's lines about an army of mercenaries:

What God abandoned, these defended
And saved the sum of things for pay.

176

But we came from the secular West, and so, for God substitute the government of the United States, or NATO, or even Western civilization. When honor failed, or patriotism or simple courage, there were always the free lances.

I spoke to the troops.

I said, "We have been using blind maps for your briefings. But there isn't one of you who can't read the damned things, and I know there has been talk. All right, the talk is probably on target. I won't confirm or deny it just now. You all know we are going to do something risky. Don't make it riskier by mixing with the civilians. I want you to keep to yourselves when we get to Kasserine. There won't be many women, and those there are will have things to do that will not include sleeping with soldiers. So stay away from them. Stay away from the technical adviser's crew, too. They could spot us in a minute. All right, we'll be on those trucks for the rest of today, so keep your personal gear with you. We'll get to Kasserine around midnight. Saddle up."

Ware and Tinker led their commandos down the gangway and into the trucks. Strachan was on the dock directing traffic. I looked for Ann. I didn't expect her to be on the pier, and she wasn't. Why, then, did my disappointment irritate me so sharply?

Louis took One Commando down to the trucks, and I said good-bye to Wilson. "I hope I'll see you again, Captain," I said. "Mr. Strachan will tell you when."

Wilson regarded me with doubtful, soft brown eyes. "Best of luck, Mr. Quary. I hope everything goes well with you." He smiled. "And thank you for the bonus."

I heard Agron's voice behind me. He had only Elie with him. The other two Israelis had gone down to the trucks with Two and Three Commandos. So far so good, I thought. They are obeying my orders. I only hoped they could continue to obey them. If there was any problem at Kasserine or down at the pumping station, the solution could get nasty. I didn't intend to leave any unguarded loose end behind us when we crossed into Libya.

We watched for a moment while the ship's hoist lifted one

Stallion from its lashings and swung it over the dock. Arab workers had the first flat-bed in position for it, and the helicopter was lowered onto it with much more skill and efficiency than the shouting and hand-waving from the stevedores had indicated. Sergeant Washington was down there overseeing the business of making the aircraft secure. On deck, Penny was bossing the preparation of the second Stallion. There was nothing left for me to do on *Kaliph*. Agron, Elie, his shadow, and I went down the accommodation ladder and into the crowd on the pier.

The sun was hot in the sheltered canyon between the warehouses on the pier and the ship's steel sides. Elie looked about him at the swarm of sweating Arabs with an expression of deep suspicion and loathing. There was no real conflict between Tunisia and Israel, but the Arab-Jewish antagonism was real enough. It showed in Elie's face.

Strachan, a bull horn in his hand, appeared beside me. "Did you have a good crossing?" he asked.

"Calm as a millpond," I said.

"Good. I hate traveling by ship." He lifted the bull horn and shouted to the gang foreman, "Abdullah! Tell those people to handle those crates more carefully!" The stevedores were giving some of our ammunition boxes a fierce banging about. The English-speaking Abdullah screamed and gesticulated at his men, pummeling one or two of them with a piece of rope he carried.

"I wonder what the union would say about that?" Strachan remarked with a grin.

"Where's Redding?" I asked.

"He's in Tunis with some government blokes. He'll be in Kasserine tonight. They're flying him down in a Tunisian Air Force Lear Jet. VIP treatment."

"Penny and Washington will need some help setting up the helicopters," I said.

"That's taken care of. There's a Tunisian Air Force crew standing by for them at Borj el Amiri. That's about thirty kilometers from here. They'll have the choppers assembled by tonight, and your pilots can fly them down to Kasserine in the morning."

178

"I want to be south of Jenien by tomorrow night, or next morning at the latest. Some of us will fly down, the rest will go by truck. Any problems with that?"

"None I can see," Strachan answered. "You can keep these trucks. I've sent a thousand gallons of fuel for the Stallions on ahead. When you get to the pumping station, you can send the vehicles back with the Arab workers."

"We shouldn't take Arab workers down south," Agron said.

"Oh, hello, Gershon," Strachan said. "I didn't see you lurking there. No ragheads south of Jenien? Why? They don't know what's going on."

"Agron is right, Strachan," I said. "We'll drive the trucks ourselves. One more thing. I have a note from Ziegler about finding a combat cameraman. I don't have time for that." Or the inclination, I thought. "If he really wants to film, he'll have to come up with someone himself."

Strachan wiped sweat from his ruddy face with a sodden handkerchief. "Cinematographers are expensive, Quary."

"It's up to Redding and Ziegler," I said.

"Filming was a stupid idea in the first place," Agron said testily.

I looked at him with interest. Was it possible that the smooth brown spook was growing nervous as the prospect of action drew near? He seemed agitated by the crush of Arab workers, the noise, and the heat. It was the first indication I had had since meeting him in Malibu that he had ordinary nerves and apprehensions.

We waited on the dock until the Stallions had both been secured on their flat-beds and the remainder of our gear stowed in the line of waiting trucks. Louis reported to me when all three commandos were aboard and ready to travel.

"There are sandwiches and beer on the trucks, Sergeant Brown," Strachan said. "You don't know how tough it is to get brew into a Muslim country. So appreciate it on the ride to Kasserine." To me he said, "I have a jeep at the end of the pier."

I turned to Agron. "You ride with us. Send Elie with Louis."

He started to protest, but I cut him off. "You don't need

179

anyone to watch your back. Let's go." And I made my way through the ripe-smelling throng to the end of the pier, where the jeep, painted desert tan and marked with the Eagle Films logo, waited for us.

The journey to Kasserine took us south and west, toward the Algerian border, to Souq el Arba, a squalid market town of mud-brick buildings sweltering in the sun, then south to Qalaa Khasba, a village on the railroad from Tunis to Kasserine.

"The damned train tracks are going to be a problem for Harry," Strachan said. "There was no railroad running through the Kasserine Pass in 1943, but he insists on a genuine location for the shoot."

"What will he do?" Agron asked.

"He's had me order down two bulldozers to cover the rails over with sand until the shooting's done." Strachan grinned tolerantly over Redding's extravagance. "It's going to raise hell with the Tunisians' railroad schedules, but that's the way Harry is when he wants something done. He was greasing the shaft in Tunis today. He had an audience with Mzali, the lord high executioner, otherwise known as the prime minister, of this desert wonderland." He gestured at the low, barren hills through which the poorly asphalted two-lane road ran. "He took a sackful of dinars with him, so I assume he'll get his way. Sometimes I think there's a little raghead in Harry. He's the most convincing bargainer I know. But then, that's hardly news to you two gents."

Behind us came our convoy of four-by-four trucks—all of them Dodges built in 1942 for the U.S. Army and abandoned here as surplus when the war moved on across the Mediterranean to Italy. The amazing thing was that the French and then the Tunisians had kept them in usable condition. The trucks and the jeep in which we rode were more than forty years old.

I commented on this, and Strachan said, "This is a poor country, but Bourguiba kept it going—and even prospering—by get-

180

ting the most possible out of not very much to begin with. The other ragheads might carry on about the jihad against the West, but not the Tunisians. If any Arab country can be said to work, this one does."

Perhaps it was the Carthaginian influence, I thought wryly. The Romans smashed their armies, pulled down their city, and destroyed their nation, but their genes were still here, mingled with those of the desert Bedouin and a dozen conquerors who came and vanished over the centuries. The people of Carthage had been Semites, seafarers, and merchants. Their city had once been a Phoenician colony. They had loved money and power and a high standard of living. They had been, in fact, a great deal like Americans. And their ghosts were here.

The country around us had little to recommend it except its history. It had been fought over by Romans, Carthaginians, Goths, Vandals, Berbers, Arabs, Europeans, and Americans. The place names struck chords of memory. I could recall with great clarity the lectures on the Allies' North African campaign given at the Academy. A grizzled old brigadier general, retired but wearing his uniform to give his lectures, refought a war that ended before I was born. I saw again the names now on the map I held in my lap: Sfax, Gabes, Gafsa. Kasserine, Mateur, Bizerte. I thought then, as we rode in Strachan's aged jeep across this ancient land, that there was probably no place in the world a soldier who knew the history of his vocation could travel without encountering terrible, familiar names.

I found myself hoping that my small force would not put Point X and Barqin into the history books as the flash point of another full-blown war. Things almost as strange had happened before. If it took place here, and to us, it might well be the last time it would happen for a thousand years.

21

After Qalaa el Jerda, a mud-brick village surrounded by played-out mines, the road to Kasserine climbs to a low pass through the hills before beginning its long, serpentine descent toward the desert. In the deepening dusk we could see isolated stands of scrubby trees, dwarfed and scarcely worthy of the name, but still unusual in so barren a landscape. From the eastern end of the pass the lights of the Eagle Films location at Kasserine stood out like a beacon. The village of Kasserine showed only a few yellow lights, but the shoot location could be seen from thirty miles away.

I had changed places with one of the troopers and was riding in the cab of One Commando's lead truck. Beside me sat Louis and the Arab driver. In the back, the men slept or sat drinking the last of the beer.

I was troubled by something Agron had said to me before I made the shift. He was traveling on a French passport, because his Israeli nationality would have caused endless troubles with the Tunisian authorities. The fact that he had a choice of papers only served to reinforce my conviction that he was an intelligence officer, and that was all right. I had grown accustomed to the idea of working with a spy at my back. But he had informed me that he would need to go to Tunis in the morning if I really required updates on the satellite photographs we were using to plan our strike at Point X. I didn't like the idea of letting him out of my sight for a day or more, and I liked even less the prospect of him unwatched in Tunis. He declined to say where in the city he would make the contact for delivery of the photographs, and there was no way I could force him to divulge that information. An Israeli intelligence mission in an Arab country, even one as reasonably disposed as Tunisia, was always at risk and would certainly refuse to cooperate if by so doing it might be blown.

I had to give the matter of this trip to Tunis some careful thought. I had gone to considerable trouble to keep the Israeli in view. Setting him free to go where he chose for a full day in Tunis was unacceptable.

As we started down from the pass, our driver indicated the lights far ahead and said, "Kass'reen, *m'sieu*." The French influence was strong in Tunisia, even thirty years after their retreat from North Africa.

Louis asked how far. In his pidgin French it came out: "*Combien kilometre?*"

"*Quarante—quarante-cinq,*" the driver answered.

Louis said, "Jesus, Casey. Look at the size of that camp. Isn't it *something*, what money can do? Redding has taken over this country."

"Not quite," I said. "But he's got a pretty fair grip on it."

Louis stretched his legs and said, sighing, "I never realized folks lived the way Harry and his people do. I could get used to it, real easy."

"Forget it," I said. "It takes lots more money than we'll ever have."

"Ain't it the truth. Like the old song says, 'You'll never get rich, you son of a bitch.' "

"This one isn't for money, Louis."

Louis said, grinning, "How come we get such great jobs, Major?"

"Nobody twisted your arm, Louis."

"Hell, I couldn't let you come all this way alone. Who'd look out for you?"

"Don't think I don't appreciate it," I said. "I wouldn't have come without you."

"The hell you wouldn't have. I saw the way you lit up when they put it to you."

"Well," I said, "I talked a lot and told people what they should do. Now it's put-up-or-shut-up time."

Louis laughed and opened the thermos bottle to pour the last of the coffee into plastic cups. We shared it with the driver.

"Harry saw my DSC, you know," Louis said suddenly. "In my luggage. You should have seen the way he looked at it."

"Why not?" I said. "It proves you're a card-carrying hero. That's the one thing he'd like to be." I finished my coffee and crushed the cup. "Hell, I wish *I* had a DSC. But I was out of it when hero time came. You weren't."

"I'm serious, Casey. He took it out of the case and held it like it was a diamond. There were tears in his eyes. I swear it."

"He's a strange man, Louis."

"I guess so, Casey. Did you notice, in Malibu, there's not one picture of him in that fancy house of his. Not one. I thought movie stars were all on an ego trip. But it's as if he bought that house with everything in it and just moved in."

Of course that wasn't the way it was, but I understood what Louis meant. The Malibu house held all of Redding's personal possessions—even Ann, I thought bitterly—but almost nothing of himself.

"The Porsche whale-tail?" Louis said. "It's almost brand new. It has about two hundred miles on the clock. He never uses it."

"Maybe he hasn't time, Louis," I said. "He keeps a hell of a schedule."

"Sure he does. But that's not what I mean. It's as though he is two people. There's Harry Redding the star, the Hollywood top gun. Then there's another Harry Redding. I can't put my finger on it, but he's nothing at all like the guys he plays in his pictures. I sort of mentioned this to Ziegler, but he just clammed

184

up tight. He probably knows Redding better than anyone does, but he isn't talking about him."

"They've been together a long time," I said. "There's bound to be a lot between them they don't share with anyone else." I've said often that I am not a sensitive man, but I had been around Redding and Ziegler long enough now to know that they were, in their own way, as wise about each other as Louis and I were. I didn't find Ziegler a particularly likable man, but then, we were only associates, not friends. "Besides, Louis," I said, "they are movie people. Creative types. They're different from you and me."

Louis looked at me, his dark face limned by the dim lights of the truck's instrument panel. He gave me a broad grin. "Now that, Major," he said, "is an absolute fact and no mistake."

We pulled into the Eagle Films camp a short time before midnight. It was still brightly lighted by strings of lamps fed by diesel generators rumbling away out in the service area. There were rows of tents, big ones. Strachan had had prefabricated buildings trucked and flown in to hold the tons of movie gear *Kasserine* required. Some of the film people were asleep, but most were not. As we drove down the dirt street between the rows of tents we could hear Arab music from Radio Tunis blasting away and competing with hard-rock tapes being played by the Americans on their Japanese portable hi-fis. People came out of the tents and buildings to watch us arrive. Any arrival was an event of casual note at this stage. The company was just setting up, and until principal photography began there was only grunt's work to do.

Beyond the tent area I could see the airstrip. On it were two vintage Dakotas, wearing olive-drab paint and U.S. Army Air Forces markings. Parked next to them was a Tunisian Air Force Lear Jet—likely the one that had brought Redding down from Tunis after his meeting with Prime Minister Mohammed Mzali.

Farther down the line in the darkness were two Heinkel-111 German light bombers, property of the Spanish Air Force but wearing black crosses and swastikas for their part in the movie-to-be.

We drove straight through the camp to an area set about six hundred yards from the airstrip. Here there were empty tents for us, some field kitchens, stacks of wooden boxes, and piles of lumber. The entire area was surrounded with concertina wire that gave it the look of a POW camp. Next to a sign designating this "Unit Two Area" stood five Sherman tanks, a dozen half-tracks, and several more tan-painted tanks that had to be looked at carefully to see that they were Shermans that had been disguised with plywood panels to look almost exactly like 1942-vintage German Tigers. These vehicles were, I supposed, only the first to arrive of the dozens that would be used in the film.

As we pulled into the opening in the concertina, we were hailed by a detachment of dark-faced soldiers, in Tunisian Army fatigues, carrying FLN assault rifles. In the distance I could see a bivouac for at least three full battalions. The Tunisians there were gathered in groups around small charcoal fires. Except for their clothing and weapons, they could have been a legion of Hasdrubal's army waiting for Scipio Africanus and his Romans to arrive.

For the next hour and a half we unloaded our special equipment inside the wire and then parked the trucks next to our tents in our own motor pool. When that was done, Tunisian Army cooks brought a late supper from the field kitchen, and I told Louis to bed the men down.

Then, with Strachan and Agron, I walked back to the main camp to report to Redding and Ziegler that R Force had arrived in Kasserine.

Redding was up and out of his tent to greet us when we arrived. A transformation had come over him. Ziegler told me that it was what he did before starting a film to "get into" the part he was going to play.

The most obvious change was that he had cut his hair. That

sounds like a small thing, but after seeing dozens of films about World War II in which the soldiers all resembled the Beatles or Jesus Christ Superstar, one begins to understand that for a modern film star to give up his shaggy locks is a sacrifice of major proportions. Redding had been skinned down in a genuine GI cut. He wore a pair of U.S. Army GI trousers and a woolen shirt with staff sergeant's chevrons on it, and there were GI combat boots on his feet. He was a far cry from the long-haired body builder with the RPG-7 I had seen in the screening room back in Century City.

In his tent were a GI footlocker and a metal rack on which hung an olive-drab pot helmet, a GI field jacket with chevrons, a mess kit and gas mask, some spare uniforms—all woolen, because that was what GIs wore in North Africa in 1943—and a perfectly cared-for Thompson submachine gun, the weapon of choice for noncoms of that era. If I hadn't known better, I would have imagined that I had fallen through some kind of time warp into that piece of the world forty-five years ago.

The other side of the big tent, however, was strictly modern times. No GI cot for Jerry Ziegler. Instead, there was a comfortable safari bed with an innerspring mattress. His clothes were also displayed on a rack, but they were all Eddie Bauer safari gear: bush jackets and tailored bush pants and several pairs of assorted desert boots. There was a desk and a camp table with a personal computer, which had been plugged into an electric console that was in turn wired to the camp's diesel-powered electrical system. I noted that there was a large battery-pack backup for the system. Ziegler had moved in a bar, too, and a bank of radiotelephones. To cross the center line of the tent was to jump across four and a half decades.

Though shooting on *Kasserine* was not due to start for a week, Harry was ready. There were script pages on the table and on the olive-drab blanket on his cot. To an uninformed observer it would have appeared that he had no thought of Point X.

That would have been wrong. Point X and his secret army were very much in Redding's mind. He had been deeply worried about the bug we had found in my suite at the San Germano, and we had talked about it. But, in the end, what was there to be said? I had talked about it on the ship with Agron, too. But discussion was pointless. We didn't know who had bugged the suite. We could guess that it was Central Intelligence or Mossad or even, for Christ's sweet sake, some rival movie company who wanted to know what Eagle Films was up to in the deep desert. But we didn't know then, when we found the bug, and we didn't know now. So I had stopped talking about it.

Redding wanted to meet all the men tomorrow; he wanted to meet them individually. I had to kill that idea—again.

"Not here, Harry. You'll get them talking, and you'll start all sorts of rumors in the camp. I don't want our group singled out for any special attention. We are Unit Two. Period. When we start work down south, you can come down and meet the people, as I told you in Naples. That will please them. You can even see us off."

Both Redding and Ziegler saw the wisdom in that, but the former's disappointment showed. Ziegler said, "Look, Harry. Quary is right. We've got a planeload of press coming down. Quary and the rest will be gone by then, and you can slip down to Jenien after the media people are gone."

The mention of a media invasion made me uneasy. It wasn't unexpected, of course. I had been warned that there would be at least one troop of reporters on hand eventually. In a business that lived and died by publicity, one had to expect that sort of thing. I was only happy that they had not arrived at Kasserine before we had.

Talk of the press made me think about Ann. I assumed she was now in Bizerte or Tunis, but I didn't want to ask. Not in this company. I knew I wanted very much to see her at least once more before we crossed into Libya. I didn't know how I was going to manage it, but I intended to try.

We discussed Agron's wish to go to Tunis in the morning. I had made his job more difficult by keeping him with us on the trip down to Kasserine, but the idea of him on his own and unwatched behind us was still about as appealing as a loose cannon, and a storm rising, would be to a sailor.

"I need two hours in Tunis," Agron said. "No more than that."

"I'll have Penny or Washington fly you there and back in one of the Stallions," I said. "If they arrive as scheduled."

"They'll be here early," Ziegler told me. "I spoke to the operations officer at Borj el Amiri at eight-thirty. The TAF crews will be finished late tonight, and your pilots will test-fly the aircraft at first light. If all's well, they'll be here by nine o'clock tomorrow."

I looked at Agron. His face, as usual, told me nothing. I would have given much to be able to follow him to Tunis and see where he planned to get the updated photographs of Point X. I couldn't even suggest that Louis go with him. Louis and I would both be needed here in the Kasserine camp to prepare for our move south. And, in any case, all Agron had to say was that his source would deal only with him alone. It was probably true.

"All right," I said. "But I want you back here no later than 1400 hours. If we can manage it, we may start south then, instead of waiting until morning." To Ziegler I said, "Can you put it out that Unit Two is leaving Kasserine to scout some other locations?"

"No problem. The word is already around that you are a special unit for some aerial shooting. Will you have room on your helicopters for some minicams? If you're supposed to be doing air shots, you'd better have cameras aboard. And we really should have footage of the rescue. It's too good to pass up. We can make a bundle selling the rights to the networks later."

Strachan said, "I don't want to throw cold water, but what if it's a disaster?" He looked at me apologetically. "I'm sorry, Casey. But we have to consider the possibility."

"I agree," I said. "Personally, I don't care one way or another about filming. I said so in Malibu. I just don't want anything or anyone messing up when we go in. If you have someone who can film, it's fine with me. But don't give me anyone we'll have to nursemaid. There won't be anyone to do it. And *everyone* carries a weapon. There will be no noncombatants in R Force."

"That might be a problem," Ziegler said thoughtfully. "Cinematographers are a touchy lot. They might not like being shot at or carrying a weapon."

"I appreciate their scruples," I said. "If they've got them, they ought to keep them—and keep them out of R Force. There's no bargaining on that point."

"We'll talk about it, Jerry," Harry said quickly. "The filming decision isn't that important. It will keep."

Ziegler showed some displeasure, but, as always when Harry spoke, there was no dissent.

We walked back to the Unit Two area under a clear, starry sky. By the time we went in, the nights would be dark. Redding and I walked behind the others.

He said, "Don't worry, Casey. Jerry will always do what I ask him to do."

"I've never doubted it," I said.

"We go way back, Jerry and I. I couldn't have made it without him." He gave a soft, almost sad laugh. "I'm not that sure I would have wanted to. Jerry always smooths the way for me. It's one of the things he does well. He does many things well."

I could think of no reply to that, so I made none. The relationship between Redding and Ziegler was not one of the things I had spent much time thinking about.

Ann, however, was. I asked where she was.

"In Tunis, Casey. She has plenty to do before you go."

"I thought Ann's job was publicity," I said. I had hoped she'd be in Bizerte, and I was disappointed to find that she was not here in Kasserine. "The last thing we need is publicity."

"If you're good at that job," Harry said, "you're as skilled at keeping things out of the press as getting them in."

"Is Ann that good?"

"Ann is *very* good, Casey. Better than you know."

But not better than *you* know, Harry, I thought bleakly. I knew her body, and would remember for the rest of my life that night in California. But Harry knew her mind and her spirit a thousand times better than I ever would. The thought was a dismal one. I had spent years looking for a woman like Ann, and when I found her I had been too stupid, too insensitive, to know who it was I had found. I had taken her like a stud in Malibu, and then I had begun to fall in love with her. I saw now that it might have been wiser if I had gone about it the other way around.

22

Around nine the next morning, the Sea Stallions appeared, flying in formation and looking altogether too military for my peace of mind. They landed on the edge of the airstrip in a flurry of dust and noise a hundred yards from where Agron and I waited for them. Ziegler had telephoned Ann in Tunis to tell her that one of the helicopters would be at Tunis-Carthage International Airport until one in the afternoon and that she would be able to hitch a ride if she planned to come down to Kasserine. I hadn't heard Ziegler's end of the conversation, but I assumed that he had told her why the Stallion would be returning to Tunis.

When the dust had settled, I went out to talk to Washington and Penny and hear their reports on the condition of the Stallions. AviaAlpha had done well by us. Both pilots were pleased with the condition and performance of the aircraft. They had come down loaded with odds and ends of gear, including the SCR-1220 I would use to stay in touch with General Stanley in San Francisco. We loaded the boxes onto a truck and sent them off to the Unit Two area, where Louis, Ware, and Tinker were getting R Force into their Afrika Korps finery so they could disappear among the extras—Tunisian soldiers and European bit players—already in the Kasserine camp.

I took Washington aside and told him he was to fly Gershon Agron back to Tunis for a couple of hours. "Do you think you could keep an eye on him without being seen, Luther?" I asked. "I'd like to know where he goes."

I picked him because he could pass for a Berber.

"I'll give it a shot, Major," he said.

"I've told him he has to be back at the aircraft in two hours, but it's bluff," I said. "We can't leave him in Tunis."

"I'll see to it he's aboard, sir," Washington said.

"Miss Ann Maclean may be flying back with you, too," I added. "Look for her."

"Affirmative, Major."

I signaled for Agron to join us. His opaque eyes gave nothing away, but I had good reason to think he was not happy that I had separated him from his Israeli paras. I said, "Luther Washington will fly you. He'll have to file a flight plan with Tunis Air Traffic Control by radio, so be sure you don't keep him waiting for the return flight."

"Yes, Major," he said.

"If the photographs you are after are not available, don't wait for them. I want us to be on the way south by dawn tomorrow at the latest."

"Or by tonight?" He favored me with a mirthless smile. My having advanced the departure time from Naples had surprised him, and he obviously did not like surprises.

"One thing more," I said. "Ask your source about the bug in the San Germano. If his men were responsible, tell them I want no more—repeat *no more*. There was the killing in London and then the bugging. That's two incidents too many. Am I making myself clear?"

"Perfectly, Major," Agron said. "Perhaps it was my friends who were responsible. I don't think so, but the possibility exists. I will deliver your message."

"Thank you, Agron," I said. "Have a nice flight."

———

Instead of going back to the Unit Two area after watching the Stallion lift off and head northeast toward Tunis-Carthage,

I went to Redding's tent to tell him that Agron was on his way.

It was too crowded and busy in the tent to do any talking, so we walked around the camp. I had never seen anything quite like it. Redding's organization was something rare in film making. To begin with, he was not just the star; he was also the director and the principal producer. Ziegler had the title of executive producer, which meant that he handled finances and local disbursements and whatever else Redding wanted done. But Eagle Films *was* Harry Redding. The astonishing part of it was that he could parcel himself out with enough skill and precision to handle a small invasion of Qaddafi's Libya and at the same time put a major big-budget film on track.

Scattered about the Kasserine location were platforms stacked with sound equipment and Panaflex cameras, lights and reflectors, power-generating equipment and booms. There were portable dressing rooms, toilets, prefabricated offices, and vans and trucks containing tons of machines, tools, and lumber for set construction. Tracks were being laid in a tangle across the floor of the actual Kasserine Pass, where dollies carrying booms and cameras would film the action from a dozen different viewpoints. Extras and workmen swarmed over the site, mingling with Tunisian Army soldiers in both U.S. Army and Afrika Korps uniforms.

Assistant producers and directors, each one of them responsible, with his people, for some part of the preparations for filming, stalked about shouting instructions through bull horns. From the airstrip could be heard the daily inspection run-ups of the ancient German bombers, which had been reinforced by a second flight of Heinkels just after the departure of our Sea Stallion.

There were commissary tents set up to feed the multitude, tank trucks of water for drinking and bathing, gangs of carpenters hard at work on mysterious constructions, high platforms, and wooden trackways connecting the various areas of the camp. At the motor pool, there were more Shermans and what appeared to be a full squadron of antique Tunisian Chieftain tanks being converted with plywood and paint to resemble German Tigers.

It was stunning to consider that all of this activity depended on one man. If Harry Redding was to slip and break a leg, Kasserine would slow to a crawl. If he had a heart attack, this entire enterprise would cease to exist. In two weeks, three at the outside, this narrow pass between low hills would return to the desert and the Bedouins. All that would remain here was what had been here before the arrival of Eagle Films: sand, rock, the desert wind, and history.

"What do you think of it, Casey?" Redding asked. "This is *my* army."

"Rod Strachan moved all of this in four weeks?"

"Give or take a few days. *Kasserine* will come in on time and on budget." He looked at me intently. "And we'll get our other job done, too. It is very important to me."

"And to me," I said.

"I know that. Is there anything else you need before moving south?"

"Only the cover story, to explain our leaving here so soon after the arrival," I said.

"You're going south for some supporting shots and to scout locations—as we decided earlier. People don't ask too many questions on a foreign shoot. They've got too much to do."

We walked past the Arab village and out into the pass. The corps of assistant directors had already begun to dot the landscape with bits of orange tape on thin poles to mark out camera angles for the Panaflex crews. The tapes blew in the morning breeze.

Redding stopped to survey the ground, his tawny eyes fixed on the southern entrance to the pass. "Think of what it must have been like, Casey," he said in a hushed voice. "The II Armored Corps came into the pass thinking the Germans were miles away, but they were waiting here, Rommel's best. It was the first real firefight for the U.S. Army in North Africa. They were green troops, Casey. Most of them kids. Draftees fresh from the States." He looked at me with a half-smile that had no mirth in it at all. "Why is it always like that, I wonder."

"It's an American tradition," I said dryly. "Bull Run, the Argonne, Pearl Harbor, Kasserine, Chosin Reservoir, Tet. The list is as long as your arm, Harry."

"But not Point X," he said intently. "We've done our homework this time, haven't we, Casey?"

"We've done what we can."

"I want to win this one," he said fervently. "I want us to succeed."

I looked around. The ground on which I stood had been soaked with soldiers' blood, most of it my countrymen's. Yet it was now a *movie set*. The tiny orange flags were the choreography of an illusion Harry Redding would present to the people of America and the world. The illusion would be spectacular and heroic, but no matter how brilliantly conceived and executed, it would be false. Heroism—that quality Redding sought so hard to portray—was not a matter of images. It was a personal thing, a testing of inner strength and belief in the face of great risk. Would he ever understand that? Ann had told me that he was a physical coward. Strangely enough, some of the most heroic acts I had ever seen had been performed by men filled with fear. There must have been dozens of such acts here, that day in 1943, most of them unrecognized, but real for all that. Could a man such as Redding, who had never been tested, ever really understand the essence of the thing he wanted so badly?

"The critics say I'm always refighting lost battles," he said. "I don't think that's true. It's that I've become fascinated by the things men do in war." He smiled at me again, this time in his familiar self-deprecating way. He squatted down, scooped up a handful of dirt, and let it run through his fingers. "But you don't think I ever get it right, do you, Casey?"

"Movies have a structure, a plot," I said. "Wars don't."

"You don't think much of what I do, Casey."

"Harry," I said, "you deal in illusion. I can't."

We looked up at the barren hillsides that had been, on that

196

long-ago day, dotted with German eighty-eight-millimeter cannon and infantry.

"Sometimes," Redding said, "reality frightens me."

"Me, too," I said. "I've felt that way in combat."

"Really, Casey? I didn't think it was like that for people like you and Louis. You are bona-fide heroes. You take charge. You shape events."

"That's nonsense, Harry," I said. "A man becomes what you call a hero because in real life he can't rewrite the script." I stared at the desert pass. "That's what happened here forty-three years ago."

Redding looked up at me with a slight smile. "There is a scene in the movie *Zulu*—you know, the one that introduced Michael Caine. A detachment of Welsh Borderers is caught at Rorke's Drift by a force of ten thousand Zulu warriors, and one of the troopers asks the sergeant major—Nigel Green, it was—'Why, Sergeant? Why us?' And the old soldier just looks at him and says, 'Because we're 'ere, lad. Because we're 'ere.' It's a beautiful bit of film, Casey." There were tears in his tawny eyes. I should have laughed at him, but I couldn't. I was touched; I saw that he was struggling with the concept of commitment, dealing with it in the only terms and images he understood.

I realized then that Harry Redding *was* America, as America had become in our time. Our people somehow had come to rely on *image* as a surrogate for reality. Even the media, the celebrants of trendiness and superficiality, were caught in a psychological maze of their own creation, just as Redding was. They—and he—tried to show the world as it was, but the result was a montage of images flashing across movie and television screens, seen for a moment and then forgotten as other images jostled today's events aside to make room for tomorrow's.

Redding could weep for two actors playing a powerful dramatic scene because he was a sensitive man. But the gulf between that scene in a film and the reality of battle required a leap of understanding that was clearly beyond him. He wanted desperately to know what it was like to face real tragedy, but all that he could conjure was a dramatic image.

He got slowly to his feet. When he looked at me, I had the feeling that he had been reading my mind, that he was aware I sympathized with him but held him lightly. He smiled with infinite sadness and said, "Have you read much of F. Scott Fitzgerald?"

"Some," I said. "Not all."

"He didn't lead a very heroic life, Casey. But he wrote something that has always made me think he knew what things cost. He wrote: 'Show me a hero and I will write you a tragedy.' That's rather grand, isn't it?"

The way he said it disturbed me somehow. It was as though he had given me a glimpse of the inner man beneath the public figure.

I said, "Why so interested in heroes, Harry?"

He smiled and said, " 'Because we're 'ere, lad. Because we're 'ere.' "

23

Louis said, "I snooped as ordered, Major."

I had told him to make sure Agron's Israelis were kept busy and then to make a complete search of his gear. I didn't expect him to find anything.

"What's strange," he said, "is that I didn't find anything *at all*. I mean not one item of identifiable value. The clothes were new. There were no papers, no magic gadgets. Nothing. If Agron had been born three weeks ago, he'd carry luggage like that."

I had the grim thought that as counterintelligence agents, Louis Brown and I weren't worth our pay. The problem was that we just didn't think the way spooks did.

We stood on the airstrip waiting for Luther Washington's Stallion. He had radioed in that he would be landing at Kasserine in fifteen minutes.

Spanish Air Force mechanics had the cowlings off one of the old Heinkel-111 bombers. They were tinkering with an engine. Ware and Penny stood watching them. That German bomber had probably been part of the *Luftflotte* sold to Francisco Franco ten years before either of them had been born. Bombers like it had burned London in the Blitz, almost half a century ago.

"How do they keep those old kites flying?" Louis asked.

"It's not as difficult as you'd think," I said. "It's an airplane's shape that defines its performance. If you keep the tinware in condition and have plenty of spares, the thing will last indefinitely." The Spaniards maintained their antiques. As long as films were made about World War II, the Heinkels earned more hard currency than was spent on keeping them flyable.

The whacking sound of an approaching helicopter alerted us. Soon the clumsy shape of the Sea Stallion appeared over the barren hills to the northeast. Luther was exactly on time.

We stood by while the chopper landed in a storm of dust. The engine died, and the rotors free-wheeled. When the fuselage hatch opened, Washington was the first one out. And then came Ann. Her head was bare, her hair blowing in the breeze from the still-turning rotors. She wore trousers and a bush jacket and carried a briefcase. When she saw me, she waved and ran across the sandy ground. I wanted to take her in my arms, but I settled for a handshake, because that was what she offered.

"Casey," she said, "it's so good to see you. I was afraid you might be gone."

"Not without my flying machine," I said. What I meant was: Not without seeing you once more.

"We have to talk," she said.

"All right. You say when."

Washington and Agron were approaching. One of Ziegler's assistant producers drove up in an Eagle Films Bronco. He said, "Miss Maclean? Mr. Ziegler is waiting for you."

"Where will you be, Casey?" Ann asked.

"Here. Or in the Unit Two area."

"I'll get back to you. It's important."

"Right," I said, and watched her drive off toward the main camp.

Agron carried a cardboard file folder. His manner was tense and agitated—not at all like that of the Mr. Cool I had grown to dislike so. He handed me the file and said, "You should look at these right away, Quary. You are not going to like what you see."

"I'll look at them back in the Unit Two area. Not here," I said.

200

"We had better call an officers' meeting. I have some other developments to report." He seemed genuinely distressed.

Washington looked chagrined. He shrugged imperceptibly to indicate that his attempt to shadow Agron had come to nothing. Well, that was to be expected. He was a helicopter pilot; I had given him a policeman's assignment.

As Agron looked around, I said, "Elie is with the troops, sorting gear. Louis will drive you back to the area."

"Quary," he said, "we are going to have to start trusting each other."

I ignored this and turned to Louis. "Officers' call in fifteen minutes. Tell the others."

"Sir," Louis answered.

Agron turned toward the pilot. "Thank you for the transport, Mr. Washington. I hope you enjoyed your tour of Tunis." Agitated as he obviously was, the son of a bitch could not resist needling Washington and, by inference, me. Luther looked as though he would love to throw a punch.

I said, "Do you need to talk to Redding or Ziegler?"

"No," Agron said impatiently. "My information is only for the force."

"All right. Carry on, Louis," I said.

Louis gave me a salute and walked off toward the jeep with Agron.

When they had driven off, Washington said, "I'm sorry, Major. I couldn't stay with him. He lost me in five minutes."

"Never mind. I didn't think it would work, but it was worth a try. You were outmatched." I put a hand on his shoulder. "Is the aircraft all right?"

"Four oh, Major. What time do we fly?"

"Be ready to go any time after 1500 today." I was extremely anxious to examine the new photographs, especially given Agron's concern. "Tell Penny to get his bird ready right away. I'll get the word to you both as soon as possible."

Most of our people were inside the Unit Two perimeter making a final check of their weapons and gear. Colonel Tinker had doled out the Uzis and ammunition that morning, seeing to it that each man's kit matched his assignment at Point X. Louis had already given out the crossbows and RPGs to members of One Commando, which would spearhead the night attack we were counting on to give us the advantage of surprise.

I planned to move One Commando south by air, with the equipment we would need to make our staging camp. Two and Three Commandos would travel south by truck with the house-keeping gear. We had concentrated men with engineer corps experience in Tinker's command.

But now I wondered if our planning was about to go out the window. Agron's agitation implied that there were changes to be made, radical ones.

I told Washington that if the Spaniards or the Tunisians on the airstrip grew curious about our movement, he was to say that Unit Two was flying to Kairouan to set up a shoot in the desert. In the general confusion of a motion-picture location the departure of some sixty-odd men shouldn't attract much attention.

I went over to where the Spanish mechanics were working on the Heinkel and collected Ware. "Come along," I said. "Meeting in fifteen minutes."

"What is it with Agron? He looked sour when your sergeant took him off."

"New pictures," I said, indicating the folder in my hand. "I don't think he likes what they show. I'll tell you at the meeting."

We walked back to the Unit Two area. I left him when we reached the tent I shared with Louis. I wanted privacy to absorb any bad news the latest reconnaissance had turned up.

I sat on my cot and spread the photos out on the blanket. Agron was right. The pictures showed what could be the first indications of a potential disaster. Point X was undergoing changes.

The high-angle photos showed a maze of vehicle tracks that had not been present in the earlier shots. Trucks—it was impossible to guess how many, but I estimated at least a half-dozen—had been brought to Point X from the track between Bir Mraja and Hasi Labres, two abandoned settlements just north of the old BP concession. If the vehicles were still at Point X, they were inside one of the dilapidated galvanized-iron buildings near the abandoned drilling site. That was bad enough, but there was worse. The low-angle shots showed Bedouin women and children working in a level area between two large sand dunes. They were placing flare pots in a square, preparing illumination for a helicopter landing zone that would be used at night. Another photograph, taken from a wide angle, brought a coppery taste to my mouth. Spaced out around Point X in an equilateral triangle were three surface-to-air missile batteries. One had been camouflaged with netting, and the others were about to be, but the satellite's pass had been well timed to expose them before they could be hidden. Ironically, the missiles were American Hawks, old heat-seekers but deadly efficient for all their obsolescence.

My first fear was that our haphazard security had broken down completely, and the Libyans and their friends were preparing a hot welcome for R Force. But sober consideration ruled that out. The site was being prepared for a possible air attack, not for an assault by light infantry—which was, actually, what R Force was. The preparations were twofold: air defense and possible evacuation. The meaning of the flares was plain: the Libyans were making ready to move their hostages. The SAMs were intended to discourage any interdiction of that movement.

I sat with the photographs before me and just stared at them. Like those I had seen in Malibu, they were in full color. They seemed slightly grainier than the first set, as though they had been taken by a satellite with a slightly different imaging system. But the detail was excellent, the printing first-rate. They had been time-coded in Roman characters, showing that they had been made barely twenty-eight hours ago. The speed with which Mossad had obtained them, duplicated them, and rushed them across the length of the Mediterranean to some stand-by spook in Tunis was impressive. The pictures lacked the Most Secret Mossad rubric I had noted on the first set, but even that showed planning and foresight. Tunisia was at odds with Qaddafi's Libya and most of the more radical elements in the Arab world. But nevertheless it would not go well with any careless spy caught with photographs of Israeli origin in his possession. Hence the prints were politically neuter.

What the pictures told me was that we had to make a decision now, without delay. A great deal was happening at Point X, and none of it good. The Libyans were preparing to move the hostages, possibly under fire. If that was allowed to happen, Redding's army might just as well reembark on *Kaliph* and return to Naples. No wonder Agron was not his customary, irritatingly superior self. I gathered the photos into the file and headed for the mess tent where R Force's leaders and Agron waited for me.

———

There was tension in the air when I joined them. Agron was not the sort of man who volunteered information, but he had been talking to them, I was sure. Ware was pulling at his mustache, and Tinker had taken out an evil-smelling pipe and was chewing on it with his large horsey teeth. Louis looked somber, which was not his usual style.

"All right, gentlemen," I said formally. "I have the recce photographs Agron brought from Tunis. I want you to take a look at them." I passed them down the mess table.

"Bloody hell!" Ware said.

"You can see they've been busy," I said. "Comments? Colonel?"

Tinker said, "I don't like those SAM batteries. Hawks, aren't they?"

"Yes," Agron answered. "Probably bought through some ex-CIA pensioner."

"They're set up to defend against air attack," Louis said, "not against choppers flying contour."

His interpretation—accurate, I thought—was the best news in a very sorry file.

"The point is, Casey," Ware said, "*why* are they doing it? Why now?"

"I can tell you that," Agron said. "Your Sixth Fleet has been cruising in and out of the Gulf of Sidra for a week or more. The Libyans think they might go in after the hostages."

"Is that conjecture?" I asked. "Or did your friends in Tunis give you hard information to back it up?"

He stared at me with those black, guarded eyes. It struck me that our spook despised Americans. I couldn't begin to guess at his reasons. Plenty of Israelis resented their nation's dependence on the United States. Others hated being pushed and prodded by the U.S. Congress in what they considered repeated interference with their foreign policy. But there was a personal element, too, in the cold look I was getting.

"I think they are planning on moving the hostages," he answered.

"We can see that," I said. "You'll have to do better."

He seemed undecided, but only for a moment. "All right," he said. "The rumors about secret negotiations are all true. Ever since they moved the hostages out of Lebanon, there have been communications between Amal and Israel and the U.S."

"We know about the rumors," I said. "They have been flying around for months. What is different now?"

"There is a deadline," Agron said.

"There's always a bloody deadline, Agron," Ware said impatiently. "The ragheads love them. You can't buy a rug from one without blathering about deadlines."

"Their demands are different this time," Agron said. "They demand that Israel dismantle Dimona and destroy all nuclear weapons."

"That's not exactly news," Tinker said, fingering his pipe.

"But this may be," Agron said, looking at me. "The United States wants Israel to agree." He turned to stare around the table at each man in turn. "Israel is going to refuse."

A heavy silence filled the tent. It muffled the distant sounds of activity on the movie location.

"Go on," I said. "There has to be more."

Agron shrugged. "Oh, there is a great deal more. When the deadline expires without a commitment from Israel about Dimona, a number of things will happen very swiftly. First, the United States will demand to be told why Israel has not kept to a promise the State Department believes it extracted from the Israeli government. Second, Israel will go on a war footing—again. But this time the nuclear weapons at Dimona will be assembled and armed. Third, Qaddafi will begin to move the hostages to some secure military base. He will move them one or two at a time, by land and by air, to prevent a rescue mission by the Sixth Fleet. And he will execute them secretly, because they will have become an embarrassment." He turned his gaze back to me and asked, "Is that enough? Do you want more?"

"When does the deadline expire? Exactly."

He looked at his wristwatch. "Fifty-one hours from now."

Louis blew his breath out explosively. "Holy shit. That tears it."

The two Brits looked stunned, and well they would. When I had looked at the new pictures, I guessed it was going to be bad, but I had no idea it would be this bad. Fifty-one hours barely gave us time to move to the pumping station, assemble our forces, complete briefing, fly the Stallions in to someplace out of range of the new SAM batteries, and mount an attack. There would be no time for practice, no time for special training of the assault teams. And we would have to be gone from Point X before Qaddafi's army and air force began arriving in strength to move the hostages out.

I looked at Agron bleakly. "What is the present situation at Barqin?" I asked.

"As far as I know—I emphasize that, Quary—*as far as I know*, nothing has changed there."

How completely did Agron's controllers inform him? Did they tell him what, if anything, they knew about Soviet intentions? Compartmentalization was the first principle of intelligence work. The domino theory could be a real menace to average supergrade intelligence officers. Keep the dominoes well apart, and if one falls it cannot topple others. A less elegant way of putting it was: No one can beat out of your spook what he has never been told. In the field spies die alone and ignorant. I didn't envy Agron his profession.

"All right, gentlemen," I said. "I thought we would have ten days to train and fine-tune the operation. We have fifty-one—" I looked at my watch—"fifty hours and forty minutes to get in and get out. Louis, pass out the silencers. Tinker, we're going to have to reschedule the transport. Only the heavy stuff goes by truck, everything else by air. Load only the absolute necessities. Take the ammunition, the heavy weapons, and the fuel for the Stallions and get under way with what men you need from Three Commando as soon as you are loaded. The Stallions will be ready to go at 1500. Louis, assemble One Commando and get them to the airstrip on the double. The men are to carry their personal weapons only. Tell Washington and Penny they will have to fly three shifts. Two Commando goes first, then the rations, water, and light gear, then the rest of Three Commando. I'll go with the last of the troops. Colonel, when you load the fuel on the trucks, leave enough here so that we can top off the Stallions each time they come back for a load. I'll talk to Redding and tell him we will have to steal one of his Panaflexes to make it look right, just in case some of Qaddafi's flyboys come snooping." I asked Agron if there was any chance that would happen.

"A good chance. Qaddafi's started deporting Tunisian workers again. But mostly by way of Tripoli and Banghazi. He doesn't want them coming back by way of the southern border."

"What about patrols?"

"A few police units. They have orders to shoot."

"That's very comforting," I said. "Do they patrol at night?"

"Almost never."

"We'll have to check when we get to the pumping station," I said. "We'll do a little patrolling ourselves. It will give your paras something to do."

Agron's face showed no expression, no emotion at all. I didn't

207

like the idea of isolating myself in the desert at night with Agron and his sabras, but I had to find out about them before we crossed into Libya. Louis would have to cover my back. He had done that often enough before, and I was still alive.

"All right," I said. "Let's move it."

"Question, Major," Ware said. "When do we go in?"

"Tomorrow night," I said. "I'll lead One Commando in the first foray, against the nearest SAM battery."

I took a jeep and drove out of the Unit Two area to Redding's tent. He wasn't there, but Ziegler was. I told him what we had to do. I didn't tell him why, not all of it, only that Agron's pictures indicated movement at Point X.

Ziegler's eyes glittered with alarm. He was a man who believed in plans and schedules. He had to. And he grew nervous when faced with improvisations.

"I thought we had almost two weeks to get ready," he said.

"I thought so, too. I was wrong."

"You need one of the Panaflexes?" I suppressed an impulse to smile. Whatever else was happening, Ziegler had a picture to make, and he bridled at giving up one of his precious seventy-millimeter cameras. But I remembered how he had said, that first night in Malibu, that the footage we might make of the rescue would be worth a fortune. Ziegler had his own set of values and priorities.

"The Panaflexes are needed here, Casey. I hate to send one just to make things look right."

"Just give me something to fool any snoopers, Ziegler. Remember, we are supposed to be a second-unit crew."

"Suppose I send a couple of hand-held cameras. Will that do?"

"Send whatever you want," I said impatiently. "Just make sure they can be identified from the air."

"You expect to be seen?" The thought reawakened his alarm.

"It's possible," I said.

"I'm having second thoughts about all this."

I said harshly, "Tell them to Harry. If he wants to scrub R Force, he can do it. He's paying the bills."

"Harry would never do that," Ziegler said. His plump face was covered with sweat. I had seen that reaction before, many times, when a moment of decision approached. But I agreed with him about one thing: Harry Redding wouldn't back out now. We had talked of commitment out there near the pass. He had made his commitment. Win or lose, his army was going to war.

"I'll be here until about 2100 tonight—that's nine o'clock— and then I'll fly out with the last Stallion. If Harry wants me, he can find me at the airstrip," I said.

As I started to leave, Ziegler said, "Ann wants to see you, Casey."

"Where is she?"

"Somewhere with Harry."

I wanted to see her, too, but without Harry, and I didn't have time to find her in the mob of actors, technicians, and extras milling around the *Kasserine* set. Time had become critical.

Ziegler picked up a walkie-talkie and spoke to someone. "Is Ann Maclean there?"

A radio voice said, "She was just here with Mr. Redding. I think they are on the way to the press tent."

The press. Jesus, I had forgotten that Ann would be having a planeload of reporters fly in soon.

Ziegler said, "Find her and tell her that Quary will be at the airstrip."

"Right, Mr. Ziegler."

He put down the walkie-talkie and said, "I'll get those cameras over to you right away. Can we use them? I mean—"

I couldn't keep up with his rapid shifts of fear and enthusiasm. The thought of carrying a camera crew into Libya with us had seemed remotely appealing in Malibu. Here it sounded like an

209

awful idea. Well, the final decision could be made tomorrow night.

I helped myself to one of Ziegler's telephones and called the Unit Two area. Tinker answered.

"Colonel," I said, "is Louis nearby?"

"Right here, Casey. I'll put him on."

Louis said, "Here, Major."

"Set up the SCR-1220. I need to touch home base."

"Right," Louis said.

Ziegler looked puzzled. "What was that about?"

"Soldier talk," I said. The satellite link with San Francisco wasn't any of his business. I started to leave the tent.

"Things aren't unraveling, are they?" he asked.

"Only a little," I said, and hurried out.

24

Murphy's Law says that whatever can go wrong will go wrong. In the military life that is a statistical certainty.

The first thing I saw when I reached the airstrip was Harry Redding's technical adviser, Colonel Jonathan Cathcart, USA (Ret.), standing beside Penny's Stallion and giving the ex–Coastal Command pilot a grilling. Cathcart was a gray-haired officer of impressive appearance and impeccable connections. His family had provided the United States Army with three generations of officers, none very distinguished but all retired as colonels or better.

Ziegler had hired Colonel Cathcart when the planning for *Kasserine* began because he had actually served with General Fredendall's armor in the battle.

The problem was that the good colonel had been out of the army for a long time, and his stint with Eagle Films not only meant money to him, but also gave him an opportunity (he undoubtedly believed) to command again.

He was commanding Derek Penny now, in no uncertain terms. He did not know what a Brit helicopter pilot was doing on this airstrip, because no one had cleared it with him. He regarded the desert-tan paint and the silly little white Afrika Korps palm tree on the Stallion an outrage. There were no helicopters in the Luftwaffe in North Africa in 1943. In fact, there were no helicopters anywhere except at Wright Field at the time of the Kasserine battle. Therefore *what*, in the name of all that was right and accurate, was that machine and its sister ship doing on the same airstrip as the Dakota and the Heinkels? Would Mr. Penny explain forthwith?

Penny saw me coming and pointed me out to the colonel. I heard him say, "Here's Major Quary, sir. He can tell you anything you want to know. I have bags of work to do, Colonel."

Cathcart turned to face me with perplexed anger in his bright-blue eyes. The man was seventy if he was a day, straight as a ramrod and as fixed in his ways as though he ran on rails.

"Major Quary, is it?"

The last thing I had time to deal with was an old man's hostility. But military habits are ingrained. "Afternoon, Colonel. The Stallions won't be in the picture."

"You are damned right they won't be. I heard you were here, Major. May I ask you why?"

"Mr. Redding wanted a second-unit company, Colonel," I said. "It was a last-minute decision."

The Colonel looked about suspiciously. "What are you doing?" About a third of the members of One Commando, resplendent in their Afrika Korps finery, had assembled, ready to carry their equipment aboard Washington's Stallion. They had their Uzis slung, muzzle down and menacing. To a soldier, they presented a glaring anachronism, uniforms and weapons belonging to different generations of armed men.

"We are going to Kairouan for a shoot in the desert, Colonel," I said. "Nothing very special."

"But there was no fighting around Kairouan," Cathcart said positively. "None in that part of the desert at all. It's all wrong."

"Harry Redding's idea, Colonel," I said, growing exasperated. "He signs the checks and he writes the script."

"Those are Uzis your men are carrying," the old soldier said accusingly.

"They're the security detachment," I said.

212

Another file came double-timing from the Unit Two area. And, of course, they, too, were armed to the teeth with modern weapons.

"What the hell is going on here, Major?" Cathcart looked angry now. Irascible he might be, but he was no fool. "What are you going to do with these men?" It had been to avoid such questions that I had warned all hands to stay away from the technical adviser.

"Hello, Colonel Cathcart," Ann said. She had materialized, it seemed, out of the dusty air. Harry was with her.

"This is all incorrect, Mr. Redding," Cathcart said. "The weapons and aircraft didn't exist in 1943. If you use them in any way, you'll look foolish."

"Oh, I know that, Colonel," Harry said, flashing that brilliant smile that was so familiar to filmgoers. "Rod made a mistake. The weapons are for the security force, though. Didn't Major Quary tell you?"

"He told me. It is a peculiar security force, Mr. Redding. Wearing those German uniforms. Very strange, sir. Very."

Harry said easily, "Economics, Colonel. We are going to get double use out of these men. When we shoot, they put aside those machine guns, pick up Mausers, and they are extras. We have to save money where we can."

Cathcart was far from mollified. But three generations of military life breeds men who know when authority speaks, even in a friendly voice. "Yes, well, I see." He could not help a Parthian shot, however. "I didn't know you had hired Major Quary for special assignments." He didn't know me, and he didn't approve of me.

Harry said soothingly, "Whatever Unit Two films will be screened for you, Colonel." He glanced in my direction and then, with a hand on Cathcart's shoulder, said, "There are one or two things about the battle I'd like to go over with you, sir. Can we go to my tent?" He gently led the old soldier toward the jeep in which he and Ann had arrived at the airstrip.

When they had gone, Ann said, "Casey, I have to talk to

213

you." She looked worried. I wondered if it was because I was going in ahead of schedule.

"I thought you were getting ready for the press," I said.

"That can wait. This is important."

Her presence overwhelmed me. It struck me that, ever since our night in Malibu, I had been sliding down a steepening emotional slope. I had thought more about Ann Maclean in the last few days than I had thought about all the women I had ever known. A loveless man can be badly disoriented when, at last, he falls in love. I realized that the answer to the question Harry had thrown at me so unexpectedly in Naples was: Yes, I am in love with Ann. I no longer cared whether or not she was, or ever had been, Harry's woman.

"Let's walk," I said.

There was a thin, high overcast of dappled silver clouds in the sky. The pallid sun made small shadows under our feet. Ann had never looked more beautiful. Her desert clothes only served to accentuate her femininity. Her dark hair blew in the soft wind as we walked away from the airstrip. I wanted to get her away from the crowd, take her in my arms and tell her about my self-discovery. I needed to say to her that I would do what I had been hired to do, but that when it was over I wanted her to be part of my life. A man who has lived as I had isn't really equipped emotionally or intellectually to deal with the kind of love I felt for Ann. I didn't know how to say what I wanted to say.

We walked away from the camp toward the pass. I had so little time, and I was half convinced that she must somehow feel what I was feeling.

But when she spoke, I was in for a shock. She wasn't thinking about Casey Quary in love. Far from it.

She said firmly, "You are going to have to cancel the operation, Casey."

"*What?*" I must have sounded stupid.

214

I came slowly to earth. This wasn't a woman worried about a man she cared for. This was something else. Something tougher. Something *professional*. It struck me like that, swift as a lightning bolt.

"You can't go in, Casey. I mean it. It's too soon. Too dangerous. Believe me."

I reined myself in hard. "What are you talking about, Ann?"

She looked really distraught. I had to give her that.

"Explain," I said. "The schedule was always open. The decision about when to go in was left to me." My voice sounded flat and dead. Something inside me had curled up and blackened, like a scrap of paper in a fire.

"I know," she said. "I tried to get Harry to cancel, but he won't do it. He says he gave you the authority, and if you say go, it's go. You can't do it, Casey. Something has happened."

I stood staring down at her. She was like a stranger. "*What* has happened?" I asked.

"Can't you just take my word for it? Please, Casey. You have to call it off."

I said harshly, "Gershon Agron's new photographs say the Libyans are going to move the hostages. We have to get them out before that happens."

"Casey, don't argue with me. Just believe what I'm telling you. You have to call it off." She had begun to sound desperate, and it infuriated me, because it meant that she was not what she seemed to be, had never been, not since before the beginning.

I took her by the shoulders and held her, not gently. "Where were you in Tunis?" I grated. "Who did you see there?"

She looked at me pleadingly. "Don't do this, Casey. Don't make me tell you. *Give it up*."

"Like hell," I said. "Not without something better than this to go on." I released her with a shove, and she staggered. "Talk to me," I said. "I mean right now."

The words came haltingly. "I visited the British Mission, Casey. That's all."

"But something's come down from there. Is that it?"

"Yes. The men in the car in London were KGB, Casey. They weren't Libyans or Israelis. Word came through this morning."

I said flatly, "The man who was killed was a British agent." I don't know how I knew it, but I did. The certainty was like a stone caught in my chest.

"Yes."

"He followed me from Zurich. Why?"

She closed her eyes before answering. "Your people weren't sharing intelligence about Point X. MI-6 had only an amateur in the field. So they put a professional on you. And the KGB killed him."

"*You*," I said. "The amateur."

"Yes. They asked me because I was working for Harry."

I felt as though the temperature of the air had dropped twenty degrees. "They got wind of Harry's private war and asked you to spy on him," I said. "Jesus. You make me sick."

"Listen to me, Casey. Please listen."

"To what?"

"Six months ago the chief resident of the KGB in Ottawa defected— Are you listening to what I am saying? You look as though you'd like to kill me."

"Go on."

"Before he was sent to Canada, he was in Active Measures at Moscow Center. Canadian intelligence has been debriefing him at a safe house in Toronto and sharing information with MI-6. The CIA wants him, and there's been some sort of squabble. Oh, I don't know, it's all so crazy—"

"Is that the amateur speaking?"

"Don't, Casey. Please hear me out. London says he's beginning to talk about Barqin—some plan the Russians have to rid themselves of an embarrassment. Some of the analysts think it's connected to what we are planning to do. Others say no, it couldn't be. The fight between the Canadians and the CIA is making things go very slowly in Toronto. London thinks you should take no chances and cancel."

"It was you who had our phone bugged in Naples, wasn't it?"

Ann nodded miserably. "I had to keep them informed, Casey. In return they promised to share what they knew."

"Does Harry know who you work for?"

"No. He thinks I'm having second thoughts because of my feelings for you."

Ten minutes earlier I would have given a great deal to hear her say that. Now it was ashes.

"What does London recommend the Israelis do about the negotiations?"

"They think they should give up Dimona."

Maybe London was right, I thought. The Israelis had been very cautious about even admitting their nuclear capability, but the dismantling of the Dimona facility might well please the British Arabists who still dominated the Secret Intelligence Service. But from the American point of view, surrender was no answer at all. There was no assurance whatever that giving in to the hostage takers' demands would result in the release of the Beirut embassy staff people. Quite the contrary. There was every reason to believe that giving in to the kidnappers' demands would produce only more demands. Ann's London controllers saw it one way; an American—any American—would see it differently.

I said, "We go in as scheduled."

"Casey, *please.*"

"Tell me what London knows about Agron," I said.

"I asked them to check on him when we were in London. So far, it seems that he is just what he says he is—an Israeli businessman and a Mossad agent. That's all they've got." She put a hand on my arm, but I moved away from her. I couldn't help it. Love and anger can get pretty well tangled sometimes.

I said, "Your people lost a man in London. What was he supposed to be doing? Was he instructed to take me out? That would have stopped R Force in its tracks."

"Casey, *no.* They wouldn't do that."

"It's the sort of thing spooks do. Didn't you know?"

"They wouldn't."

"Then the KGB made a mistake. They thought they were hitting me."

Ann looked dismal, her face drawn, close to tears. "I don't know. I don't *know*. I've never been in a situation like this."

"Don't cry, Miss Maclean. That *is* your name, isn't it? Spooks don't weep over small errors like that."

"Damn you, Casey. Stop it."

I made a show of looking at my watch. "It's late. I have things to do. Tell London Quary says thank you for the advice, but they know where they can put it."

I turned and walked away from her. From the direction of the camp, Louis came running to tell me that the satellite link was ready and that General Stanley was expecting my transmission.

25

As I hurried back toward the Unit Two area with Louis, I felt a throb of pain in my chest and had to pause. Louis, who was older than I and an absolutely perfect physical specimen, had double-timed all the way from the camp to where Ann and I had been standing. He wasn't even breathing hard. He regarded me with a concerned frown.

"Something wrong, Casey?"

I straightened with an effort and drew in a deep, painful breath. "Nothing," I said. But it *was* something, and I knew exactly what. That fragment of a Soviet mortar shell that showed up every time I was under an X-ray machine was nudging the working machinery in my chest. It had picked a rotten time to start migrating.

"Stop staring at me, for chrissake, Sergeant," I said. "Let's go."

We went on, but Louis set a slower pace. It irritated me, and as soon as I could I began to jog. I was damp with sweat when we reached our area.

The place was a hive of activity. Trucks and jeeps were being loaded with our supplies. Troops were checking their packs and forming up to march to the airstrip.

Ware appeared and said, "Luther Washington is ready to fly, Casey."

I said, "Go, Ware. Set up a perimeter at the pumping station. Keep the men under cover as much as possible. And tell Washington to get back here as soon as he can make it."

"Affirmative, Major," Ware said, and saluted. He looked like a Prussian in his new Afrika Korps outfit, all desert tan and silver piping. He wore the collar tabs of a master sergeant of infantry.

He ran for a jeep already loaded with men and equipment, and they headed for the break in the wire and the track to the airstrip.

I could see that Louis had set up the SCR-1220 behind the meeting tent. He had put a trooper—an ex-Ranger—on guard.

"Casey," Louis said, "what's the matter with you and Ann Maclean?"

"Not a thing," I said shortly, and started for the satellite link.

Louis stopped me. "You can take a minute. What's going on with you two?"

I had a savage impulse to knock his hand away and tell him to mind his own goddamn business, but his concern was so transparently obvious I couldn't just fob him off with a snarling answer. Louis knew me better than any man alive, and he had eyes. He had a fairly good notion of what I felt for Ann.

I said bitterly, "She's a spook, Louis. A British spook."

"I'll be damned," he said softly.

"It doesn't matter," I said, and headed for the SCR. I relieved the Ranger on duty and sent him on his way. Then I settled down to operate the keyboard of the satellite transmitter.

I wrote: QUARY TO STANLEY BREAK WAITING BREAK BREAK ENDS.

For a moment there was no reply on the small computer screen. I snapped at Louis, "Is that dish oriented properly?" The unit had an eighty-centimeter parabolic antenna that had to be pointed at one of the geosynchronous military satellites stationed over the central Atlantic.

Then letters began to appear on the screen, scrolling upward. They were originating in a hospital room at Letterman, half a world away. They were going to another geosynchronous satellite over Central America, leaping across space to the Atlantic satellite, and then down to this equipment that would shortly be dismantled and carried by a single man in a backpack. In the process, the signals were being encrypted by the satellites and then decrypted by the miniature computer in front of me.

The message came swiftly: STANLEY TO QUARY BREAK REQUESTED INFORMATION NOT YET AVAILABLE BREAK AM WORKING ON IT BREAK EXPECT RESPONSE ON YOUR NEXT TRANSMISSION BREAK MOST URGENT BREAK MOST IMPORTANT BREAK SIXTH FLEET ENGAGING IN FREEDOM OF THE SEAS EXERCISE GULF OF SIDRA BREAK LIBYAN RETALIATION COULD INVOLVE HOSTAGES BREAK RISK FACTOR YOUR MISSION ENOR-MOUSLY RAISED BREAK SUGGEST YOU DELAY PLANNED ACTION UNTIL SITUATION CLARIFIES BREAK BREAK ENDS.

I stared at the message.

Louis had read the screen, too, and he looked at me. "What do we do, Major?"

"You saw Agron's photographs," I said.

"You're going in as planned?"

"The Libyans will be watching the navy."

I knelt at the SCR in silence for a moment. I had a bitter thought. Somewhere these messages were being stored away. If we went ahead and the Point X operation turned out to be a fiasco, hard copies—classified at the highest level available, no doubt—would be laid before the President of the United States. General Stanley, or his shadowy sources in Washington, would have to say: "We warned them, sir."

I typed rapidly: QUARY TO STANLEY BREAK RISK ACCEPTABLE BREAK FORCE COMMITTED BREAK WILL REPORT SOONEST BREAK BREAK ENDS OUT OUT.

"Dismantle the unit, Sergeant Brown," I said, getting to my feet. "Then get yourself over to the airstrip."

"Yes, sir," Louis said. He smiled thinly at me and murmured, "And I thought the Rubicon was in Italy."

———

I flew south in Penny's Stallion on the final flight of the move of R Force out of Kasserine. I rode in the copilot's seat, crowded

221

even there by the last-minute packs of equipment we had thrown aboard, and barely conscious of the silent men behind me, all of whom were as crowded and uncomfortable as I was.

Not long before, an hour after nightfall, I had waved off Washington's last flight, loaded with men and deadly equipment. I ordered him to fly the last trip on the deck—just above ground level—to check out the light-enhancing pack and goggles Louis had bought in North Carolina. We had two sets only, one for each pilot. They consisted of a lens system mounted on a helmet, behind an electronic light intensifier—the same sort of setup sometimes used on night snipers' scopes. They could take whatever ambient light existed (and even on the darkest night there was some) and enhance it so well that images could be seen as clearly as if it were daylight.

The colors were wrong, of course, tending to the glowing green, but the equipment made it possible for pilots to fly the contours of the land at fifty feet or less. Penny was doing it now, looking like a spaceman in his intensifier helmet and whooping delightedly from time to time as he lifted the cumbersome Stallion over some unseen ridge line or sand dune.

For a passenger it was unnerving. There was just enough starlight for an occasional patch of white sand or a contrasting darkness blotting out the low desert stars to be seen without the electronic eyes. I could feel my toes curling inside my desert boots each time we changed altitude. I couldn't see them, but I knew that we were flying over hills and dunes that ranged from fifteen hundred to two thousand feet in elevation, and our altimeters, set to sea-level zero, never once showed more than twenty-one hundred. What the men in the troop compartment thought about all this zooming and dipping through the desert night I could not imagine. I could only assume that they didn't know how low we were flying or they didn't care.

The men were huddled around portable radios trying to catch a Voice of America broadcast and getting only Arab music from local stations. The word on the "freedom of the seas" exercise being run by the Sixth Fleet in the Gulf of Sidra had begun to get around the Kasserine camp in midafternoon. Despite the probability that the Libyans would be swarming like bees around a disturbed hive now, the news that the United States was taking some position against a radical Arab country gave all of R Force a jolt of adrenaline.

So far, Radio Tripoli had broadcast only the news that the hated Americans had crossed the "Line of Death" and were being "repulsed" by the Libyan armed forces. There were claims of "several" American jets shot down, but those had been greeted with derisive laughter by the men of R Force.

I had discussed the new developments with Tinker, and he had concluded that, on balance, the sudden military activity to the north of us was all to our advantage. It would concentrate any potential Libyan power along the coast of the Gulf of Sidra, several hundred miles from our line of advance.

Two and Three Commandos should already be at the pumping station, our staging area. On this last trip, the Stallion carried One Commando—twenty men—and the remainder of our supplies. The rear of the troop compartment was piled high with cases of ammunition for the Uzis. Since those mean compact weapons could spew a thousand rounds a minute on full automatic, the hundred and twenty thousand rounds I had obtained through Dieter Lang were none too many if it should come to an all-out fire fight with the kidnappers at Point X.

Penny handled the big Stallion expertly. We were carrying a heavy load of men and equipment—actually a larger load than we would carry into Libya in about twenty-two hours—but he made the clumsy aircraft dance across the dark desert. It had been a long time since I had flown a helicopter, and I had no desire to fly this one. I did the copilot's chores on the flight deck, tasks that almost any member of R Force could do under the pilot's supervision. Penny and Washington were both capable of flying the Stallions without that sort of backup. I did it to keep my mind off the rock and sand streaming by unseen fifty feet beneath the helicopter's wheel pods.

The robot-headed figure beside me said, "These light enhancers are bloody marvelous, Major. I've never used them before."

"Wonderful," I said. I hadn't thought to ask him if he had ever flown contour at night with image-intensifiers. I had assumed all military chopper drivers had used them. But Penny, learning on the job, was having a grand time, and I had to believe he was in control. If I was wrong, there would soon be bits and pieces of Stallion and men scattered all over the low hills. On the chart this area was marked with blue block letters reading: "Maximum elevations believed not to exceed 2,500 feet." Penny had flown the route twice before now, ferrying men and equipment to the pumping station, first in daylight and then at dusk, all without optical enhancement. This trip was the only rehearsal he would have for tomorrow night.

The big Stallion was not very fast. We showed an indicated air speed of 190 knots. If need be, another twelve to fifteen knots could be squeezed from the old Pratt and Whitneys, but not enough to run away from a Soviet-built gunship. Sand dunes and contours became less threatening when you thought about that.

I hadn't seen Ann again before leaving Kasserine, nor had I seen Harry. The sudden activity along the Mediterranean coast, where a kind of mini-war could be erupting between Qaddafi's nervous jet jockeys and the Sixth Fleet, had caused excitement among the movie people and the reporters who had been flown in. Some criticism of the American action had come from that group. Redding would have had them on his hands, so I made no attempt to see him before I boarded the Stallion to leave the Kasserine location. I couldn't allow myself to think about Ann at all. Of course I thought about her constantly.

I leaned closer to Penny and asked, "Could you fly lower if you had to?"

He turned his hugely helmeted head, which made him look like a giant insect on the dimly lighted flight deck. "A bit, I imagine," he said. "Want me to try?"

"How high are the sand dunes on the other side of the border?" He would have seen them on his earlier trips.

"Ten to fifteen meters trough to crest."

"Tomorrow we may have to," I said. But there was no point risking an accident now.

On the international frequency there was no radio talk. Tunis-Carthage Air Traffic Control had no interest in us. They were too busy keeping civil airliners out of the air space over the Gulf of Sidra. British Airways still flew into Libya, as did Alitalia, Air Maroc, and Middle East Airlines. None of their planes would be in the air now. The U.S. Navy had issued an advisory that the air space over the Gulf of Sidra was being used for "military exercises," and Radio Tripoli made it sound as though World War III were beginning.

I tried to imagine how the news was being received back home. I had grown so accustomed to the United States doing nothing but growling after each terrorist outrage that I couldn't even begin to imagine what the public response to this sudden muscle flexing by the fleet would be.

I should have been better prepared, I thought. The hijacking of a TWA aircraft had produced only bluster from the Administration. But the navy had pulled off a coup when it forced down the *Achille Lauro* hijackers. Now the Administration had ordered the fleet to defy Qaddafi's Line of Death. What next, I wondered. How long would it be before retaliation escalated? There was an air of carefully measured fury in what was taking place in the gulf right now. It made the rescue of the diplomats being held at Point X critical. R Force seemed suddenly to have become an accidental part of some larger plan.

We were in a weird position. The Tunisians might love Harry Redding and Eagle Films, but I had no illusions about what would happen to any survivors of R Force if our invasion of Libya turned into a disaster.

I seemed to be the only member of the force who was worried. I saw us starting a small Arab war, which could trigger an Arab-Israeli war, which could start the dominoes falling all the way to Moscow and Washington. It was right and proper that I should be worried. That was part of a commander's job. Until H-hour. Then it would be time to put doubts aside and go for it.

Penny said, "I'm going up now, Major. Jenien is right ahead."

He put the Stallion into a climb and removed the image-intensifier helmet from his head. At three thousand feet above the desert even the night world took on a proper shape. There were bright stars, a horizon, and the folded land below us looked as though it were in its proper place. There were some lights, a very few, because there are not many villages this far south in Tunisia. And the lights were dim and widely spaced, because electricity is a luxury. Far off in the west, on our starboard side, could be seen the tiny, flickering pinpoint of yellow brightness that marked a stack on the Algerian border where natural gas was being flared off from wells in the oil fields in the Erg Oriental. Ahead and below, the Tunisian saheer was dark and seemingly empty, but Penny clicked the switch on the Stallion's radio and a square of lights began to form on the ground about six miles south of us.

As we drew nearer I could see that there were other lights softly glowing behind canvas shields. Penny brought us in high and made a broad, shallow circle. He flashed his position lights as briefly as he had the radio. "I don't want some windy bloke thinking we belong to the bad colonel and using an RPG on us," he explained.

We made our approach from the south. As we began to hover and then descend, I could see the camp. There were fires and electric lanterns and a few tents to shield our more lethal equipment. There were men moving about the landing zone, but not many of them. Louis, Ware, and Tinker were enforcing field discipline.

I stretched my legs wearily. I was leaden with fatigue, and my chest still ached dully. I desperately wanted some sleep, but knew there would be little time. Besides, the moment I slowed down a bit I would start thinking about Ann, and that wouldn't do me, or anyone else, the slightest good.

But we were all here at last, south of Jenien, in our staging area. Sufficient unto the day, I thought. Tomorrow night I would be putting my chosen profession to its ultimate test, once again.

It was strange. Harry Redding had made it all possible. He had conceived the operation, had done what no one else in our country had been willing or able to do, had hired me and the men behind me and below, had paid for the weapons and the aircraft. He had become a sovereign state in a small but quite possibly deadly way. Yet I didn't think about him seriously. Perhaps it was because he was far to the north getting ready to make his movie, and I was here according to a shorter and tighter scenario, one that would be acted out with real bullets and real blood.

Then the Stallion rocked on the ground, and the rotors stirred up the familiar storm of dust pierced by beams of flashlights and lanterns. We were down, and Louis came running through the swirling debris to unlock the flight-deck door.

"Welcome, Major," he said.

26

Tinker had done a professional job of setting up the camp. Three large tents had been pitched to give the men shelter through the coldest part of the desert night, though few were sleeping. Each man had been issued emergency rations with two canteens of water. Washington's Stallion was under camouflage, and even before Penny's helicopter was unloaded, Tinker had a crew of men spreading a canopy of desert netting over it. A field kitchen had been set up, and the men were fed in shifts—rough fare and hardly up to the cuisine being consumed at Kasserine by the film people. Tinker's years in the British Army hadn't exactly made a gourmet of him, but his troops never went hungry. "A good mess and plenty of latrines," he said, "have won many a battle." He reminded me of my father, who used to contend that a soldier should keep his stomach full and his bowels open. Family military wisdom, applicable to any army.

Louis had put out pickets, two-man teams, each with a hand-held radio. We were less than a mile from the border. The sand sea that could be seen dimly in the light of the rising moon lay in Libya.

I made a tour of the outposts with Ware and Louis. I had a quick look at the platforms Tinker had cobbled together to look like camera stations. He had inspected the real movie locations

228

at Kasserine carefully, and he had imitated them in miniature, with stakes driven into the ground and colored markers. From the air, R Force's temporary camp stood a good chance of passing for the base of a film unit of the company in the north. A really close look might make an observer wonder, but we didn't intend to allow such a look. Any Libyan pilot venturing low across the border would receive a welcome from a Czech grenade launcher—not the best antiaircraft weapon in the world, but effective in experienced hands.

The night was chilly, and there was the flinty odor of the desert in the air. What wind there was blew in from the southeast, and it carried with it the bitter tang of the Sahara. We were on the very edge of the great sand sea that stretched across the northern reach of the continent.

I met Agron in the mess tent. He had changed clothes and was wearing, as we all were, the sand-colored uniform of the old Afrika Korps. It was an ironic touch for a Russian Jew—turned–Israeli, and it wasn't lost on him. "Heil Hitler, Herr Major," he said sardonically.

"The uniform becomes you, Agron," I said.

He favored me with a short, harsh laugh. He was tense, nerves finely drawn. I could sense it. Approaching combat has its effect. I was reacting in much the same way, and so were the others. With Agron, however, there was something else I couldn't identify. Each man faces danger in his own private way, and, moreover, Agron was a complicated personality. I intended to keep him near me, and if he faltered or made a wrong move, I would stop him, even if I had to kill him. Civilization recedes in direct ratio to the distance from battle.

"I want to do a recce across the border before dawn," I said. "You will come with me. You can bring your sabras along."

"Very well," he said. "Name the time."

"Sunrise is at 0530 hours. We'll go at 0400," I said.

"How far will we penetrate?"

"Only a few miles. Washington can fly us. Any problems with that?"

"None."

His lean brown face showed nothing. No questions. I knew he was wondering why I would want to do a patrol so near the main strike. I *wanted* him to wonder. My concern was not for the lie of the land just across the border. Since we knew there were no Libyan military installations along this part of the line, he could sense that the patrol was a test. I intended to present him and his three Israeli paras with a chance to kill me. Or try to. If his intention was to sabotage R Force, I meant to give him an opportunity before we were irreversibly committed. If he declined, it did not necessarily mean that it wasn't his eventual intention. Somewhere out in the sand sea were the hostile Libyans at Point X, beyond that the Russians at Barqin. There were all sorts of possibilities, most of them bad. Slow down, I told myself, one damned thing at a time.

At 0330 hours I was awake and dressing. Louis had already gone to alert Washington to get the helicopter ready. In the predawn dark I put on my harness and settled the extra magazines into the canvas pockets. I checked the action on my Uzi and fitted it with a silencer. Silenced weapons—properly called sound-suppressed weapons—are a violation of the Geneva Convention, but we live in a time when such considerations are for moralizing about after the fact—and after discovery. Every army on earth now uses illegal weapons, which tells more about the state of the world than about armies.

I walked across the stirring encampment in my Afrika Korps uniform. Suited up like this, a single army corps of the Wehrmacht had kept the Mediterranean in turmoil for three years and had very nearly taken Egypt from the British. Would the ghost of Erwin Rommel be laughing to see what we were doing now?

The whine of the Stallion pierced the early-morning dark. I

230

could see the blue glow of its jet engines as the former Marine warmed it up.

Louis, Agron, and his three paras were waiting for me near the helicopter. In the high flight deck, Washington was bent over his checklist. Ware and a few of the men of Two Commando had gathered to see us off. To Bertie I said, "Keep someone on the radio link. We won't break silence unless we run into something we can't handle. If we do, we'll try to stay low until tonight, and you can pick us up then."

"Sir," Ware said, all military now.

I looked at Agron and his sabras. "Let's get aboard."

"May I say something, Major?" he asked.

"Go ahead."

"I don't understand why we are doing this. There is no need."

"I think there is. Get aboard."

We filed aboard the Stallion, and Ware slammed the hatch. I signaled for Washington to wind it up, and the rotors began to turn. The dark interior, lit only by a single red battle lamp, smelled of sweat and jet fuel. I made my way to the flight deck, sat down next to Washington, and held the folded chart I carried under the map light. "Let's go, Luther," I said, and the Stallion lurched into the air.

We were into Libya before we reached five-hundred-feet altitude. The sky was clear and spangled with stars. I told Washington to hold his present altitude and angle south, staying at first within gliding distance of Tunisian territory and then, as we left behind that tip of Tunisia that hangs like a wedge between Libya and Algeria, to descend to two hundred feet and circle to the east to avoid the Libyan air base at Ghadames.

The last batch of satellite photographs Agron had provided showed no activity at Ghadames. I suspected that the current squabble with the Tunisian government had caused the Libyan Air Force to move whatever had been stationed there north toward Tripoli. Muammar Qaddafi was nothing if not predictable—always assuming one expected the worst. When he quarreled with the Egyptians, he moved his airplanes and armor east.

When it was the Tunisians who annoyed him, he moved his forces northwest. Now, with the Sixth Fleet cruising in force in and out of the Gulf of Sidra, a body of water he claimed as Libyan territory, he had to be in a state of mingled fury and panic. Almost certainly, the bulk of his military strength had raced for the coast.

I went back into the troop compartment and spread the ONC chart on the floor of the aircraft so that all could see it.

"We are flying over the oasis of Baldat Tuatah," I said, pointing to it on the chart. "Note this low range of hills to the southeast. We are going to land there and do a recce along the high ground that overlooks the western part of the Hammadah al Hamra—the northern rim of the sand sea. Point X is about a hundred and fifty miles southeast. I want to know if the Libyans are patrolling the hills. We'll land, because I don't want the chopper spotted. We'll do a foot patrol for an hour. Thirty minutes for the north, thirty for the south. If everything is clear, we'll head straight back. If not, we'll have to see what area they have under surveillance so that we can by-pass it tonight. Questions?"

"Do we fight?" Louis asked.

"Only if we're spotted," I said. I looked across the chart at Agron, flanked by his three silent sabras. "Understood?"

Louis smiled. "Harry would love this, Major. It's straight out of *Freefire Zone.*"

I was grimly amused by the comment. When Louis sat in that Century City screening room watching Redding's impossible heroics, he had been quick with his laughter. But a couple of weeks' association with Redding had made him suspend his disbelief. I guessed it was because in all of us, even the professionals, there existed a hidden wish that war *could* be the way Redding's films portrayed it—glamorous and brave and satisfying: the realm of heroes. But that was only possible in situations in which the director could shout "Cut!" and the dead rose to fight another day.

Agron was watching me, and there was just the ghost of a

smile on his thin lips. Because he had been associated with Redding's world longer than I, perhaps he understood what I was thinking.

I folded the chart, tucked it into my map case, and returned to the flight deck to give Washington his instructions.

It was still very dark when Washington put us down near the crest of some jumbled hills overlooking the edge of the saheer. We spilled out of the chopper and spread a camouflage net over fuselage and rotors.

It was cold. These hills were hardly hills at all—the ridges no more than three hundred feet higher than the saheer to the east—but the wind was stronger here. At midday it would be like a blast from a furnace; in the predawn the wind had a brittle chill.

We set out immediately along the ridge line, seeking a vantage point that would give us a clear view of the expanse of sand stretching out to the east. Washington remained with the Stallion.

I ordered Agron to take the point. I followed him at a distance of twenty to thirty feet. Then came Avram, Elie, and Ariel, with Louis bringing up the rear. I had the sabras behind me, but Louis was behind *them,* his Uzi charged and ready. It was a foul way to conduct a patrol, but this was as much a test as it was a scouting mission. As I walked along the rocky ground in the darkness, I had a tight feeling at the base of my spine. If Agron's young men chose to kill me, they could cut my body in half in less time than it would take to tell about it. The soldier pays a high price for imagination, and if you have been pierced by metal before, there is memory to contend with.

From time to time Agron would signal a halt, and I would join him to study the terrain below the hills with night glasses. The saheer seemed empty, as lifeless and desolate as the surface of the moon, but there were nomad Bedouins in that wasteland, people whose way of life had not changed in more than a thousand years. They still lived by the laws set down by their prophet in the seventh century. And there were men with the same rigid outlook living in fortresses and palaces in the north, men who had at their disposal most of the terrible weapons of our age. It was a frightening thought.

Somewhere to the southeast, beyond the dark desert horizon, beyond Point X, lay a scientific complex busily creating the material of Armageddon. How, I thought, could the Russians have allowed themselves to be put in such a hazardous position? The answer was politics, of course, and the changing currents of the Cold War. Events interlocked like the links of a chain. If the United States and the USSR had not begun to quarrel after World War II, there would have been no diffusion plant in the Sahara forty years later. There was a kind of madness in the way human beings conducted their affairs.

A hint of light tinted the eastern sky, the false dawn of the deep desert. Agron studied the dunes below the hills. Nothing moved there but sand dust swept by the wind. He said, "We should be out of here by sunup."

"If there are patrols, we have to know the routes and schedules." We would be returning this way tomorrow, and we could have both hostages and casualties with us. If the Libyans were prowling the saheer on foot or in helicopters, we needed to know it.

"There are none," Agron said.

So speaks the spook, I thought. "We will make sure," I said. "Move out."

———

Thirty minutes' march from the Stallion we angled to the south, down the jumbled slope of the low hills. The false dawn faded, and for a time the night grew very dark, too dark even for our night glasses.

We had circled around to within two miles of the waiting Stallion when Agron raised his hand to halt us. He signaled that we should take cover, and we all went to ground. I listened, but the loudest sound was my own steady, heavy heartbeat. Agron summoned me forward with a hand movement. I signed for the others to remain where they were and scrambled along the ground.

Agron pointed to the south. We lay on a small shelf, protected by a rocky outcrop. Below, and some sixty yards away, hidden from the others by a fold of ground, stood a Russian-built utility vehicle resembling a jeep. The hood was up, and two men in uniform were bent over the engine, their shapes outlined by the glow from a flashlight. A two-man desert patrol. But from where?

I tried to recall the features on the chart in my map case. At Baldat Tuatah, over which we had flown earlier, a wadi named Awwal made a narrow cut through the hills. Where the wadi reached into the beginnings of the sand sea there were at least a half-dozen dots marked "Abandoned Camps." These were either places where Bedouins had been and gone, or long disused oil exploration camps. There was water in such places if one knew where to dig for it. A deep *qanat*—an underground aquifer—could often be found in the vicinity of dry wadis. Somewhere nearby there might be a bivouacked unit to which these two soldiers belonged. Since the vehicle was not armored, it was likely that it was only part of a larger force, probably a section or even a platoon with armored personnel carriers.

I looked at my watch. It was 0510 and very soon now the sun would appear like a sliver of fire on the eastern horizon, and the sudden desert dawn would be upon us.

The two soldiers' murmured conversation was carried toward us by the predawn breeze. I signaled for Louis and the sabras to join us. They moved up silently. I could smell the acrid sweat set in their uniforms.

In the growing light I saw the whip antenna on the vehicle. One of the soldiers stepped back and lit a cigarette. His face was pale in the flare of a lighter. They were between us and the Stallion, which lay on the far side of the low hills.

One of the soldiers laughed and punched the other on the arm. They had no idea that there was anyone within miles of them. I raised my glasses and studied them. They were dressed in camouflage fatigues. The smoker handed a canteen to the other, who stepped away from the open engine compartment and drank. He said something that brought more laughter from his companion. They were young.

I said softly, "Russians."

"Shee-it," breathed Louis.

"They are a long way from Barqin," I whispered to Agron. "How do you account for that?"

"I don't," he said.

"I want them alive," I said. "And I don't want them to use that radio."

Agron's dark eyes were veiled. After what seemed a long time he nodded slowly. "Yes," he said.

I sent Louis back along the way we had come and told him to crawl to the ridge line and cover us from there. Avram and Ariel I sent down and to the right. I tapped the silencer on my Uzi, and they attached theirs. The Russians below had abandoned their effort to revive their disabled vehicle. But they made no immediate move to use their radio. Like soldiers in any army they were sloughing off their duty because they were unsupervised, smoking and drinking and stealing some private time. I wondered what they carried in that canteen and guessed that it wasn't water.

"Let's go," I whispered. "Slowly." Flanked by Agron and Elie, I rose to a crouch and moved down the slope. I was within a dozen yards of them when one of the Israelis off on the right made a noise. The Russians stopped chattering and stood for a moment in confusion. Their weapons were in the rear of the vehicle.

I rose to my feet and ran at them, Uzi held level. Agron was slightly behind me, and he shouted something at them in Russian. They were startled and badly frightened. Perhaps they thought one of their officers had found them. One came to attention in a sort of foolish parody of a parade-ground move. Agron opened fire.

236

The Uzi made a whooshing sound. The bullets shattered the windshield of the vehicle, made a clatter as they scored and gouged the steel sides. The two Russians spun away as though they had been snapped from an invisible catapult. Their uniforms shredded. Their blood made a black rain in the dawn light. When the burst ended, there were two piles of rag and wetness on the sand three yards from the shot-up vehicle. Behind me Elie uttered some Hebrew expletive.

I wheeled to face Agron. *"What are you doing, damn you!"*

I could see his face clearly now. It was a tight mask, covered with sweat.

"He reached for a weapon," he said in a tight voice.

Louis and the others appeared and stood looking at the slaughtered Russians and then at Agron and me.

"He went for a weapon," Agron said again.

"He sure as hell didn't make it," Louis said.

I looked at the vehicle. The radio was a shambles.

Agron slowly removed the empty magazine from his Uzi and replaced it with another. In one burst he had fired eight hundred rounds of nine-millimeter steel-jacketed ammunition.

I walked over to the dead soldiers. On their tattered uniforms were the badges of a corporal and a private. And the blue collar tabs of a Spetznaz unit. If this was an example of their best, I thought grimly, the Soviet Army was in trouble. But long duty in an alien land did strange things, even to good soldiers. I picked up the canteen. It had been punctured by several rounds. I wet my fingers with its contents and tasted.

"Vodka?" Avram guessed.

I nodded and dropped the canteen.

Agron spoke to Avram in Hebrew, and the sabra gave a barking laugh and nodded. He took a note pad from his pocket and wrote something on it in Arabic. He offered it to Agron questioningly. Agron said "Yes" in Hebrew and slipped the paper under the twisted windshield wiper.

"What's that?" I asked.

Agron had regained his composure. He said, "It is a message

237

the desert Bedouins often leave with the dead after they have robbed and killed them. From the Koran. 'He looses the thunderbolts, and smites with them whomsoever he will.' If the Soviets find them, they will blame the Bedouins. Perhaps." He shrugged cold-bloodedly. "It is worth a try, all things considered."

"I told you I wanted them alive." It wouldn't have taken much more for me to put a bullet in him.

Agron shrugged again and turned away. All the way back to the Stallion and on the return flight across the border, not another word passed between us.

———————

I called an officers' meeting in the shelter of a camouflaged helicopter at noon. It had some of the characteristics of a court-martial. Agron was included, but Louis had him under guard. He and his sabras had been disarmed.

I let Tinker run the meeting as presiding officer because I was far from open-minded about what had happened. I had the pilots attend and Ware and Sergeant Green.

I said, "We go in at dark. But before we commit I want a judgment from all of you." I looked around the circle of faces. Those who hadn't been on our patrol were discomfited and puzzled. I described the mission in detail with particular emphasis on Agron's slaughter of the two Russian soldiers. "I told Agron I wanted them alive, for questioning. He opened fire without orders."

Agron said again, "They went for their weapons."

Tinker asked Louis, "Is that true, Sergeant?"

Louis looked regretfully at me and said, "I don't know, Colonel. I didn't see it."

Tinker addressed Ariel. "Did you fire?"

"No, I did not." Elie and Avram shook their heads in agreement.

"It was too risky to leave them alive," Agron said. "They were Spetznaz."

"They were *drunk*," I said.

"I'm not so squeamish as you, Major Quary," Agron said. "And they did go for their weapons."

Ware asked, "You were a *refusenik* in Russia?"

Agron nodded curtly.

"What about your family?"

In a flat voice, Agron said, "They are in a gulag. Or dead."

"I have heard," Tinker said, "that the Soviet authorities are hard on the families of *refuseniks,* but I have never heard that they imprison or kill them, Agron."

"When I joined Mossad, the authorities retaliated."

Everyone was silent at that. They looked at me. To them it seemed natural that this man who had had his family brutalized should hate Russians enough to kill when he had the chance.

"What do you want to do, Quary?" Tinker asked. It was plain to see I would not have support if I chose to take serious action against Agron. They were disturbed by his action and his disobedience of orders in the field, but their Western sense of fair play was now involved. I was ready to leave him behind when we started for Point X, but my officers wouldn't approve. I needed their unquestioning trust. There was no time for discussion, philosophical or otherwise.

"Give him his weapon, Sergeant Brown," I said. "This meeting is over."

———

Louis came to me twenty minutes later. "I know you don't like the guy, Casey, but we need him and his Uzi and his guys."

"Louis," I said, "we're on a string. I don't know who is on the other end. That son of a bitch does. I'd like to beat it out of him."

"I'll watch him, Casey."

"Yes. Do," I said.

"Something else is bothering you," Louis said. "Do you want to talk about it?"

I didn't, but I felt he had a right to know. I reminded him of what I had discovered about Ann Maclean. "Everybody is using us, Louis. I should have told Redding."

Louis got a strange, guarded expression on his face. "No, I don't think so, Casey. Harry needs for this to be something of his own. It means everything to him."

"I didn't know he confided in you, Sergeant."

"I think he would rather have confided in you, but he felt you wouldn't understand."

It was a strange thing for Louis to say, but I didn't want to pursue it. I was still caught in my anger at Agron's murder of the Russians. His action had obviously convinced the others of his pathological hatred of his former countrymen, but it didn't ring the same for me. And he was here—my problem—whereas Redding was back at Kasserine, on the other side of that impalpable wall that separates the real from the make-believe.

———

At about 1500 that last day, a Tunisian Air Force Mirage flew over us, very high. From the radio broadcasts we were picking up we heard that Tunisia had gone on alert because of the mounting tension in the Gulf of Sidra. The Sixth Fleet was moving at will across and beyond Qaddafi's Line of Death, intent on provoking him. Radio Tripoli was claiming several American jets shot down, but none of the foreign broadcasts confirmed the claims. The Libyans broadcast a communiqué from Qaddafi's headquarters now and then, followed by long minutes of martial music.

On the military frequencies, there was nothing we could get so far south. Agron used one of the radios to try to pick up Russian transmissions from Barqin, but either he failed to find the proper frequencies or the Soviets were lying low. Their presence in the north was common knowledge. They had advisers in great numbers with the Libyan Army, and there had been Soviet naval units in the harbor at Tripoli. But both the British and French radio reports that we picked up noted that the Soviet warships had quietly departed and the regular Soviet military advisers had absented themselves conveniently from areas likely to come under attack. Tinker voiced what most of us were thinking: The Soviets had had previous knowledge of the Sixth Fleet's intentions and wanted nothing whatever to do with any fighting to protect Libya.

It made me wonder what the Politburo intended to do about the inconvenient installation at Barqin. But that wasn't my problem. Point X and my troops were.

I was tempted to set up the SCR-1220 and communicate with General Stanley. But my last message from him didn't encourage another contact until we were actually inside Libya. At this point I didn't even want to argue about a recall order. I was only a few hundred miles from Ambassador Lyman and the other hostages. I intended to get them out.

In late afternoon Louis reported that One Commando was ready for action, Two and Three would be within a half hour. Sunset was shortly after six, and it would be full dark one hour after that. Seven-thirty—1930 hours—was our H-hour.

The camp was silent. The men had been fed earlier and had retired to their shelters. Throughout the day, Tinker had had troopers, with the cameras, move around the site as though setting up or shooting, on the off chance that a Soviet satellite might be overhead. Now that activity had come to a halt, and there was a tense stillness in the air.

At 1900 Louis said, "Here we go again, Major. Watch yourself, okay?"

I looked into the face of the closest friend I had. Louis Brown was a handsome man, big, robust, alive. He'd said it all—"Here we go again"—and I smiled broadly at my cherished comrade

241

in arms. "And you take care, too, Sergeant. Don't be too big a hero."

"Casey," Louis said, with a strange half-smile, "this is really a job for Delta Force, isn't it?"

"Of course it is, Louis."

"But instead of being in Delta, we're in the movies."

"We are deniable, Louis," I said. "It's that kind of world."

Louis looked at me intently. "That kind of gives Harry some rights, doesn't it? I mean, shit, he could end up in Leavenworth."

"Improbable. No one tried to arrest Perot for getting his people out of Teheran. Of course, that was a *successful* operation."

"And no one got shot up or killed. We've already greased two Russian kids."

The story of the morning's patrol and the meeting afterward had gone the rounds of all the men in R Force. It had heightened the tension, but no one had voiced any criticism of what had been done. I wondered what Ann and Redding would say when they heard about it. Perhaps, in Redding's case at least, it would make him understand that what he had set in motion was not a film script.

But when I said that to Louis he looked at me pointedly and said, "Casey, I think you're misjudging Harry. This isn't make-believe to him."

Ware appeared at the entrance to the tent. He was already rigged out for combat, in dark flash paint and Afrika Korps black combat smock, which Strachan had had made for us in Italy. His harness supported an arsenal of lethal gear Rommel's men had never known: concussion grenades, spare Uzi magazines, night glasses, and his own Royal Marines pigsticker, a nasty serrated black blade a foot long with a guard that incorporated steel knuckles. In a fight, you'd want this man on your side. His face was set in rigid lines, all trace of his natural clownishness gone.

I had a quick memory of his wife, Jean, in their flat in Knightsbridge, drinking too much and happy that I was taking Bertie off her hands for a time. Had she ever seen *this* Albert Ware?

Had the other salesmen at the Rover dealer's any idea of what sort of being prowled their London showroom? Not likely.

He said formally, "Sir. Two Commando is ready for your inspection."

"I'll be there right away, Captain Ware," I said.

He stamped to attention and departed.

I said to Louis, "I'll inspect One Commando now."

"I've already done that, Major. They are all set to go. Colonel Tinker has Three Commando ready to load up."

I unzipped the canvas duffel containing my combat gear, and Louis did the same with his. The sun was setting, and darkness was descending. As Louis and I had done many times, in many places, we dressed for action.

27

The sky had turned to a purple darkness, and the first stars were emerging when the entire force gathered at the helicopters. The surrounding hills had lost their dun coloring and lay like the bodies of dead prehistoric animals all around us. The temporary camp was abandoned. We had brought almost no unneeded gear with us from Kasserine, only the field kitchen and the tents. They would be left behind for the wandering Bedouins to find. We showed no observable lights of any kind, nor would we until the operation was over.

"Gather around," I said. The men formed a deep circle around me.

"I have gone over our plan with your officers," I said, "and they have explained it to you. Now I want to say something to you that's personal." I looked around the circle of faces. The flash paint and the dark battle smocks made each man look like every other one. For all of that, I was acutely aware that these seemingly anonymous soldiers I was about to commit to battle were individual human beings, who could bleed and die. I knew something else. From this time onward, what mattered was the mission. That was why the military texts seldom spoke of people and almost always spoke of "effectives" when the subject was soldiers in the field.

"We will not be returning here," I said. "From Point X we will fly directly to Sfax and deliver the hostages to *Kaliph*. Most of you will go with them to Spain. The rest of us will return the Stallions to Kasserine and rejoin the Eagle Films company." This was a part of the plan I had not shared with anyone but Strachan. Our security had to hold until the Ambassador and his people were safely out of the Arab world. Even Tunisia was suspect. Doubly so at this moment, when the U.S. Navy was bruising Arab sensibilities in the north.

I felt I should say something about that. "You have all been listening to the radio reports about what is happening in the Gulf of Sidra. We have good reason to think that a high percentage of Libyan forces has been rushed up there to meet the threat. I can't promise you that we won't run into any Libyan reinforcements, but I can tell you it is likely the nervous Colonel is putting as many soldiers as he can manage between himself and the Sixth Fleet. That can't help but make our job somewhat easier." I avoided completely any speculation as to whether the coincidence of our operation's so exactly matching the timing of the navy's sail through the Gulf of Sidra was luck or design. If they wanted to think everything had been planned to work out this way, I wasn't going to say it wasn't so. It could boost morale to know that there were three U.S. aircraft carriers and their battlegroups sailing off the Libyan coast.

"You are all professionals," I said. "I trust you to do your jobs." I heard myself growing a bit heavy-handed. A surfeit of inspirational speechmaking is something I could always do without. "If we do our job just right, Harry Redding will probably give each of us a lifetime pass to any Eagle movie. Think about that when we reach Point X."

They grinned at me like kids. The men in R Force were hardly that, but every one of them was feeling the adrenaline that comes before the start of combat.

"All right," I said. "Let's go."

The helicopters came to life, engines whining, rotors stirring up a storm of dust and sand. The troop-compartment ramps dropped. I stood in the darkness watching the shadowy lines of men filing aboard. I saw the camera carried aboard. I thought grimly that the film might make interesting viewing for Muammar Qaddafi and his Soviet advisers if our assault failed.

I looked at my watch. We were starting exactly on time. The first objective, which I had assigned to myself and the men of One Commando, was the nearest surface-to-air missile battery. It had to be destroyed so there would be a gap in the defenses through which we could withdraw.

Ware, the last to go aboard Penny's Stallion, stood on the lowered ramp and gave me a salute. I returned it.

Louis came to me and said, "We are ready, Major."

I took one last look around the dark campsite. Canvas tent flaps snapped in the wind from the helicopters' huge rotors. That was all that remained to give evidence that we had ever been here.

Evidence. I said to Louis: "Tell the cameraman that if things go bad he's got to destroy the film."

I settled the night battle smock more comfortably on my shoulders and went up the ramp into the crowded interior of Washington's helicopter. He closed the ramp, and for a few moments we were in nearly total blackness. As my eyes became accustomed to the dim glow of light from the flight deck, I could make out the faces around me.

The Sergeant fed power to the engines, and we lurched into the air and headed for Libya.

─────────

We had been airborne for five minutes when the red battle lights in the troop compartment came on. Washington said over the intercom, "We've crossed the border, Major Quary. I'm going down now." It was my cue to come to the flight deck and act as observer.

I picked my way over the seated men. There was little chatter. Each man seemed locked into his own thoughts. I'd seen this momentary isolation many times. I had shared it. In Vietnam, when we were heading for a hot landing zone, no one made the terse, quotable remarks that were the stock in trade of screenwriters. A few men were smoking, others sat with their heads against the vibrating bulkhead, their eyes closed, fixed on inner visions.

On the flight deck, I slipped into the copilot's seat. Washington, in his image-intensifier helmet, was now a man from outer space. The altimeter hovered around two thousand feet. That put us less than a hundred feet above the low hills.

The air war chart was clipped to Washington's thigh, illuminated by a tiny red light on a flexible stalk. He had drawn a circle around the position of the westernmost missile battery and a course line, with the headings in and out marked on it.

I peered out the side window, looking for our second Stallion. The light had gone completely from the sky, and there was nothing visible beneath us. But presently, as my eyes adjusted, I could see the blue glow of jet exhaust. Penny was keeping station on our left.

"Where are we?" I asked.

Washington tapped one of the crosshatchings on the course line. We had already covered almost a third of the distance between the border and the missile site. I looked up and forward through the Plexiglas panes of the hull above the flight deck. It was purely reflex. If we were going to be intercepted by a MiG or a Sukhoi, we would never see our attacker. It was even unlikely we would see the heat-seeker missile that could kill us.

"How are the troops riding, Major?"

"No sweat, Marine," I said.

Luther's teeth showed in a smile under the mask of the helmet. "This is better than dusting for Medflies in the San Joaquin Valley, Major."

"You should never have left the Corps, Luther," I said.

"Yeah, right. It was a mistake. But I had twenty in, and I figured I'd try the world for a while. I think maybe I'll re-up if we come through this."

I thought about the army and how much it had meant to me. General Stanley hinted that I, too, might be taken back if all went well. But this was no time to make plans for the future.

"We are past the hills, Major. I'm going lower," Washington said. "I'm going to hide this fat mother in the dunes." He reached overhead and flicked a panel switch once, signaling Penny to drop into line astern. A single blip of the navigation lights entailed less risk than a radio transmission. We were now within sixty miles of the battery, ninety from Point X. The plan was to land two miles short of the battery and hold the Stallions there while One Commando took out the Libyans manning the missiles and deactivated them. Once that was accomplished, I would call the choppers up and reload my men. Then we would fly directly to Point X and perform what the textbooks so neatly refer to as a "vertical envelopment."

I hoped that the defenders were inexperienced in formal warfare and would, for a few critical moments, mistake our Stallions for Soviet-supplied Libyan helicopters. By the time they realized we were not the transport for whom they had built the pads, we should be able to silence the interior guards, collect our people, and be on the way out. I was relying heavily on the laxness and overconfidence brought on by an isolated and secret location, and by Arab reluctance to face a pitched battle with a heavily armed force.

But first must come the missile battery. We couldn't penetrate any deeper into the saheer without making the air safe for our lumbering Stallions. And the battery must simply drop off the communications net without sending a warning that it was under attack. That meant stealth.

"Ten minutes, Major," Washington said, not taking his electronically enhanced eyes from the dark terrain ahead.

I left the flight deck and returned to the troop compartment, where I killed all but a single red battle lamp. "We'll be down in ten minutes," I said. "I want my team ready at the ramp. The rest of you spread out and establish a perimeter. If anything out there comes within five hundred yards of the choppers, kill it. Use the silenced weapons first. If they don't handle the problem, go for broke. All right, missile team to the rear of the compartment."

Louis joined me, carrying one of the crossbows he had bought in Fayetteville. There were five others in the team I had selected to attack the battery with me. All carried silenced Uzis.

The man carrying the shoulder-held minicam had backed onto the step between the troop compartment and the flight deck. I could see from the red light on the camera that he was shooting, using infrared film. The presence of the camera brought back the world of make-believe I thought I had left behind at Kasserine.

Washington said through the interphone, "Four minutes, Major." I feel the Stallion's altitude changing as he hopped a dune and searched for a suitable trough into which we could settle.

"Two minutes." The sound of the engines changed, and the nose pitched up as Washington prepared to put us down.

The red light on the minicam went out, and the man holding it pushed by to stand with the others ready at the ramp. He was shorter than I by a great deal. As he passed me, I caught his arm and turned him so that I could see his face.

Three things happened all at once. The Stallion's undercarriage touched the sand. The ramp dropped, opening onto Stygian darkness. And I recognized Harry Redding.

In the next moment the troops were charging out of the helicopter, Redding with them.

Fifty yards from us I could hear, and almost see, Penny's Stallion landing. The downdraft from his rotors was throwing up a sandstorm, and I covered my nose and mouth with my scarf and signaled my team to assemble on me.

In all the time I had served with Louis, I had never been so angry. I caught him by his harness and rasped, "*What the hell*

249

are you playing at?" I never doubted for one moment that it had been he who had connived with Redding to bring him along. It was such a stupid, dangerous thing to do, and so out of character for an experienced soldier that my fury almost choked me. What made it even worse was that from this moment on we were on a split-second schedule. There was no time for recriminations and problems of discipline.

Louis said, "Damn it, Major, it's *his war.*"

"Put him back in the helicopter. Tell Washington to see to it that he *stays* there. That's a direct order, soldier!"

It was all I could think of to do. The very thought of a civilian like Redding stumbling about in a night action against positions of unknown strength made my stomach churn. And it was not only that. Worse was the realization that Louis Brown, a man I had soldiered with for years and to whom I owed my life, could be so reckless and irresponsible for the sake of a celluloid hero.

Louis vanished in the darkness. I collected the other members of the assault team and checked the compass course to the missile battery.

Louis reappeared with Redding. I had to resist the impulse to hit them both. The latter was fully done up in our hybrid German battle gear. His face was spattered with flash paint. His eyes were wide. And I wanted to hammer him into the sand.

I said, "If I could send you back, I'd do it. But listen to me. I want you inside that chopper *now,* and I want you to stay there. Is that understood?"

"Casey," he said breathlessly, "it wasn't Louis's fault. It was my doing. Only mine."

"Well, this is *my* doing. Get your ass aboard that chopper."

"Casey, listen. I'll stay out of the way. I can shoot if I have to—"

I screamed to keep from hitting him. *"This isn't the goddamn movies, Redding.* Get him out of my sight, Sergeant, and let's move out!"

Redding said quietly, "All right, Casey," and walked back to the ramp of the Stallion with Louis.

28

Slogging through deep sand in darkness for two miles is not a task for a man in a fury. I had the team spread out behind me, and we moved across the steep dunes with reasonable speed despite the sand sliding away under our feet as we climbed from trough to crest.

Our night vision was by now as good as it was going to get. Each time we reached the top of a dune I signaled a short stop while I searched the terrain ahead with my night glasses. We had one Starlight scope with us. Louis had fitted it to the Barnett crossbow he carried. With the other members of the group lying just behind the crest of each succeeding dune, I used it from time to time to check the darkness ahead.

It took us forty minutes to come within two hundred yards of the battery. It was well within the time I had allotted myself for this mission.

The Libyans had put the battery on the slope of a wadi, and the nasty-looking snouts of the SAMs in their launcher were dark against the paler sand. From what I could see with the Starlight scope, they had stacked a double row of sandbags around the launcher, but there was no redoubt around the radar trailer or the parked Russian vehicle used to move the battery and its auxiliary gear.

The dish on the radar was stationary. The missile crew was not in any state of alert. I could see two sentries limned against the slope of the wadi. They were smoking and talking in low voices that carried clearly across the dunes.

The normal crew for a SAM unit is a dozen men, but if there were that many at this site, most of them had to be inside the radar trailer. It was too early in the evening to expect them to be asleep. Their blackout discipline was poor. Light leaked from the open door.

I gave a hand signal, and we moved forward on our bellies. When we were within sixty yards of the battery, I signaled a halt. Louis lay near me just under the crest of the last dune before the wadi. I surrendered the crossbow to him. He was the special-weapons artist, not I. I held up two fingers and pointed left. Then I raised my silenced Uzi, set it on semiautomatic, and sighted on the door of the radar trailer.

Louis raised the Barnett and sighted through the Starlight scope. The laminated-steel bow made a soft musical sound. I heard the short arrow strike its target with a thunk. The remaining sentry gave a puzzled yell and stood. Louis had reloaded, and he aimed and shot quickly. The second sentry went down without a sound.

I leaped to my feet and signaled again. Five shadows rushed past us. I followed at a run, weapon leveled.

A figure appeared in the doorway of the trailer, outlined against the light. He shouted a perplexed question, received no reply. I fired a three-round burst that was almost soundless, and he fell.

My desert boots pounded on the sand. I felt the change under my feet as the footing grew firmer when I reached the wadi.

One of our people, quicker than the rest of us, leaped the low line of sandbags around the launcher. He fired at the trailer, and I could hear the bullets striking. From inside there was a shriek of mingled pain and alarm.

The others of the team spread out, searching for unseen Libyans. They found none. Then I was over the sandbags, a concussion grenade in my hand. I pulled the pin, released the lever, and threw it inside the trailer. It was a four-second fuse, and the interior of the trailer lit up almost immediately. The explosion was confined, but it blew off the door and sent it spinning into the darkness.

I looked inside. Papers were scattered everywhere, burning. The radar and communications gear was in ruins. There were seven mangled dead Libyan soldiers sprawled out. One, who might have thought of himself as a fedayeen, had tried to smother the grenade with his body. He had only partially made it. He was headless. The trailer's interior stank of cordite, blood, and feces.

I found an undamaged fire extinguisher and sprayed CO_2 on the fire. I didn't need a blaze that could be seen from fifty miles away.

Outside the trailer, my people were deactivating the missiles, smashing the guidance systems and the heat-seeking warheads. Louis appeared and asked formally, "Shall we disable the vehicle or use it, Major?"

It was an unnecessary question. Our plan called for a short click on our radio frequency to bring in the Stallions. But it was Louis's way of probing through the anger he knew I was feeling about his connivance with Redding.

"Just break it," I said. "And let me have the radio now."

Louis handed over the transceiver. We stood for a moment, filled with unexpended adrenaline. The short, sharp engagement was like many others in which we had participated. Though the Libyan soldiers had not been able to get off a shot, there had been the old familiar—and addictive—tang of danger. It was a thing Louis and I had shared many times. It reminded us of who we were.

"Louis, you shouldn't have done it."

"It meant so much to him, Casey."

"Well, he's in it now," I said. "But I can't have you babysitting him. There's too much to do." Louis understood this. He was my most valuable soldier. And I needed him to watch my back. "He stays in the helicopter when we hit the LZ," I said. "You see to it he understands that."

"I'll tell him, Major."

I looked around the missile site. Smoke was still coming from the interior of the radar trailer. I was as certain as one could be under the circumstances that the Libyans had not managed to get off an alarm. Our attack had been swift and silent. I signaled for Louis to join the other team members at their work of destruction.

I held the radio to my ear and listened. There was no signal from the Stallions, and that was right. None was expected. I clicked the transmitter button once, then three times. In return I received two clicks, a pause, and then one.

Ten minutes later, the first Stallion was landing next to the ruined missile battery.

Now was the time to make contact with General Stanley. The force was fully committed. There could be no recall. But I wanted him to know this so that he could tell our government that while the Sixth Fleet was baiting Qaddafi, there was an American-led team far to the south doing what needed to be done to recover the hostages.

I hated to take the time. With the Stallions on the ground and the force concentrated around the wreckage of the missile battery, we were terribly vulnerable. But it had to be done.

I set up the SCR-1220 and typed our QUARY TO STANLEY BREAK HAVE DESTROYED ONE PERIMETER MISSILE BATTERY BREAK WILL ASSAULT PRIMARY OBJECTIVE IMMEDIATELY BREAK BREAK ENDS.

The computer encrypted the message into microbursts and sent it on its way across the world. Almost immediately there was a response. The message spelled itself out on the dimly lighted liquid crystal display: WEEDEN TO QUARY BREAK STANLEY DIED TWO HOURS AGO BREAK.

I took that like a shot under the heart. I knew that John Stanley

254

was a desperately sick man, and yet I had said to him, in effect, "You have involved me in this scheme, now I want you involved, too. Right at the center." The old man had wanted it. I had no doubt about that. But it had killed him. It was even possible that my last transmission, from Kasserine—which had told him that I had the bit in my teeth and would do as I chose rather than as he or my government ordered—might have been the final strain his damaged heart could not handle.

The satellite-link computer began printing again: KOPINSKY FAMILY UNKNOWN TO REFUSENIK ORGANIZATIONS BREAK USE EX-TREME REPEAT EXTREME CAUTION AGRON BREAK LIBYA ATTACKED ELEMENTS SIXTH FLEET BREAK FLAGSHIP AIR HAS SUNK TWO LIBYAN PATROL BOATS BREAK ALSO DESTROYED TWO COASTAL MISSILE BAT-TERIES BREAK TRIPOLI STUNNED RAVING BREAK STANLEY LEFT NOTE QUOTE CASEY REMEMBER FARRAGUT MOBILE BAY UNQUOTE BREAK BREAK ENDS.

I had more of the pieces, but the damned puzzle was getting larger, thornier, and more intricate with every passing minute. At least I knew General Stanley's personal view. Admiral David Farragut's famous rallying cry was "Damn the torpe-does! . . . go ahead!" I took a deep breath, and my finger moved on the computer keyboard: QUARY TO WEEDEN BREAK UNDER-STOOD BREAK BREAK ENDS OUT OUT.

Five minutes later our helicopters were in line astern at fifty feet above the desert floor. I sat beside Washington, my Uzi across my knees. I had said nothing to anyone about the information from Weeden, back in San Francisco. It struck me that the faceless captain, to whom I had paid no attention while visiting General Stanley, was unlikely to be the National Guards-man I had assumed him to be. Defense Intelligence Agency was more likely his unit. Spooks again, I thought bitterly. Our operation was stiff with them.

"How did it go, Major?" Luther Washington asked. He had

not had a chance to look over the shambles we had made of the desert missile battery.

"Piece of cake," I replied.

Agron appeared, crouching beside the pilot's chair. I half turned to look at him. So there was no dissident Kopinsky family in a gulag or anywhere else. Was that what Ann expected to learn from the defector in Canada? That left only two options: either Agron was simply an Israeli agent or he worked for the Soviets. There were no other choices.

He said, "Redding is aboard."

I had almost forgotten about that grandstand play. Agron thought he was telling me something I didn't know. In the dim light from the Stallion's instruments, his deep-set eyes were even more opaque, more unreadable. "If he is captured, it will be a disaster," he said. "He would be worth more than the hostages they have now."

It was a strange commentary on the nature of our time that what he said was exactly right. A world-class movie star on a military mission falling into the hands of terrorists would create far more turmoil than kidnapped diplomats. But I didn't like the way Agron said it—as though he had an obvious solution to the problem.

"Nothing is going to happen to Redding," I said. "He isn't going to be captured. And he isn't going to be shot in the back, either."

Agron gave me a slow, feral smile. "What a low opinion of me you have, Major Quary."

I gripped his battle smock in one hand and held it. "You're so right. I'll be watching you. Every damned minute."

"I expect that," he said, and waited calmly for me to release him. The man had the personality of a thin steel wire: cold, resilient, with a harsh cutting edge. I had felt it when I saw him sitting on Redding's terrace overlooking the Pacific, and my dislike had grown steadily since that day. And every step of the way we had had to rely on his information. I had the angry feeling that he was the only man in the entire force who really knew what was happening.

I could see Elie, crouched in the forward section of the troop compartment, watching us.

I let go of Agron and pushed past him, past Elie, and made my way to the rear of the aircraft where Redding sat with Louis.

I studied his painted face, trying to read what I saw there. Fear, yes. Ann had told me that he was a fearful man. Yet here he was. Was he looking for a way to challenge and conquer his personal demons?

"Casey," he said, "I promise I won't do anything to endanger the mission."

"You don't know what would endanger the mission," I said. I glanced about the red-lighted interior of the Stallion. The men were watching us with interest. By now, I was sure, they all knew that the cameraman with us was Harry Redding. He was a false note. He added a touch of unreality. Given who he was and what he was, he endangered the mission simply by being here.

"General Stanley is dead," I said. "He died a couple of hours ago. Captain Weeden is in charge at Letterman." I ignored the shock on Redding's face, but I realized that he had been counting on Stanley in almost the same way I had. The General had given our assault on Point X a kind of legitimacy. We were on our own now. I looked at Louis. "Agron may be a double agent for the KGB. Stand by to disarm him," I said. "If he resists, kill him."

Redding's face showed shock again. I thought savagely, You want to know what it's like, Redding? Then pay attention. It gets very bloody sometimes.

I turned and made my way back toward the flight deck. One of the troopers, an ex–Green Beret named Muller, stopped me and said, "That's Redding, isn't it, sir?"

"Think of him as an observer, soldier," I said, keeping it light, "just along for the ride. He has a right to see how we're spending his money."

I was rewarded by a smile, and the knowledge that the word would get around that I'd intended him to be here all along.

But when I reached the forward bulkhead I felt a touch on my shoulder. It was Louis, who had followed me.

257

He said, "Shall I take him now?" He meant Agron. It was typical of Louis that he required no second order, no confirmation. In this environment, he was a killing machine.

"Not yet. I don't want a fire fight inside the chopper." I looked across the troop compartment at Agron, now sitting on the deck with his silenced Uzi across his thighs. He was watching me speculatively. "I'll tell you when," I said.

Louis nodded and sat down on the deck, watching Agron in exactly the way Agron was watching me.

I climbed back to the flight deck and sat down in the copilot's seat. Washington turned and tapped a headset hanging from the control console. I put it on and heard his drawling voice. "We are getting a transmission from Kasserine," he said. "It's in the clear. You'd better hear it, Major." He switched over to the command net, and suddenly I heard a familiar voice.

"—an announcement from Jerusalem. I will say it again. Casey, hear this. There has been an announcement from Jerusalem. They have released transcripts of all the negotiations. With Amal, with Syria, with Libya. Israel has disclosed the kidnappers' demands and has rejected them. Can you hear me, Casey? God, I hope you are getting this." Then Ann went through the whole thing again. "Please turn back. Please turn back. I've had word from Canada, and we can't find Harry. Listen to me, Casey. Canada's guest says the man we talked about is one of theirs. Did you get that, Casey? *One of theirs.* Turn back. Please turn back—"

I sat there with an acid taste in my mouth.

"Five minutes, Major," Washington said. He had heard all of the Kasserine transmission, of course. "Go or no-go right now, sir."

So it was all coming into the open, just as Ann had warned me it would. Israel had refused absolutely to consider dismantling the plant at Dimona. There had never been any real doubt about that, but now it was public knowledge. And she was also trying to warn me about Agron. Within five minutes—less, now—of Point X.

"Major?"

"We go in," I said. "Redding is with us. I want you to see to it that he stays in the aircraft." Then I hesitated, but only for a moment, before deciding. I said, "Gershon Agron is KGB."

Washington's expression was hidden by the grotesque helmet he wore. But I could imagine it. Any soldier has to be shocked when he recognizes frantic improvisation, the thin edge of the wedge of disaster.

I went back into the troop compartment, signaled to Louis to cover me. When I spoke to Agron, I had the muzzle of my Uzi level with his midriff.

"Drop your weapon," I said. *Do it now.*"

Redding started to speak, but Louis silenced him swiftly, though his eyes never left Agron and me.

Agron took the strap of his Uzi from his shoulder. Very slowly, very carefully. "So you found out. What a pity."

The others, watching, didn't know what was happening or what our conversation meant.

Elie made a small movement, and Louis covered him instantly. Protecting me in action was something he had done for so long that it was second nature to him.

I said to Elie, "He's KGB. A double agent, soldier. Won't Mossad be proud?"

Elie, a Saiyeret commando, must be accustomed to dealing with Arab terrorists inside Israel. But this had to be something different for him. How quickly he decided to believe me would govern whether or not he would live. There was no time for long discussions.

Washington's voice came over the intercom system, and the red light over the raised ramp began to flash. "Two minutes, Major! We're getting some small-arms fire!"

We were losing the element of surprise. Not completely, but losing it. Someone on the ground had identified the Stallions as unfriendlies.

I scooped up Agron's Uzi and handed it to Elie. "He stays right here. See to it, soldier."

Agron put his hands on top of his head and looked at me calmly. "It's too late, Quary. Believe me. It is too late."

"Stand in the door!" the intercom ordered.

There was a snapping sound, and the troops hunched instinctively. A round had pierced the fuselage, but no one was hit.

There wasn't time for anything more, because the Stallion touched down hard and the ramp dropped. To Elie I repeated, "*He stays here,*" and to Redding, "Stay with Washington," then I was down the ramp and into the Point X compound.

As I went I had one last look at Redding's face. It was frozen into an expression of shock, fear, disbelief, and exaltation: the expression of any soldier hearing, for the first time, the sound of guns.

————

There was light in the compound. It came from one of the buildings fifty yards away. Dark figures in combat fatigues were pouring out of the building, and they were tumbling into the sand as they were met with concentrated fire. Penny's Stallion was down, the ramp falling. Troops poured out and scattered, firing as they ran. Two Commando had the mission of silencing the Libyans' communications, and the men moved swiftly toward the building we had decided contained the radios.

Although we hadn't achieved complete surprise—they had heard the Stallions approaching—they had had no time to prepare a proper reception for us. I had, for no more than a moment, wondered what Agron meant when he said it was too late. Our attack was succeeding, and that was enough for me.

Followed by a team of six troopers from One Commando, I ran across the open compound toward the largest building—the one we thought sheltered the hostages.

Tinker had been given the job of setting up a protective perimeter around the choppers and destroying anything or anyone that threatened them. They were huge and vulnerable, squatting like grounded birds in the compound.

260

There had been no way to tell Tinker or Ware about Agron, or about Redding, for that matter, and I felt the risk deeply. But the first priority was locating the hostages from the Beirut embassy and getting them aboard the aircraft. I led my people through the cordon at a run. The air crackled with gunfire: the flat, snapping noise of Kalashnikovs and the strange sound the Uzis made, as though a giant deck of cards was being riffled by an enormous gambler. There were shouts and cries of pain, curses and shouted orders.

I crashed through the door into the galvanized-iron building shouting: *"Americans down flat! Stay down!"*

There were pressure lamps burning inside. A figure in mottled battle dress was struggling to charge a Kalashnikov. I shot at him, and he went sprawling, spraying dark blood. A man in grimy white shirt started to rise from the floor, and I whirled, Uzi ready, and stopped myself just in time. *"Down! Stay down!"*

My troopers fired across the floor as more figures burst in from a side entrance. They, too, wore the mottled fatigues Arab militiamen affected. The massed fire cut them down, made a sieve of the tin wall, and shattered a smeared window.

I slung my weapon and shouted, "Lyman! Ambassador Lyman!"

One of the prone figures on the earth floor waved a hand. "Here. Here—"

Outside, in the compound, the sound of firing slackened. But farther off, on the perimeter, a fierce fire fight was going on. And to the rear of the building, something had begun to burn. I heard the thump of concussion grenades then silence. Someone—it sounded like Ware—shouted for his men to "Cease fire! Cease bloody fire!"

"Ambassador! Get everyone up and ready to move out," I shouted.

A bearded man tottered to his feet. Others began to stand. "Look out!" I don't know which of them yelled it, but a uniformed figure stood with them. The figure had a face with a drooping mustache, dark cheeks framed in curly black hair, and wild, hate-filled eyes. He leveled his AK-47, not at us, but at the hostages. He took the time to scream out a battle cry, "*Hez-bolllllaah!*" That was his fatal error. Or perhaps he had deliberately drawn attention to himself, assuring his own martyrdom. One of my men blew him literally to pieces with a three-second burst.

The hostages immediately dropped to the ground again and had to be coaxed to rise. So far, none of them had been hit. If one was looking for miracles, that was surely one. Perhaps Allah really was the Merciful, the Compassionate.

I caught the Ambassador by an arm and shouted in his ear, "Are all your people here?"

"No. They took two out this afternoon. Lenard and Darrow. Just this afternoon—" He seemed confused, and I couldn't fault him for that. He was trying to get himself under control. He asked, "Are you Delta Force?"

"Something like that. Where did they take them?" I asked.

"To the headquarters building, I think."

"The tin shed across the compound?"

"Yes."

I thought about the way our fire teams had shredded the metal walls of that shed and cursed under my breath. I hoped we hadn't done the same thing to two American hostages.

"I don't know why they did that," the Ambassador said. "It's been months. They were treating us well—" He had been a prisoner long enough to begin to identify with his tormentors. It was a common reaction among captives, but it grated on my soul to hear him. "At least, they hadn't been beating us. Not for a while. I don't understand what changed today. Maybe they knew you were coming."

"If they had known we were coming, you would be dead," I said. I selected three of the men who had come into the shed with me and ordered them to move the hostages out and into Penny's helicopter on the double. "The rest of you come with me," I called, and headed out and across the compound toward the building beyond the grounded helicopters.

As we ran through Tinker's perimeter, I shouted to him that

the hostages were coming out and to hold his fire. Then we were through and running at the shot-up headquarters building.

There was a fresh burst of gunfire somewhere behind the large building that had held the hostages. Louis had taken twenty men from One Commando in a sweep around that perimeter to meet any attackers coming out of the bunkers that had been dug in the sand a couple of hundred yards from the camp center. What we couldn't risk was the enemy swinging their anti-tank weapons around so that they could have the helicopters under fire.

I heard grenades exploding and the rushing sound of Uzis. The return fire sounded light and disorganized. I thought of Louis and murmured a prayer. He had been in so many fire-fights. Each time the odds lengthened.

I put that out of my mind and charged what was left of the headquarters building. Somewhere I heard high-pitched scream-ing and that ululating noise Arab women make when they are terrified or happy or simply lost. The fighting had spilled over into the Bedouin camp. I thought about the children and hoped for their safety.

Suddenly, flames rose from the direction of the camp, turning the scene into a firelit hell as, followed by my fire team, I reached the shot-up building. Behind us something moved, and one of my people opened fire. A spotted animal, a goat or a dog, exploded into a smear of blood and entrails. "Christ!" the trooper said.

I kicked open the door and slammed my back against the wall, but there was no gunfire from inside. One of my team shone a light inside. The place had been reduced to kindling by bullets. Two men in fatigues lay on the floor, bloody and dead. They had parts missing.

In the distance the firing slackened, started again. The Libyans were fighting, but they couldn't win now. Not unless they could destroy our helicopters, and Tinker was not likely to allow that.

I kicked open a second door and burst through. This room had not been so badly torn to pieces, though there were holes in the walls here, too. On the floor lay a fancy Sony video camera. Whoever had been using it had dropped it, probably at first sounds of shooting.

Lying on his side, still bound with wire to an overturned chair, lay one of Lyman's people, a middle-aged man. The side of his head was missing. He had been shot at close range with a heavy-caliber pistol or rifle, and the exit wound took half his skull and a third of his face. Around his neck was wired a crude sign lettered in English: *Death to America! Death to Spies of the Great Satan!*

I felt my stomach churn. Not at the blood and brains on the dirt floor, but at the sure realization that the murder had been videotaped and that the tape was undoubtedly still in the discarded camera. That was what we had come to: featured players in a kind of Grand Guignol, a theater of the mad.

"Get the camera," I ordered, "and cut him loose. We are taking him home."

It was then we heard a thumping. Instantly the Uzis pointed at the source, a closed narrow door.

"Hold fire," I said, and pushed the door open with the muzzle of my weapon. It was a dark closet stinking of urine and feces. On the floor was the missing American, bound and gagged with wire and adhesive tape. His face showed signs of savage mistreatment—mouth swollen and bloody, eyes almost shut. Plainly he had been intended as the next victim. The plan was simple enough. Having finally realized that simply holding the hostages would not get them what they wanted, the terrorists were preparing for the media blitz they had so long delayed. They held a dozen Americans. That probably meant twenty or thirty tapes. Interrogations, beatings, pleas by the hostages, murders.

"Carry them both," I said. "Let's go."

I led the way back into the firelit night. The shooting had stopped completely. The only sound was the moaning of the wounded and the roaring of the fire consuming the Bedouins' camp. The Bedouins themselves had run off into the desert. Across the compound I could see Ware's Two Commando with a group of fifty or more Arab prisoners, disarmed, most of them wounded. There was no fight left in them.

I jogged across the sand to Ware and asked for the bill.

"Three men slightly wounded. *Sir.*" Ware was totally a Royal Marine, for tonight at least.

Louis's team came out of the dark at the double. One Commando had some wounded, too, but none who needed carrying back to the Stallions. I began to congratulate myself on the luck of R Force. A half-dozen wounded, none killed, all the hostages but one recovered alive.

But the thought came too soon. From where I stood, the burning Bedouin camp lay northwestward, and the flames were dying down. But quite suddenly, due east of us, the sun seemed to rise. I can describe it no other way. A column of fire rose like a reverse bolt of lightning into the sky. Something enormous had been exploded. The pillar of fire rose without sound. It climbed into the starry desert sky, blotting out the stars. At first I thought it was a nuclear explosion, but the colors were wrong. And as the sound rolled over us at last, it was a rumbling, complaining thunder that lacked the ripping scream of a nuclear blast. The tower of flame had been made by a huge quantity of conventional explosives carefully triggered to burn every gram in the instant of ignition.

The explosion had obviously taken place minutes before we saw it. In fact, we had seen only the tower of flame and debris rising perhaps a hundred miles distant. There was not the slightest doubt in my mind that what we were witnessing was the end of Muammar Qaddafi's nuclear diffusion plant at Barqin.

As we stood fascinated by the distant display, Louis gave voice to the obvious conclusion: "The Israelis must have taken Barqin out," he said.

It was a logical assumption. They had done such things before. Once, they had bombed an Iraqi reactor, and more recently they had flown a thousand miles to take out Yasser Arafat's PLO headquarters on the outskirts of Tunis.

But the assumption, no matter how logical, was wrong. And we found it out when Agron and Redding appeared on the ramp of the nearer Stallion. The Israeli had an arm around Redding's neck and an Uzi jammed under his chin.

"Stand back, Quary," he said. "You lose after all."

I could see it as though I had been there. Possibly Elie had had doubts and hesitated. Washington's main responsibility had been the aircraft, and surely his attention had wavered. And Agron, a fine-tuned and highly trained spook, had taken advantage of them to grab Redding and a weapon. That's all it would have taken, and it was my fault. I should have killed Agron the moment we landed.

Redding said, "He used the radio, Casey."

Agron drove the muzzle of the Uzi upward into Redding's throat. "That's enough. Be silent now."

"What do you want, Agron?" I asked. "What's the price?"

"I want you to wait here. Exactly where you are now." He was facing the fading glow in the eastern sky, and suddenly bits and pieces began to fall into place. It all gets very simple and straightforward when the puzzle maker hands you the last piece.

Agron was KGB, all right. From the beginning. Because he was Jewish, or pretended to be, and because he was a *refusenik*, or pretended to be, Mossad had swallowed him whole. A measure of how important that glow in the sky was to the Soviets was the fact that the KGB had thrown Agron into our operation like an ante in a poker game.

It seemed likely that he had kept KGB informed of every move we made. Likely? Hell, it was a dead certainty. From the beginning—from before the beginning probably—the wet-affairs specialists on Dzerzhinski Square had been active planners of R Force's amateurish assault on Point X.

"Let Redding go, Agron," I said quietly. "I give you my word you can wait here for your Russian friends."

That brought a cry of outrage from Avram and Ariel. I had forgotten them. Mossad had assigned them to Agron never realizing he was a double agent. And now the third member of their team was undoubtedly dead inside the Stallion, along with Luther Washington. Perhaps their sense of betrayal was even stronger than mine. After all, I had never been easy with Agron. They had assumed he was an Israeli patriot.

Whatever they had assumed, they reacted recklessly. They raised their weapons, but Agron leveled his and shot them down without an instant's hesitation.

Louis Brown, the consummate soldier, reacted before I could. He crashed into Redding, shoving him back against Agron and rolling them off the ramp to the ground. But Agron was fast, deadly. He dropped the muzzle of his Uzi and fired. It was a microburst, three rounds, four at most, and then the Uzi ran dry. Before he could reload, I had him. I fired and sent him tumbling.

Redding came to his knees. But Louis did not. He lay face down in the sand by the helicopter's ramp, and I knew it was bad.

Jimmy Green, the medic, and I reached him at the same time. Green rolled him over gently. Louis's Afrika Korps battle smock was wet and sticky. I cradled his head, unable to speak. Green was unfastening his gear, cutting away the soggy cloth covering his massive chest.

Louis looked up at me and said faintly, "Son of a bitch, Casey." He sounded more surprised than hurt. And then he died.

29

It seemed to me that time moved at a crawling pace as I knelt there beside the ramp with Louis Brown's body in my arms. And as the seconds slow-marched through that firelit slaughterhouse, I had all the time in the world to rethink our situation and reach some understanding of all the things I had failed earlier to discover.

Of course, Gershon Agron was a double agent. How else had he been able to supply such accurate intelligence? The original satellite photographs he had given us were undoubtedly American in origin. But what of the second set? The CIA and Mossad—and quite likely MI-6 as well—had had good reason to encourage the formation of R Force and its use to recover the hostages. We were the most deniable force imaginable. If it all went wrong, who could blame Western intelligence for the failure of so quixotic an operation?

But *of course* Agron had had a slightly skewed set of objectives. That fire etched against the sky in the distance was the confirmation of a plan far more complex and cruel than anything we had concocted in Harry Redding's war room overlooking the Pacific. The Soviets, in a fit of stupid adventurism, had given Libya a dangerous toy—a nuclear diffusion plant. Now, a decade later, the plant was producing weapons-grade uranium, and it was a deadly danger not only to Colonel Qaddafi's enemies, but also to his friends in Moscow.

I could imagine the glee with which the men in Dzherzhinski Square had received Agron's progress reports. Intelligence services are not known for the efficiency of their operations. They only appear to be clever. But we had given the KGB all it needed to solve the Kremlin's Libyan problem.

Agron had informed his control of the hour and minute of our arrival at Point X. It remained only for the Soviet Spetznaz troops at Barqin to blow up Qaddafi's dangerous toy at the proper moment and blame it on us. The elegant solution to their problem was so beautifully simple. *Of course.*

It seemed almost too perfect, but only from our perspective. It wasn't a coincidence that R Force had been manipulated by American intelligence to strike at the very moment the Sixth Fleet was conducting its freedom-of-the-seas exercise in the Gulf of Sidra. That enhanced our odds. But had anyone in Washington guessed that the Soviets might time their destruction of Barqin to match both the navy's actions in the north and R Force's incursion in the south? I suspected that no one had, and that it was the Soviets who stood triumphant at the peak of the pyramid of deception.

It had cost them Gershon Agron—or whatever his real name was. But what of that? He would always have been expendable to the KGB.

I looked at Louis's still face and thought: I should have been wiser, more clever. I should have known.

Only moments had passed since he fell. The troops of R Force were all around me, and the hostages, too, and Redding, looking stunned and lost, and not one of them knew what was to come next. But I did. *Of course.*

Within minutes, not more, there would be gunships from Barqin, and possibly Spetznaz paratroopers, too. When you bloodied a scapegoat, you didn't leave it alive. It would take a bit of corpse moving, but not much. The Russians would fall on us, and there would be *no* survivors. Before the sun rose again our bodies would be scattered through the wreckage of Qaddafi's nuclear facility. The Soviet commander would tell the Colonel, with regret, that his small detachment of Soviet soldiers had been unable to prevent the plant's destruction. But he would give him the remnants of R Force, which had connived with the U.S. Navy, to put on display in Tripoli. *Of course.*

Because I hated spooks and politicians and all their works, I had failed in a commander's most elementary duty. I had not foreseen what the Soviets might do. I knew they were at Barqin. I knew the nuclear plant had become an embarrassment to them. I knew they needed not to alienate the Libyans. And Ann had tried to warn me.

But, just like Redding, I had wanted desperately to play soldier. Nothing else had really mattered to me except this chance to fight one more time.

God, I thought, what a price tag my fantasy carried. I looked down at Louis, and my eyes grew blurry with tears. I could hear him saying: "Expensive, Casey. And if you don't get your ass in the saddle *right now,* it is going to cost a lot more."

"Casey—"

Bill Tinker was kneeling beside me. His face showed concern under the paint and grime. I had the strangely inappropriate thought that he was too old for this kind of thing, and so was I.

Behind him was Bertie Ware. There was a smear of blood on his cheek. He said, "Washington's dead, Casey. There's no one to fly his kite."

"I can," I said. I straightened. My legs ached. It was as though I had crouched over Louis for hours, but it had been no more than a few minutes. The compound was darkening as the fire consuming the Bedouin camp died down. I could still hear women screaming, but from far away. I looked at the carnage R Force had created. The kidnappers were scattered among the dead Libyans.

"Tinker, what are your casualties?"

"Two hit. One badly, but we have him aboard the aircraft."

Two plus Ware's three wounded. Six dead. By the book our

assault had been cheap, dirt cheap. But you didn't figure the loss of friends by the book.

"Get as many of your people as possible in with the hostages. Tell Penny to forget Sfax. He's to head straight for Kasserine. Make it fast. I think we're going to have company here. The Soviets have blown up Barqin, and they'll be coming for us. Move out, Colonel."

"Right," Tinker said. He began to call orders, and the people milling about the shattered compound streamed toward the Stallion.

Ambassador Lyman appeared again, limping.

I said, "Are you hit?"

"Only a nick." He still looked shocked. "Who *are* you people?"

"The ones who came after you. Now, sir, please get aboard the helicopter."

"God bless you," he said, and went aboard.

I picked Louis up in my arms and staggered under his weight. He had once done the same for me, but I had survived. I carried him into Washington's Stallion and laid him down on the floor of the troop compartment, next to Luther. Ware had covered him with a tarpaulin. You'll never have to dust another field, Warrant Officer Washington, I thought. I gave you a choice, and you took it. I felt as though my chest was filled with stones.

I heard Penny's Stallion start up. Through the open door I could see people crowding aboard.

Redding appeared at my side, and suddenly I was burning with rage. "You had to play hero," I said, hating him. "I should shoot you myself."

I pushed past him and stood on the ramp. Tinker had managed to load almost everyone into the other helicopter. Discarded weapons and ammunition cases littered the ground.

Ware came running up to me. "They're fully loaded, Casey. There are about a dozen people left. Can you really fly this thing?"

271

"I could once," I said. "We'll see." I waved at Penny. "Lift off! *Go!*"

The heavily laden Stallion's rotors raised a storm of dust as the aircraft lurched into the air, backed across the compound, turned, and began to climb, very slowly, into the night.

"Get everyone aboard, Ware," I said. "We've got to haul out of here."

I climbed up to the flight deck and sat in the left-hand pilot's seat. The maze of switches and dials stared back at me. It had been years since I had flown a Stallion, and then only as a copilot. Most of my flying time had been in tiny Loaches and gunships.

I managed to find the right handles and buttons. The engines whined into life, and the main rotors began to turn. Penny's Stallion was gone—safely airborne or crashed in the desert. There was no way of knowing.

And then a rocket burst in the center of the compound. Steel fragments clattered against the sides of our Stallion. White fire spun and arced from the site of the explosion. Two more rockets struck. One leveled the tin building that had contained the hostages, and great jagged sheets of torn siding sliced through the air. A Soviet Hind gunship, its undersurfaces lighted by the explosions, roared over our heads, very low.

You're too late, you Russian bastards, I thought savagely. You have to kill us all, and you can't do that now.

Unless there was another gunship lining up to blow Penny's helicopter out of the air somewhere out in the dark.

"Bertie!" I called. "Get one of those RPGs up here on the double!"

One of the troopers from Two Commando struggled to the flight deck carrying a rocket-propelled grenade launcher, and Ware followed with a steel case of six rounds. The men on the ramp took cover against the thin sides of the fuselage as still another rocket exploded in the compound. It was nothing short of a miracle that our large, ungainly aircraft had not been hit. We wouldn't remain that lucky for long.

Ware banged me on the shoulder and shouted, "Everyone's aboard, Major!"

I hit the switch that closed the ramp at the rear of the troop compartment. On the rising ground between the compound and one of the useless bunkers the Libyans had built, I saw a large troop-carrying helicopter landing. It carried Libyan Air Force markings, but the troops alighting from it were Spetznaz. You could tell from the precise way they moved to deploy.

I shouted back to Ware, "Get some fire on those hostiles, Captain!"

Almost immediately, I heard the sound of Uzis firing through the ports on the side of the Stallion. I fed power to the engines and clutched in the rotors. We were light, and we began to lift.

To the trooper I said, "Break out that window." He leaped to obey, pounding on the latches with his bare hands. "Use your weapon, man!" I shouted.

He forced the right-hand window with the butt of his Uzi. A storm of wind from the rotors' downdraft filled the flight deck with dust and swirling debris.

I turned to call over my shoulder for another man to help the gunner serve the RPG. A Stallion wasn't meant to fly through an environment of close-order combat. It had been designed to transport troops into protected areas near to, or within, fire bases. It was too big and too defenseless to fly in a killing zone. But here we were—and here we would stay unless we improvised.

We had reached an altitude of about twenty feet when we began taking heavy fire from the Spetznaz swarming over the shattered compound. Someone in the troop compartment shouted and cursed. "Captain Ware is hit!"

"Get your head and shoulders out of that hatch," I shouted to the gunner. "Use the RPG on that chopper on the ground!"

The man was one of Ware's ex–Royal Marines. He didn't need further instructions. He hoisted the RPG to his shoulder and, half in and half out of the cockpit, got off a rocket. The backflash lighted the flight deck like a giant strobe. Below, amid what appeared to be a flickering star field but was actually the muzzle flashes of about two dozen assault rifles firing at us, there was a red-and-yellow explosion. Our gunner's first shot had struck the Russian troop carrier just under the huge double rotors, and the aircraft erupted into a volcano of burning jet fuel and exploding ammunition.

There was a wild cheer from the men in our troop compartment. Pieces of the Russian chopper rose a hundred feet into the air. They spun like fiery pinwheels just outside our Stallion's windshield.

I shoved hard on the collector, diving through the flying debris. Another miracle—we didn't hit anything. We flew through unscathed and headed northwest, engines screaming at one-hundred-percent power. We left the fires of Point X behind, and I eased the Stallion down to fifty feet. Thin moonlight vaguely illuminated the crests of the dunes below. I didn't attempt to fly in the sand troughs. I wasn't that skilled, and there was no point in attempting to hide now. We were running for the Tunisian border and didn't care who knew it.

I shouted to make myself heard over the noise and wind in the flight deck. "Good shooting, Marine!" I tugged at his trouser leg to bring him down out of the slipstream.

He fell heavily across the back of the copilot's seat. The RPG crashed to the cockpit floor. In the red light I could see blood from a wound under the man's chin. A bullet from below had gone through his throat and up into his brain.

Ware, one arm bound to his body, thrust himself into the cockpit. He looked at his trooper and said, almost mildly, "Bloody hell."

Someone pulled the dead Marine back into the troop compartment.

I said to Ware, "Get someone else up here to use that RPG in case they send a gunship after us." An air-to-air combat between a Hind gunship and an old Sea Stallion could end only one way, and I knew it. But we were too near to pulling our operation off, and we had spent too much on it, not to keep fighting. And they *would* send a gunship; I was certain of it. The Russian plan had been excellent, but they had arrived minutes too late to catch both of our aircraft on the ground.

Ware said, "We have other casualties back there, Major."

There was not much I could do about that. Either Green could patch them together until we were safely down in Tunisia or they would die.

Flying the Stallion was a handful for me. Airmanship isn't something you forget, but techniques get rusty from disuse, and the aircraft had suffered some battle damage. We were lurching about the sky only half under control, but we were moving away from Point X, away from Barqin, and toward Tunisia. We had killed one of the Russian helicopters, and it was unlikely that the Soviets would call in help from the Libyan Air Force. That was the good news. The bad news was that the other Stallion, with all the hostages and most of our men, might be under attack. I had to find out, so I broke radio silence.

I began to call Penny on our operational frequency. There was no reply. But suddenly I heard Kasserine on the air. It was Ann.

"Casey, what's happening? Can you read me?"

"I read you," I said into the microphone. "We have Russian gunships on us. Tell the Tunisians we need help." There was almost no chance that the Tunisian Air Force would scramble fighters and create an even messier international incident. But if the Russians were listening, it might give them something to think about. I decided to make it worse for them. If we went down under their guns, at least their actions at Barqin would not go unreported.

"Ann, listen to me," I radioed. "Make certain Ziegler hears this. The Soviets have destroyed the nuclear facility at Barqin and attacked us at Point X. We got the hostages out, but they are in the other Stallion and may have been shot down by Soviet gunships. Did you get that? Louis is dead. Redding is with me. Tell Ziegler to get us some help."

Another voice came on the air. It was Ziegler's. "Casey, is Harry all right? Can you hear me? *Is Harry all right?*"

I shouted into the radio, "Get on to our embassy in Tunis and tell them we won't make it without support."

I would have said more. I would have asked for the whole of the Sixth Fleet's air group if I had thought it would do any good.

But we were still sixty miles or more from the Tunisian border and nearly seven hundred from the Gulf of Sidra. Time was running out. The Soviet Hind gunship carries a very effective search radar. The wonder of it was that we'd gotten as far as we had.

Apparently we were destined to go no farther. The fiery streak of an air-to-air rocket came at us out of the darkness.

I gave one last call. "We're under attack again," I said, and then forgot the radio, because there was a crumping explosion above and behind, and the Stallion became almost unmanageable, yawing wildly and vibrating.

I saw another rocket go by us and burst on the ground ahead. We were so low we flew through the debris, and the windshield over the flight deck starred and cracked. I shouted to the people in the troop compartment, *"Hang on! We're going down!"*

I fed full power into the rotors, trying to make the big aircraft hover. It was impossible. We had serious damage, and I couldn't keep it on a straight heading. It kept sliding off to the left, trying to pitch on its side. The altimeter warned me there was almost no air between us and the dark desert.

Something struck the ground, and the aircraft pivoted through almost three hundred sixty degrees. The rotors overhead struck and disintegrated. The fuselage bounced hard, twisted. I could hear the men behind me yelling. Two more air-to-air rockets struck near us, lighting the desert as they exploded. Then we smashed hard into something yielding—a steep sand dune. I felt myself thrown violently against the safety harness, and there was a bolt of pure agony in my chest. The crash had done something to the piece of Soviet metal there. I remember thinking that it was ironic that a wound I got in the jungles of Vietnam was going to kill me years later in the Libyan saheer.

———————

I opened my eyes and saw Green looking down at me. The light came from the burning wreckage of our Stallion a few hundred yards away. I felt a deep, throbbing ache in my chest.

"I think I'm leaking in there," I said in a whisper.

"I think you are, too, Major. Don't move around."

"Where are the others—?"

The medic shook his head in disbelief. "Everyone managed to get out." There were shadowy figures all around me. I could recognize Ware, with Redding squatting near him. I had a crazy desire to laugh. He was cradling the RPG across his thighs and had a necklace of rockets hanging across his chest. Where had I seen that before, I wondered vaguely.

Ware came over and knelt next to me. "We're up the bloody creek, Casey. It must still be a hundred kilometers to the Tunisian border. But you got us down. I don't know how, but you did. For all the good it will do us now."

"Where are the Russians?" I asked.

"The buggers made a couple of passes at the wreck and hit it with rockets. But they didn't land."

"They'll be back as soon as it's light," I said. "With troops. You have to get the men moving, Bertie."

"Casey, be reasonable. We have six Uzis. The rest were in the Stallion, with the ammunition and the water. We have a hundred kilometers to go. And you can't be moved."

"To hell with that. Get the men ready to move."

"You won't get a hundred yards from here, Major," Green said.

I looked at Bertie. "Did you get Louis out of the Stallion?"

Ware shook his head. "I'm sorry, Casey. There wasn't time."

I turned my head and looked at the still-burning wreckage of the helicopter. It was down to charred stringers and a tangle of twisted metal. I didn't realize it, but tears were streaming down my cheeks. I could see Redding behind Ware, that silly necklace of RPG rounds hanging around his neck. This is what it is really like, Harry Redding, I thought. How do you like it?

I tried to rise, and the pain exploded in my chest again. I dropped back on the cold sand. So we both stay here, I thought— Casey Quary and Louis Armstrong Brown. The way it was always meant to be. "Captain Ware," I said, "get the men ready to move. That's an order. And you, Redding, give me that goddamn RPG—"

Ware moved away to whisper with Green. The rest of the men crouched around us silently. I looked straight up at the sky and was shocked to see that the stars had faded. Powder-blue morning light was starting to unveil the saheer.

Ware was making the rounds of the men, speaking to them in low tones. I tried to shout at him, "Damn it, Ware, this isn't a democracy! Follow orders!" I forced myself to sit and then to kneel. It felt as though something was sawing at my lungs. I tasted blood in my mouth. And then I fell back again, and the growing light of morning vanished.

I was back in Vietnam. I could hear the characteristic whack-whacking sound of helicopters. I had been hit by NVA fire, that was obvious. My chest felt as though it were on fire. Each time my heart beat it was as though a knife were being worked through my body. Where was Louis? He had saved me once before, so why wasn't he with me now?

And then the dream fell to pieces, and I knew where I was. The sky was turning white. In the east it was the color of newly minted silver coins. And from the east came the helicopters. A Hind gunship leading a big Sukhoi troop carrier.

Ware had disobeyed me, the insubordinate Brit bastard. He had the men dug in along the crest of a tall sand dune. The smoldering crash of our Stallion sent a plume of smoke up into the still morning air. Louis Brown's funeral pyre. Luther Washington's, too. No more crop dusting for Luther, no more medals for Louis. Those things were finished now, and so was I. So were we all, it seemed. The two Soviet aircraft were black against the metallic sky.

I lay helpless and useless, facing the last battle of my life empty-handed. My perception was slightly blurred. I could feel the pain, but it seemed to belong to someone already dead. Green had stabbed me full of morphine, I supposed. That was a hell of a way for a soldier to die, doped up and weaponless.

I called out in a paper-thin voice, "Give me the RPG, Harry. Give it to me."

He appeared with the weapon. His face was drawn and white. Had he imagined it might end like this when he first listened to Gershon Agron? I remembered him climbing the stairs from the beach at Malibu, the late twentieth century's kind of hero, all image and unreal dreams. This patch of Libyan desert was a far piece from the imitation forests of Vietnam or the barren pass at Kasserine forty years after the battle ended. I felt sorry for him.

"Help me," I said. "Get me up."

He tried. I'll give him that. He really tried. The two Soviet helicopters came on, and their mechanical approach must have terrified him, but he did try to help me hold the RPG.

I couldn't make it. There was no chance at all. I cursed Ware for not taking the weapon from him and giving it to a real soldier. But Ware had been too concerned with deploying the command he had inherited. Or perhaps it had seemed the natural thing to leave the rocket launcher in Redding's hands. After all, half the world had seen Harry Redding carrying his favorite weapon in living color and Panaflex photography.

I knelt on the sand again, trying to breathe through the blood leaking into my lung. I said, "Give the launcher to Ware, Harry. Don't let the big chopper land."

It was an incredible moment, clear and glowing. Redding, livid with fear, but somehow in command of himself, his tawny eyes bright, almost fevered, said, "I know what to do, Casey."

He shouldered the RPG and began slogging his way up the face of the sand dune. Twice he fell in the loose footing, but he kept going.

The Hind gunship swept over us, low. I could see the pilots in their heavily armored flight deck. They passed overhead and then backed away to hover, covering the approach of the troop carrier.

They saw Redding climbing the dune with the RPG, and they read the situation more quickly than I did, or any of us. They

279

opened up with a burst of Gatling-gun fire that passed over his head and flattened the crest of the dune.

I thought he would drop the rocket launcher and take cover. Most men would have. Almost any *soldier* would have, too.

But Redding didn't. He kept on struggling to the top of the dune, the RPG on his shoulder.

The pilots of the big Sukhoi saw him, too, and veered sharply away. They knew their danger. Another burst of the Gatling gun struck the sand below where he stood. He stumbled, but did not fall.

Then he leveled the RPG and fired at the Sukhoi.

The rocket-propelled grenade was at the limit of its range when it struck the big helicopter just forward of the tail rotor. The aircraft burst into two pieces and a shower of fragments and flame. The fuselage, out of control, reacted to the torque of the huge rotors by flinging itself into a wild series of gyrations, which spewed burning fuel across the dunes. It spun into the ground near the wreck of our own Stallion and dissolved into a ball of oily fire.

Our men let out a ragged cheer, and those who had weapons began firing at the gunship. I could see the bullets pocking but not penetrating the armored hull. The Russians backed away, climbed for altitude.

I yelled at Redding, "*Get down! Take cover!*"

He didn't do that. He loaded another round into the RPG from that necklace of grenades around his neck, just as he had in his movies. I really don't think he was afraid. Not then.

The gunship came in on a firing pass, and this time it didn't miss. But neither did Redding. He stood and aimed and fired an instant before the torrent of Russian bullets cut him down.

His grenade struck the armored windshield of the Hind, failed to penetrate it, bounced up, and then struck the armored housing of the main rotor. It exploded there. It didn't bring the Hind down, but it scrambled the complicated working of the rotating hub, and the aircraft became nearly unmanageable. It veered off to the south, struggled for height, and then ran to the east.

I dragged myself along the sand until I reached Redding. Even in death the man had style. The rain of bullets from the Gatling gun had missed him. All, that is, but one, which had passed through his chest and killed him instantly.

On his face was an expression I had never before seen on a man killed in battle. It was—how can I put it?—a look of discovery, of satisfaction. Perhaps only real heroes die with that look. Or is that only a soldier's fantasy? I will never know for certain, but I will believe it for the rest of my life.

30

There is little else to tell of Harry Redding's R Force and the assault on Point X. When he played his self-cast part and shot down the Russian Sukhoi and drove off the gunship, the war was over—though I was in no condition to realize it.

I was in and out of consciousness, ripped up inside by my old gift from the USSR. But I was far from dying. Green stayed with me, worked on me, and kept me functioning.

The wonder of it was that my hopeless demands for help actually brought us a pair of Tunisian Air Force F-5s and a helicopter. They arrived an hour after Redding had disposed of the Russians. Ziegler had put all the pressure of which he was capable on the American Ambassador to Tunisia, and he, in turn, had persuaded the Tunisians to risk an incursion to take us out.

There are enormous ironies in war. If the Soviets had used the gunship on us better, Redding might never have killed the Sukhoi. If they had come an hour later, the Tunisians would have turned back and left us to die in the desert.

I never knew whether the Soviet plan to blame us for the destruction of Barqin was a KGB operation or something the GRU dreamed up. I suspect it was the latter. Soldiers, and that includes intelligence divisions like the GRU, tend to favor flamboyant plans.

In the north, the United States Navy, having proven its point that the Gulf of Sidra was international waters, not Muammar Qaddafi's private lake, was withdrawing toward Malta in leisurely fashion.

If the fires that lighted Barqin and Point X for one night were noted by the satellites high above the earth, no one remarked upon them. The naval scuffles in the Gulf of Sidra absorbed the attention of the world's news media.

Our number-two Stallion had flown direct from Point X to Kasserine, carrying all the hostages to Tunisian safety. At the moment Redding died, the hostages he had planned so hard to save were—all but one—landing among the movie people at Kasserine. The Russian Spetznaz pilots had chosen to follow us, rather than Derek Penny's machine. It was a fatal mistake for them. For Redding, too.

I don't feel free to make any profound comment about Harry Redding. Only that in the end, when it counted most, he was a hero. As I rest in my hospital room in Washington, recovering from the operation I should have had when I left Vietnam, I think a great deal about him. Beyond the shadowy legends that rumor might breed, he will never get recognition for what he did in Libya. But I know, and so do the survivors of R Force.

Ann spends a great deal of time with me. She has "retired," she says, from MI-6. I hope she is speaking the truth, because I don't intend to let her get away from me. Not ever.

It is a bitter thing for a man like me to admit to having been wrong. But I think now about how very certain I was—before we went to Point X—that I had the answer to the sickness that pervades our time. Be firm, I said, strike hard and often and all will be well. I have discovered that it isn't that simple. Point X, and what it cost, proved it. But we were soldiers, Louis and I, and we did what we could. Ann believes that. I think I do, too.

Ann listens—often with smiles, sometimes with tears—as I reminisce about the lives and times of Casey Quary and Louis

Armstrong Brown. She knows my loss, and helps me to bear it.

We sometimes talk about Harry and Ziegler. Harry's death has turned Jerry into a ghost. I wish I could make him understand that Harry, in those last terrible moments, found what he had probably been searching for all of his life.

F. Scott Fitzgerald said, "Show me a hero and I will write you a tragedy." Perhaps. But to a soldier, Harry Redding's death was no tragedy; it was a kind of triumph. All his life he'd wanted desperately to be the kind of man he played on the screen, and in the end he was. There are worse ways to die.

Fitzgerald didn't, after all, write Harry Redding's valedictory. It was Housman—Housman all the way:

For round me the men will be lying
    That learned me the way to behave,
And showed me my business of dying:
    Oh who would not sleep with the brave?

Epilogue

[Front page, *The New York Times,* April 2:]

AMERICAN HOSTAGES FREED
Diplomatic Pressure Brought
by Tunisians and Algerians

WASHINGTON, April 1—The United States Ambassador to Lebanon, Edward Lyman, and ten members of his staff taken hostage by Arab militants sixteen months ago, have been freed through intensive negotiation by Tunisian and Algerian diplomats. One member of Ambassador Lyman's mission is reported to have died while in Arab custody.

The diplomats, now undergoing debriefing by the State Department, have refused comment on their captivity and on the means used by pro-Western Arab governments to free them. . . .

[Lead story, front page, Entertainment
Section, *Los Angeles Times,* April 3:]

DEATH OF HARRY REDDING
SHOCKS FILM INDUSTRY
Future of Eagle Films Uncertain

The accidental death of superstar Harry Redding on the set
of his film-in-progress, *Kasserine,* has stunned the motion picture
world.

Redding, winner of an Oscar for Best Actor, whose vivid
portrayals of American veterans and soldiers as heroes stirred
equal measures of praise and criticism among his co-workers,
died while performing a hazardous stunt in his planned wartime
epic. A spokesman for Eagle Films noted that Redding was a
perfectionist in film making, and often performed his own stunts.

Jerome Ziegler, Executive Vice President of Eagle and Executive Producer of *Kasserine,* told the *Times* that all work on
the new film was suspended pending "a serious appraisal" of
Eagle Films' future.

An obviously grief-stricken Ziegler told media representatives
in Tunis, "I cannot imagine Eagle Films continuing without Harry
Redding. It is impossible that anyone could even attempt to take
his place. He was unique."

Plans for a televised memorial service will be announced. . . .

[Personalities Section, *The Army Record,* July 20:]

QUARY—MACLEAN

Married, Fort Myers Post Chapel, July 18: K. C. Quary, Lieutenant Colonel, USA, to Ms. Ann Maclean of Malibu, California.